WHEN OUR WORLD ENDED,
THEIR MISSION BEGAN

STEPHEN KNIGHT
EARTHFALL

THE WOMAN'S FACE *is still mostly smooth. The only signs of her true age are an array of laugh lines that crinkle whenever she smiles, which she does quite a bit, finding something humorous in almost every situation. Her hair is a tawny blond, its rich color diminished somewhat by the encroaching grays, the ones she's just not vain enough to try to hide behind the quick fixes of bottled hair products. The woman—and more importantly, the man who adores her—knows that youth and vitality are more about what's on the inside than what's on the outside. The interior is what's important, and only a precious few intimates get to see that. The exterior? Hell, everyone else on the planet can see that, free of charge.*

The girls look like both of them, a mix of her fair skin and honey-colored hair, but with his eyes and nose. He thinks the nose looks much better on them than on him. It confers an impression of quiet, regal strength that makes him wonder how they'll fare in the coming years when boys begin to circle around them. Would they take the males on head-to-head as he would, or would they instead use the mother's good nature and occasional guile? He finds he almost can't wait to find out, but he knows these things will happen sooner than he'll want. It's not going to be easy watching them winnow away the list of suitors until they find the right ones. And when that happens, they won't be his little girls any longer.

He pulls open the screen door on the small house they leased on the plains of Kansas, where the land is flat and seems to go on forever, broken only occasionally by trees or telephone poles that stand a silent vigil in the heat of the midday sun. From somewhere in the humid, sticky distance, a crow caws, and he feels a momentary portent of dread flutter across his heart. But why? The day is perfect, the weather calm, and his family waits for him only a few steps away in the small kitchen. He enters the room, and the girls shriek with delight as they leap toward him with no hesitation, even though he's been gone for so many years of their lives that he sometimes feels he barely knows them. His wife's smile is broad and welcoming, and her dark eyes twinkle as she turns from the kitchen counter, forgetting about the lunch she had been about to serve.

"Well, it's about time, stranger!" she says, laughing, her voice bright and clear.

Behind him, the crow caws again.

He awoke to the total darkness that could be found only beneath the surface of the earth. He lay in his rack and listened to the sounds of the base: the gentle whisper of climate-controlled air moving through the ductwork, the muted sounds of equipment operating, the occasional footfalls in the corridor outside his quarters as someone walked past. The clock on the nightstand read 0246. He wasn't officially on duty for over five hours, but he knew he wouldn't be sleeping much more.

The dream. Always the dream.

Sometimes when he awoke, he was filled with an overwhelming despair that made him contemplate suicide. So easy, so amazingly easy, to end it. The varieties of method to his self-inflicted demise were endless. Gunshot. Overdose. Hanging. Slashing his wrists and bleeding out in the shower. Or simply accessing one of the emergency exits, where he could climb up to the surface and let God do His work as he walked back to the house.

Other times, he awoke clear-headed and mostly free of the numbing despair. But the sad loneliness was always there, followed by the shame that he had failed to execute the one mission that mattered most. That failure left him an empty shell most days, making him into little more than a ghost that haunted the base. The vitality, the zest for life, the need to serve and carry out his sworn duties ... all fell by the wayside, washed out of him like the rays of the sun could diminish the colors of an old photograph.

Why, he always asked himself as he lay alone in the darkness in small, cramped quarters. *Why them? Why not me?*

The base had no answer.

1

THE WASTELAND WAS as dry and barren as the surface of the moon. Over the course of decades, the topsoil had been bleached by the sun's searing rays, the soil converted to chalky dust. No vegetation remained, for no life could exist in a land where the earth and air had been poisoned by nuclear weapons. Sandy ridges and wind-carved rock stood mute sentinel to the passage of time. Despite the fact the land was completely lifeless, the casual observer—had there been one—might still have considered the wasteland austerely beautiful.

Hidden beneath a pulsating brown-black mass, a vast cloud stalked across the forbidding wasteland like some hungry beast stirring after a long hibernation, the horizon but a memory. Tens of miles across, the ferocious sandstorm grew larger by the second, illuminated by sporadic flashes of lightning. Riding the stiff breeze, the storm's top rose almost seventy thousand feet into the dry air, which no longer enjoyed the benefit of an ozone layer to strip away harmful radioactive particles emitted by the distant sun. The storm surged forward at more than sixty miles per hour, devouring the land before it, ravaging the wasteland even further with cyclonic winds full of debris that could strip a man's flesh from his bones in minutes.

Despite the hostile environment, the powerful storm, and the radiation—both man-made and heaven-sent—there was life.

A gigantic, eight-wheeled, all-terrain vehicle bolted across the gently rolling landscape, trailing a rooster-tail of dust. While the vehicle raced away from the storm, it became briefly airborne as it crested a small ridge before it slammed back to the parched earth, rocking on its heavy-duty suspension. The rig's turbine engines roared as they propelled Self-Contained Exploration Vehicle 4 along at almost sixty miles an hour. It wasn't fast enough. The monstrous storm continued to close, and the gap between its amorphous leading edge and the dirty vehicle slowly narrowed.

Strapped into the driver's seat, Captain Mike Andrews kept his eyes rooted on the desert landscape outside the thick viewports. His left hand kept the rig's control column pushed fully forward, and the system's drive-by-wire technology translated the action into full power to the rig's large, knobbed tires. The ride was far from comfortable, of course. Even though the SCEV had been designed to withstand harsh punishment in the field for months at a time, there was a limit to what suspension technology could dampen. Hurtling along at old highway speeds across broken terrain was one of the things it couldn't handle.

"Hey, listen, the temperature's going through the roof on number one," Choi said, squirming slightly in the copilot's seat beside Andrews. He was a few years younger than the vehicle commander, but his even temper and genuine likeability made him an asset in the field during the long reconnaissance runs they made four times a year. Now, though, Choi was obviously agitated, and not just from the SCEV's violent progress over the landscape that had once been western Kansas. It wasn't the close proximity of the storm causing him discomfort, either. Andrews knew the chance the vehicle might be forced to spend days waiting out the storm within only a few miles of Harmony Base was getting to Choi. Hell, it was getting to him as well. After thirty-three days in the field, all Andrews wanted was to get back to Harmony and soak in the small bathtub in his quarters. The SCEV's accommodations were fairly excellent, but confining eight people inside a vehicle that had less than four hundred square feet of living space for a month was enough to make anyone long for privacy.

Choi pointed out the temperature tape on the multifunction display set in the instrument panel between the two men. Andrews only glanced at it, but he could see the number one engine's temperature had spiked dramatically over the past few minutes.

"Listen, if you don't back off soon, you're going to blow number one," Choi said.

"Like hell, Tony. The computer'll shut it down first. But so what? That's why we have two engines in these things." Andrews patted the lip of the SCEV's gray instrument panel. "Hang in there, babe. Almost home, just hang in there."

"Yeah, that's gonna work."

Andrews looked at the weather radar display. "It'd better, man. That storm's a hot one, and if it catches us, we'll lose the base's homing beacon. No way I'm backing off now—this is our only shot."

"So what are we going to do if number one shuts down? The storm'll catch us for sure."

"Spencer!" Andrews shouted.

"What up?" A small, squat man appeared in the door that separated the SCEV's cramped cockpit from the not-so-cramped work area in the center of the vehicle. By regulations, the pressure doors separating the three compartments were supposed to be closed, but with the vehicle lurching and bucking across the terrain, Andrews just didn't have it in him to make what already felt like a coffin even smaller. If he was in the back, he'd have a tough time not blowing chow all over the place.

"One's getting close to thermal shutdown, but I need it," Andrews told the crew chief. "What can I do about it?"

Spencer looked at the multifunction display, then tabbed through the couple of screens. He grunted and returned the display to the main situation page. "Particle separator's shitting the bed, which means the engine's taking in dirty air. I can suppress the alert and raise the shutdown threshold, but the engine's gonna fry. Walleyes won't be happy about that," Spencer added, referring to the commanding officer of the base's vehicle section by his informal—and completely impolite—nickname.

Andrews considered his options. So far in his career, he'd been able to steer clear of Colonel Larry Walters's wrath, which he had visited upon every other SCEV commander over the past decade since the Sixty Minute War. Walters was a ticket-punching chump, one of the Old Guard, and Andrews didn't much care for him. But he was a superior officer, even if he was far too old to be a full-bird colonel. But there was no retiring to Tampa or Sun Valley or Bangkok anymore, which meant Andrews and every other SCEV skipper would have to deal with Walters's shit until he dropped dead from old age or was relieved of command.

In the end, Andrews figured that if he was going to have a run-in with Walters, it might as well be over something fairly major, like burning up the core of a precious SCEV powerplant.

"Do it," he told Spencer. "A direct order, and if you want me to use my code to access the vehicle engineering module, I'll be happy to do it."

"Nah, I got it. Just back me up when someone tries to nail my ass to the wall. Gimme a sec, I'll use the station back here." With that, the swarthy crew chief returned to the multipurpose workstation located only a few feet away. Choi looked back at him, then at Andrews.

"You're putting him on the line, Mike," he said softly.

"He's not doing shit, I'm the one who doesn't want to be out here in this storm," Spencer said. "You see the size of it? That thing'll last for a week before it blows out, and frankly, this thing smells like a can of farts. And I want out."

"The fart smell would be mostly *your* fault, Spencer," Leona Eklund said, her voice carrying to the cockpit over the roar of the rig's engines and the various creaks, groans, and scrapes caused by the vehicle's transit over the rough terrain. Andrews had to grin. It was true; one of the biggest drawbacks to crewing with Todd Spencer was the fact he emitted an exceptionally vile amount of swamp gas, no matter what he ate, and no matter what medication had been prescribed to prevent it. Whatever foulness lurked inside him, Spencer's body tried valiantly to eject it through his sphincter.

"Yeah, yeah, too bad all of us can't fart potpourri like you do, princess," Spencer said. "Captain, I've raised the threshold on number one, but listen, you've got maybe three, four minutes until it fails. Keep that in mind."

"Roger that, Spence. Thanks."

An alarm went off then, sharp and strident—the lightning strike indicator flashed in the corner of one primary display as the storm behind them fired off great discharges of electrostatic energy, one of the things that made the great sandstorms that plagued the former Midwestern United States such a terror for the SCEV teams to deal with. Not only did they pack hurricane-force winds, they also cast off powerful cyclones and great bolts of lightning that homed in on virtually anything metallic. Despite the vast amount of advanced technology that went into insulating the SCEVs, they were still comprised of a good deal of metal.

Brilliant light flared outside, and for an instant Andrews saw the SCEV's shadow grow remarkably long before the pulsing illumination. The lightning strike indicator blared again, and then the lights inside the rig dimmed momentarily. Andrews thought he saw whiplashes of the electrical discharge roll across the SCEV's blunted nose like St. Elmo's fire, spectral and wraithlike. The cockpit displays fluttered for a moment as they reset themselves from the pulsing effects of the charge, but it was the sudden *BANG!* and the sound of the number one engine winding down that held Andrews's undivided attention.

"Talk to me, somebody," he said. "I've got power falling off up here. Spencer, did that particle separator finally fail and take the engine with it?"

"Negative, it's better than that. Looks like that lightning bolt invoked a compressor stall in the same engine," the crew chief reported. "I'm looking into it. Choi, reset the ignition switches and secure the generator. I'll run the restart from back here."

Choi reached up to the overhead panel and did what Spencer asked. He missed a switch combination because the vehicle was rocking hard over uneven ground, but he managed to get it right on the second shot. Outside the viewports, thick dust began to swirl. The rig's speed was dropping past fifty miles per hour, and the storm was catching up to them. Andrews kept the sidearm controller fully forward, but the SCEV was delivering only as much speed as her remaining engine could generate.

"Spencer, talk to me," he said.

"Working on it."

"We're in max commo range," Choi said. "Maybe we ought to let the base know we're coming?"

"Spencer?"

"Still working on it," Spencer said. "Call Harmony, Captain. Spend some time chatting up someone else—I'm busy."

Andrews pressed the red transmit button. "Harmony Base, this is SCEV Four. We're inbound on a course of three-three-five magnetic. We're on a storm run, and we'll require immediate entry by north lift. Over."

Over static broken only by cracks and the whistling, sporadic pops that synchronized perfectly with the flashes of lightning outside, Andrews heard a tinny voice in his headset.

"SCEV Four, this is Harmony Base. Roger your SITREP. You're cleared for north lift. Over."

"Roger that, Harmony. Make sure it's lit up like a

Christmas tree. Visibility's going to suck substantially by the time we get there. Over."

"SCEV Four, Harmony. Lift is on its way, and it will be fully illuminated. Over."

"Harmony, roger."

Andrews turned to Spencer. "I'm not seeing any torque increase on number one up here, Spence. No pressure, but that storm's right on our ass and we'll be losing the beacon pretty soon. After that, it's up to my Mark One Eyeballs and a compass to get us to the lift."

"Yeah, yeah," Spencer said. "Keep your shirt on."

"Come on, man! Get that damn engine started!" Tilly Rodgers called from the back.

"Yeah, get it squared away!" Leona added.

"Blow me, both of you! I'm working on it!"

Choi paged through the system's status pages on the multifunctional display. "Engine's too hot, man. The computer's sitting on it like an eight hundred pound gorilla."

"Spence, what's the problem?" Andrews asked.

"It's too hot! The computer won't let it torque up enough to turn over," Spencer said, frustration evident in his voice.

"Point for me," Choi said.

"Spence, you said you could raise the thermal threshold so that it would keep on running."

"And I did, but the engine's got its own onboard computer, and it's getting in the way. The only way that's going to change is if I rip up the floor and yank the module from the side of the engine, but that means we'll have to stop." The SCEVs had been designed to allow even major repair work to be conducted from the inside, so that its crew wouldn't have to step outside into extremely hazardous conditions to replace a transaxle or computer chip. But that meant pulling up the deck, and doing so would invoke safety overrides that prevented the machine from moving. Either way, the storm would overtake them.

"Just do whatever you can do," Andrews said. "Including getting out and pushing. Choi, give me the numbers?"

"Electromag interferometer's pegged at two thousand volts. Distance from leading edge is one thousand meters, rate of closure one hundred thirty-four klicks per hour. It'll take us down in less than three minutes."

EARTHFALL

"All right, you guys, hang on back there. It's not going to get any smoother." Andrews patted the SCEV's instrument panel once again. "Come on, baby, come on ..."

"Four, this is Harmony. Lift is up and illuminated. Over."

"Much obliged, Harmony. We'll be coming in hot. Over."

"Roger that, Four."

Daylight ebbed outside the viewports. Swirling dust blew across the thick glass, and Andrews glanced down at the infrared picture in the upper left corner of the functional display. The dust was thick enough to mute infrared images, which meant they would soon be blind.

So I guess this means all we'll have left is a compass.

An alarm chirped, and engine one suddenly came to life, its growling whine slowly building to a crescendo. As soon as it began delivering power to the rig's transmissions, the SCEV suddenly felt more nimble—or as nimble as a forty-ton vehicle could.

"Spencer, you're the *man!*" Andrews said. "How'd you manage to get it started?"

"Busted into the engine's integrated computer and shut down the thermal module," Spencer said. "I did that because I'm brilliant and all, in case anyone was wondering."

From the back came a chorus of jeers. Andrews toned them out as he raised his voice.

"Listen, folks, sorry, but I'm segmenting the vehicle," he said. "Embrace the suck." As he spoke, the two pressure doors that separated the rig's three compartments slid closed. Andrews and Choi were sealed off in the cockpit.

"So how're we doing this?" Choi asked as the big SCEV swayed from side to side. The leading edge of the storm had caught up to it, and the winds were battering the slab-sided vehicle.

"We run like hell and hope we can make it to the lift before the storm shuts us out," Andrews said. "But if we screw it up and drive right into the side of the lift, then at least we won't be around to listen to Walleyes."

"If 'we' screw it up? Who is this 'we' you're talking about, white man?"

"Attaboy, Choi, back me up all the way."

The SCEV had lost too much ground to the storm.

Even as it accelerated forward, bumping and crashing over the dry landscape, the storm's leading edge enveloped the vehicle, shrouding it beneath a shifting, inky darkness that made Andrews think the rig had just been swallowed whole by some sort of land-borne leviathan. Choi activated the rig's infrared systems, but it was of little help; the swirling dust reduced the amount of heat that could be read by the high-tech device's super-chilled planar array, rendering it as effective as Andrews's eyeballs.

"The suck has arrived," Choi said.

"We're still on course, and the GPS says we should be at the lift in a minute or so," Andrews told him. "Keep your eyes open."

As he drove, Andrews flipped on the SCEV's array of high-intensity floodlights. They gave him an additional twenty or thirty feet visibility now that the sunlight was being pared down by the storm, but he still couldn't see comfortably. All he had to go by were the instruments, and even the military-grade GPS satellites that had been launched prior to the war were accurate only to within ten feet. If visibility was reduced much more, they could drive right past the lift without anyone noticing it.

"There!" Choi said a moment later, pointing out the diamond-matrix viewport. "Right there, I see the strobe! You got it?"

Andrews leaned forward. The straps of his four-point harness dug into his shoulders as he looked at the heads-up display. Sure enough, there was a very faint winking in the darkness ahead. Bands of dust would obscure it entirely, then lessen for just an instant to allow him to perceive more light. He compared the flashing with the GPS location on the multifunction display. If it was right, then he was nearly on top of the box-shaped lift.

He yanked back on the sidearm controller and stomped on the brakes. The SCEV slewed crazily as its wheels locked up, sending it skidding across the dry, sandy ground.

It came to a rest only feet away from the lift's open entrance. The lights inside the large cubicle gleamed dully, their tepid illumination no challenge to the storm's all-encompassing darkness.

"Yeah, I got it," Andrews said.

"Could you have stopped a little more, you know, artfully?" Choi asked.

Andrews released a long sigh. "Probably, but why make it easy?"

He coaxed the SCEV into the waiting lift. The vehicle bumped slightly as it crossed the threshold, its array of high-intensity fog lights illuminating the big cubicle's interior. A layer of dust already coated the floor, masking the yellow positioning circle painted on the elevator's flat floor. Andrews pulled the SCEV into position by memory and triple-clicked the TRANSMIT button on the sidearm controller. The pulses from the rig's radio were read by the receiver inside the lift, and the elevator's thick, double-pocket pressure doors slid closed, shutting out the dark, seething fury of the storm as it reached full force. Yellow strobes flashed outside the rig's viewports as the atmospheric scrubbers came on, venting radioactive dust and other airborne particulates from the air inside the elevator. After a few moments, an alarm sounded over the radio, three strident tones. At the same time, the strobes outside turned from yellow to red. The SCEV bounced on its stiff suspension for a moment as the elevator commenced its descent.

"Bay Control, this is SCEV Four. We're secure and on our way down for an in-and-out. Over," Andrews said over the radio.

"Roger that, SCEV Four. Welcome back to Harmony Base. Over."

"Roger that, Harmony," Andrew replied. "It's good to be back." With that, he and Choi finally relaxed, sinking back into the padding of their seats. Through the pressure door behind them, they could hear the rest of the crew applauding. It was good to be home—even if home was a windowless, subterranean fortress buried over a hundred feet below the Earth's surface.

The SCEV Decontamination Center was their first stop after the elevator doors opened. The chamber was large and well-lit, the floor comprised of thick grating that creaked slightly beneath the vehicle's weight as it trundled out of the lift. Andrews brought the rig to a halt inside a painted circle in the middle of the room and, once again, yellow strobes flashed. On the way down, Choi had opened the shield doors that separated them from the rest of the crew, and Spencer entered the tight cockpit and crouched between the seats. He examined the instrument panel critically, even though the displays were shown on his own station directly aft of the cockpit.

"Is there a problem?" Andrews asked the engineer as he looked out the side viewport and verified the rig was dead center in the circle. "Left side, check."

"Right side, check," Choi responded, verifying the SCEV's position from the right side.

"Had a few tweaks on one of the differentials," Spencer said, paging through the system situation display in the center of the console. "I just want to verify it from up here. You mind?"

"So long as you don't fart," Choi said.

"No sweat, I'm saving it for later." Spencer paged through the display menus. "Yeah, it registered on this station, too. Looks like I'm going to be tearing this baby apart for the next couple of weeks."

"Knock yourself out, little brother," Andrews said. "We're not going anywhere soon."

"SCEV Four, Bay Control," a voice said over the radio. "Stand by for external decon. Over."

"Light us up, Bay Control. Over. Spencer, any reason we can't start the recovery checklist, or is there something else you need to do?"

"Negative, I'm good. Let's get on the checklists." Spencer retreated to his station as the strobe lights outside turned from yellow to red. Several robotic arms descended from the decon center's ceiling, each equipped with a large nozzle. The SCEV crew began their arrival checklists, and the arms sprayed the vehicle with thick streams of detergent-laden water. They weaved about the rig in a complex pattern, hitting it from every angle and blasting away the hazardous dirt and grime the vehicle had accumulated during its run. As Choi read off the checklist items and Spencer verified settings and switch positions, Andrews looked out the viewports, watching as filthy water cascaded down the rig's sloped nose. SCEV Four was being sprayed with more water than it had encountered in over a month of field time. The thought depressed him. In fact, the entire act of returning to Harmony empty-handed left him feeling hollow. Everyone in the base had been counting on them to return with some good news, with reports that, over a decade after the Sixty Minute War, humanity was flourishing somewhere in what had once been the United States of America. Failing that, people wanted some evidence that Harmony Base wasn't humanity's last outpost.

Andrews hated to be the one to disappoint them.

"Yo, Captain, you with me?" Choi asked.

Andrews looked up, surprised to discover he'd zoned out during the checklist procedure. "What?"

"I said, 'secondary generator switch to standby position.' I can see it is, but you know, you have to respond."

Andrews sighed and checked the switch both visually and by touch. "In standby." His voice sounded tired even to his own ears.

2

MAJOR GENERAL MARTIN Benchley sat behind his desk and paged through the series of consumption reports on his tablet, reading them without even really seeing them. After years of doing so, he knew what the base's usual rhythms were, what readings were wrong, and what consumables were being wasted. It was not unusual for him to operate on autopilot. But when he realized he'd scrolled through to the end of the document without retaining *anything*, he knew he would be revisiting the data once again. Benchley sighed and rubbed his eyes. Other senior officers might have been content to review the executive summary and sign off but, as the commanding general of Harmony Base, he didn't have that luxury. If something went wrong or if some vital resource was being squandered, he was the last line of defense. His position mandated that he always remain vigilant—no matter what.

He regarded the array of flat-screen displays that adorned the wall opposite his desk. He could view any common area inside the base from his office, everything from the engineering spaces to the dining facilities to the corridor outside. He had watched the arrival of SCEV Four on one of those very monitors. The dusty rig had made a gutsy run for the elevator despite a last-second mechanical glitch, even though procedure mandated they shut down and wait out the deadly tempest before trying to gain entry to the base. He'd already heard from Colonel Walters, the eternally dissatisfied head of the vehicle maintenance area, who'd ranted for some time about the fact that Andrews was obviously disregarding procedure and putting his crew and their precious, thirty-seven-million-dollar Self-Contained Exploration Vehicle at extreme risk. Benchley shut Walters down as gently as he could. While he was essentially correct—Benchley himself had mandated that procedures be followed to the letter, as they might be the only thing standing between life and certain death—the fact of the matter was, the general was eager to get his hands on the SCEV team's report. They had concluded the first long-range reconnaissance survey of the central United States since the Sixty Minute War, and

Benchley was not alone in wanting to discover what they had learned.

The base was the last remaining holdover from the old Cold War. Originally initiated during the Reagan Administration, Harmony had been designed to restore the United States after a possible thermonuclear conflict with the Soviet Union. Full of seed stocks, cryogenically suspended animal embryos, staffed with brilliant scientists, engineers, and competent military tradesmen, tacticians, and troops, the subterranean outpost had been designed to be self-sufficient for fifty years. The place was one of the very largest hardened sites ever created. There was enough room for almost a thousand people. Its warehouses were stuffed full of everything that might be needed: freeze-dried and vacuum-sealed foods, petroleum products that had been treated with long-term stabilizers to ensure their combustibility, thousands of books in both paper and electronic formats, tools, building materials, even precious stones and gold, should those become necessary to whatever post-apocalypse society might spread after the bombs dropped. No stone had been left unturned.

Harmony had fared well, even during the tightest budget periods, when political administrations had been tempted to suspend money for the long-running budget. The base had always had a surfeit of hardcore proponents—in the halls of Congress, the military, and the private sector—to ensure its survival. But the base's most surprising benefactors turned out to be the terrorists behind September 11, 2001. They had helped renew interest in the multi-billion-dollar installation during a time when America was more interested in the peace dividend caused by the dissolution of the old Soviet Union. The attacks on American soil had galvanized those holding the black project's purse strings into action, and the money had started to flow once again. Harmony was retrofitted and restocked with the latest technologies, a trend that continued and even accelerated once the diseased Russian Federation finally died, and the progeny of the old authoritarian Communists rose again. The cycle began anew, the United States of America once again faced a monolithic threat.

When the war finally came, it punished not just America, but the entire globe. The event began without warning, as far as

Benchley could tell. One moment, he was contemplating his upcoming retirement, the next, he was ordered to seal the base as the missiles tracked across the sky. As mushroom clouds bloomed across the planet, Harmony was finally good to go on its mission.

For the past six months, the SCEVs had been setting off into the field, conducting their surveys. After a decade of isolation, it was time for Harmony Base to enact the second part of its charter: *Quando mundum finit opus nos incipiet.*

When the world ends, our mission begins.

What Benchley and everyone in Harmony Base wanted to know: *Are we alone? Are we all that's left?* That was all they cared about now, after almost a decade of isolation, biding their time beneath the Earth's surface and—

A chime sounded, and Benchley looked up at the bank of monitors again. Four hours after SCEV Four's arrival, Captain Mike Andrews stood in the corridor outside, flanked by two enlisted MPs. As he watched, a crowd of passersby tried to extend their congratulations to Andrews, so many that the big MPs stood no chance of holding them back. Andrews appeared to accept the attention as stoically as he could. Benchley noted the slump to the younger man's shoulders and the drawn, almost pained expression on his face when he acknowledged the presumably good tidings extended by the others. Benchley wondered if Andrews's expression held all the answers he would ever need.

He feared exactly that.

Benchley rose and walked to the office door, his powerful stride belying his sixty-six years. He had been ready for retirement before the Sixty Minute War, with only two weeks left on post before rotating out and ending his service with the United States Army. Of course, the launch of several nuclear weapons against the US had put his retirement plans on hold—forever. He opened the metal door and it slid inward on well-oiled hinges. Benchley had no secretary. She'd been on leave before the war struck, and he hadn't seen any reason to replace her. He crossed the small outer office, opened the door to the corridor, and waved inside the three men waiting in the hall.

"Come in, Andrews. You men mind waiting in the outer office while I debrief the captain?" The two MPs shook their heads in unison.

"No, sir," the senior man said.

"Thank you. Go ahead and make yourselves comfortable." Benchley ran a hand over his close-cropped silver hair and motioned to his office. "In there if you will, Captain."

"Yes, sir," Andrews said. He carried a small nylon bag with him as he stepped into the office. Benchley followed him in and shut the door.

"Have a seat, son. Good to see you home safe and sound. Looks like Mother Nature threw you a last-minute monkey wrench, eh?"

"Yes, sir." Andrews settled into one of the visitor's chairs facing Benchley's desk only after the general had set himself. "But that's what happens when you try to keep a schedule."

"Indeed. All right, we'll keep this short. I know you've been away for quite some time, and you're probably eager to get back to life."

Andrews opened the nylon bag and pulled out a binder and two thumb drives. He handed the items over to Benchley, who placed the electronic devices on his desk. He opened the binder, which was Andrews's written log of SCEV Four's sojourn through the wasteland. The logs kept by every SCEV commander constituted the sole remaining paper in Harmony Base. Benchley flipped through it quickly, scanning the neat print.

"It's all collated, sir. Lieutenant Eklund's analyses are complete, and Engineer Spencer will have the—"

"Let's cut to the chase, Andrews. What did you find?"

Andrews hesitated for a long moment, then released a heavy sigh. "I'm sorry, sir. The mission was a wash."

Even though he had been ready to hear it—or thought he had—the news hit Benchley like a physical blow. He sagged back into his chair and looked across the desk at Andrews. For his part, the young captain returned his gaze with forlorn eyes.

"That's ... damned disappointing, Andrews. I'd hoped a long-range recon would turn something up. We *can't* be the only survivors of the war ..."

"And we probably aren't, sir. We've just been looking in the wrong places." Andrews appeared more animated now, shrugging off the depressing reality of his report in a way that only the young could. "The Pacific Northwest is our best bet. Everywhere from Los Angeles to New York was hit with at least one nuclear device during the war, and anything that wasn't was covered by the fallout. The winds are still hot outside, even ten years later—the only place anyone could possibly survive outside of hardened bunkers would be in the Northwest. You give the word, sir, and I'll have my rig ready to roll in three days."

Benchley smiled despite himself. Andrews was a true go-getter, perhaps the one SCEV commander he trusted above all others. He was thorough, meticulous, and smart enough to know when to flex the rules a little bit to get something done. Best of all, he was a keen motivator, a trait that years of being trapped underground, slaves to repetition and outright boredom, had almost been eliminated in the Harmony Base culture. Andrews still had it, however, carrying his enthusiasm like a badge. Even though he had little but bad news to report, the young officer was rallying himself to charge out into the field and try again. In the process, Benchley noticed his own sagging spirits being lifted by Andrews.

Thank God for this boy, and all the others like him.

"I appreciate your can-do attitude, Andrews. Really. I'll give your request full consideration, but my instinct is to stick to the schedule for now. In the meantime, myself and the rest of the command staff will go over your findings. Expect to be fully debriefed on Friday, which should give you enough time to get your personal affairs in order."

Andrews looked disappointed. "Your call, sir. But we're ready to jump out on this one. I mean, we're *really* ready and—"

Benchley held up a hand. "I get it, Mike. I get it. I have to consult with the rest of the command staff before I make any sweeping changes to the recon schedule, and you know that. I really will consider making the change, but I need to discuss it with the rest of the team. Trust me on this one, okay?"

Andrews smiled wryly. "Trust has never been a problem here, sir. But if you don't mind me saying so, you might be acting a little too ... *conservatively* about this."

"Me? Conservative? Bite your tongue, Captain—I'm practically a flaming liberal regarding issues like this." Benchley rose to his feet and smoothed out the blouse of his Army Combat Uniform, the standard duty dress in Harmony Base.

Andrews practically rocketed upright, instantly standing at attention.

"Anyway, congratulations, Captain. After thirty-three days in the field, I can absolutely and without reservation confirm that you and your crew have done well. Now go home. You look like hell."

Andrews saluted. Benchley returned the gesture, then held out his hand. Andrews took it, his grip firm. The grip of an adventurer, Benchley thought. If there was a post-apocalyptic Lewis and Clark, Cook, Perry, or even James T. Kirk, Mike Andrews was that man.

"Thanks, sir. Let me know if there's anything in the log that needs clarification," Andrews said.

"Of course. Now get out of here," Benchley said. "You have a young wife to see." He hoped his smile didn't reflect the heaviness he felt in his heart. If Andrews noticed, it didn't show. In fact, the reference to his wife seemed to rejuvenate him. To Benchley, it appeared Andrews couldn't get out of his office quickly enough. The captain stepped out of the office and allowed the heavy door to clang shut behind him, and Benchley slowly sank back into his chair. He put a hand on the logbook before him, palm down, as if he could somehow distill all the disappointment and thrashed dreams without having to actually wade through the reports.

He shook his head slowly. There was nothing to be gained by putting off the bad news.

The lights inside Andrews's quarters were off, masking the small dwelling in the pervasive, all-encompassing darkness found only deep underground. He slowly closed the door behind him, latching it quietly.

"Command: lights, twenty percent," he said. Though his voice was as soft and quiet as he could make it, it still sounded harsh and loud inside the apartment's stillness. The AI executed his command, and the overhead lights slowly brightened until the small living room was bathed in a pale amber glow. For a moment, Andrews just stood in place, looking around the small apartment. Though it was tiny, it was practically a palace compared to an SCEV, and he luxuriated in the surfeit of open space. He stepped around the decidedly no-frills couch to the kitchenette and tugged open the door of the small refrigerator. He smiled when he saw four bottles inside. Rachel had managed to score them from one of Harmony's brewmasters, another engineer who worked in the Core. She probably had to work double shifts for a week to pay for the veritable liquid gold, but that was the kind of woman she was. The end of the world had ensured that there would never be such as thing as a free beer, which meant she would have to pay for the goods with labor. Andrews ran a hand through his dark blond hair and considered the bottles greedily. He desperately wanted one right now, but there was a time for everything. Though it took a surprising amount of self-control, Andrews refrained.

Instead, he headed for the small partition on the far side of the apartment, the bedroom, which occupied a space less than six feet wide by eight feet deep. Andrews stopped at the bedroom's narrow entrance and listened. The AI had left the lights switched off here, and in the pitch-black darkness that dominated the tiny bedroom, he heard Rachel breathing. Slow, even, and deep. He stood still and waited for his eyes to adjust. After a time he could make out her slumbering figure, barely a silhouette beneath the linens. He continued to watch her sleep, her face turned away from him, her dark hair spilling across the pillow like a waterfall of shadow. Her work uniform lay in a crumpled heap at the foot of the bed, and he bent over and picked it up. Smoothing out a few wrinkles, he opened the microscopic closet set into the wall and hung the single-piece uniform on a hanger. He did the same with his own duty uniform, then carefully crawled into bed and stretched out beside his wife. Despite his best efforts, she stirred; after all, who wouldn't if they felt someone slinking into their bed when their husband was away?

"Mike?" she asked, voice blurry from what Andrews guessed was too much work and too little sleep. Before he could say anything, Rachel bolted upright in the bed with a gasp, reaching for him with one hand. She felt his face in the darkness, and he kissed her fingertips.

"Miss me?"

"Mike! Oh, God—" Her embrace almost crushed the breath

from him, and Andrews laughed at the ferocity of it. Thirty-three days was a long time for a man to be away from his wife, and it was good to see she felt the same way.

"Easy there. Don't break the merchandise, hon."

"I'm so sorry!" There was genuine regret in her voice, which puzzled Andrews.

"It's no big deal."

She laughed and pulled away from him long enough to take his face in her hands. "No, no ... not about that. I'm sorry I didn't meet you at Receiving. I must have slept through the pages. I worked the overnight shift as well as the morning shift, and I just stretched out for a quick nap, but—"

Andrews put a finger to her lips. "Rachel, it's no big deal. So I had to walk another couple of hundred feet to see you. Not a problem. Really." He kissed her gently. "Anyway. *Did* you miss me, or is there something else we need to talk about?"

"I don't want to talk," Rachel said, pulling him close. She wrapped her legs around him and gripped his shoulders with an intent that Andrews was well familiar with.

3

THE COMMAND CENTER of Harmony Base was a high-tech affair, a dimly lit room populated by workstations and displays of all sizes and brightness. From here, the personnel on duty monitored the condition of the subterranean installation, home to almost a thousand people. All internal metrics were captured and stored and, if necessary, reviewed. It was mostly mind-numbingly boring work, a repetitive process of staring at screens, monitoring the internal affairs of Harmony Base, and keeping the occasional eye turned toward the happenings on the surface over a hundred feet above their heads. But studying the surface was even more boring. Ever since the Sixty Minute War had essentially eradicated the ozone layer, solar radiation continued to bombard the planet, causing the Earth's surface to waste away even further. Beyond dusty rock and parched earth, there was almost nothing left outside to see. Not even a *cockroach* remained alive out there, so it was a rare circumstance for something outside to merit any discussion beyond *Hey, look at how big that dust storm is*, or *Well, it might not look like Kansas ... but it still is.*

"Sorry, Colonel, but do you have a second?"

Corrine Baxter looked up. Barney Rosen, the lone technician manning the External Observation Station located in one corner of the Command Center was facing her direction, leaning back in his chair. Baxter simply stared at him for a moment before responding.

EOS wants to talk?

Baxter pushed away from her desk at the back of the Command Center and stood. She straightened her uniform and walked over to the EOS station.

"What is it, Rosen?"

"We've just detected another tremor, ma'am. One point four on the Richter, same general epicenter as yesterday."

Baxter had to think back to the morning briefing to recall what the sallow-faced technician was talking about, but she did remember that several small tremors had been detected in the direction of the Colorado plains. That area was relatively stable—tectonically speaking—so the sudden uptick in activity was interesting, but not considered threatening in any way.

"You sure we're not talking about equipment failure here? It's been a long time ... Can tectonic sensors go bad?"

"They can, but they've passed all the diagnostics," the technician said. "For my money, they're working fine, ma'am."

Baxter didn't know what to make of that. "Okay. Do you think the quakes pose a threat to the base?"

"Oh, no. I wouldn't say that. I just want to make sure someone in the command group is aware of them, that's all. I would usually just log it and let it go, but since it's a pretty repetitive event," the technician pointed at one of the graphics on his workstation display, which showed a bar chart of tectonic occurrences over the past few days, "it seems like this is info you might want to look at for yourself, ma'am."

"Ah. All right, then. Forward the data to my station. I'll look it over."

Rosen pressed a button. "Done, ma'am."

"Thanks."

Baxter walked back to her station and slid into the high-backed chair. Her shift was over in ten minutes, and she would hand over the task of overseeing base operations to a junior officer while she knocked off for a straight eight. Just the same, she called up the tremor readings on her workstation and reviewed the graphs and the baseline assessment Rosen had conducted. Seismology was certainly not her forte, but the fact was Harmony had been positioned in western Kansas because the area was thought to be tectonically stable. Even if it wasn't, the base had been designed to survive a near-miss ground strike from a nuclear warhead in the forty megaton range, so she wasn't very concerned about earthquakes.

She bundled up the data and forwarded it to General Benchley. This was something he should know about.

Andrews sat at the small dining table in his quarters, drinking a cup of coffee. Rachel was in the shower, and he heard the water splashing across her body as she prepared for another day of work. Usually, a spouse would get a free day or two after an SCEV team had come back from the field, but the cost of the beer was high: Rachel had to cover for a sick coworker as part of the deal. They'd each had one of the beers last night. While they were good—fantastic, actually—Andrews was no longer convinced they were worth the price Rachel was paying for them.

The shower was turned off, and Andrews got up from the table. He brewed another cup of coffee for Rachel and set it down for her, along with a piece of toasted cinnamon bread— plain was how she liked it, which Andrews thought was boring as hell—then slid back into the plastic chair. He didn't have to wait for long before she emerged from the bathroom, stark naked, a towel wrapped around her hair.

"Morning, sweets!" she said, smiling at him brilliantly. "Sleep well?"

"Like the dead—you really tired me out last night." Seeing her in such a state of undress caused a flush of heat to surge through his groin. Rachel Andrews, née Lopez, was one of the most beautiful women in Harmony Base, and somehow, Andrews had gotten lucky enough to score her as his wife.

Rachel looked at him and her smiled widened. "Uh-huh ... doesn't look like it to me, mister." She pointed at his crotch. "If I'm not mistaken, it looks like you're pitching a tent in your bathrobe."

Andrews laughed and turned away from her, crossing his legs. Carefully. "Don't worry, I won't make you late for work."

"We'll see about that. But maybe I'll get dressed now, just in case."

"Your call, babe."

She walked to the bedroom, intentionally shaking her ass a bit, making him laugh. He heard her open the closet in the bedroom and pull out a work uniform, then listened to the rustling noises as she dressed.

"So, what did you find?" she asked from behind the bedroom partition.

"Nothing."

"What do you mean, nothing?"

Andrews sipped some more coffee. "All we found were burned-out cities. Collected a ton of scientific data that doesn't mean crap. Put a few thousand miles on the rig, and somehow, we didn't kill each other after more than a month driving around looking for life."

"You didn't find *anything*?" The disappointment was obvious in her voice.

Andrews sighed. "Well, we did find some fortified communities that survived the initial war. But once their supplies were exhausted, they had to abandon them. We don't know what happened to them, but the fortifications were empty." He paused for another sip of coffee. "Cheyenne Mountain's gone. Looks like it was hit with several ground strikes. The area was still way too hot for us to go EVA and check it out."

Rachel walked to the table, fully dressed. She slid into the chair opposite him and looked at Andrews with sad, dark eyes. "So ... we're all that's left?"

Andrews shrugged. "I don't know. We still think the Northwest is the best place to look, but the command staff wants to take baby steps and start local."

"Jim Laird's rig is going to head northeast," Rachel said, sipping her coffee. "Up the Ohio Valley, or something."

Andrews grunted. "Wrong direction, but at least the powers that be are thinking we need to stretch our legs. When did you find that out?"

"His rig was moved into vehicle prep last week. Kelly told me that was the plan."

"Jimmy's a good commander. If there's anything to be found out in that part of the country, he'll find it."

Rachel hesitated. "Kelly also mentioned something else," she said, finally.

"Do tell."

"Word has it that Benchley might create a new staff position. Director of Field Operations."

Andrews snorted. "More management, huh? Hooah, just what this place needs."

Rachel ignored his remark. "Babe, you'd be a natural. You're a great leader, and you have an eye for detail. And it's a base position—limited field time involved."

"Me? A base position? Rachel, you know I'm no paper pusher. I'm still young, and the field work is—"

"Important, I know, I know. Look, Mike, it's been ten years.

I think we're *it*. We're all that's left. You're putting yourself at risk for nothing."

Andrews looked at her over the rim of his coffee mug. "We've been through this," he said calmly. "I have a great crew backing me up. As long as I keep my head and don't do anything stupid, the field work's as safe as working in the Core—"

"That's bullshit." The anger was clear in her voice, and her eyes flashed with barely restrained fury. Andrews sighed inwardly. There was no winning this argument, and as long as he remained in command of SCEV Four, he was always going to spend part of his time home bobbing and weaving.

"Rachel, it's *not* bullshit."

"Yeah, right. Would you sing that song if your parents had bought it out in the field? Don't think so, Mike. Don't think so at *all*." She rose, turned to the sink, and fairly flung the remains of her coffee into it. She rinsed her mug as Andrews got to his feet and came up behind her, slipping his arms around her waist.

"That happened when the war was just going down. No one knows the full story—"

"Wake *up*, Michael!" Rachel put her hands on the counter and looked toward the ceiling. She sighed, and Andrews knew it was only a moment or so before she totally blew her top. "Mulligan and Benchley were serving together before we were born! The old timers cover for each other all the time, and you know that!"

Andrews squeezed her and spoke calmly into her ear. "And what does that prove, hon? What does that even mean, if it's true? Nothing. The fact of the matter is, what I do for this installation is as safe as it can be. What happened to your parents is the exception ... not the rule."

"Just because the only fatal rig accident happened over ten years ago doesn't mean it can't happen again. And it sure as hell doesn't mean it can't happen to you." Slowly, she turned inside his arms and looked at him, her brown eyes locking with his blue. She put her arms around his neck. She was cooling off, and Andrews allowed his gut to relax slightly. "Look. I'm sorry. I didn't mean to jump into this right away, I just got carried away."

"Don't apologize. I hear what you're saying. I really do." Andrews pulled her closer and kissed her forehead. "Listen ... I want that northwest recon. If anyone's still alive on this continent, that's where they'll be. After that, if this position you're talking about comes around, I'll speak to Benchley about it. Seriously."

"That would be nice," Rachel said softly.

Andrews kissed her. "I know this hasn't been much of a marriage. All we've had are little honeymoons in between deployments. That's my fault, and I'll try my damnedest to change that."

"You might as well. After all, it's the only marriage we've got. Right?"

Andrews smiled at her. "Right."

A chime sounded over the apartment's speaker system, followed by a neutral male voice. "The time is zero six fifty." Rachel sagged into his arms when she heard the announcement.

"Duty calls. I'll see you tonight, okay?" Andrews gave her a big hug.

"You sure will. What'll you do today?"

"Spend some time in the Commons, then head for the SCEV bay and check on the teardown of the rig. That's Spencer's job, but I want to keep my hand in, make sure everything's going as well as it can."

Rachel nodded slowly, her face impassive. She kissed his neck, then broke their embrace. "Well, enjoy it, I guess. I'll catch you at seventeen hundred."

"Okay. I love you, baby."

Rachel headed for the door. "I know you do." She pulled open the heavy door and stepped into the brightly lit corridor. When she turned to pull it closed, she looked at Andrews and smiled. "Get some more rest. I have plans for you later."

"Oh, goody!" Rachel laughed and closed the door. Andrews fairly collapsed into his chair and regarded the cold remnants of coffee in his mug. He put it back on the table and leaned back.

"Welcome home, you stupid jerk," he said to himself.

The Core was a huge, three-story chamber in the bottom of the base. The center of the floor was dominated by a wide platform, atop of which sat three wailing turbines contained inside soundproofed compartments that only served to dull the roar. If the personnel inside the base formed its soul, then the turbines were absolutely Harmony's heart. Without the life-giving power they generated, the base's inhabitants would have perished long, long ago. As such, the turbines and their associated systems were supported by dozens of technicians, and more were trained on their operations and maintenance every year. It was essential that the turbines remain operational twenty-four hours a day, 365 days a year. Without them, Harmony Base would cease to exist.

At noontime, Rachel walked across the floor to where Jeremy Andrews stood, talking to another engineer. She stood off to one side and waited to catch her father-in-law's eye, not wanting to interrupt the conversation. Jeremy looked and scanned the floor, his brow furrowing when he saw Rachel.

Jeremy finished his conversation, then headed toward Rachel. He looked at her with concern written all over his face. "You look like you've been put through the wringer. You all right?" Jeremy asked. "All of these shifts are doing you in. Don't think I haven't noticed."

"I'm fine," Rachel said. Jeremy Andrews was the base's engineering officer, one of the most senior civilian personnel in the base. Because of that, she had to be perhaps even more diligent in her duties. Despite the fact he was her husband's father, it wouldn't do for her coworkers to think she might be using family status to her unfair advantage. Keeping this in mind, she still asked, "Do you have a second? I, um, want to talk to you about something."

Jeremy smiled, the skin around his eyes crinkling. "Sure—anything to avoid work. You're on your break, right? Your station's manned?"

"Full up," Rachel said.

"Cool. Let's hit the lounge."

Jeremy led Rachel to a gangway, and she followed him up its narrow length to the next level. While he was about the same height as his son, Jeremy Andrews was about thirty pounds heavier, and the metal steps creaked slightly beneath his weight as he vaulted up the gangway. Despite his age and the expanding paunch that encircled his belly, he still moved fast, and Rachel had to hurry to keep up with him.

The lounge was located on the Core's second level. It was a bright room, and the tables and chairs were positioned before the thick windows that overlooked the Core. Rachel was happy to see the room was unoccupied. Jeremy immediately headed for the small refreshment area in one corner and grabbed a mug from a rack on the wall.

"Want a cuppa?" he asked, pointing at the coffee station.

"Sure, that'd be great." She really was tired from working so many double shifts, and the coffee would help her get through the rest of the day.

"Are you scheduled tomorrow?" Jeremy filled two mugs with dark coffee as he spoke.

"No, I'm off. Why?"

"Good. I was going to insist you take the day off. Listen, getting those beers for Mike was great and all, but they're just not worth two weeks of double shifts. Don't do that again. I'll talk to Dominick about it as well—he's a jerk for pushing you into that sort of an agreement. It's great that he can trade for a couple of days off so he can brew more beer, but when he starts pushing people into corners and performance suffers, I'm calling him on it."

"I'm fine, Jeremy. Really."

Jeremy handed her a mug of coffee, and she accepted it gratefully. He raised his own mug to his lips and looked at her for a moment as he sipped it. "You're fine? That's horse crap. You're dead on your feet." Before she could respond, he waved the matter away with one hand. "Anyhow. Most young married people would be doing handstands after their dear mates returned to the fold. Why aren't you?"

"Am I that transparent?"

Jeremy laughed and walked toward the windows. "Not at all, but I've been there. Before Meg died, that is."

He put his hands in his uniform's pockets, and Rachel could see his reflection in the glass. At the mention of his wife—her mother-in-law—who had died from cancer almost three years ago, a vaguely haunted expression flashed across his face. He hadn't wanted her to see it, she knew, but he had been foiled by the glass before him. He turned back to her and smiled easily, all traces of loss and loneliness gone from his face. "And I have an inkling as to what makes my son tick. So ...?"

Rachel sighed and shrugged. "I guess I'm acting like the little wife, as disgusting as it sounds."

"I don't know what that means. I know you probably go through a little or a lot of hell every time Mike takes off in that rig of his. Hell, I get queasy myself. But you know that his work is vital, right? That it's part of the core reasons for this base's existence?"

"Yeah, I'm up on all that. It's still a tough thing for me to deal with, and it screws up every homecoming. I just can't stop myself from trying to convince him to try his hand at something else. Even *I* realize what a nag I've turned into, so it must be ten times worse on the receiving end."

"The answer's easy—stop."

"I can't."

He sipped more coffee as she joined him at the window. "Then you're going to have a hell of a fight on your hands. I know Mike. He acts loose and easy all the time, but the fact of the matter is, he has one stiff neck. You try and bend it, he's going to stand up and give it back to you one day, and that won't be pretty." He paused. "But your position is absolutely understandable, given what you've gone through."

"Thanks. He thinks so, too. But he's convinced himself the rigs are the safest things around—"

"They are," a deep, rough voice said. Rachel's heart seemed to freeze in her chest, and if she hadn't been caught by surprise, she would have kept her gaze rooted on the turbine platform below. Unfortunately, she turned.

A tall, imposing man stood in the break room's corridor doorway, his pale eyes fixed on hers like he was tracking a target. He had a hard-edged, handsome face, bordering on old movie-star looks, but it seemed lived-in, a facade covering up decades of Rachel didn't know what. Command Sergeant Major Scott Mulligan was the base's senior enlisted man and a contemporary of the Old Guard—a relic.

Jeremy jumped in quickly. "Mulligan! What brings you to our cherished inner sanctum?"

Mulligan turned his inscrutable gaze toward the burly engineer. "My feet, of course." He raised the notepad he held in one hand. "It's time to go through the quarterly physical security review, which is on your calendar, Major."

"I thought that was tomorrow," Jeremy said.

"I guarantee you it's today, sir. And it'll be as routine as always—I'll ask you the same boring questions, you give me the same boring answers, we'll review the same boring data, and finally, we'll both sign the same boring attestation forms."

"Doesn't get any more exciting than that, does it?" Jeremy ran a hand over his face, then nodded to the tall sergeant major. "All right, then. Let's get to it." He put a hand on Rachel's shoulder. "Can we continue this later?"

"Sure," Rachel said, and she put her coffee mug in the sink. She couldn't get out of there fast enough.

"If it makes you feel any easier, Andrews, I can confirm for you that what Captain Andrews says is completely true—the SCEVs are about as bulletproof as any mobile system can be," Mulligan said to her as she turned for the door.

Rachel broke stride. It was rare for Mulligan to address her; the big enlisted man was usually too aloof to interact in a meaningful way with the New Guard, the people like herself and her husband who'd been brought to the base as children before the war. Now he had done so twice in rapid succession, and it provided Rachel with a sudden opportunity.

"Is that so, Sergeant Major? What's it like to kill people in them?" The sudden snarl in her voice surprised her. Like so many others, on some level she *feared* Mulligan. He was too different; he embodied too much legacy. He was an example of what had gone wrong in the world before the Sixty Minute War, a complete anachronism whose uniform still sported the patches of Army Special Forces. Everyone was on their toes around Mulligan, even members of the command staff, so when Rachel suddenly faced him down, she was perhaps the most shocked of all.

There was no backing down now. She stared at Mulligan, who stared back at her without any display of emotion. The moment dragged on, and Mulligan kept quiet until Jeremy opened his mouth to speak.

"It's not as easy as you might think," Mulligan said finally.

The bland response unnerved her and, for a moment, Rachel was afraid she might burst into tears. Instead, she managed to hold them back long enough to fix the tall soldier with a withering glare. If he recognized the hatred she felt for him,

Mulligan gave no indication. His only response was to look back at her with his usual flat, disinterested gaze.

Finally, he turned back to Jeremy. "We should get to work, Major."

Rachel stormed out of the break room and back into the never-ending din of the Core. She bolted down the narrow gangway, shoving past a burly electrician plodding up the metal stairs. The man had to flatten himself against the bulkhead so she could get past, and Rachel jostled him mightily. She would apologize to the electrician later. Right now, she needed to get to the restroom on the main floor and hide in a stall, so no one could see her tears.

4

AFTER HAVING BREAKFAST in the Commons Area, Andrews rode one of the elevators to the SCEV Maintenance Area. Virtually as wide as the entire base below it, "the bay," as it was called, was the single largest room in the installation, housing Harmony's remaining nine Self-Contained Exploration Vehicles. The tenth rig had been lost in the immediate aftermath of the Sixty Minute War under circumstances that remained unclear, though Andrews had of course heard the rumors that placed the blame squarely on Scott Mulligan's shoulders. The fact that Rachel's parents had perished in the same incident was not lost upon him, but Andrews wasn't about the past. He let Mulligan and Benchley and even his own father dance with that. Andrews was all about the future.

One portion of the bay was dedicated to assembly and repair, and SCEVs Four and Five were already there. Andrews made a beeline for his vehicle just as a ceiling-mounted crane lifted the bulky Mission Equipment Pack from the vehicle's back. The MEP was what made the SCEVs tick; loaded with all manner of sensors, a low-slung radome that housed a millimeter-wave radar, and a retractable pod that held six AGM-114R Hellfire missiles, the MEP had been designed to be modular. That way, a pack could be taken from one vehicle and attached to another should the rig's original pack have a systems failure. Removal of the pack after decontamination was also the first step in performing rig maintenance, and Andrews was not surprised to see Todd Spencer overseeing the operation. Standing with his feet spread and hands on his hips, Spencer struck a pose that was almost dictatorial. He shouted at the crane operator and the technicians who mounted the MEP to the crane, reminding them that they were handling millions of dollars of equipment—which would probably be worth billions now, if currency still had any value.

"Sergeant Spencer! Don't you crew chiefs ever sleep?" Andrews asked as he stopped beside the engineer and looked up at the MEP dangling from its truss.

Spencer only glanced at him. "*Buenos dias, Capitan.* Yeah, I caught a straight eight after we rolled in. I wanted to get cracking on that engine you guys blew. 'Scuse me for a second..." Spencer hurried over to where another maintenance technician was prying open an access panel on the SCEV's fuselage. "Hey, McCready! What're you doing? Since when do you just *pry* open an access point like that? You're going to bend the plate!"

Andrews watched as Spencer harangued the tech about the proper procedure required to open access plates, pointing out that said procedure was even written on the surface of the plate itself. Andrews shook his head. Spencer could be a little too much at times.

"Hey, Mike! Welcome back!"

Andrews took a slap to the back that was hard enough to make him take a step forward. He whirled around, startled. Jim Laird, the commander of SCEV Five, clapped his hands together as he snickered.

"Man, you should see the look on your face!"

"Kiss my ass, Jimmy. You scared the shit out of me."

"Sorry, sorry. How's it going?" Laird stuck out his hand, and Andrews shook it. Laird was about an inch taller than Andrews, and while Andrews could be described as broad-shouldered, Jim Laird was built like an old-time linebacker. And where Andrews was definitely Caucasian, Laird was anything but. "Philly black," he'd said about his ethnicity when they were kids.

"Tried to catch up to you yesterday, but you'd already made it back to quarters," Laird continued. "I figured I'd wait. Didn't want to interrupt anything important and have Rachel boot me in the nuts."

"Probably a good choice," Andrews agreed. "How're you doing, man?"

"Fair to middlin'. Getting ready to head up to Minnesota and see what we can see." Laird nodded to SCEV Five. The rig Laird commanded was an identical twin to Andrews's, the only difference being a black number 5 painted on its white fuselage. "Should be a couple of weeks of wall-to-wall excitement."

"There's lots of storm activity all across the Midwest," Andrews said. "Get ready for it. How far up do you think you'll go?"

"All the way to the Canadian border, if we can make it."

"Damn, guy. You go!"

Laird smiled. "As far and as fast as I can, pal." He paused. "So, scuttlebutt is you guys rolled snake eyes."

"Why, Captain Laird, I'm surprised at that statement. You know the command group will release the findings of my last mission in due time," Andrews said, tongue firmly in cheek.

"Come on, guy, throw me a bone here."

Andrews chuckled. It was true, he was technically not allowed to discuss his mission's findings with other personnel, but that regulation was regularly ignored every time an SCEV crew returned to the fold. That Laird already knew the mission was a wash less than a day after SCEV Four's return certainly indicated someone was chattering. Andrews took Laird by the elbow and led him several yards away from the two rigs.

"We found jack shit," Andrews said, turning back to watch the two SCEVs, one being torn down after a mission, the other being readied to jump into the field. "We found a couple of strongholds, but they'd been abandoned years ago. Even the best prepared survivalist couldn't hold out for a decade."

"You find bodies at those sites?"

Andrews nodded. "At some, yeah."

"But not at all of them?"

"We only found three, Jim. Two were full of bodies, the last one was empty ... but it *had* been occupied. Plenty of signs of habitation. They must've taken off for greener pastures, but no idea where they went. Or if they survived."

Laird was silent for a moment. "Well, maybe they made it. Maybe they headed northwest."

Andrews shrugged. "No evidence to show that, but yeah, maybe they did. The only way to crack that nut is to actually go there. I brought it up to Benchley again yesterday, but it doesn't seem like he's going to go for it. At least, not yet."

"Keep at it, man. You're the guy with the inside—"

The floor lurched beneath their feet, and Andrews staggered slightly. Laird reached out and grabbed his arm, but whether to steady Andrews or himself, he didn't know. Overhead, the chamber's ceiling creaked ominously, and SCEV Four's MEP swung from the crane like a pendulum. Andrews stumbled again as another jolt ran through the bay; the emergency lights flickered on and off, even though the main lights remained steady. Spencer started yelling at the crane operator, shouting for him to drop the MEP back on the SCEV. The technicians holding the MEP's guidelines looked amongst themselves as the base seemed to sway beneath their feet, the movements growing more forceful by the second.

What the fuck is going on?

"It's an earthquake," Laird said, as if reading his mind. "Oh, man, we're going through an earthquake in *Kansas!*"

Andrews looked around the prep area, listening to the creaks and groans of stressed superstructure that only grew louder. The vehicle elevator doors warped and flexed in their frame; a moment later, the frame itself seemed to undulate, twisting right to left amid the cacophonous rending of metal.

Oh, man ...

The Core exploded into chaos. Alarms blared as the base rocked on its shock-absorbing system, a series of gigantic fluid-filled cylinders designed to aid the base in surviving a near-miss from a nuclear ground strike. The absorption system was very much on Jeremy Andrews's mind as he slogged to his workstation. Could they survive an actual earthquake, one that continued on for more than just a handful of seconds? He suspected he was about to find out.

He slipped on his headset and immediately starting barking orders. "Let's get all the stations secure! Spool down turbine three, relegate it to standby status! Davies, Kadaka, get me the numbers on the well!!"

All around the Core, technicians staggered to their stations or fought to maintain their footing. He heard metal tear, followed by an explosion of steam. Above the creaking and rumbling, someone screamed, and Jeremy looked up in time to see a figure flying through the air amidst a rapidly expanding cloud of steam. A steam pipe had exploded, the force of the explosion blowing one of his engineers right off the third level. As he watched, Benny Okabe fell to the bottom floor, arms pin-wheeling. Jeremy could see his face plainly, and his expression was blank. Okabe landed on the other side of the turbines, and Jeremy was thankful the turbine housing was tall enough that he couldn't see the impact.

A klaxon wailed, loud and strident above the din of the earthquake rattling the base like a child's toy. Either someone had hit the emergency cutoff on the turbine platform, or the Core's AI had initiated an automatic shutdown of the three systems independently. He looked down and was surprised to see he had done it himself—he didn't remember lifting the plastic shield and throwing the red switch beneath it. It was too late. One of the turbine housings tore loose from its mounts and rocked back and forth; from inside it, several crashing explosions could be heard above the racket as the turbine array destroyed itself, its rotating components disintegrating as they contacted the housing's interior.

Then the main lights went out. Several people cried out in shock and fear as sudden darkness descended upon the great chamber—he was one of them. The emergency systems snapped on, bathing the area in pale, tepid illumination. There was another series of concussive blasts, and he could feel them this time. Jeremy clung to his console as the floor beneath his feet continued to undulate. He looked around, peering into the shadows where the illumination from the emergency lights couldn't penetrate. Was there smoke coming from the battery room?

The flames that erupted from the room confirmed Jeremy's suspicions. Another alarm sounded as the fire suppression system activated, blasting the room with heavy, dust-like fire retardant. But it wasn't working.

Then, just as suddenly as it had started, the violent, side-to-side jerking subsided. If it wasn't for the alarms, the emergency lights, and the acrid, deadly smoke filling the air from the battery room, it might have seemed that the earthquake had never happened.

"Secure the battery room door!" Jeremy shouted as another of the battery units suddenly exploded, causing more people to cry out in terror.

The command center was a pit of confusion illuminated by red emergency lights. Major General Martin Benchley clung to his workstation even after the earthquake had subsided, shaking in fear. The base creaked and groaned in the void left by the earthquake, and Benchley looked around the room. Several operators and technicians had taken cover beneath their workstations, cowering in their foot wells. Alarms rang. Displays flashed a series of situational alerts, and Benchley looked at the screens on his own workstation. The turbines were offline, and the base was operating on emergency power only.

Snap out of it! Get in the game!

"Operations!"

"Go for Ops, sir," said Cheadle, the officer manning the ops console.

"Let's get standard light restored, then tell me how badly we're hurt. Damage control teams need to get out and start making their assessments. Reports go to Colonel Baxter, ASAP."

"Roger that, sir."

"Is anyone in the center injured?" Benchley rose to his feet, pushing aside his fear. He had to show everyone the Old Man was still playing his A-game, and no one was going to listen to anything he had to say while he was clutching his workstation like it was his mother's apron strings. He looked around the command center as the lights suddenly brightened. Several bulbs flickered for a moment, then shone bright and strong. Benchley sighed in relief that no one seemed hurt.

"Cory, are you all right?" he asked Baxter. She had fallen to the floor on the other side of his workstation. A small cut on her dark cheek oozed blood, and he reached for her. Baxter shrugged off his hand and smiled tightly.

"Still operational, sir," she said.

"Sir, I have a preliminary report," the operations technician said.

"Let's hear it."

"The base is running on auxiliary power only. We've got enough juice for lights and air, but that's about it."

That wasn't what Benchley wanted to hear. "What's the word from the Core? When will primary power be restored?"

"I'm trying to get a hold of someone down in the Core, but there are several fire alerts down there. I think they're pretty busy, sir."

Benchley looked at the situation display on his workstation. Sure enough, several fire sensors had been tripped in the Core, and several more throughout the base. There were fire indicators illuminated on each of the installation's seven floors.

"All right, let's wait for the damage control teams to report in. Any word from medical?" he asked Baxter.

"Nothing yet, sir."

Benchley grunted. He feared what news the coming hours might bring.

5

EVEN THOUGH THE main elevator wasn't working, Andrews and the others managed to escape the SCEV prep area through a stairway that led to the next level of Harmony Base. Emergency lights glared in the gloom, and intercom announcements were strident but informative: There had been an earthquake; engineering was working on restoring essential power; seriously injured personnel were to be transported directly to the base's medical section on level three; all non-essential personnel were to return to their quarters or the Commons Area on level three and await further taskings.

"Guess that's us," Laird said. "Unless someone needs an SCEV at the moment."

"Sounds like," Andrews said. They were on level two, the first floor beneath the SCEV bay. Despite the fact it was an admin level, it was buzzing with activity. Several injured personnel were being carried down the corridor on stretchers. The elevators were under inspection, so they were out of commission. That meant the injured had to be transported down the four stairways located in each corner of the floor.

"I'm headed for the Commons. What about you?" Laird said.

"The Core. Rachel was on shift."

Laird made a sound of commiseration. "Damn. I'll go with you."

Andrews waved the notion away. "Nah, don't worry about it. I'm sure she's fine, but I'm going to head down there and check things out. Gives me the opportunity to heckle the old man, too."

"You sure?"

Andrews nodded and slapped Laird on the shoulder. "I'm cool, man. Really."

Laird looked at him levelly for a long moment, then returned his nod. "Okay. If you need me, I'll be in either the Commons or my quarters."

"Hooah," Andrews said. They hurried back into the stairwell. Laird peeled off on level three, heading for the huge

Commons Area, Harmony Base's main social and dining hub. Andrews pressed on, pushing past people coming up from the base's lower floors. Several were injured, many were near panic, and all of them had drawn-out expressions of grim foreboding etched into their faces. No one had been prepared for an event like this, and Andrews felt exactly the same way.

It took almost an hour to get down to level five, which was where the uppermost level of the Core could be accessed. Security guards turned him away, informing him the area was currently off-limits to anyone without an engineering specialty. They knew who he was, of course, and that his father was the base's engineering officer, but still they refused him admittance.

"I just want to know if my family's safe," Andrews told the senior trooper guarding the fifth floor entrance to the Core.

"I know your father is all right," the soldier said. "I saw him myself. I don't know about your wife though, Captain. Sorry. All section commands are supposed to be posting casualty lists, so ..." The soldier shrugged and looked over at the second guard for verification.

"That's probably the best thing you can do right now, sir," the other soldier agreed.

Andrews looked past their shoulders, but there was little to see. People were coming and going from the Core; those leaving were injured or heading to other parts of the base with toolkits and spares in hand, while those entering were apparently hurrying in to supplement the remaining workforce. There was the acrid hint of smoke in the air, a particularly foul-smelling, chemical sort.

"Do me a favor, guys ... You see Rachel Andrews, tell her I'm fine and I'll be in the Commons. You know who she is, right?"

"Oh, yeah," the first guard said. "We'll tell her if we see her, sir. Don't worry. Same message to your father?"

"Roger that. I'd appreciate it."

"Consider it done, sir."

Andrews nodded and reluctantly turned away from the doorway. He briefly considered going down to the sixth floor and trying his luck there, but it probably wouldn't work. The guards had their hands full already; they didn't need some junior officer trying to bull his way past them when they had orders.

So Andrews joined the procession of people moving up the stairs, pressing himself against the wall when damage control or medical teams came past, granting them priority access. It usually only took a minute or two to get to the Commons level, but due to the crush of bodies and their slow gait, it took ten minutes. It was perhaps the longest ten minutes of his life, and Andrews felt a particularly furious sort of irritation blossom in his chest. While he was no stranger to impatience, he was used to being in control of himself, being capable of reining in his emotions before they got the best of him. It was something all of the New Guard had to become familiar with. Being raised underground and told they were humanity's last hope and the seeds for a new United States of America, patience was something that had been inculcated in them from their earliest years. While the Old Guard wrestled with claustrophobia, boredom, and even outright hostility, the New Guard was able to look past those things and face the future with a calm, even gaze. The Old Guard couldn't do that, at least not as reliably as the younger people. The Old Guard had grown up in wide open spaces with lovely blue skies. The only clouds that came their way sprinkled rain or snow, not radioactive particles that could damage cellular reproduction and cause uncontrollable cancers.

Andrews sensed a strong undercurrent of frustration running through the crowd. Only a few hours ago, everyone had been carrying on with their subterranean lives, hoping and praying the SCEV teams would find other pockets of life that Harmony Base could work with to rebuild the nation. Now, that mission seemed to be a very distant goal. Survival was once again at the fore.

When he finally stepped into the Commons Area, he wasn't surprised to find it packed tight with people. Even though it had been designed to accommodate virtually the entire base, it was rare for so many people to be in the cavernous room at one time. As he walked through the crowd, occasionally acknowledging someone he knew, he decided it wasn't as packed as he'd initially thought. There was still enough room to move about, so long as he was careful and took care not to stomp on someone's foot or get hit with a chair as someone stood up from a table.

"Mike!"

Andrews turned. Leona Eklund pushed toward him through

the crowd, her lean, athletic frame giving her more than enough dexterity to wend her way through the occasional mass of bodies and, when required, the power to shove her way past. Like himself, she'd been brought to the base at a very young age—four years old, to be exact. Now nineteen, she served as his executive officer and was commissioned as a first lieutenant in the United States Army. Her curly dark hair hung free around her shoulders, and her narrow-featured face turned his way, her deep brown eyes locked on him. Someone—one of the Old Guard, he remembered—had mentioned to him once that Leona was built like a saluki, lean and all angles. Andrews had had to look it up, but he found that a saluki was a breed of dog built for racing. He agreed with the description. Leona did seem to possess the same poise as the dogs he had seen in the videos.

"Lee, you okay?" he asked.

"Yeah, I'm good. What about you?"

Andrews shrugged. "Tried to get down to the Core, but it's under lockdown. I heard my dad's all right, but don't know anything about Rachel yet."

She looked at him for a long moment. "I'm sorry about that. It must be terrible."

Andrews shrugged, wondering if the worry was as visible on his face as he feared it might be. "I'll make do," he said lamely. "You see anyone else from the team?"

She nodded. "Everyone's accounted for, except for you and Spencer."

"He's fine. We were in the SCEV prep area when the quake hit. They'd just started pulling our rig apart. I'm glad it wasn't on the elevator—it looks like it got whacked big time. The doors practically collapsed inward."

"Sounds bad. Did Five leave?"

"No, not yet. Both rigs are still in the prep area."

Leona nodded and started to say something else, but the screens surrounding the Commons came to life. A shiver ran through the assembled people, and everyone turned to the nearest screen. Andrews was no different; his heart started to race, and he and Leona both turned to stare at the closest screen. The casualty reports were in alphabetical order, so Andrews didn't have long to wait. There was no listing for "Rachel Andrews." He didn't allow himself to fully relax until the listing progressed through the Ls and there was no "Rachel Lopez," either. When he saw that, he released his breath in a trembling sigh.

The list is going to be continually updated, he told himself. *Just because she's not on it now, doesn't mean she won't be on it later.*

Adding a small cast of desperation to his thought was that there were almost thirty names on the list. Thirty names, and he knew them all. Thirty people who had been killed during the earthquake. He had grown up with four of them, and one of them, a woman named Sally Kesserman, had been one of his dearest friends when they were younger. He remembered that at first, they played long games of tag in the base, stealing off to areas few adults could get into as they hid from each other and giggling in the darkness, the antiseptic corridors of Harmony Base infected by the sounds of their running feet. Only three quarters of the base was inhabited, so it gave them lots of space to play in, and Andrews remembered they had actually gotten lost twice in the labyrinthine installation. Then later, when they began to mature, they discarded the games kids played and spent the time just talking, just hanging out with each other. While they had never been mutually attracted to each other, the friendship they developed was a strong one.

But over the decade that had passed since the Sixty Minute War, Andrews had watched Sally grow up. She had become a serious-minded woman, a quartermaster's assistant, her brow always furrowed by the rate at which the base's consumables disappeared. While Andrews was in charge of connecting the base with any outside settlements that might exist, her job was to remain below ground and count beans. She was in charge of worrying, something she'd never had a penchant for when she was younger.

Other than meaningless chitchat, Andrews hadn't kept up with her for the past several years. That he would never have the opportunity to talk to his old friend again left him feeling hollow and guilty.

"So many," Leona said, her voice soft. Sobs broke out around the Commons. In such a small community, the loss of thirty people meant that everyone had lost someone. The bottom had just dropped out of several people's lives. Andrews looked around numbly. He felt it, too.

Oh, Sally ...

He looked at Leona, her face tightly drawn. She had always been a super-confident sort, the type of person who never let her true feelings show. He remembered when she was maybe twelve years old, when she and her family had arrived at the base. The rest of the kids would sometimes make fun of her gawky figure, thin features, and lank hair. If the teasing had ever bothered her, she'd never given any of them the satisfaction of seeing it. As he grew older, Andrews found he admired her for that trait, which he himself had never been able to master. But even Leona had her limits, and the sudden notice that thirty people had checked out for the long dirt nap had pushed her past them. Tears glittered in her eyes as she continued to stare at the displays. Andrews put his arm around her shoulders and gave her a squeeze. She stiffened at the sudden contact, but Andrews kept his arm around her to let her know she wasn't alone in her grief.

"You all right?" he asked.

Leona relaxed suddenly. She bowed her head, as if embarrassed by her tears, and tried to hide them by wiping the back of her hand across her eyes. "Yeah, I'm okay. I just wasn't expecting there to be so *many*."

Andrews looked at the scrolling fatality list and wondered idly at its power. Millions had died well in advance of these thirty, but it was these thirty that he knew. In the grand scale of things, the passing of thirty souls could perhaps be considered inconsequential. But in the small community of Harmony Base, it was as if an entire nation had just been ripped asunder.

"Hang in there, Lieutenant," he said. "Just hang in there."

Leona raised her head and looked at him, a bit of the old fire back in her eyes. "Because it's probably going to get worse, right?"

"It might," he agreed softly. "It just might."

Leona nodded and looked back at the displays. She reached up and touched his hand, the one that was still wrapped around her shoulder. "Thanks for this, but you don't want anyone to get the wrong idea."

Andrews smiled lamely and released her. "I don't think anyone even noticed."

"I know. Thanks for helping." She flashed him a sudden smile. "Really."

"Free of charge."

"Andrews," a voice called from behind him. "You need to come with me right now."

Andrews turned as Colonel Larry Walters stepped up beside him. He was shorter than Andrews by quite a bit and, true to his nickname, the colonel was in fact somewhat wall-eyed; his left eye wandered a bit off-center, enough so that it was difficult for people to know which eye to look at while they were speaking to him. He was a small-boned sort, and his steel gray hair was cropped so close to his skull that Andrews wondered why Walters never went for broke and just shaved it bare.

"Sir?" Andrews said automatically, even though he had heard Walters perfectly. The truth was, his heart had skipped a beat. Why was Walters here? Had something happened to Rachel? Had he come to find Andrews before her name was released on the casualty list?

"I need you to come with me," Walters said again, impatiently. He looked past Andrews. "You too, Eklund. Follow me."

"Where to, Colonel?" Leona asked.

He fixed her with his imprecise stare. "Follow. Me." He turned and pushed through the crowd without saying anything else. Andrews nodded at Leona, and he headed after the bantam officer as quickly as he could.

Andrews was surprised to find Walters had led them to the commander's conference room. That the room was full was no shock—the base had just been hit by what appeared to be a major catastrophe, and he expected all the senior department heads to be present. What he didn't expect was for Jim Laird and his exec, Kelly Jordello, to be in attendance, any more than he would expect Leona and himself to be summoned. What did SCEV teams have to do with the earthquake?

"Andrews and Eklund, sir," Walter said as he stepped into the room. General Benchley sat at the head of the long table opposite the entrance, and he made eye contact with Andrews and Leona as they entered. It was standing room only. From the corner of his eye, Andrews saw Rachel sitting at the far end of the table.

"Very well," Benchley said. "There's not a lot of room left, so you folks come in as best as you can."

"You heard him, get yourselves squared away," Walters said. He folded his arms and leaned against the wall beside the door. Andrews and Leona pushed themselves inside and grabbed a patch of wall to lean against.

"Jeremy, if you could get started, please," Benchley said.

Beside him sat Sergeant Major Mulligan, and Andrews thought the big Green Beret didn't look happy. He was practically crushed against the edge of the conference table, and the look of utter disdain on his face was priceless. Andrews might have smiled at the sight if Mulligan hadn't looked in his direction. He turned and looked over toward Rachel. She smiled at him vaguely.

The far wall illuminated suddenly; it was actually a huge LED monitor. A vector graphic diagram of Harmony Base appeared on the display. Overall, the representation was in green, but several areas of the base were red. Andrews saw one of those areas was the SCEV bay, where the rigs were stored when not in use. The prep area above the bay was still mostly green.

"All right, folks. As most of you know, several areas of the base have been badly damaged. Most notably, the geothermal exchange system and the auxiliary power cells, here and here." Andrews watched as his father walked up to the display and tapped the indicated areas. "We're operating under emergency conservation procedures, which gives us essential systems power for eight days, max. After that, we're on lifeline support, but without the batteries, we're not looking at much more than another five days or so before the CO_2 levels reach critical. In short, we'll all suffocate down here unless we can get the main systems back online.

"The supports that hold the heat exchanger pumps in place were damaged by the earthquake, leaving them without any reliable stabilization. When those units are operational they vibrate quite a bit, and without the supports, the conversion pumps would be smashed to pieces against the sides of the shaft."

Jeremy manipulated a control on the remote, and the display

changed to show a graphic of the heat exchange system located almost a mile beneath the base. A long shaft had been bored into the Earth's crust to where the planet's molten core provided enough heat to turn water into steam. That steam was then pumped under pressure to the turbines in the Core, providing them with the necessary fuel to power Harmony Base. The steam would condense back into water, which was then replaced in the ground, ensuring the cycle of availability was more or less continuous. Even though he wasn't one of the base's powerheads, Andrews knew all about it. After all, his father was in charge of maintaining the system and had architected improvements in the few years before the Sixty Minute War shut the door on everything topside.

"These supports were designed to meet exacting tolerances, and their operational lifespan is supposed to be a century or more. They're very dense, and due to their metallurgical properties, they're not something we can manufacture in one of our machine shops. We don't have the foundry skills to do it."

"So what's the big reveal?" Mulligan asked. Benchley cast a glance at him, but the sergeant major gave no indication he noticed. Jeremy sighed and clasped his hands behind his back.

"The big reveal is this, Sergeant Major: if we don't get replacements, we can't turn on the geothermal exchange pumps. And without those pumps operational, there's precious little power to scrub the air, run the water, or operate the lights. In short, we're kind of fucked."

Colonel Baxter rubbed her forehead. "Mister Andrews, that sounds kind of extreme."

"It's an extreme set of circumstances, ma'am."

"But this base was designed to withstand a near ground-strike from a nuclear weapon," Baxter said. "How could an earthquake result in this much critical damage?"

"A nuclear strike is pretty much a short-lived event, Colonel," Jeremy said. "The earthquake discharged even more energy than a nuclear weapon over a greater period of time, albeit over a much larger area. As such, the base was going to take one in the snot locker. We just didn't expect it to take out our teeth with one punch, as it were."

"These supports ... we don't have replacements? It seems like something of this nature, a component that's critical to the survival of the base, should be in our supply chain somewhere."

"That made sense in the 1980s, ma'am. But after the fall of the Soviet Union, this installation wasn't exactly considered a primary project any longer. Interest in it was renewed after the terrorist attacks of 9/11, and the base went through some substantial refurbishing to bring it up to date. But the general architecture of the geothermal exchange system was left untouched. We've done some modifications to make things more efficient here and there, but overall, the system is still using technology from the 1980s. And since the supports were designed with such a long lifespan, the replacements were never shipped."

"*Are* there replacements, sir?" Mulligan asked.

Jeremy hesitated for a long moment. He looked down the length of the table at Benchley. The general sighed loudly and ran a hand over his steel gray hair.

"Tell them," he said.

"There were," Jeremy answered. "I mean, as far as I know, there still are. In California."

The assemblage took in its collective breath and released it in one long sigh.

"California." Mulligan's voice still sounded flat, even over the din of the restive group. "As in, the Beach Boys' California?"

"That's the only one I know of," Jeremy said.

Mulligan snorted and leaned back in his seat, crossing his arms over his barrel chest.

"And this is why we're here," Benchley said, looking around the room. He made eye contact with everyone. "This installation has just gone through an extremely powerful event, one that rivals the lethality of the Sixty Minute War. Actually, it casts even that circumstance in deep shadow. As you've just heard from Mister Andrews, Harmony Base is now faced with the possibility that the earthquake might very well be a terminal event." He paused to let that sink in for a moment. "We've already lost people. We may lose more in the coming hours. And if we don't act quickly, we might lose everything inside of two weeks."

"You need us to go out and secure replacements," Andrews said suddenly.

Benchley turned to him and nodded. "Correct, Captain. As

it stands, SCEVs Four and Five are the only rigs in the rig prep area. The lift to the SCEV bay is currently out of commission, and best estimates are that it will take more than a day to repair. So those two vehicles are going out into the field to secure replacement supports." He pressed a button on a desktop controller, and the wall display changed to show a route from Harmony's position in western Kansas to San Jose, California. "I realize that Four has just come back in from the field and was in the beginning stages of post-mission teardown. Obviously, the rig will be reassembled after the more pressing maintenance items are tended to. Once completed, both vehicles will depart as soon as possible for California. Andrews, you'll serve as mission commander. Captain Laird will serve as mission deputy commander. Eklund and Jordello will remain rig XOs. You will be accompanied by Engineer Spencer, Mission Specialist Choi, and Missus Andrews here, who is familiar with the supports." Benchley nodded toward Rachel, sitting at the far end of the table next to Jeremy.

Andrews blinked. "Uh, sir, she isn't qualified for field work, and we won't have time to train her up—"

Benchley held up one hand, cutting him off. "I understand your dilemma, Captain, but I want someone on hand who can not only identify the supports, but also identify which ones are good and which ones are bad. Bringing back defective parts isn't an option. We won't have another chance at a do-over." The general paused. "I'm also adding Command Sergeant Major Mulligan to the mission roster."

Mulligan's eyes widened. "General, I'm an instructor—"

"—who is fully current in SCEV operations, and in light of your Special Forces background, I feel it's prudent you go." Benchley faced Mulligan directly. "Any questions on that, Sergeant Major?"

Mulligan glared at Benchley for a long moment, then slowly shook his head. "Good to go here, General."

"Excuse me, sir?" Kelly Jordello, Laird's executive officer, spoke up. She was short and curvy, with long blond hair she kept tied back from her face. A vivacious sort, she was full of energy and had been something of a tomboy in her youth, a quality that had attracted Andrews to her in their teen years. He'd tried to woo her, but it had all been for naught. Kelly's preference was for other women, and while such a revelation was hardly enough to raise even an eyebrow in the base's small society, Andrews had been heartbroken for a month when she finally rebuffed him. But as they grew older, they developed a casual, low-maintenance friendship that made up for their embarrassing past.

"Go ahead, Lieutenant."

"You've named only eight crewmembers. You *are* assigning more faces for the spaces, right?"

"Negative on that. Should one vehicle become disabled, then the second rig can take on the remaining crew without overloading its life support systems. I know half-crews will increase everyone's workload, but it's unavoidable. Colonel Walters will provide the required electronic navigation updates for both rigs, and he has already ordered every available vehicle engineer and crew chief to the prep area to assist with rig stand-up and certification. Andrews, you and Laird will be responsible for ensuring all tier one safety checks are completed, but I encourage you to skip the nonessentials in order to take to the field as quickly as possible. Understood?"

Andrews looked at Laird, and the other commander nodded his assent. "Roger that, sir. We'll try and streamline things as much as we can."

Benchley nodded. "I appreciate that. I understand this is a sudden thing to drop on you. Normally we spend months planning each jump into the field, but I'm sure you understand we have no choice here. I wish I could provide you with more information, but we have nothing further. Get your affairs in order—you'll be leaving as soon as possible. Colonel Walters will be your conduit to the command group for any last minute issues. I know everyone has a great deal of work to do, so if there's nothing else, you're all dismissed to tend to your tasks."

The assemblage stirred to life. Andrews stepped out of the conference room and waited in the corridor. Leona followed him, and he turned to her.

"You mind heading up to the prep bay and checking in with Spencer? Make sure he knows what's going on, and that he has everything he needs. Remember, we had a twitchy differential. Let's get that replaced and tested. As soon as the rig is put back together, start a full component test. I want even the line replaceable units bench-tested. All right?"

"Got it," Leona said. "Anything else?"

Andrews looked past her shoulder as Rachel emerged from the conference room. Her uniform was covered in grime; clearly, she'd been busy on some sort of repair before she'd been pulled into the conference. Leona followed his gaze, then looked back at him.

"I'll see you later," she said, and headed down the corridor.

Andrews looked at Rachel and, from her expression, he could see she knew he wasn't happy that she'd been assigned to the mission.

"So ... now I get to see you at work, huh?" She smiled sheepishly.

"Don't be so damn sure," he said. "There's got to be someone else who can be assigned to this. You can't be the only person who can tell us not to bring back a rusty support."

"There's more to it than that, and Jeremy is the one who selected me. Listen, I'm not exactly thrilled to leave right now. There's a lot that has to be done, and going on a road trip through post-apocalyptic America was always pretty low on my to-do list."

Jeremy stepped out of the conference room, staring at his data tablet with a frown. He looked up when Andrews grabbed his arm and pulled him away from the exit. His frown deepened.

"Save it, Mike. I know what you're going to say. Rachel's the best asset to validate—"

"Dad, she doesn't know jack about SCEV ops, and she's terrified of them. You know that. Asking her to saddle up with the rest of us is *majorly* away from goodness."

Jeremy sighed, and he glared at Andrews angrily. "Stop bitching about it. This is how it's going to be played, Mike. I'm sorry if you find this personally inconvenient, but we don't exactly have a lot of choices here. Benchley asked for the best person available to ensure that good replacements are brought back, and that person just happens to be Rachel." He looked at her. "You're good with this?"

"Mostly," she said. "I'll do whatever you need me to do, Jeremy."

Jeremy looked back at Andrews. "Any further questions, Captain?"

Andrews sighed. "No, sir."

Jeremy relaxed a little bit, and he squeezed his son's shoulder. "I know it's asking a lot of you, and I know that adding Rachel to the mix is going to make it tough for both of you personally. But there's no choice in the matter, so you might want to try and make it as easy as possible by making sure she gets spooled up on the broad strokes of SCEV operations. All right?"

"Yes, sir," Andrews said. There was no use fighting it. His father was right, and the stakes were high. Better to just soldier on and get it done.

"Good," Jeremy said. His tablet pinged, and he had another crisis to tend to.

In the conference room, Benchley took a moment to compose himself before the next session started. He still had a slew of damage reports to go through, and the road ahead looked bleak and desultory. He noticed Mulligan beside him at the table, staring at him with his dark gaze. "Is there something I can do for you, Sergeant Major?" Benchley asked.

"Field duty, sir? *Me?*"

"You'll be needed, Mulligan."

"How so? I haven't been in the field for over ten years, sir. I'm an old geezer. And Rachel Andrews happens to hate my guts for—"

"And whose fault is that?" Benchley asked, irritation plain in his voice. He took a moment to dial it back a bit before continuing. "Scott, I'm sorry. I understand the deployment will be rough, but I want your experience on tap. We don't know what these people might run into out there. Your background and your skill set might be a very welcome addition, should things go even further into the shitter."

Mulligan snorted derisively, and Benchley found he couldn't contain his irritation any longer. He fixed Mulligan with an icy stare.

"As you still wear the uniform of the United States Army, you should be able to recognize an order when you hear one, Sergeant Major. Am I clear on that?"

"Hooah," Mulligan said. "With your permission, sir, I guess I ought to get to it."

"An excellent idea."

6

THE VEHICLE PREP area was a beehive of activity as a veritable army of maintainers, engineers, and SCEV crews crawled all over the two rigs. Andrews was in the thick of it himself, overseeing the reseating of SCEV Four's Mission Equipment Pod on the rig's broad back. Over the past nine hours, all the systems in the pod had been tested and certified as good to go; those that had failed were serviced until they were in the green. Even the MEP's complement of six Hellfire missiles had been replaced, and the millimeter wave seeker heads on each had been retuned to ensure perfect accuracy. That was a first; Andrews couldn't recall a time when he had seen every missile replaced before a mission. Sure, he'd seen one or two swapped out after failing a test, but the entire complement? Never.

"Why is patience a virtue?" Spencer shouted over the din of activity as he slid out from beneath the rig with another technician. Their coveralls were stained with oil and grime. "Why can't 'hurry the fuck up' be a virtue?"

"You can't push this stuff," the other maintainer said. "It's got to go slow—you know that."

"Slow is a comparative term."

"Hey, Spence!" Andrews barked as the MEP was locked down on SCEV Four's back. "What's the problem?"

Spencer looked tired but alert. He only had eyes for the rig, and he turned and scoured his high-tech baby for any defects related to the positioning of the MEP.

A dedicated man, Andrews thought.

"No problem, Captain. We swapped out the number one engine and the particle separator, along with the forward differential, which we'd already talked about. I was just busting McCready's balls. He moves like an old lady when it comes time to turning a wrench."

McCready frowned. "Dude, that's so not true."

Andrews saw that McCready was just about run out from working God knew how many hours straight, and Spencer's riding him wasn't helping. He slapped Spencer's arm with the back of his hand. "Hey, why don't you knock off for some chow.

I don't want you guys getting so damned tired that you're seeing double and making phantom adjustments."

"Yeah, yeah, just let me check the pod. Once that gets squared away, we've got the green light as far as I'm concerned. Everything else after that just involves bold type safety checks." As he spoke, he walked away from Andrews. He pulled an LED flashlight from inside his grimy uniform and shined it up at where the MEP joined the SCEV. He ran the beam all along the join, and Andrews knew he was looking for irregular gapping, something a junior technician could do.

"Spence, let someone else do that," Andrews said. "We've got five other SCEV crew chiefs here. They can take care of the MEP."

"My rig, my duty."

"Spencer, this isn't a gentle suggestion," Andrews said. "Knock off for a meal. If you drive yourself into the ground now, you'll be no good to me out in the field."

"Just a second, sir." Spencer hadn't paused in his inspection of the SCEV for one second, and he gave no indication he was going to stop for something as pedestrian as a meal. McCready looked from Spencer to Andrews and back again.

Andrews took four quick steps and seized hold of Spencer's arm, forcing him to stop and look at him. Spencer's brow furrowed in annoyance.

"Hey, Captain, if you want this tub ready to leave on schedule then—"

"Let. Someone. Else. Do. This. You've been going at this for hours straight. I want you to take a break. Don't fucking argue with me, Spencer, *just do it.*"

Spencer blinked. Andrews had never spoken to him like that before. He'd never had to. It shocked him as much as it did Spencer, but that was what it took to get through. Spencer nodded slowly.

"Okay. Okay, if you feel that strongly about it. No problem," the burly crew chief finally said.

"Glad you see it my way. Don't come back for at least twenty minutes."

"Sheesh. Okay, Dad." With that, Spencer walked off.

"What about me, sir?" McCready asked.

Andrews looked at him. "What do you do, again?

Propulsion systems, right?"

"Roger that," McCready said. "Transmissions, differentials, all that stuff."

Andrews shrugged. "You don't work for me, so if you're done, you're done. Check with your boss."

McCready put his hands in his pockets and walked away. Andrews turned and looked up at the MEP that straddled his vehicle. He certainly had the chops to check for defective seals himself, so he grabbed a step ladder and went to work.

The hours passed slowly and, before he knew it, Andrews had spent twenty of them in the prep area, going over SCEV Four and, when time permitted, SCEV Five. Laird's rig was in tip-top shape; it had undergone the full evaluations before SCEV Four had returned and was within days of jumping out. Little needed to be done except stock it with consumables, then it would be ready for the field.

"You look like hell," Laird said at one point. "You should knock off for a while, man."

"Can't," Andrews said. He felt exactly how Laird said he looked. His eyes were scratchy, and they burned as if they were orbs of flame. He felt at once jittery and bone-weary, and he was having trouble focusing. It wasn't that he wasn't capable of working long hours—in the field, everyone did. But the tasks he had to conduct required concentration and severe attention to detail, and performing such tasks back-to-back for hours only accelerated his exhaustion. He'd already cut his crew loose and instructed them to get some rest. Even Spencer had sacked out for a bit, albeit in one of the narrow bunks in the back of SCEV Four.

"Bullshit," Laird said. "I watched you dismiss your entire crew, man. You need to get some shut-eye yourself, otherwise you're going to be one messed-up cat when it comes time to jump out."

Andrews rubbed his eyes. He knew Laird was right. Besides, he had about a gigabyte of regulations corroborating exactly that in his tablet. But he just couldn't bring himself to knock off. SCEV Four was just in from the field, where it had been ridden hard, and now it was being sent back out before it had even entered the proper maintenance phase inspection. Andrews wasn't sure he could sleep even if he *did* step out of the prep area.

He started to respond when movement in the cockpit of SCEV Four caught his attention. He rubbed his eyes again, then looked up at the thick viewports. Someone was sitting in the rig's pilot seat.

"That would be Mulligan," Laird said, following Andrews's gaze. "Your newest, bestest pal."

Andrews grunted. He hadn't wanted Mulligan on the mission any more than he wanted Rachel. He was saddled with both of them, despite the fact that they would be at each other's throats the entire time. To help alleviate this, Andrews and Laird had agreed that Rachel would crew on SCEV Five, while Mulligan crewed on Four. They would also work off-shift from each other; Mulligan would get the first shift, while Rachel would get the third. That would help prevent them from even hearing each other over the radios. Andrews thought it was all very childish, but he knew why Rachel felt the way she did, and there was no reasoning with her. Her wounds were years old, but the scar tissue was still extremely sensitive. Andrews didn't need her picking at it any more than she already did.

"What's he doing up there?" Andrews asked.

"Going over startup and shutdown procedures. It's been a while for him, you know."

"Yeah, I guess so." Suddenly remembering something, Andrews turned to Laird. "Hey, Engineering was supposed to bring up two motorized dollies, one for each rig. We need them to—"

"Move the core supports, I know. And yes, both arrived, and one is in the aft storage compartment of each rig." Laird nudged him in the ribs. "Dude, go take a nap, would you? I've got the duty on making sure your rig is prepped and ready to go for the next few hours, all right?"

Andrews looked around the prep area. Despite the hour, it was still humming, and SCEV Four was receiving most of the attention. Panels had been pulled open, and the equipment that lay behind them was undergoing thorough examination. Maintenance crews walked all over the top of the rig, checking antennae, infrared systems, lights, and high-frequency comms—

anything they could get at.

He focused his attention on the figure sitting in the cockpit of his rig, and put his hands on his hips. He sighed, and Laird sighed as well.

"Man, you'll have days to sit and chat with Mulligan. Get some rest, Mike."

"I will." He walked toward the SCEV's open airlock door, the lower half of which formed a short stairway up into the airlock itself. As he mounted the stairs, he half-turned his head, just long enough to see Laird shrug and turn his attention to more pressing matters.

Andrews hauled himself inside the Self-Contained Exploration Vehicle. The quarters were tight; the airlock was supposedly big enough for two people fully suited in Advanced Mission Oriented Protective Posture IV gear, which was true— presuming one of them was a circus midget. The inner airlock door was open, so he was able to step right into the rig's second compartment, which housed the engineering and science workstations, as well as the crew's microscopic "living area"— the portion of the SCEV where they would eat and do whatever it was they fancied when not piloting the rig, conducting experiments, or sleeping. A small dinette was set against the left bulkhead, opposite the kitchenette, which consisted of an over-and-under refrigerator and freezer, a convection/microwave oven, a sink, and storage cabinets. When not in its stowed position against the overhead, a twenty-inch LED display could be lowered to face the dinette as well. The SCEV had thousands of hours of movies, games, and other programming available, though it was all over ten years old.

The compartment floor was opened up, and several technicians were going over the rig's transmissions from the interior access points. Andrews saw the drive shafts that connected the rig's multiple differentials. The panels were opened all through the vehicle, even in the sleeping compartment in the back, where Andrews clearly heard Spencer sawing wood despite all the activity occurring right next to him. The technicians held data tablets, which were directly linked by DIN connections to the SCEV's maintenance access harness, and they compared settings.

"Hey, guys," he said. "Mind if I step in?"

"You're good to go, sir," one of the technicians said, barely glancing up.

"Why aren't you guys using the wireless?"

"It's saturated, sir. We've got a couple of dozen techs working this rig over, so all the access points are taken." The technician touched the cable connecting his tablet to the rig's data bus. "It's this, or nothing."

"Roger that. I'll leave you guys to it, then."

The technicians didn't acknowledge him further, so Andrews stepped over the gap in the floor beyond the airlock and turned to his right. Squeezing past the engineering and science stations, he made his way to the cockpit. The door was very narrow, so he had to bend slightly and rotate his shoulders. He knew Mulligan was sitting in the left seat—the command seat—so he turned toward the copilot's seat on the right side of the cockpit.

"Sarmajor," he said, slipping into the cockpit and lowering himself into the confines of the copilot's seat.

"Evening, Captain," Mulligan said. His voice was its usual basso rumble, and he turned his clear, green eyes toward Andrews, watching as he slipped into the seat. "You've been at it for quite a while, sir. Shouldn't you be getting some rack time?"

Andrews waved away the suggestion. "I'm good, Sarmajor. What are you up to?"

Mulligan pointed at the forward instrument panel, where the wide touchscreens glowed. On the center display, the computerized checklist was up and available, and several items had already been marked green.

"I'm going through the safety checklist. Even though we were instructed to skip the nonessential checks, I'm going through as many as possible. When I leave the cockpit, I intend to leave it sterile—with your permission, no one gets in or out until we're ready to jump out. That way, we'll preserve the vehicle status."

Andrews grunted. "Uh, you *are* aware that the rig's still being torn apart and put back together, right, Mulligan?"

Mulligan looked at him expressionlessly. "Yes, Captain, I'd caught onto that. This is how we did things back in the day, when there was the chance we wouldn't have time to run through checklists and the like, but recognized there was a high-threat level that could mandate equipment use right off the cuff."

"I understand, Sarmajor. But these vehicles are going to be accessed right up until we leave ..."

Mulligan shook his head. "Untrue. We'll go into a rest cycle before we jump out. I've already been over that with General Benchley. He agrees that we'll need a bit of downtime before we leave, after everyone's been burning the candle at both ends trying to get these vehicles ready for departure."

Andrews blinked, surprised. *Just how much pull does Mulligan have, anyway?*

"I don't see how that's possible, Mulligan. We need to get to California ASAP and—"

"The *successful* completion of the mission is what's important, Captain, and if Harmony can give us six hours to get some rest to increase the chances of mission success, then the command group is all for it. After all, we're the last card these people have to play." The big man paused for a moment. "I take it that Benchley or Walters haven't talked to you about this yet?"

"No. Not yet." He tried to keep his composure, but he was already getting irritated with Mulligan. What he said made sense, but he should have discussed it with Andrews first before going to the command group. As the mission commander, Andrews was the one who should be lobbying for such things, not a command sergeant major, even one as storied as Scott Mulligan.

Mulligan must have been able to read his mind. "You and the other officers were all wrapped around the axle trying to get the rigs up and mission capable, sir. I decided to go to the command group on my own initiative, figuring that it was something you wouldn't have time for. Sorry if I stomped on any toes."

Andrews was mollified a bit by his apology. "No ... no, that's cool, Sarmajor. Thanks for doing that. I hadn't even thought about it." As soon as he said the last bit, he felt a surge of embarrassment.

Mulligan didn't appear to notice. "No problem on this end, Captain."

"Yeah, well ... thanks again." Andrews hesitated for a

moment. "Listen, Mulligan. I wanted to talk to you about Rachel."

"All right."

"You know what her problem is with you, right?"

"Sure," Mulligan said without looking away. "I killed her parents."

The big enlisted man's response was so casual, he might have been discussing the merits of his favorite color. That flustered Andrews even more; he was so taken aback, all he could say was, "You *did?*"

"They were in SCEV One with me, Captain. Is that what you want to talk about?"

Andrews considered that for a moment. "Do you want to tell me about that?"

"No, sir. I do not."

Andrews nodded. "I just wanted to tell you that I know there's going to be friction, so Laird and I are working to keep the two of you apart. Separate vehicles, separate shifts, all that stuff. If we can manage it right, you guys won't even have to talk over the radio."

"That's great, sir. This deployment is going to be a real ball-buster, so I appreciate you taking these measures on the behalf of your wife and myself."

Again, Mulligan's demeanor was so damned nonchalant and his responses were so glib that Andrews found he was getting pretty pissed off. And Mulligan's presence was going to make a lot of people uncomfortable, most notably Rachel. Scott Mulligan was feared by most, and revered by a few; for his part, Andrews was starting to finally get a handle on him. The guy was just an asshole.

"You know, Sarmajor, it might be better if you were to unass and stay in Harmony," he said. "I'm pretty sure the mission would go a lot more smoothly without the rest of us having to keep an eye on the drama meter and all."

"I agree with that, Captain. Maybe you can speak to Benchley about that, since he's the one who ordered me to be added to the roster? Come back with orders from him to unass, and I'm gone—otherwise, I'm going along for the ride." There was a certain coldness to Mulligan's voice that Andrews found intimidating.

"I'll see what I can do, Mulligan. But from where I'm sitting? You probably aren't the best asset for this mission."

Mulligan shrugged. "Like I said, I agree. But it's not my call, Captain."

Andrews shrugged and changed gears. "I like what you said about sterilizing the SCEVs. We've never done that before. How can we enforce it?"

"Easy. I post guys with guns with orders to shoot anyone who doesn't have authorization to touch the vehicles," Mulligan said. "Pretty old world, but also pretty effective."

"You're kidding me," Andrews said, shock evident in his voice.

Mulligan frowned. "If someone presses your buttons hard enough, you'll find killing them is pretty easy." He seemed to take stock of Andrews's distress, then sighed and looked at the displays before him. "Listen, no one's going to get shot, and I know no one's going to maliciously fiddle with the rigs. But we'll want to prohibit physical as well as electronic access to them while the crews are in their rest period. Posting armed guards is an effective deterrent."

"If you say so, Sarmajor."

Mulligan looked back at Andrews once again. "I say so, sir. Now, if I were you, I'd hightail it out of here and look to get an audience with Benchley, if he's available. If not, then I'd take the opportunity to get some rest."

"Roger that, Sarmajor."

Benchley felt like death warmed over as he went through the latest damage control reports at his desk in the command center. Even though the chamber was dimly lit—all nonessential systems had been ordered shut down to preserve energy, and that included a fair share of overhead lighting—the center was fully staffed, everyone busy coordinating the ongoing emergency responses. Benchley was shocked by just how badly damaged portions of the base were. While the big ticket items were obviously the loss of Harmony's primary and secondary power generation systems, the devastation to the SCEV bay elevator, for instance, was simply stunning. It could take *weeks* to restore that platform's capability, and Harmony had only one central vehicle lift. Benchley shook his head. *So much for contingency capabilities.*

He must've zoned out for a moment, because the next thing he knew, Mike Andrews was standing at attention before the desk. Benchley blinked, trying to clear the cobwebs from his head. He rubbed his chin and felt the rasp of razor stubble there. What the hell was Andrews doing here? Benchley tried to straighten up in his chair. He looked old and rumpled, he knew. Hell, he *felt* old and rumpled.

"What's up, Mike?" he asked finally, not terribly surprised by how rough his voice sounded.

"Wanted to talk to you about Sergeant Major Mulligan, sir." Andrews relaxed minutely and looked around the command center quickly. "I know you wanted Colonel Walters to be the relay between the team and the command group, but I'd just as soon drop this one on you myself. Can I bend your ear for a moment, sir?"

"And what about the most interesting man in Harmony Base did you want to talk about?" Benchley placed his elbows on the desktop and leaned forward, trying to at least appear interested. He already knew Andrews was going to try to get Mulligan off the mission. Andrews could be a very persuasive young man when it suited him, and Benchley knew his rationale would be sound. He found himself confronted with two possible responses. The first option was to explain his decision to the mission commander in a way that he could break down and digest, which would have been a tough thing for Benchley to do even if he wasn't running on fumes. The second was to just shut Andrews down right away. He was a company grade officer, and he was mostly still a receiver of orders, not an issuer. Benchley decided to opt for expedience.

"Sir, you know some of the personal history between Mulligan and—"

"Everyone needs to get over it, right now." Benchley kept his voice even but stern. "I'm aware of the conflicts between Mulligan and your wife, and I obviously consider that friction to be survivable. Both Mulligan and your wife have skills that might be needed—therefore, they go. Anything else?"

Andrews blinked. His overall expression did not change, but

Benchley could tell his response had caught Andrews flat-footed, and the SCEV captain didn't know what to do. Benchley was pleased when the other man decided to press on. Mike Andrews had stones. No other SCEV commander would run right back to the line after being shoved back.

"He might have the appropriate ratings, sir, but he's not one of us. He's going to get in the way, and he's going to be stepping on everyone's air hose the entire way out and the entire way back. In my opinion, he poses a *substantial* risk to this mission's success."

Benchley leaned back into the confines of his chair. "Under normal circumstances, Andrews, I'd agree with you. You know I'd never assign Mulligan to anything other than a training mission to keep his ratings current. That man's wired pretty tightly, but he's a consummate professional in his field, and he just might very well be a force multiplier in this circumstance."

"Sir, I don't get it. He's a Green Beret. Those guys ran around blowing stuff up and making a lot of people fall over dead. How can he possibly add any value to what we do? Please, sir, help me out here."

"Army Special Forces was about a lot more than 'blowing stuff up and making a lot of people fall over dead,' Captain. There's a specific heritage of service embodied by that branch, and part of that heritage involves making substantial personal sacrifice. Mulligan hasn't forgotten any of that. Hell, he's probably been waiting for the past ten years to bang some of the rust off those old skills of his. The non-killing ones, I mean."

"Uh ... sounds great, sir, but—"

Benchley held up a hand. "But nothing, Captain. He's going. Sorry it's a personal inconvenience for you, but do us all a favor and figure that shit out, all right?" Benchley looked at Andrews significantly, and he knew his expression alone would have been enough to tell Andrews he'd run out of altitude on this one. "You get where I'm coming from on this, Andrews?"

Andrews brought himself to attention as smartly as he could. "Yes, sir. I get where you're coming from. Sarmajor Mulligan's on the roster, and that's how it's going to be. I'll get everything squared away, sir."

"Outstanding, Andrews. Simply outstanding. Anything else?"

"No, sir," Andrews said woodenly.

"Then get some rest, Captain. Colonel Walters tells me the rigs will be locked down within the hour, and that your mission jumps out at zero eight hundred tomorrow. That gives you five hours of rack time. I suggest you make the best of it."

"Roger that, General." Andrews saluted. Benchley sighed at the unnecessary formality—he was seated, after all—but he got to his feet and returned the salute. There was no need to piss Andrews off any more than he already had. He would have his hands full in the field, and Benchley needed him as focused as possible. He watched as Andrews slipped out of the center, defeated, then sank back into his chair.

"Mulligan's going," Andrews told Rachel later as he held her in their darkened quarters. Aside from the commotion of ongoing repairs, the base seemed unusually quiet; the customary noises of working machinery that moved air and water and powered lights were mostly absent, and Andrews thought the void made the darkness a bit spooky.

"Benchley wouldn't talk with you about it?" she asked after a long moment.

"He talked to me. Well, more like I listened to him talk, but that's what it came down to. Mulligan's on the roster, and this is what it's going to be." Andrews kissed her neck tenderly, breathing in her smell. Even though she hadn't had a hot shower in the past day or so, she still smelled great. "If it means anything, I talked to Mulligan as well. He doesn't want to go either, but he has to roger up and do what he's told."

Rachel said nothing.

"We just have to get through it, babe. We get those supports and get back here so the lights can be turned on again, and that's all there is to it. Mulligan isn't important, and he's not going to do anything to screw this up. This is his home, too."

"Let's get some sleep," she said finally. "We have a long day tomorrow." She turned away from him and faced the wall, presenting him with her back. Andrews sighed. He knew why she was pissed, but there was nothing he could do about it.

"Good night," he said.

She didn't answer.

7

"WE SEEM TO be spending more time here than usual," Jim Laird said when Andrews stepped into the vehicle ready bay. It was already full of people, most of them standing around and waiting. Spencer looked agitated, and it didn't take a social scientist to figure out why. When Mulligan had said the rigs were frozen, he hadn't been kidding; armed guards had kept the SCEV maintainers and crews away from the waiting rigs.

"Okay, what's the SITREP here?" Andrews asked.

Laird pointed at the waiting SCEVs. "Rigs are frozen, and no one goes near them until you give the word. You're the mission commander, so both assets are under your operational control." He sniffed and crossed his arms over his broad chest. "They wouldn't accept my authority to grant the crews access, so we were waiting for you. I was about to have you paged over the intercom, actually."

Andrews checked his watch. "Hey, I'm a half hour early."

"Yeah, I'll make sure you get a commendation for that."

Andrews ignored Laird's slightly pissy tone. "Oscar, are you in charge of the guard detail?" he asked one of the sentries. He was a tall, broad-shouldered staff sergeant of Hispanic extraction, and his dark skin was covered with a slight sheen of sweat.

"Yes, sir," Oscar said.

"We'd like to access the rigs now, and start the pre-launch checks. Any problem with that?"

"Negative, Captain. You're good to go, sir."

Andrews waved to the waiting maintainers. "Let's get it done," he said.

"About fucking time," Spencer groused.

"Orders, man. I got orders," Oscar told him. "Major Alexander gave 'em to me, but you know where they really came from? Mulligan, man."

"Ah, screw him," Spencer said testily.

"Yeah, good luck with that," Oscar said. "He'll rip your little wiener out by the roots and slap you across the face with it."

"Spencer, knock off the shit and do your job," Andrews told him. He asked Laird, "All essential personnel present?"

"Waiting on Mulligan. And your wife, actually."

"She'll be here in fifteen. We don't need her or Mulligan for the vehicle checks, so let's get started."

"Hooah."

The maintenance crews went to work making the final checks. Andrews made a quick walkaround of SCEV Four, checking the various sight gauges and ensuring the fluid levels were right on the line, the tires were in proper condition for an overland hike, the infrared turrets were clean, and the heavy duty shock absorption system was in good repair. He had no problem shouldering maintainers aside so he could crawl into the inspection spaces and put his own eyes on target. Getting his hands dirty was never something he'd been afraid of, and within minutes they were covered with grime and grease. He removed several axle bellows and checked them for any residual grit from the rig's last trip, and he was happy to see they were as clean as if the rig had just rolled off the assembly line. Crawling out from beneath the vehicle, he glanced over at SCEV Five and saw Laird doing the same thing, and just as aggressively. Good. While he'd known Jim for as long as he'd known anyone, he'd never crewed with him before, and he was glad to see the broad-shouldered officer was as dedicated to mission prep as he was.

Andrews took some time to clean as much of the grime from his hands as he could before climbing the short stairway to the rig's interior. There was no need to make it any dirtier than necessary just yet; there'd be plenty of time for it to get messed up during the mission, and he preferred to keep the living and working spaces as pristine as possible.

Inside, Tony Choi and Leona Eklund were already conducting functionality checks of the environmental systems, and another technician still had the floor pulled up in the sleeping area, going over the last third of the transmission system. Andrews nodded to his crew, then looked past them at the technician servicing the tranny.

"Hey, Halderman. Make sure the holding tank has been emptied, all right?"

Halderman smiled. "You're good to go on that, sir. Everyone is free to pee with abandon."

"That's what I wanted to hear, thanks."

Andrews pushed himself into the cockpit and slid into the left seat. The rig was still running on external power, so activating the instrument panel was as simple as flipping a switch on the inverter panel. Chimes sounded as the instruments powered up, and the screens came to life as the rig's array of computers booted. Once the power-on test was completed, a schematic of the vehicle appeared on the center display. He could see every panel that was open on the rig's exterior, the status of every system, the level of every fluid reservoir—and he was happy to confirm that Halderman had been correct, the rig's poop tank was reading as empty. The SCEVs were powered by a sophisticated hybrid powerplant, using two variable-speed turboshaft engines for propulsion that in turn charged an array of batteries that would keep the rig going for a couple of days in the unlikely event both engines shit the bed. Andrews ran all the pre-ignition checks but stopped short of actually starting the rig—even though there were at least two pre-positioned caches of fuel along their route, he had no idea if they were still accessible, or if they'd been raided in the war's aftermath. In light of that, they'd need to preserve every drop of fuel in the tanks.

Spencer stuck his head inside the cockpit. "Hey, *el Capitan*. We're good to go on the externals. I'm going to have them pull external power once you give the word. And the big guy is coming up now." The crew chief pointed out the thick viewport windows.

Andrews looked through them and saw Mulligan sauntering toward the rig, a scowl on his face. The maintainers gave the big NCO a wide berth, wary of his foul expression.

"Take another walkaround, just to be safe," he told Spencer. "I'll let you know when you can disconnect the external power supply."

"Roger that." Spencer ducked out of the cockpit, and Andrews paged through the menus on the system display, checking off items that had been completed. A moment later, he felt a presence hovering over his right shoulder. Andrews looked up, even though he knew who it was. Mulligan looked down at him with eyes that were about as warm as a polar ice cap.

"Sergeant Major," Andrews said by way of greeting.

"I see you weren't successful in getting me pulled off the

roster," Mulligan said.

"No, I wasn't."

"Regrettable."

Andrews pointed to the right seat. "I take it you remember the ignition procedures?"

"I'm not that out of it, sir." Mulligan crouched down as he pushed himself into the cockpit and lowered himself into the copilot's seat with surprising dexterity. Andrews was impressed. The cockpit was extremely tight, and the close quarters made taking a seat almost an exercise in gymnastic torture. That a man of Mulligan's size was able to slip into the copilot's seat almost effortlessly made it seem as though he'd spent a lifetime crewing on SCEVs.

"Something wrong, Captain?"

Andrews smiled and shook his head. "We're good, Sarmajor. Maybe you can show Choi how to enter the cockpit like you did—it's a pain in the ass when he kicks the center console and flips the radio frequencies."

"I'll make a note of it."

Andrews slipped on his radio headset and, from the corner of his eye, saw Mulligan do the same. "Leona, are we buttoned up back there?"

"Roger, we're secure throughout the rig," Leona reported from the second compartment. "All floor panels are replaced and locked, and only crew are aboard at this time."

"Roger that. Mulligan, bring the APU online, if you would."

Without consulting the procedure, Mulligan reached to the overhead console and flipped two switches. From inside the SCEV's belly, a groaning whine sounded. The rig's auxiliary power unit came to life and, as soon as it began delivering the proper amount of current, the rig's onboard computer shut off the external power supply. SCEV Four was now running on full internal power.

Andrews reached for the control column beside him and pressed the red radio button. "Five, this is Four. Are you guys ready to crank? Over."

Jim Laird's voice came back a moment later. "Roger that, Four. Ready whenever you are. Over."

"Roger. Light 'em up." Andrews motioned for Spencer, who was standing outside just off the SCEV's nose, to pull the external power cable. Spencer reached forward, unlocked the cord's head, then removed it and held it up for Andrews to see. Beside Spencer, SCEV Five's crew chief did the same thing and showed the disconnected cable to Laird. Andrews shot Spencer a thumbs-up.

"Crew, prepare for engine start," he said.

"Ready for start back here," Leona reported.

Andrews flipped the switch to start the rig's first turbine engine. Since the powerplants were equipped with a fully automatic digital engine control—FADEC—there was no need to worry about the potential of a hot start, when fuel would begin to burn prematurely, causing a fire. The FADEC system managed the entire startup sequence, keeping the starter motor blowing cool air throughout the engine's turbine section until the appropriate pressure level was reached and the fuel/air mixture in the engine's compression area could be safely ignited. Once that happened, the engine spooled up rapidly. The turbine's whine was clearly audible, even through his headset's ear cups.

"Clean start," Mulligan reported. "T^5 is good, exhaust temperature's normal." Mulligan made the same report after the second engine had been activated and spooled up.

"Thanks. You good to go on the post-start checklist?"

"Yes, sir."

"Thank you, Sarmajor." Andrews glanced over at Laird's rig. "SCEV Five, this is Four. Ignition positive. Over."

"Four, this is Five. We're operational on this side. Over."

"Roger that. Break. Bay Control, this is SCEV Four. We're about ready for departure. Over." As he spoke, Andrews saw the maintenance crews packing it up, pulling their rolling tool chests away from the two vehicles. Fuel and power lines had already been disconnected and were being reeled up onto their spools. The two SCEVs were technically free to maneuver. From the corner of his left eye, he saw SCEV Five's outer airlock door cycle closed. A slight but noticeable change in air pressure tickled his eardrums as his own rig was buttoned up. Once the airlock doors were closed, the SCEV became "inflatable," meaning it was slightly pressurized to keep its interior clear of any biological or radioactive contaminants it might encounter while roving about on the surface.

"SCEV Four, Bay Control. You're clear for lift one at your

discretion, though we would appreciate it if you could expedite your departure. Over."

Expedite our departure? "Well, I guess they can't wait for us to get gone," Andrews muttered.

"They're having to burn more energy for the ventilation system," Mulligan said. "The rigs running are dumping a lot of poisonous exhaust into the bay, and running the fans and scrubbers for more than a few minutes is a bit of a luxury they really can't afford."

"Ah, right. Thanks for that, Sergeant Major."

"It's what I'm here for, sir. Post-start checklist complete. Want to grade my work?"

Andrews glared at the bigger man, but if he was at all affected by Andrews's irritated expression, Mulligan didn't show it. If anything, Andrews thought he detected a ghost of a smile threatening to form on the big NCO's weathered, Hollywood-handsome face. He remembered years ago overhearing his mother mention how Mulligan looked like a super-sized Charlton Heston, and he'd made it a point to watch one of the actor's old movies. Sure enough, the resemblance was uncanny.

"No, we're good," Andrews said, turning away. "Bay Control, SCEV Four. Roger, we're rolling now. Over."

"Roger, SCEV Four."

Andrews pushed the control column forward a quarter inch, and the rig slowly trundled forward, its big, knobbed tires rolling across the steel plank floor. A soldier with illuminated wands guided Andrews around the idling bulk of SCEV Five and pointed him straight toward the huge cargo elevator that would take the vehicle to the surface. As the rig rolled forward, following the yellow lines on the floor, the soldier saluted—the usual sendoff whenever a vehicle departed Harmony Base. Mulligan returned the salute as Andrews steered twenty-eight tons of composites, aluminum, titanium, steel, assorted plastics, rubber, and human bodies toward the waiting elevator.

The elevator brought the rig up to the dry surface in less than two minutes, but it was among the longest couple of minutes Andrews could remember having lived through. He found he was suddenly gripped by a fear that the lift might fail due to undetected quake damage. Getting hung up would be bad, but if the lift suddenly sheared off the rails and plummeted back into the base, the result would be lethal. He breathed a heavy sigh of relief when the elevator made it to the surface and stopped as fluidly as it always had.

He then remembered the elevator needed to make another trip, and that it would be bearing his wife. *Here's hoping Five makes it up, too.*

When the thick doors slid open, harsh sunlight slashed at Andrews's eyes, partially blinding him despite the sunglasses he wore. The viewports polarized automatically, darkening against the brilliant light. Andrews blinked away the glare and pushed the control column forward. The SCEV lumbered out of the elevator and onto the parched, dusty ground.

"Warning: External radiation level—four point two sieverts."

Andrews silenced the alarm with his right hand as he brought the SCEV into a sweeping left turn. The rig bumped slightly over the terrain, and Mulligan kept his eyes on the displays.

"So four point two sieverts, that's bad, right?" he said.

"You gotta be kidding me, Mulligan," Andrews answered. He tightened the SCEV's turn, pulling the rig around until it was pointed back at the elevator. He braked the rig to a halt, just as the elevator's doors slid closed. Then the entire cubicle disappeared, descending back into the ground as another set of doors slid closed, sealing up the shaft. To the rig's right, a tall electronic surveillance mast rose over a hundred feet into the air. It was dotted with all manner of antennae, which could monitor signals across the entire electromagnetic spectrum. Other than the blast doors that covered the elevator shaft, the ESM mast was the only physical indication Harmony Base even existed. As Andrews watched, a dry wind gave birth to several dust devils that swirled around the idling SCEV.

"I am kidding you, sir. I'm aware that four sieverts equals lethal radiation exposure, resulting in acute radiation syndrome and death in unprotected individuals." Mulligan smiled humorlessly. "Tell you what, I'll skip the levity for the rest of the trip."

"That would be great." Into his headset, he added, "Bay Control, this is SCEV Four. We're on top and holding for SCEV Five. Over."

"Roger, SCEV Four. Five will be on its way in just a minute. Over."

"Understood, Control." As they waited, Andrews scanned the instrument panel. The SCEV's systems seemed to be operating perfectly. Nevertheless, he loosened his shoulder straps a bit and leaned around the bulkhead that separated the cockpit from the rig's second compartment. He saw Leona and Spencer sitting at their duty stations, directly behind the bulkhead and across from the inner airlock door.

"Spence, how are we looking?"

"We're in great shape. All systems are doing fine." The swarthy crew chief added a double thumbs-up for emphasis. "How are things up front? The Sarmajor hypnotized by all the pretty blinky lights?"

"Keep that up, Sergeant, and I'll introduce you to some *really* pretty blinky lights," Mulligan said, holding up a big fist.

Spencer barked his characteristic laugh and turned back to his station. Leona looked at Andrews and gave him a pale smile. Andrews smiled back and faced forward, tightening his straps.

"Here comes Five." Mulligan pointed out the viewport. Through the thick, shaded glass, Andrews saw SCEV Five haul itself out of the elevator, which had just risen from the ground.

"Let's get this show on the road. Guys, we're getting ready to roll," he said, then eased the control column forward. "SCEV Five, this is SCEV Four. Over."

"Go for Five. Over," Laird responded via radio.

"This is SCEV Four. Come around to heading two-seven-seven and let's make best speed for the west. Over."

In the darkened command center, General Martin Benchley sat at his command console in the rear of Harmony Base's nerve center. On one of the displays embedded in his station, he watched as the two Self-Contained Exploration Vehicles accelerated away, heading for the distant western horizon.

And with them go our hopes and dreams.

He sensed a presence behind him and turned. Corrine Baxter looked past him at the monitor, her brow furrowed, the worry plain on her face.

"Think Andrews'll be able to pull this off, sir?"

Benchley thought about it for a moment. *Really* thought about it. When he did that, he found he didn't care much for the answer, so he fell back to the usual platitude an officer in his position would be expected to make.

"He has to, Colonel. There are no other alternatives."

8

THE TWO SELF-Contained Exploration Vehicles rolled across the shattered landscape, making their way westward as fast as they could. Several roads and interstates were still marginally navigable; even though the war that had decimated much of the United States had been violent and almost completely lethal, it was the aftermath that had caused the most damage. The deadly fallout that had descended across the Midwestern portion of the country had worked its dire magic over the course of days and weeks, giving sickened populations the ability to try to travel. As such, the roadways near major cities and towns were choked with automobiles of all types, from thrifty economy hybrids to tractor-trailer rigs hauling sixty-foot trailers. While many of these tie-ups had already been mapped, once the SCEVs moved past the areas that had previously been reconnoitered, they found themselves confronted time and time again with impassable traffic jams, columns of motor vehicles that were now nothing more than rotting sheet metal and delaminating fiberglass. Occasionally visible behind the dusty, grime-covered windows of several vehicles, the mummified remains of humanity could be seen.

The two rigs had to backtrack from those impassable snarls and strike out overland. But the SCEVs had been designed for just such a voyage. Patterned after the venerable HEMT-T A3 tactical truck used by the military, the SCEVs were able to roll across fields and over hills without much incident. So long as soft ground was avoided and treacherous ravines were skirted, the two rigs pushed on, fording dried-up creeks and virtually empty riverbeds when necessary. Overhead, skies the color of cobalt gleamed, free of any sort of storm activity. It was an austerely beautiful sight, but still, the day was lethal with radiation from the war and that which descended from the heavens, thanks to the decimated ozone layer.

The vehicles drove on, bouncing and jouncing across the terrain, unperturbed by the deadly conditions. Their turbine engines wailed, and their big, knobby tires bit into the dry soil, leaving long plumes of dust that rose into the air behind them.

As the sun slowly set, the day died another death as night reigned supreme. The SCEVs did not stop; their floodlights cut a swath through the gathering darkness, illuminating the terrain ahead with brilliant light that would have blinded anyone who looked directly at them.

If anyone had been alive to witness the event, of course.

Mulligan sat in the command seat on the left side of the cockpit, the control column in his left hand. He kept his eyes on the instruments, maintaining a watchful position and scanning the radar display that mapped the terrain beyond the pool of light cast by the rig's floodlights. Leona watched him from the corner of her eye for the first hour of their shift together, then finally just looked at him directly every now and then. If he noticed, Mulligan said nothing. He merely continued to do his job, which was to oversee the rig's progress across the darkened landscape. Leona had to admire his single-minded determination. It had been years since he'd been out in the field, but he handled the rig like a pro, always skirting barely noticeable breaks in the terrain that might have slowed their progress to a crawl. And he did so without the ham-handed acceleration and braking that someone like Tony Choi would have subjected them to. Mulligan knew how to keep the SCEV on course, and obviously knew the value in making the trek as comfortable as possible.

Finally, the big sergeant major stirred. He reached inside one of the pockets on his Army combat uniform blouse and pulled out a long, cylindrical tube. Holding one end in his mouth, he unscrewed the cap on the other end, then reversed it and tipped it back. At first, Leona thought it was some sort of beverage in a decidedly unusual-looking container. Instead, it was something she hadn't seen in years—a cigar.

"You're not going to actually *smoke* that thing, are you?" she asked, a little shocked. "It's against regulations, you know ..."

"Lieutenant, sometimes the only good regulation is a broken regulation."

Leona was properly scandalized. "You're kidding," was all she could say. "Do you realize what that will do to the CO_2

scrubbers? Not to mention the smell—"

"Relax, Lieutenant. I know all about the delicate balance of the rig's environmental systems. Don't worry, I'm not going to light up. I only do that on special occasions." Mulligan chewed on the end of the cigar. "If one ever happens to pop up, that is."

"God—you actually *do* smoke those things? How can you stand to do that to your body?"

Mulligan scanned the instruments, then looked out the viewports. "After everything we've been through, ma'am, one might think a little secondhand smoke wouldn't be high on your list of worries."

"Everything's high on my worry list, Sergeant Major."

"Yeah, I remember you always being the high-maintenance sort. Even as a kid in basic, you always wanted to know why things were done one way and not the other. But like I said, you're safe. I'm not going to light the thing." Mulligan seemed to think that ended the conversation. He continued to drive and make his instrument scans with a metronomic regularity that Leona actually admired. While Command Sergeant Major Scott Mulligan was a riddle wrapped up in an enigma, she was surprised to see just how disciplined he was.

"Well ... where did you get it?" she asked after a long pause.

"I grew it."

"You did? Where?"

"I have a small portion of the hydroponics farm allocated to me. I grow a tobacco plant there, and harvest it when the time is right. Then I make my own cigars." Mulligan switched the cigar from one side of his mouth to the other. "Not as good as a Cohiba Edicion, but they get the job done."

Leona nodded and scanned the instruments herself. She had nearly another three hours before she took the left seat and Choi came forward to take the copilot's seat. "I see."

Mulligan said nothing.

"So ... what did you do before the war, Mulligan?"

"I defended truth, justice, and the American way."

She smiled at that. "Why do you always act like such a hard-ass?"

"It's no act, Lieutenant."

Feeling suddenly bold, Leona pressed on, even though the big man's body language seemed to indicate he wasn't particularly interested in chatting. Just the same, this was the first time she'd ever been in close proximity to the mysterious senior NCO of Harmony Base. If he thought he was going to go for a couple of weeks without interacting with the rest of the crew, he was severely mistaken.

"So other than being a soldier, what else did you do? Were you ever married?"

Mulligan's only reaction was to reposition the cigar in his mouth. In the glow of the flat panel displays on the instrument panel, Leona thought she saw a glimmer of a scowl flit across his face.

"What's the matter, Sergeant Major—couldn't get a date?"

Mulligan finally turned to her. His face was as devoid of emotion as the surface of the moon was absent of air, but his tone was anything but sedate. "Lieutenant, keep this up and the only thing you'll get out of me is a severe whipping from an enlisted man. We're not here to get to know each other on a personal level—we're on a mission. As such, I would respectfully recommend you concentrate on the current mission essentials, which at the moment are backing me up on the instruments and assisting in terrain avoidance, while ensuring the rig's systems are checked according to schedule. Is that clear, ma'am?"

Leona clenched her teeth, a little pissed off at his tone. He was perilously close to insubordination.

So what're you going to do, try and pull rank on Mulligan? Yeah, do that. It'll be all sorts of fun.

"I read you, Sarmajor," she said.

"Hooah," Mulligan said simply, then turned away from her and peered out the viewports. Leona watched him for a moment, then sighed and leaned back in her seat.

It was going to be one very long mission.

"So how's it going?"

Rachel's voice sounded distant and remote over the headset transceiver Andrews wore as he lay stretched out on one of the bunks in the rear of SCEV Four. He had strapped himself into the narrow, slightly bowed bed in a bid to keep from being pitched to the deck should the rig roll over some broken terrain, and he'd asked Rachel to do the same. While it was a small thing, she had no experience with SCEV operations, and ignoring even mundane details like that could get her killed.

"Everything's good on this side," he told her, speaking softly even though he was alone in the compartment. "You getting by over there?"

"Sure. Jim's patient with me, and Kelly's giving me some pointers. Tony's doing the same, but I think he'd rather be over on your rig than stuck over here." Rachel paused. "Come to think of it, so would I."

"Non-starter, babe. Separation of church and state and all that."

"Oh, I'm your church now? Or am I your state?" she asked, a playful lilt in her voice.

"Well, I do worship you."

"Such a sweet talker you are."

"Isn't that why you married me?"

"Yes. Well, that and the fact that you're great in the sack."

Andrews laughed. "Now, now ... keep it clean. The channel's encrypted, but you can never be sure."

Rachel laughed as well. "I know, I know. Besides, I have to start my shift in a few minutes. I'm taking right seat."

"Who has left? Jordello?"

"Yeah. She's going to show me the ropes for the next few hours."

"Well, try not to roll the rig, all right? That's Choi's job."

Rachel laughed again, then grew serious. "How are things with the asshole?"

Andrews frowned, put out by her derogatory language. "Mulligan's been fine. Professional. He's getting the job done, and he's keeping to himself. He knows he's an anachronism out here, so he's not pushing any buttons." That last part was a bit of a lie, for he felt that Mulligan was smirking at them on the inside. The senior NCO certainly didn't try to hide his smug aloofness, and that bugged Andrews quite a bit.

"Don't trust him, Mike."

"I've got my eye on him, babe. Don't worry about it."

She snorted. "How can I *not* worry about it? You're over there, with him—"

"Easy, now," Andrews said, not wanting the conversation to

devolve into another one-sided shit-flinging contest. "I know the guy's history, and we've been over this already. He's not going to screw things up. Take it easy, Rachel."

After a long pause, she said, "I'm trying."

Andrews was suddenly painfully aware of the distance that separated them, and he found he very much wanted to hold her in his arms—not just to help ease her distress, but because she was so close to him, yet so very far. As much as she worried about him crewing with Mulligan, he found it difficult not to obsess over her being in the field as well. He'd had the training and had volunteered to be inducted into the US Army after the war, so field time was part of what he was all about. For her, it was an entirely accidental occurrence, and he feared for her safety, despite the fact that Jim Laird was as competent at SCEV ops as he was. Kelly Jordello and Tony Choi were able hands, as well. There was no lack of practical experience surrounding Rachel, and Andrews really couldn't have asked for her to be protected by a better team.

"Hey, be glad you're not over here. Seriously," Andrews said, "you don't have to smell Spencer's farts. The guy has no class. He just blows 'em all over the rig. I don't know what the hell it is he's eating, but it's practically chemical warfare over here."

Rachel laughed, but it sounded false, forced. Andrews sighed. There wasn't any way to help her relax, and that made him feel even worse about things.

The rig slowed suddenly and bumped to a more-or-less gentle halt. It was time to change shifts, which meant Mulligan would be surrendering the left seat to Leona, while Spencer moved forward to occupy the copilot's seat. Outside, SCEV Five would be rolling to a stop as well, and Rachel would have her first opportunity to act as a rig copilot.

"Okay, I guess this is it," Andrews said. "You take care of yourself, babe."

"I will. What are you going to do now?"

"Get some sleep. What else is there to do? In six hours, I've got to stand up and prepare for my next shift."

"Right. Well, sleep well. Pleasant dreams. I love you, Michael."

"I love you too, hon. Take it easy, all right?"

"I will. Good night." And with that, the link went dead.

Andrews leaned back in his bunk and pulled the headset off, listening to the sounds of the crew change. A moment later, the pressure door at the head of the compartment opened, and Mulligan stepped inside the sleeping area. He flipped on one of the overhead lights, and Andrews screwed his eyes shut against the sudden brightness. Mulligan made a brief, apologetic noise, then walked to the rear of the compartment where the head was located. He pulled open the door, stepped inside, and closed it behind him. Andrews heard the lock click into place.

A moment later, the SCEV started moving again. Andrews hoped Mulligan didn't piss all over the place, and if he did, that he'd have the decency to clean up after himself.

Hours later, Mulligan awoke in his bunk. The sleeping area had been designed to accommodate persons of average height and weight, and he found the bunks were just a bit too short to comfortably house his six-foot-six-inch frame. Therefore, he was forced to sleep curled up, something that he found unpleasant, given that he needed to be strapped in as well. That alone made for a less than restful sleep. Even though he had long since grown used to the jouncing and bouncing of the SCEV as it plowed across the landscape, he found that his head would invariably strike the side of the bunk's hard plastic shell, and that always jolted him awake. He moved the thin pillow a bit in a bid to gain some protection, but that could only last for so long. Mulligan consigned himself to being tired and even more grumpy than usual over the next several days.

And if the lack of sleep wouldn't to him, then the voyage across the burned-out remains of the United States most certainly would.

For years, he had been confined to the sterile environment of Harmony Base, with only a few brief sojourns to the surface to maintain currency in his SCEV ratings. He had grown used to the barren wastelands surrounding the base's training range, and he had never strayed from it, even when the desire to turn to the east and drive all out possessed him with such fury that he feared he might do just that.

But watching the irradiated world pass by as the SCEV drove mile after mile after mile, Mulligan felt a queer sense of derangement settling over him. For a decade, he had existed as virtually nothing more than a phantasm stalking the corridors and gangways of Harmony, a hollow man whose soul had been laid to waste. But he hadn't really set eyes on what devastation had been wrought, on the totality of the destruction. It was more than just the detonation of multiple nuclear weapons across a vast swath of the country; it was the long-lasting effects of the fallout, the decimation of the ozone layer—or "ozone process," he now knew—and the contamination of what seemed to be the entire biosphere. Even beneath the heavy mantle of his despair, Mulligan had still thought—had still *hoped*—that humanity had managed to persevere. But after laying eyes on the skeletal remains of cities and towns and not seeing so much as a single *bird* in the cobalt skies, the small ember of hope he carried was virtually extinguished.

We're all that's left, he thought.

He glanced across the small aisle and saw Eklund lying in the bunk across from him. She was awake, but as soon as he looked in her direction, she closed her eyes and pretended to be asleep, probably depending on the dim light to hide her indiscretion.

Mulligan snorted. "Something on your mind, Lieutenant?" he asked, raising his voice over the engine noise.

She didn't answer, apparently choosing to believe that if she pretended to be asleep, he would let her be. Mulligan considered pressing it, but settled for twisting over onto his other side and presenting her with his back. Regardless, he felt her gaze on him again and knew she watching him as if he was on display.

Just another animal in the zoo, he thought.

"Go to sleep, Lieutenant," he said. And then he closed his eyes and followed his own order.

AT LONG LAST, the two SCEVs made their way across the Sierra
Nevada mountain range and into the smaller foothills that
surrounded the Santa Clara Valley. Andrews and Mulligan were
once again helming SCEV Four, the sixth time they had shared
the rotation. Andrews found that the big sergeant major's
disposition hadn't changed greatly during their time together,
though he did continue to restrain himself from engaging in any
non-mission discussions. Not that there was a lot to talk about
it; even though Andrews was greatly interested in Mulligan's
history with Rachel and her parents, it was clear he wasn't going
to get anything out of the older man. Beyond discussing the
vistas outside the rig's viewports or the texture of the landscape
revealed by the terrain-mapping radar, Andrews had little choice
but to leave Mulligan to his own devices.

Early in the afternoon of the sixth day after leaving
Harmony Base, the rigs made it to the valley.

Andrews brought the rig to a halt on the valley's rim. From
the corner of his eye, he saw SCEV Five slowly ease to a stop
beside them.

Below them lay the weathered skeleton of San Jose,
California. Parts of the city were mounded over by great dunes
of sand; others had been blackened by long-extinguished fires
that left almost nothing behind. It was obvious the city had
suffered at least one direct ground strike, for they could see a
large crater that was ringed by layers of shattered debris that age
and weather had made virtually unidentifiable. The rotting
husks of cars and trucks lay scattered about and, in the distance,
Andrews thought he could see the twisted skeleton of a downed
airliner laying in the dusty emptiness of a street from which all
structures had been blasted away. To the north, the cities of
Santa Clara, Sunnyvale, and Cupertino were vague and
indistinct, hidden behind veils of wind-blown dust.

Andrews took in the vista and let his breath out in one long,
drawn-out sigh. Leona slipped into the cockpit and knelt
between the seats. She stared out of the viewports, and Andrews
glanced at her. Her expression was blank and unreadable,

revealing nothing of her internal thoughts. Andrews looked beyond her, to where Mulligan sat in the copilot's seat. He was surprised to see a glimmer of emotion in the big man's eyes, which he tried to conceal immediately when he realized Andrews was watching him.

"Come here before the war, Sergeant Major?"

Mulligan snorted and turned away, looking out the viewport to his right. "Yeah. Hasn't changed much, I see."

Leona glanced at Mulligan as well, and her brow furrowed. She seemed to sense the man's internal turmoil and she looked to Andrews, as if seeking guidance. Andrews shrugged and shook his head.

Don't bother with it, Lee.

Leona looked back at Mulligan again, then reached forward and grabbed the control yoke for the forward-looking infrared system. She panned the FLIR from left to right, watching the imagery it returned in a small window on the center display. She stopped the device's slew suddenly and made a curious sound in her throat. Andrews glanced down at the display as she thumbed the zoom.

Framed in the small picture was a short, twisted tree with pale green leaves.

"Life," Leona said.

Mulligan looked at the display and cackled suddenly. "My God, is that all we get? That thing's twice as ugly as Charlie Brown's Christmas tree."

"It'll do, Mulligan," Andrews said, trying to keep the irritation out of his voice. "It'll do."

The rigs picked their way down into the valley, pushing the wrecked hulks of dead cars out of their way as they sidled down the remains of a cracked street. On either side of the roadway, the dilapidated remains of tract housing stood silent watch over the vehicles' progression. Many of them had been flash-burned by the nuclear blast that had hit the area, and the ensuing shockwave had ripped off roof tiles, broken windows, and shattered chimneys, but for the most part, the structures had fared well. They were lifeless and uninhabited, of course. While the instruments indicated the radiation level was substantially lower in this part of California than it was in the Midwest, they would have been absolutely lethal even in the short term for several years after the war. Andrews watched one Mediterranean-style house slip by as the SCEV trundled past, its windows missing, the tattered remnants of what had once been über-expensive drapes flapping about in the mild breeze. The dwelling had likely cost millions of dollars, but its construction was cheap and its walls thin, so there was little doubt it had extended the lives of its occupants by only minutes, if that.

Finally, when the two vehicles had picked their way through the shattered city's outskirts and into the municipality itself, Andrews brought SCEV Four to a halt.

"Five, this is Four. Over."

Jim Laird's voice came over the radio immediately. "Go ahead, Four."

"We'll push on ahead and see if we can find the target site for those supports. You folks hold here and wait for us to report back. We'll be in protective posture four at all times. You getting our transponder data? Over."

"Roger that, Four. We're getting everything. Uh, you sure it's wise to split up at this time?"

Andrews looked over at Mulligan. "Sarmajor, opinion?"

Mulligan shook his head. "Your wife is in Five, and she's the subject matter expert for the supports we need, so it makes sense to play pathfinder for them."

"Hooah." Into the radio, he said, "Yeah, Five, this is how we'll play it. If we run into any trouble, you'll be the first to know. Over."

"Roger, Four. We'll stand overwatch here."

"Later, Jim."

"Happy trails, Mike."

"Walters is going to love the nonstandard radio communications," Mulligan said. "You do know he listens to the recordings?" Like all the measurements taken by the rig's instruments, radio communications were likewise recorded, stored in one of the rig's many black boxes.

"Screw him." Andrews pushed forward on the control column. The SCEV slowly accelerated down the road, leaving the other rig behind.

"That's the spirit, Captain." Mulligan was smiling faintly when Andrews glanced over at him, but he didn't say anything further.

Andrews drove on, cutting through streets and vacant lots where he could, or using the SCEV to batter through old, dead traffic when necessary. The rigs were built to be as tough as tanks and, so long as he didn't do anything stupid, SCEV Four could take the punishment he was giving it. If the rather strenuous workout of pushing through tons of pitted sheet metal and delaminating fiberglass bothered him at all, Mulligan said nothing. He merely divided his time between monitoring the instruments and keeping an eye out for any obstacles Andrews might have missed.

It was during one of those times that Mulligan slapped the lockout switch on the center console and seized the copilot's control column. Andrews was locked out; the controls on his side of the cockpit were frozen in place. Mulligan stomped on the brakes and wrenched the rig hard to the left without any warning. Andrews heard Spencer shout from the rear of the SCEV, where he was still getting some rack time. He hoped the crew chief had strapped himself into the bunk, otherwise he would be bouncing all over the place.

"Mulligan, what gives?" Andrews demanded when the SCEV shuddered to a halt amidst a spreading cloud of dust.

Mulligan pointed out the viewport. "Sinkhole."

Andrews saw a clump of cars on the roadway ahead of him. The street canted down the face of a small hill, and the vehicles were piled up near the base, as if they'd all been caught in the same accident.

"I don't see—"

"Look past the cars, Captain." As he spoke, Mulligan slowly reversed the rig back up the hill. Andrews leaned forward and peered through the thick glass. Sure enough, just on the other side of the pileup, he could see a yawning maw of blackness. It was just barely visible, but when he knew where to look, there it was.

"Holy shit."

"Don't sweat it, sir. I'm sure you would've figured it out before we went over the edge and woke up taking harp lessons from Saint Pete." Mulligan continued reversing the rig as Spencer practically leapt into the cockpit.

"What the *fuck* is going on, Sarmajor?" he bellowed before Andrews could say anything.

"Hello, Sergeant Spencer. Come up to critique my parallel parking skills?"

"Spencer, Mulligan just stopped me from killing all of us," Andrews said as Spencer sucked in air to reply. Spencer considered his words for a moment.

"Yeah, like how?"

"I almost drove us into a sinkhole. Mulligan saw the danger and acted."

"Oh. Well, good job then, Sarmajor. Happy to have you onboard."

"Shut up and go back to sleep, sweetheart." Mulligan brought the SCEV to a gentle halt. He turned and looked back at Spencer with hard eyes. "And the next time you take issue with something I've done, I strongly urge you to discover the proper tone of voice to take when you bring it to my attention, son."

Spencer looked at Mulligan for a long moment before a big, shit-eating grin slowly spread across his face. "Hooah, Sarmajor." Even Spencer, who was about as sensitive to the human condition as a water pump, could figure out that screwing around with Mulligan was a fast road to hell.

"Okay, I'll take it again, Sergeant Major." Andrews reset the lockout switch and grabbed the control column on his side of the cockpit. "Unless you have any problems with that?"

Mulligan cut his eyes over to Andrews. "None at all, sir. But I'd recommend you take that left there"—he indicated the direction with his big chin—"and follow it for another hundred meters or so before swinging a right. The manufacturing complex should be a few klicks away. You still here, Sergeant Spencer?"

"Gone," Spencer said, ducking out of the cockpit in a hurry.

"Mulligan, stop fucking with my crew," Andrews said softly as he checked the moving map display. Sure enough, an alternate route to the manufacturing complex had been highlighted.

"How am I doing that, sir? Spencer wasn't just out of line,

he was annoying at the same time. That's a transgression no one should forgive."

"If anyone's going to discipline the crew, it'll be me." Andrews brought the SCEV into a left turn. The big rig bumped up and down as it rolled over a small economy car that hadn't moved in a decade.

Mulligan stared at Andrews for one long moment, then shrugged. "Sure thing, sir."

Almost an hour later, SCEV Four finally rolled up to the manufacturing complex. Like every other structure they had seen over the past few hours, the buildings of the manufacturing complex were extremely weathered, having suffered blast damage from the strike that had hit San Jose. Andrews slowly circumnavigated the complex, looking at the sagging chain-link fence surrounding it. The fence was topped with coiled concertina wire, essentially a whirl of razor blades that, while weather-beaten, still looked sharp enough for a shave.

Leona ducked inside the cockpit. "So this is it, huh?"

"The sign says it all, Lieutenant." Mulligan pointed toward a large, badly peeling sign that read WHITNEY MANUFACTURING, INC.

"Yeah, that does make it pretty obvious, doesn't it?" Leona leaned forward and looked past Andrews's head. "That long building there must be the warehouse."

Andrews nodded and ran his fingers through his hair. Even though the rig carried enough water for them to take the occasional quick shower, he still felt dirty and grimy. "Roger that, we'll start there. I guess we'll just crash what's left of the fence." He slowed the SCEV and turned toward the sidewalk. The rig jounced slightly as its big tires met the curb, then it smashed right through the fence. Andrews worried briefly about the razor wire slashing open a tire so badly that the self-sealing compound inside it might fail to do its job, but when the tire pressure system didn't indicate anything even remotely approaching a leak, he allowed himself to relax. He kept his eyes sharp and moved his head on a swivel, scanning the area for anything that could threaten the rig as it rolled across the facility's cracked, empty parking lot. From the corner of his eye, he saw Mulligan doing the same thing. There was a metallic *click* as the sergeant major relaxed his harness's shoulder straps and leaned forward, half-turning in his seat to look out the rear of the vehicle. When he leaned back, he caught Andrews's eye.

"It's always wise to check the flanks, sir," he said.

Leona laughed. "You think there's anyone out here who's going to try and harm us, Sergeant Major?"

"I have no idea, Lieutenant. But it's wise to presume there is."

Leona laughed again, and Andrews nudged her with his elbow.

"This is what Mulligan's here for," he told her. "Knock off the pissy attitude, Lee."

Leona looked at him for a long moment, then nodded. With a blank face, she slipped out of the cockpit and returned to her station. Mulligan shot Andrews a thumbs-up, then went back to his scans.

Andrews brought the vehicle to a halt by the loading docks and pressed the red TRANSMIT switch on the control column. "Five, you copy?"

Laird's voice came back a moment later, marred slightly by the hiss of static. The air was still full of charged particles, and radio communications would become progressively more unreliable the further away the vehicles were from each other. "Standing by, Four. Over."

"Yeah, listen Five, we found the complex. We'll have to enter some structures, so I'm going to bet we'll lose voice commo for a while. I'll try and keep you updated every hour. Is that good by you? Over."

"Roger, Four. Hourly updates are good from our side."

"Outstanding. I sent you the route we took to get here, did you get a chance to review it?"

"We have it, Four. Both myself and my XO checked it out. Seems simple enough, and the computer tells us we can make it to your location in about forty minutes if we take our time. I'm presuming you left us a nice path? Over."

"Roger that, Five. Just follow the crushed vehicles and the tire tracks in the dust. You have a fix on our pos? Over."

"We have your pos as Latitude North, 37 degrees, 19 minutes

47.0316 seconds, Longitude West, 121 degrees, 53 minutes, 19.7736 seconds. How's that?"

Andrews chuckled but confirmed the coordinates anyway. "That's pretty precise, Jimbo."

"Hey, we aim to please."

"Roger that. We'll be suiting up and heading out now. We'll update you before we leave the rig, then hit you every hour afterwards. Over."

"Roger your last, Four. Happy hunting, and we hope to hear good news soon. You give the word, and I'll bring in the SME to verify your findings and we'll be on our way home. Over."

"From your lips to God's ear, Jim. SCEV Four, out." Andrews set the parking brake and looked at Mulligan. "All right, Sarmajor. Let's go through the shutdown checklist, and then let's get suited up and ready for action."

"Highly motivated, sir," Mulligan said, though his tone indicated he was anything but.

10

THE CLAMSHELL DOORS on the SCEV's starboard side opened. The lower half formed a brief ramp to the ground while the upper half tried valiantly to shade the occupants of the cramped airlock from the blazing sun, which hung high overhead. Andrews walked down the three steps to the bone-dry asphalt and felt the day's heat immediately, even through his protective suit and respirator. Mulligan was right behind him, holding his assault rifle at low ready. Andrews thought it was kind of dumb bringing weapons with them, since the chances of anyone surviving out here were simply astronomical, but the gargantuan NCO had insisted. Because security was his territory, Andrews had relented. He'd had to argue with Leona for a minute, since she was convinced it was plain nuts to carry an assault rifle around under the circumstances, but even she had to give in when Mulligan planted himself in front of the inner airlock door and declared no one would leave the vehicle unarmed.

That had ended the discussion.

Behind them, the airlock doors closed. For the next two minutes or so, Andrews and Mulligan were on their own while the airlock was sterilized; only after it had been scrubbed of possible contaminants would Eklund and Spencer be allowed to progress through it to join them. Andrews looked around, the visor of his full-face respirator polarizing against the brightness of the day.

"Well, California's still sunny," he said via his voice-activated transceiver. Everyone had transceivers in their suits. It certainly beat shouting to be heard beneath all the gear they carried.

"Some things, even nuclear wars can't change," Mulligan said. "You sure we shouldn't leave Spencer with the rig? He's the crew chief, after all."

"I want to be operational, Sarmajor," Spencer said over the radio—even though he and Leona were still inside the rig, they could still monitor the suit frequencies. "Besides, I want to stretch my legs a bit."

Mulligan looked over at Andrews. "Sir?"

Andrews sighed. Doctrinally, leaving the rig unattended wasn't wise, even though access could only be gained by entering the access code on the keypad next to the airlock door. But Spencer might be useful; he was the closest thing they had to an engineer. "No one's alive to mess with the rig, Sarmajor," he said.

"Roger that, sir." Mulligan slowly turned in a circle, taking in the entire area in one long scan.

Andrews felt like he was loafing, so he did the same, then wondered why he cared what Mulligan might think of him. At any rate, the two men found nothing even vaguely threatening beyond the day's dry heat. Andrews took it upon himself to do a quick walk-around of the SCEV, checking for any damage. The rig was filthy, covered entirely with a thick coating of dust, save for the electronic probes and viewports, which had been treated with an anti-static compound that prevented the dust from accumulating. Except for the grime, the hardy vehicle seemed to be in perfect condition. He even checked the tires for any sign of tearing from the concertina wire they'd driven over, but he found nothing worthy of anxiety. No leaks, no gouges, no indications of anything burning away, seizing up, or falling off.

When he moved back to the right side of the rig, the airlock doors opened again. Spencer and Leona emerged from the rig's cool interior, wearing their white environmental suits, air tanks, full-face respirators, and carrying Heckler and Koch M416A3 assault rifles. Knapsacks slung over their shoulders contained whatever they might need to crack open a crate or shipping container: hammers, screwdrivers, crowbars.

It didn't take long for Spencer to start bitching. "Damn, think it's hot enough?"

"Yeah man, but it's a dry heat," Mulligan said.

"That's a line from that old movie *Aliens*, right, Sarmajor?"

"I guess nothing slips past you, Copernicus."

"Yeah, well, we won't be having this funny repartee if one of us passes out from dehydration, Sarmajor."

Mulligan sighed wistfully. "Please, God, let it be me."

Leona made a disgusted sound as she pushed past the two men and tried a nearby door. It was apparently locked, and even though she shoved herself against it, she couldn't get it to budge. Andrews hurried over and tried it as well, but the door was definitely locked. It was a metal fire door, too. He sighed and looked down at the loading dock doors, but they were closed and quite likely locked as well.

"Well, I guess we'll have to do this the old-fashioned way." He reached into his knapsack and pulled out a crowbar.

"Tell you what, Captain. Let's go total old school, instead." Mulligan steered Andrews off to one side and handed him his assault rifle. He motioned Leona to stand clear, and she moved back a few steps. She looked at Andrews, who merely shrugged at her.

"How old school are we talking about, Sarmajor?"

Without answering, Mulligan walked to the door and kicked it down, almost tearing it from its hinges. He stepped to one side and peered into the darkness, minimizing his profile and being careful not to silhouette himself against the bright day. Again, Andrews thought the big man was overdoing things a bit, but after that display of strength, he didn't want to bitch too loudly.

Finally satisfied all was well, Mulligan returned to Andrews and reclaimed his assault rifle. He jerked a thumb over his shoulder at the severely dented door.

"I learned that in Special Forces," he said proudly.

"You must've been the toast of the dinner party circuit," Leona said, her voice dripping with sarcasm.

"Indeed, I was."

"All right, all right, let's get going." Andrews slung his rifle over his shoulder by its patrol strap and stepped toward the door. He leaned into the darkness beyond and found it to be quite gloomy even after his visor brightened. He pulled a flashlight from his belt and snapped it on, panning the bright LED beam across the area as he stepped inside the warehouse and moved to his left. Mulligan was the next one in, and he held his assault rifle at the ready, the stock pressed against his right shoulder, the barrel pointed at the dusty concrete floor. The interior of the warehouse was dark and gloomy, the only light coming from several holes that had been ripped through the roof. Crates were everywhere, mostly stacked atop one another. Some had fallen to the floor and burst open, spilling their contents. Andrews walked up to one and examined the spillage. He couldn't tell what the objects were, only that they weren't what they were looking for.

"Okay, we've only got two hours of air on hand, so let's make the most of it. Mulligan, head for that office down there and look for a stock manifest that might tell us what's where."

"Roger that."

"Lee, you and Spence split up and poke around. Don't rip your suits. It's still hot enough around here that you'll wind up shaving some years off your life if you're exposed for more than a day or so, so take it seriously."

"Oh, hell yeah," Spencer said.

Leona played her flashlight around. "Let's just get going, all right? This place gives me the creeps."

"You're not going to get all *girly* on us now, are you, LT?" Spencer asked.

"What, afraid someone's going to compete with you for the Miss Universe crown, Spencer?" Mulligan asked. Leona laughed at the unexpected support, and Spencer shook his head sourly.

"And from a fellow enlisted man, no less," Spencer said.

"Everyone clear on their orders?" Andrews asked, smiling.

Everyone reported their assent.

"Okay, then. Like the lieutenant said, let's get to it."

With empty eye sockets, the nearly mummified corpse in the office's single chair grinned at Mulligan as he slowly pushed open the door and stepped inside. The sight of the skeletal remains chilled him and, for a moment, he stood paralyzed in the office doorway. He had automatically raised his rifle into an attack posture and pointed it at the human remnants, which sat half-slumped over in the chair. Most of the skin was gone, giving the sergeant major a good opportunity to inspect the corpse's many dental implants. Mulligan slowly lowered his rifle and released a quiet sigh, then stepped into the office and looked down at the skeleton. On the dust-covered desk stood an equally dusty drinking glass and a small pill bottle. Both were empty. Mulligan picked up the pill bottle and squinted, trying to make out the label, but the ink was another casualty of war. He placed the bottle back on the desk, then glanced at the computer sitting nearby. For sure, the entire warehouse's contents were there, written to a hard drive system that had probably been wiped clean by the electromagnetic pulse that shut down the entire city's power grid when the first nuke detonated. That meant the electronic search was over before it had even started. With no other recourse available, Mulligan pawed through the desk drawers, ignoring the leering skeleton. He found nothing of any great interest.

Hell, not even some pornography. Who ran this place, Jesuit priests?

He turned to the file cabinet behind him and found it was locked. He tried all the drawers, but with the same result. He considered his options: go through the keys in the desk, trying each one, or blast away the lock with his rifle. He elected to conserve ammunition and went for the keys instead. The lock was old and desiccated, but he found the proper key and forced it to turn in the cylinder. The cabinet drawers squeaked loudly as he pulled them open, and he searched through the green folders inside. Eventually, he grew weary of thumbing through them one by one, so he pulled an armful out of one drawer and dropped them on the desk. He shoved the office chair out of the way and it spun into a wall, unceremoniously dumping the rag-clad skeleton to the filthy floor. Bone rattled against concrete in a macabre, atonal symphony.

Sorry, Charlie.

Mulligan studied the pile of folders. He knew the series number of the parts he was looking for, but it took him a few minutes to figure out the files were organized by customer, not product.

So who was the customer? US Government? US Army? Harmony Base? Just plain old Uncle Sugar?

Mulligan returned to the filing cabinet and went through the last one. Sure enough, there were several folders marked *USG*.

Close enough for government work.

It took another five minutes, but he finally found what he was looking for. Shining his flashlight on the yellowed paper, he nodded to himself.

"All right, listen up! Whoever's nearest to aisle fourteen, section C, gets a free ride home," he announced over his transceiver.

"Say again?" Andrews responded. Mulligan snorted soundlessly and shook his head. Jesus, but these kids needed everything spelled out for them.

"Core supports, Captain. According to the manifest I've found, there are twenty-four of 'em in here. Aisle one-four, section charlie."

Outside in the warehouse itself, Spencer found himself, somewhat auspiciously, in aisle fourteen. Shining his flashlight around the cavernous warehouse, he walked hurriedly down the aisle. He was in section B, which if the alphabet still worked, meant the next section would be C.

And then there they were, right on a pallet on the ground. Several large metal shipping containers and, stenciled on their sides in faded yellow paint, was the legend that made him feel *coup de coeur* for the first time:

CORE SUPPORTS
MIL-STD-344
PROPERTY U.S. GOVERNMENT

"Roger, Sarmajor—I got 'em!" he said jubilantly, practically flying toward the first crate. He pulled a crowbar from his knapsack and went to work on the latches that held the lid in place. They weren't locked, but exposure to the elements had left them somewhat corroded, and he didn't want to risk ripping open his suit and exposing himself to the radiation content inside the warehouse—even though the instruments back in the SCEV had rated it was enough to cause harm after only a day of continuous exposure, the last thing Spencer wanted was to dose himself and wake up the next morning with nine heads, three arms, and no dick. Caution was the order of the day.

He was so focused on the task that he didn't notice the figures step out of the gloom from behind him until they were literally right on top of him. By then, it was too late.

A bolt of light exploded behind his eyes. He heard the crowbar sing as it fell to the concrete floor, and a curious buzzing noise flitted through his ears—he recognized it an instant later as Andrews's voice over the radio. Then the light faded from his eyes, and Spencer was left in darkness so absolute that he couldn't even scream.

"You all right, Spence?" Andrews asked when he heard the sound of metal on concrete. He was at the far side of the warehouse, but he had already started toward the crew chief's position when Mulligan relayed the location of the core supports. He heard a sharp intake of breath over his radio earpiece but, other than that, there was no response.

"Spencer? What's going on?" Andrews started moving faster, shining his own flashlight around the area. He stepped into aisle fourteen; to his left was the office and way the team had entered, to his right a patchwork of darkness broken by sunlight streaming through structural damage.

On the concrete floor, the sterile glare of an LED flashlight illuminated the bottom of several shipping crates. Andrews hurried toward the light, still holding his own flashlight in his right hand and his crowbar in his left. A small voice in the back of his mind suggested that he might be better off with his rifle in hand, but he ignored it. Spencer might have fallen and gotten hurt, but there was no need to go to guns on him. Spencer's flashlight and crowbar lay on the dusty concrete, practically right next to each other.

What the fuck?

He looked around, but there was no sign of Spencer. The dust around the pile of shipping containers was disturbed, and Andrews had no problem seeing the tread from Spencer's boots ingrained in the light coating of earth, but there were other prints there as well, prints that extended toward the rear of the warehouse ...

"Eklund, what's your position?" He slipped his crowbar back into his knapsack and grabbed his rifle. There was a rail system on the weapon's forestock, where he was able to mount the flashlight so he could handle the weapon with both hands. But the LED beam seemed suddenly insufficient. Despite the occasional hole in the roof high overhead that admitted shafts of bright sunlight, there were far too many shadows throughout the warehouse.

"Far end of the warehouse, near the loading doors," Leona

reported. "What's happened? Is Spencer hurt?"

"I don't know. I've found his flashlight and crowbar, but no sign of him. Looks like there might have been a struggle over here ... lots of prints in the dust, and they're headed your way, Lee." Andrews kept the buttstock of his M416 pressed against his right shoulder, panning the barrel across his path. "Mulligan, what's your twenty?"

Mulligan's response was terse and flat. "Far end of the warehouse from Eklund. Closing on her position. Over."

"Roger that. Lee, stay put. We're heading for you," Andrews said, "but lock and load and get your back against something. I don't think we're alone here."

"You're kidding."

"I'm not kidding, Lieutenant. Get into a defensive posture and wait for us."

The undercurrent of reluctance was all too plain in Leona's voice when she replied. "All right, all right. But this had better not be some sort of stupid test or—*oh, God!*"

A single gunshot tore through the darkened warehouse, startling Andrews even though he thought he was on the alert. Over the radio, he heard the sounds of Leona struggling with something; she made a small mewling sound, then the link went silent on her end. Andrews picked up the pace, running now, the adrenaline coursing through his system. His lungs burned as if he couldn't get enough air, even though the respirator continued to deliver what he needed on demand, the soft hiss of its operation barely audible. Despite his weapon and his training, Andrews felt suddenly vulnerable.

"Leona! Leona, report!"

There was no answer.

He bore down on what he believed to be her last position, but there was no evidence that Leona Eklund had even existed. She must have moved to a different spot, obeying his order to find a more defensible position until he and Mulligan could get to her. Andrews looked at the dusty floor, searching for any sign of where she might have been. He saw a single pair of footprints one aisle over, and he hurried over to them. They were definitely boot prints, and the tread matched his own.

"Mulligan, where are you?" he asked as he followed the trail. Ahead, he could see signs of a scuffle, and what looked like drag marks. Andrews passed through a shaft of bright sunlight, and the glare dazzled him. Gleaming in the light at his feet was a single brass cartridge from a 5.56-millimeter round. He saw no evidence of blood, so he had no idea if Leona had hit her target or not.

"Heading your way, Captain. I take it Eklund's missing as well? Over." If the big sergeant major was feeling any stress, it didn't come through in his voice. To Andrews, Mulligan sounded all business, as if he was doing something trivial, like taking out the garbage or giving a weather report.

"Looks that way. I've found signs of a struggle and some drag marks. I'm following them now. I'm about seventy-five meters from our point of entry." As he spoke, Andrews continued following the trail through the dust. Sweat ran down his back, making him feel like ants were marching between his shoulder blades. He fought off the urge to shudder.

"Negative. Halt where you are and take a fighting position. I'm on the other side of the warehouse from you—I'll be there in two minutes. Take cover and wait. We'll track Spencer and Eklund together."

Movement to Andrews's right caused him to stop and spin around. The flashlight's bright beam revealed a pair of glittering eyes peering out at him from beneath a shaggy pile of filthy dark hair. There was so much grime on the pockmarked face that Andrews couldn't tell if it was male or female, but the eyes burned with a curious combination of intelligence, fear, and disgust.

"Don't move! Remain where you are!" Andrews shouted, pointing the weapon directly at the shadowy figure. As soon as he was oriented into the fighting posture, the figure ducked and leaped behind a pile of crates, moving with the speed and dexterity of a cat. The figure was small and lithe—a child or a small woman? He moved his finger from alongside his rifle's lower receiver frame to the trigger. He had kept the weapon indexed since the safety was off, as he didn't want to accidentally shoot anyone friendly. But now, he was ready for business.

"Andrews, give me a SITREP. Over." There was a hint of emotion in Mulligan's voice now.

Andrews stepped toward where the figure had stood,

crouching slightly, rifle tight against his shoulder. "We're not alone here, Sarmajor—"

As he spoke, more shapes swam through the gloom on either side of him. Andrews reacted, spinning to go to guns on the threat to his right, but something slammed into him from behind. Andrews cried out as he was flung face-first into a metal shelving unit. The durable plastic visor on his facemask cracked, and the impact was hard enough to allow some air to leak out through the seal around his face. Ignoring the possible contamination, he threw himself away from the metal obstruction and tried to spin around. At the same time, more figures piled onto him, laying him out on his chest and trapping his assault rifle beneath his body. Hands tore at him; in an instant, the mask was ripped from his face. Andrews yelled Mulligan's name, then something struck him in the side of his head with so much force that he saw stars.

Then the world went black.

Mulligan had moved to the far side of the warehouse upon leaving the office, moving as quickly and furtively as he could. His situational awareness was low—all he had to go on was what the others had reported. As their numbers diminished and he failed to generate any actionable intelligence from Andrews's reports, the big Special Forces soldier could reach only one conclusion: he was utterly fucked.

"Andrews, SITREP."

No answer.

"Andrews, give me a click of your microphone if you can't speak."

His radio earpiece remained silent, not even a vague hiss of background static. Everyone was off the air, which meant he was the last man standing. The others were armed and had been taken down with silent rapidity, which likely meant that Mulligan was not only fucked, he was quite possibly severely outnumbered, as well as having the dubious honor of being the next target the opposing force was looking to service.

He kept the warehouse wall to his back. He realized he had made a tactical error by moving deeper into the structure to maneuver himself closer to the action and perhaps outflank the attackers. But he hadn't expected the others to be taken so quickly, and practically without a fight. That could only mean overwhelming numbers and substantial coordination. To get back to the entrance—and to the SCEV—he would either have to backtrack or cut through the center of the warehouse.

Where the others had been taken.

That's a non-starter.

He turned and slowly began to pick his way back the way he had come, taking great care to move as silently as possible. In this situation, stealth was superior to speed. The gloomy interior of the warehouse worked to his adversaries' advantage. No doubt they knew its layout quite well, otherwise their ambushes wouldn't have been so flawless. With that thought in mind, Mulligan switched off his flashlight. The return path was relatively free of obstructions, so he wouldn't need the light to help him skirt around anything in his path. Even though there were areas in the warehouse where shadows grew dark and deep, he would stick to the near-twilight areas, where he stood a chance of seeing an attacker closing on him.

As he walked, he became hyper-aware of the sounds inside the warehouse. Wind whispering through the holes in the structure. Sporadic creaks as the warehouse settled. The soft scuffling of *things* moving somewhere in the gloom.

And those scuffling noises seemed to be drawing closer.

Outstanding.

"SCEV Five, this is Mulligan. We need immediate evac. Over." Even though the other rig was miles away and the suit transceivers didn't have the power to reach it through the covering structure of the warehouse, Mulligan hoped that Laird or the others would at least catch *something*. Even a fragmented sentence or a series of clicks might cause them to come in. Jim Laird was extremely conservative, the kind of small unit commander who could be counted on to follow orders and never do anything that too risky, but this mission was far different from anything he had been given before—would he be able to break the mold and rise to the challenge? Mulligan wasn't counting on it, but Kelly Jordello, SCEV Five's XO, was a real firecracker and had an intuitive grasp of tactical situations her commander lacked. Then there was Tony Choi, the Korean kid who was all goofy on the outside but who had a core of hard steel he kept tucked away where no one could see. Even though she wasn't military, Rachel Andrews had a lot riding on this, too. After all, her husband was out here with the man who had murdered her parents, so a fragmented transmission might get her dander up ...

There was no reply. Mulligan repeated his call as he kept falling back, his head on a swivel, alert and vigilant. He repeated the call, but the result was the same—unbroken silence.

A sudden sound from above made him whirl. A vaguely humanoid shape leapfrogged across the stacked crates, passing from shadow to shadow like some kind of demented gymnast. It moved with an almost simian grace, deeply unnerving Mulligan. Was it even human?

He didn't pause to consider that he might be surrounded by monsters. He simply raised his rifle and squeezed off two rounds—*crack-crack!*—with a practiced ease that was still second nature to him, even though he hadn't fired a weapon in anger in over a decade. His skills were still up to par, for he watched the figure jerk and spin as the steel-jacketed NATO rounds found their target. It howled as it tumbled off a stack of crates and crashed to the floor, where Mulligan couldn't see it. As he moved to his right, his foot hit something—a large chunk of concrete. He glanced down at it, then quickly stepped back to his left.

He stood on the edge of a large hole in the concrete floor. Its presence puzzled him for a moment, until he saw something moving in the opening's black depths. He was surprised to find a filthy human face peering up at him. It wasn't just a hole. It was a *tunnel*.

Mulligan brought his rifle to bear, but the man in the tunnel shrieked and darted back into the darkness.

Stealth was no longer going to cut it. As the sounds of movement grew louder throughout the warehouse, drawing nearer, the big Green Beret broke into a run.

11

THE SUN WAS low in the sky, bathing the shattered city in fiery light that was beginning to turn a brilliant shade of orange. That was the thing about nuclear exchanges, Jim Laird thought as he piloted SCEV Five down a dusty avenue. They left enough contaminants in the air to refract the light in such a way that they doubled the beauty of a sunrise or sunset.

"SCEV Four, this is SCEV Five. Can you copy? Andrews, Eklund, Spencer, Mulligan, kick it back. Over," he said into his headset as he steered the big rig down the same streets SCEV Four had taken over two hours ago. He gripped the control column in his left hand, and the instrument felt slick beneath his fingers. Laird was sweating, despite the cool air blowing over him from the vents overhead.

"We should have gone in with them," Choi said suddenly. He sat in the right seat, dividing his attention between the instruments and the view outside.

"Yeah, no kidding. Unfortunately, Andrews is the mission commander, and he told us to stay," Laird snapped. He regretted his tone immediately. Choi normally served with Andrews and Eklund and Spencer, so of course he would be worried about the sudden silence that had descended over the comms. When Laird had insisted they hold station for another half hour, just in case Andrews and the others were delayed for some harmless reason, Choi and Rachel Andrews had been pretty direct in voicing their displeasure. Even Kelly had questioned the decision, though not aloud. Laird had only to look at her eyes to get that, but he had held firm. Andrews and the others were probably so absorbed in looking for the supports that they had blown past the radio check. Overreacting to that wouldn't make things any easier.

"Sorry, Tony," he said lamely.

"Don't sweat it," Choi said, and Laird had to wonder if he was joking.

Rachel entered the cockpit, and Laird had to fight not to groan. She'd been the poster child for worry and despair during the entire trip, and now circumstances had conspired to make her even more tightly wound. Laird felt the weight of her stare as she knelt between the cockpit seats.

"Anything yet, Captain?"

"Not yet, Andrews. I'll let you know as soon as things change. Now go back and strap in. There's a lot of broken ground ahead, and—"

"What the fuck?" Choi said suddenly.

Laird backed off on the control column, slowing the SCEV. "What is it, Choi?"

"Check this out!" Choi tapped the center display excitedly. "According to Four's transponder, her bearing is changing. She's *moving!*"

Laird glanced down at the display. Sure enough, the rig was moving. Dead slow, but it was definitely moving. Which didn't make any sense at all.

"Could their radio be out?" Rachel asked, a glimmer of hope in her voice. "That would explain why they haven't been able to respond, right?"

Laird shook his head with a sigh as he accelerated again. "Each rig's got three separate radios with dedicated antennas. We can broadcast on VHF, FM, and HF. The chances of all three failing are ..." He reconsidered what he was saying, and who he was saying it to. With a sigh, he glanced over at Rachel and gave her a jerky smile. It was the best he could do at the moment.

"Ah ... yeah, Andrews. They could be NORDO. Maybe that's it."

Choi was apparently oblivious to what he was trying to do. "Whatever, sir, but the engineering uplink says she's on standby, and the rig's engine isn't running. Even if they were moving on auxiliary, the entire system wouldn't be in standby. For instance, the airlock doors haven't been cycled, and the security code wasn't entered—"

"Yeah, great, thanks a lot, Choi." Laird took his eyes off the road to stare daggers at the younger man. "You're a big help, man. Keep it up."

"*Watch out!*" Rachel screamed suddenly, gripping Laird's shoulder with enough strength to hurt. Her fingers dug into his flesh hard enough to leave bruises, but the pain barely registered in Laird's mind as he snapped his eyes forward and looked out the viewports. What he saw made him swear, and both he and

Choi stomped on the brakes at the same time. The big rig shuddered to a vibrating halt as its anti-lock brakes stuttered like a machine gun. Laird and Choi both reached out and grabbed Rachel at the same time, preventing her from flying into the instrument panel as the SCEV suddenly decelerated. From the back, Kelly Jordello let out a shout, and Laird heard something go flying to the floor of the second compartment.

Then everyone jerked backward as the vehicle came to a full stop and thrashed backward on its suspension. Rachel fell back onto her ass with a cry, her feet kicking up into the air. Laird ignored her and fumbled for the parking brake before hitting the quick-release on his harness. Beside him, Choi did the same. Both men stared out the viewports as a cloud of dust slowly rolled over the rig. Before it obscured their view through the thick glass, they saw a stumbling figure approach the rig, hands held high, as if in supplication.

It was Mulligan. He looked like he'd been through one hell of a fight. Laird grabbed the seat release and kicked the seat all the way back until it smacked into the bulkhead. He hauled himself out of the pilot's seat as Mulligan collapsed to the ground outside, his MOPP suit ripped and torn, his respirator assembly and facemask gone.

Blessedly cool air whispered over Mulligan as Laird and Choi pulled him through the tight airlock and half-carried him into SCEV Five's second compartment. They'd already removed his tattered environmental suit and tossed it into the incinerator before cycling open the inner door, leaving him dressed only in his sweat-soaked Army Combat Uniform. The two men dragged Mulligan over to the faux leather settee and eased him down onto it as Kelly Jordello moved toward him with the rig's medical kit in hand.

"Gotta shower," he said to her. "I'm hot—"

Kelly shook her head, and her ponytail swayed back and forth. "Not necessary right now. You haven't been exposed for very long." She glanced at Rachel, who stood nearby. Mulligan followed her gaze and, when he saw Rachel, he could tell by the set of her jaw that she was barely hanging on to her emotions.

"Rachel, get him some water, please," Kelly said.

Rachel hesitated for a moment, then stepped over to the kitchenette and drew a cup of water from the sink. As Laird and Choi pulled off their suits, Kelly snapped on some rubber gloves and slipped on a surgical mask.

"Procedure," she said to Mulligan when he looked at her.

"Lieutenant, I need to hit the shower and decon," he said.

"You have open wounds, Sergeant Major. You'd better let me tend to those first, unless you want to scrub them out with water and bleach yourself. Are you light-headed? Nauseous? Having trouble catching your breath?"

"Well, yeah. It's been a tough couple of hours."

"You're dehydrated. Rachel, the water?" Kelly pulled out a stethoscope and unbuttoned Mulligan's soaked ACU blouse. The T-shirt beneath it was dark with sweat.

Rachel held out the cup to Mulligan. He reached for it with trembling fingers and missed it on the first try.

Kelly took the cup from Rachel and put it in Mulligan's hand. "Drink that. We'll get you loaded up with electrolytes in a bit."

Mulligan brought the cup to his lips and drank down the contents. Some slid down the wrong pipe, and he coughed mightily, almost spilling the rest all over himself.

"Take it easy, Mulligan," Laird said.

"Blow it out your ass, sir." The sound of his voice reminded him of a metal rasp being dragged across stone. "We have a bit of a situation here."

Laird apparently chose to overlook the insubordination. "Where are the others, Sergeant Major?"

"Captured, I think. Maybe even dead. I was cut off from the rig—"

"*Captured?*" Rachel said, her voice high-pitched and shrill, a perfect counterpoint to Mulligan's dry, husky rasp. "By who?"

Mulligan took a moment to drink the remainder of his water, managing not to drown himself at the same time. He cleared his throat and looked at her directly. "By survivors of the war, ma'am. Like the judge always said—when you're hot, you're hot."

Rachel stared at him for a moment as her cold dread suddenly blossomed into a hot fury. "So you just *left* them there?

You ran out on them, you fucking bastard?"

Before Mulligan could formulate a reply, she was all over him, pounding him with her fists. Mulligan took the punishment. He didn't have the strength to fight her off, anyway.

"You left them! The only reason you're here is because you were supposed to watch over them, and *you left them!*"

"Rachel, get off him!" Kelly shouted, shoving her away just as Laird and Choi grabbed her shoulders and yanked Rachel back. Laird pinned her up against the sealed inner airlock door with one thick arm, pressing it under her chin. She fought against him, but Laird just increased the pressure.

"Keep this shit up, Andrews, and I'll fucking choke you out!" he bellowed, right in her face. "Get a grip—*now!*"

Rachel's lips pulled back from her teeth as she continued to fight, thrashing and kicking, but Laird was not a small man, and he was true to his word. Rachel began to choke when he put enough pressure on her airway that she couldn't take a breath. She finally relented, but it took longer than Mulligan would have thought.

That girl's got some fire in her, for sure.

When she began to sag, Laird quickly released her and grabbed her under the arms so she wouldn't fall to the deck. After she took several ragged gasps of air, Rachel raised her head. She didn't look at Laird; instead, she glared directly at Mulligan, and the hatred he saw in her eyes was truly impressive.

"Business as usual for you, isn't it?" she gasped.

"That's it, Andrews. Knock it off," Laird said. "Can you stand?" When Rachel finally nodded, Laird straightened. "All right, I'm going to let you go. Don't go batshit again, otherwise we'll tie you up in back. You get me?"

"Yes, Captain. I get you."

Laird slowly withdrew. After exchanging a glance with Choi, he turned back to Mulligan. It was pretty obvious even to Mulligan in his current state that Laird's mind was whirling. Finding survivors of the nuclear conflict has been Laird's mission for the past decade; now that he'd nearly realized his mission, it was too much. This was something the team just couldn't handle right now.

Still, he had to explore it.

"People?" Laird asked, finally.

"Well, I wouldn't say *that*. But there are a lot of those bastards, and they're apparently none too happy to see us." Mulligan started to laugh then, a laugh that sounded a little crazy even to him. When he saw the others staring at him as if he'd lost his marbles, he got himself under control. "I'm sorry, but it's kind of ironic, huh? We've finally found life outside of Harmony. Boy, I'll bet Benchley's going to pop a boner over this."

Laird shook his head, stunned by the news. Kelly resumed her work, listening to Mulligan's heart and taking his blood pressure.

"Jesus," Laird said after a loud sigh. "Yeah, I'd probably get a little hot and bothered over it myself, if we didn't have other things to take care of right now." He rubbed his face, then crossed his arms. "All right ... we're still getting Four's transponder signal. Whoever your new friends are, they're apparently moving the rig, but we can track it down. Hopefully, the others won't be too far from it."

"Better wait for a few hours, in that case," Mulligan said. "The bad guys'll think they're secure, and we can roll up on them using the darkness as cover."

"They could be unprotected, Sarmajor. The rad count's still high enough that continuous exposure will cause damage," Kelly said as she finished taking his vitals.

Laird nodded. "Jordello's right, Mulligan. The sooner we get our people back, the sooner we can complete our mission."

Mulligan sighed. "Excuse me, sir, but do you have a plan?"

Laird hesitated. Choi and Mulligan looked at him, waiting for an answer. Kelly pulled out cotton, gauze, swabs, and antiseptic as she prepared to clean out Mulligan's wounds, something he wasn't looking forward to. He noticed that Rachel Andrews kept her eyes rooted on him, as if she was trying to stare holes through his head. Mulligan suddenly found that he was very tired of all the pussyfooting around, and decided to roll in for the kill.

"Listen, Captain—we have night vision devices, armored mobility, secure communications, and a fair amount of firepower at our disposal. But unless you play it smart, none of that's going to mean jack."

"So what are you suggesting, Sergeant Major?"

"I'm suggesting that I'm the only warfighter in the vehicle, so you might want to let me take the lead on this one, sir. No disrespect intended, but I'm the only one here who's already had his cherry popped, so I kind of know what we're going to have to do."

"You left them," Rachel said. "Why should we listen to you?"

"Because if they're not dead, I'll be able to get them back alive." Mulligan scowled. "Shit or get off the pot, Captain. We're danger close across the board. What's it going to be?"

Laird frowned, glaring at Mulligan, furious at being called out in front of his crew. Mulligan sympathized, as he would certainly feel the same way if their roles were reversed. But that changed nothing, and they probably had a lot of fighting ahead of them.

Laird couldn't keep the anger out of his voice. "All right, Sergeant Major. You've made your point. What first?"

"We break it down into manageable pieces and knock them out one at a time. Hiding the vehicle would be a great way to get started, sir. Get us out of the middle of this street and under cover."

Laird stared at Mulligan for another long, frosty second. Choi fidgeted, looking from one man to the other. Finally, Laird motioned to Choi.

"Get forward, Choi. Jordello, get that son of a bitch cleaned up and deconned. Once you're done, Sergeant Major, take some time to get yourself squared away, then tell us how you figure we're going to get this done, if you don't mind."

"Hooah, sir," Mulligan said.

Choi pushed past the settee and headed for the cockpit. Laird turned and followed him without saying another word and, a moment later, the rig started moving again.

"I'm going to clean your wounds, Sergeant Major. When I'm done, you can shower up."

"Roger that, Lieutenant. Do your worst." As Kelly started cleaning out the scratches on his face, Mulligan looked over at Rachel. She continued to glare at him, her arms crossed, her feet spread so she could keep her balance as the vehicle swayed slightly from side to side. Mulligan sighed and decided to try one last time to reach her.

"It's going to work out okay," he told her. "We'll get them back."

Rachel snorted and turned toward the cockpit. "They were dead the second you came aboard, Mulligan."

12

WHEN LEONA CAME to, she had a pounding headache that wouldn't quit and her right eye burned and itched horribly. She reached up to rub it, and the ensuing burst of pain left her gasping. She curled up into the fetal position for a time, trying to deal with the pain until she worked up the courage to try again. Gently, she ran her fingertips over her face and found the flesh around her left eye was tender, distended, and so swollen she couldn't even see out that eye. She felt like she'd gone five rounds with a heavyweight boxer, and she'd have one hell of a shiner to show for it, that was for sure.

Then she realized she wasn't wearing a glove on her hand.

Slowly, she unwound from her fetal position and looked around. She was on the floor of a dark, dirty room. It was devoid of any furniture, and the walls were dingy with years of accumulated filth. A small window was positioned high up on one wall, the glass there cracked. It admitted only tepid light, which was just bright enough to allow her to examine herself. Her environmental suit was ripped and torn, hopelessly compromised. And she had no respirator assembly—it was all gone, along with her radio, weapon, and knapsack. Her right hand throbbed, and she found a swollen knot on one knuckle. Had she hit someone? She tried to recall what had happened at the warehouse, but her recollections were disjointed and vague. She found her entire body ached, as if she'd been through a strenuous fight.

Then she remembered. Her last thought before the darkness had descended was finding herself suddenly surrounded by a filthy horde of shapes that moved through the warehouse gloom with a self-assured efficiency that told her they knew the layout of the building as well as the backs of their hands. Their garments were old and covered with dust and grime, and she had realized then that if it wasn't for the respirator mask she had worn, she likely would have smelled them coming.

Then they had attacked. Leona remembered squeezing off a wild shot from her rifle as rough, calloused hands grabbed her from everywhere, tearing off her facemask and ripping the weapon from her grasp. Then there had been the vicious blow to her face, the one that left her with an eye so swollen she couldn't see through it.

She looked up at the window as she slowly, gingerly, rose to her feet. She still wore her boots and uniform beneath the tattered remains of the suit, which was a step in the right direction. She stumbled toward the wall, wincing as a sudden tenderness in her hip made itself known. Leaning against the wall, she reached up toward the window, but it was too far for her to reach, much less look outside to get an idea of where she was.

From behind her, a door opened on creaking hinges.

Leona turned as quickly as she was able, keeping the wall to her back and slipping into a Shotokan karate stance, adopting an edge-on position that presented the right side of her body toward the newcomers while keeping the swelling on the left side of her face away from them. She already knew that contact with the swelling was immensely painful; the last thing she wanted was for someone to strike her there. She knew she would fold up like a rag doll.

As she had suspected, she was able to smell them coming. The fetid stink of unwashed bodies and clothing rolled into the room like a sickening tsunami. Leona felt her gorge rise but she fought it down silently, clenching her teeth together to prevent a groan from escaping her lips. She watched as several figures stepped into the room and fanned out on either side of the door, their eyes glittering in the darkness. They were dirty, grime-covered people, two men and one woman, while the fourth was more like a shambling monstrosity. Hunchbacked and possessed of an overly large head, the hideous creature examined her with pale blue eyes. A strand of thick, ropey drool spilled out of its mouth and rolled over its insanely thick lower lip, slowly making its way to the floor. Leona gasped at the sight of the grotesquerie, almost horrified beyond belief.

It's deformed from the radiation ... but how could something like that live?

The deformed person burbled something in its throat, then shuffled off to one side. Leona found that she couldn't take her eyes off it.

"Don't be afraid of them, dearie," a voice said from the

blackness beyond the open door. "They won't harm you."

Leona pulled her eyes off the deformity and tightened up her stance, clenching her hands into fists and them raising up before her. She watched as another figure stepped out of the deep shadow and into the nominally better light inside the small room. He was clad in dirty, threadbare clothing, but his garments seemed to be in better shape than any of the others. His hair was thinning, and his face was pockmarked with scars left from old, festering sores that had finally healed. He smiled at her, and Leona thought that he had once been a handsome man, many years ago. Now, time and the harsh post-apocalyptic environment had taken their toll. His dark brown eyes seemed to gleam with an uncanny intellect, and when he looked at her, Leona felt he could see directly into the depths of her soul.

She feared him instantly.

"Allow me to introduce myself," he said. "I am the Law. And before you even think about it, let me tell you there's is no place for you to run, even if you did manage to get out of this room. We know this city quite well, and we have your vehicle. You couldn't escape." His smile widened into a broad grin, revealing surprisingly white teeth that looked to be in fine shape. He took another step toward her, closing the distance between them to about ten feet. Leona instinctively tried to back up, but she found she was already against the wall. There was no place for her to go.

"Tell me ... who are you? Where did you come across such a useful vehicle?" the man asked. When she said nothing, he pursed his lips and feigned a crestfallen expression. "Come on, now. I'm absolutely *dying* to hear your voice."

Leona regarded him for a long moment, then slowly lowered her clenched fists. She took a tentative step toward the man who called himself the Law, and forced her dry throat to swallow.

"Sure thing," she said, right before she launched a quick snap kick right for his face.

The man avoided the blow as if he had known it was coming. The air around him seemed to pulse suddenly, to come alive with a rising electricity that quickly filled the room. Leona had never felt anything quite like it before as it enveloped her, almost like a physical thing. Then, every nerve ending in her body exploded with pain so deep and sudden that her legs gave out. Leona screamed as she crashed to the floor, jerking in a series of agonized spasms she could not control. Her scream continued until her lungs emptied of air, then she had to fight to fill them again as bright flashes danced behind her eyes. The pain was immense, as if every cut, bump, bruise, and injury she had previously experienced was only a series of tests before the main event. Her conscious mind retreated, fleeing the pain, but found nowhere to hide.

The man seemed oblivious to her torment. "I can force you to speak, you know. How do you like the pain? Should I make it worse?"

Leona's agony suddenly doubled. She threw her head back and shrieked as she convulsed on the floor, her limbs flailing, completely out of control. She felt consciousness start to fade as tunnel vision set in, and she wondered vaguely if this was going to be the last thing she ever felt—degrees of pain she had never imagined, agony so extreme it threatened to shatter her mind.

Then, as quickly as it had come, the pain subsided. Leona gasped for air as her nerve endings slowly cooled off, radiating pain like a heat sink.

Law stepped closer to her. "You didn't enjoy it? I hadn't thought you would. But that was just one of my powers, girl. A bit crude, maybe ... like a bat against an infant's skull. Want to try something else? Something a touch more *sophisticated*. What do you say?"

Leona rolled over onto her belly. It was almost an autonomous motion, as if her body was taking charge and trying to get her away from the slender man with the bright eyes who could induce such mind-numbing pain that the very thought of enduring it once again nearly drove her mad. She tried to crawl away from him, heading for one of the room's dark corners, her muscles trembling and her joints barely moving. She let out a ragged gasp when Law stuck his foot under her belly and turned her onto her back. He stood over her, still grinning manically, his eyes agleam with something Leona couldn't identify. Madness, she decided, something she'd never seen before.

"Want to see how it all ended?" he asked in a harsh whisper. "A tour of mankind's demise? It's a definite E-ticket attraction!" He squeezed his eyes shut, as if concentrating on some difficult task. Veins suddenly stood out on his forehead, and Leona could see them pulsing with blood. The air grew electric again, and she made a small noise in the back of her throat. The pain was coming, and she knew it.

But the pain never came.

Images flashed across her mind's eye—

An atomic warhead detonates over San Jose in an airburst of brilliant, blinding, malignant light.

Ear-splitting thunder cracks as streets full of people are instantly atomized, disappearing in brief puffs of flame.

A luminous shockwave tears across the city, shattering skyscrapers, flattening homes, tossing debris everywhere.

The same city, now a time-ravaged tomb.

Mangy, diseased dogs stalk the streets, devouring whatever is left that still bears meat; clouds of black flies descend upon thousands of bloated human corpses that lay baking in the hot sunlight.

The images stopped as suddenly as they had started, and Leona's mind was returned to her. She found she was weeping, convulsing with great sobs of despair and sorrow at what she had seen. Was that what it had been like during the Sixty Minute War? The fear, the horror, the destruction of inescapable death? She had spent months over the past year looking at the rotting corpses of the great cities of the Midwest, their crumbling skyscrapers skeletal and gaunt, having shed their facades and panes of glass as the rest of the settlements around them decayed. Examining those cities and the remnants of small towns, the husks of what had once been country houses and farms, she had felt a vague, disconnected sorrow for what had befallen her people, her fellow Americans, and perhaps the entire human race. But that pale mourning was hardly even a drop when compared to the vast sea of grief that now consumed her. She raised her hands to her battered face and cried into her palms, unable to do anything else.

The man who called himself the Law knelt beside her, and she could feel his lips moving against her hair as he spoke, his voice a calm whisper.

"Now. Tell me who you are, where you come from, and what you're doing here."

13

MULLIGAN SAT IN the pilot's seat of SCEV Five, the control column in his left hand as he steered the big rig through the shattered remnants of San Jose. The night was dark and deep, the only illumination coming from the cold, distant stars in the black sky. Despite the darkness, the SCEV ran without any external lighting. Mulligan had decided it would be in everyone's best interest to make the rig as difficult to detect as possible, and that meant the rig's impressive array of high intensity floodlights would remain switched off. But the darkness did not pose a substantial problem for the SCEV crew. Projected across the cockpit's forward viewports was an infrared display of the terrain ahead, which allowed Mulligan to see what lay in the rig's path as if he were a lion stalking a limping gazelle across the nighttime Serengeti.

Laird sat restlessly in the copilot's seat as Mulligan drove, staring at the same thermographic imagery. A route had been highlighted on the display, and that pale yellow line was leading them directly to where SCEV Four's active transponder said the missing SCEV could be found.

"Ah, this is a little weird," Laird said after a moment.

"Do tell," Mulligan said. He flexed his right hand against his thigh. When he'd blasted through the people who had tried to attack him in the warehouse, one of them had hit him in the hand with a piece of piping. The fourth finger on his hand had swelled up, and moving it was painfully difficult.

"Four's transponder information—the elevation value is reading negative." Laird pressed a button on the center console, and a small window opened on the infrared overlay in front of Mulligan. SCEV Four's position information was displayed in the small box and, sure enough, the elevation value was showing as negative ten meters.

"So they've taken the rig underground," Mulligan said. "Cunning bastards."

"We have detailed data files on the area. Let's see if I can come across any civil defense or zoning records that have any actionable information on the buildings in that area. You want the data window to stay open?"

"Negative, it's just making the view more cluttered."

Laird closed the window, then opened another on one of the multifunction displays in the instrument panel. Mulligan glanced over quickly, and he saw the husky captain scrolling through a map of the area.

"Bingo," Laird said after a few moments. "Says here that there's a parking garage on the next block. Right next to a civic center, and across from a light rail station."

"Same route as the one we're on?" Mulligan asked.

"Hooah, Sarmajor. We're heading right for it."

"Roger. Stay sharp, and switch off the gun safeties, if you don't mind, sir."

Laird made an affirmative noise and reached for the fire control panel. He lifted a red switch guard and flicked the toggle beneath it. When the switch moved to the ARMED position, it made an uncharacteristically loud click, followed by a distinct tone over the cockpit speakers. Anyone trained in SCEV operations would know that the turreted machine guns on either side of the SCEV's nose had just been made operational. A red targeting reticle appeared on the viewport in front of Laird, and when he moved the grip on the center console, the reticle and the guns themselves would slew onto the designated target.

"Hot guns," Laird reported.

"Roger, hot guns. Let's see what we can see. Hang on, the road's pretty torn up out there," Mulligan said as the SCEV began to bump up and down. He slowed the rig dramatically as its knobbed tires rolled across cracked and shattered concrete. All manner of detritus lay in the street and, a moment later, Mulligan saw why. Several entire buildings had collapsed. He couldn't tell what had caused the destruction, only that it seemed to be more recent than the nuclear attack that had destroyed San Jose.

"Parking garage is down the street and on the right," Laird said. "I think I can see it—there. Looks kind of messed up, but at least it's still standing."

"I've got tracks through the rubble," Mulligan said. "Lots of them. Looks like our friends actually *towed* the rig here." As the vehicle slowly approached the parking garage, Mulligan felt his heart rate increase. If ever there was a time for an ambush, this is when it would happen. He didn't know if any of the survivors that had attacked them had weaponry capable of penetrating an SCEV but, if they did, they'd use them soon. Not that the crew had any choice in the matter; urban terrain made long-range surveillance difficult, so they had to come in close, either on foot or in the rig. They'd tried it on foot earlier in the day, and it had only resulted in the disappearance of Andrews, Spencer, and Eklund.

The tire tracks led directly to a closed metal garage door. Mulligan looked at it through the infrared overlay, but the image fidelity wasn't sufficient enough for him to determine how substantial the door was. And he wasn't going to stop and check it out personally.

"Lieutenant Jordello, take control of the FLIR turret and put eyes on the building to our right. It's a parking garage, and the entrance has been sealed off. Let me know if the door looks solid, if you would. We won't be stopping, so do it quickly."

"Roger that," Kelly said from the science station on the other side of the cockpit bulkhead. Mulligan kept the SCEV moving at just above a crawl, and he looked out the side port to his left. The night was as dark as ever, and there was no sign of any illumination. No firelight, no candlelight—nothing. If the opposing force was nearby, they were certainly adhering to strict blackout routines.

"Yeah, it looks like it's a folding metal rollup door," Kelly reported after a moment. "Seems solid enough. Quite large, though."

"They must've run semi-trucks in there," Mulligan said. "You said there's a civic center somewhere around here?"

"On the other side of the garage," Laird said.

Mulligan grunted. "Makes sense. They'd roll the big rigs in whenever they had a show and offload the trailers right into the center. Okay, let's go around the block and see what we can see."

"Maybe we should dismount," Laird suggested.

"Maybe we shouldn't," Mulligan said. "The group that attacked us, they didn't have any projectile weapons—only clubs and bats and knives. If that's all they have, then they'll have a hell of a time trying to get at us as long as we remain in the vehicle. If we had more boots with us, we could do what you suggest, but we don't. Right now, our best protection is the

SCEV."

"I got you, Sergeant Major," Laird said. "But from the transponder data, SCEV Four is definitely somewhere inside there."

"I know, Captain. I know. Patience."

With that, Mulligan slowly drove around the block. He wished he felt as confident as he sounded, but he knew the situation could explode into a clusterfuck at a moment's notice. While he was comfortable with the assumption that the opposing force—OPFOR, in military parlance—didn't have much in the way of heavy weaponry, and almost certainly no antitank weaponry, there were still a dozen other ways for their night to be ruined even further. If the OPFOR managed to block off the street and prevent the vehicle from escaping, that would definitely put a damper on the presumed rescue mission.

As the rig pulled around the huge, domed civic center, the city remained quiet and dark. That made Mulligan nervous. The SCEV had doubtless made a large racket in its passage, even while operating on battery power—driving a multi-ton vehicle over rubble and not making a lot of noise was impossible. He saw no indication that anyone was going to investigate the disturbance made by the rig, but he wasn't sure if that was a positive or a negative.

Time will tell.

When Mulligan made to turn right on the far side of the civic center and head back for the parking garage, he brought the rig to a sudden halt. Laird let out a long sigh when he saw what lay ahead of them.

"Man, it's a good thing we didn't come the other way," Laird said.

Ahead, the street had collapsed. The concrete roadway had been transformed into millions of pieces of disjointed rubble, all of which lined the bottom of a wide crevasse. Despite the utter darkness, the infrared sensors revealed that the train station below the street had been exposed in the collapse. An old car lay upended in the rubble, its battered rear bumper gleaming in the wan starlight.

"Looks like an earthquake hit the city some time ago. That explains why this area is such a mess," Mulligan said.

"Then why would they bring SCEV Four here?" Laird

asked.

"Because the place is so fucked up, no one would bother to look around here. Cagey bastards." Mulligan regarded the train station for a moment. He knew that the BART system had been extended from San Francisco all the way to southern San Jose. That there was a station stop at the civic center was no surprise.

"You know, we might be able to use that," he said, pointing at the train station.

"For what? Catching a train?"

"Ingress, Captain. Ingress. There've got to be ways inside the civic center from there, and from the civic center into the garage."

Ten minutes later, Mulligan parked SCEV Five between two decimated buildings a block away from the civic center. He preceded Laird into the second compartment and went directly to the arms locker located near the second bulkhead. It was locked, of course; only rig commanders had the keys to the small arms. He turned to Laird and motioned him forward.

"You mind opening the locker, sir?"

Laird reached into his uniform blouse and pulled out a set of keys hanging around his neck on a thin lanyard. He opened the locker wordlessly and stepped out of the way. Mulligan removed four of the eight M416A3 rifles that were secured inside and set them on the dining settee. Then he reached further into the locker and pulled out a worn, black plastic case. It had its own lock, this one biometric.

"What's that?" Laird asked. "I don't remember that being there."

"That's because I took the liberty of placing it aboard before we left Harmony," Mulligan said. He set the case on the settee table and pressed his thumb against the biometric lock. It clicked open instantly, and Mulligan raised the case's lid on its hinges. Inside the case's foam-lined interior lay several blocks of white, putty-like substance, several blasting caps and their integral batteries, and two remote detonators. Mulligan examined the case's contents with a critical eye. The C4 was a bit long in the tooth, but it should still be functional, along with the blasting caps. He checked the radio frequency detonators—they were fully charged. Everything was just as he had left it.

"Sarmajor, are those *explosives?*" Kelly Jordello asked.

"Well, you could play around with one and find out," Mulligan said. "I like to be prepared, but I gotta tell you, I didn't think we'd need 'em. Captain, maybe you could start handing out rifles. Everyone should take at least six magazines with them. We have no idea what we'll run into."

"Roger that," Laird said. He reached past Mulligan and pulled out several pre-loaded magazines, then began slapping them inside the rifles.

"We can't use those! Those are *people* out there! We can't just blow them up because of some misunderstanding!" Kelly said.

Mulligan turned and looked at her directly. "Lieutenant, if we can walk in and negotiate with the people who are holding our crewmates and get out of there without firing a shot, fine— I'm all for it. But if we meet resistance, I intend to respond decisively."

Kelly glared at him. "What's the matter, Mulligan, wasn't the last war enough for you?"

"Back off, Jordello. He says he's got the skills for this stuff. Let him do what he has to do."

Mulligan looked past Kelly. Rachel stood right behind her, holding a heavy ballistic vest in one hand and a radio headset in the other. Her expression was hard, her attitude focused. It was obvious that she wasn't letting her dread over her husband and her hatred for Mulligan get the best of her anymore. She looked like a full-time player. Mulligan was caught completely off-guard by the unexpected alliance.

"Kelly, you and Rachel get suited up in combat armor," Laird said. "Sarmajor, I take it we're going to move fast and keep our exposure to the elements to a minimum?"

"Absolutely, sir."

"Then let's skip the MOPP gear," Laird suggested, which surprised Mulligan almost as much as Rachel backing him up against Jordello. "The rad count's so low we won't need it, and it'll just slow us down."

"Hooah on that, sir," Mulligan said.

Kelly wasn't letting it go. "Jim, we can't just go to guns on the first group of survivors we've encountered in—"

"We're not," Laird said. He popped a magazine inside another rifle, pulled back on the charging lever, and checked to ensure the safety was set before setting it down and moving to the next rifle. "We're going in armed, and Mulligan has operational control of the mission, but no one's going to shoot first and ask questions later. Right, Mulligan?"

"Depending on the situation, yes," Mulligan said. He turned back to Kelly. "If we're attacked, we'll need to defend ourselves. We'll give them a chance, but if they fuck it up, we absolutely *will* light them up so we can continue with our mission— remember what we're here for, Lieutenant."

"Remember what Harmony Base stands for, Sergeant Major," she shot back.

Laird sighed. "Kelly, listen—"

"Pull your head out of your ass, Jordello!" Rachel said. "We let these people get the upper hand and detain us here, or outright kill us or whatever it is they might want to do, then *everyone* at Harmony winds up taking the long dirt nap. You need to choose between the survival of everyone you know or your ideals. Let us know when you've made your decision, all right?"

Damn, that was impressive, Mulligan thought.

Kelly glared at Rachel, then looked to Laird. The captain met her eyes for a moment, then shrugged. "Andrews and Mulligan are right, Kelly. Mission first, founding principles second. The situation's pretty clear, and I think we've taken this discussion as far as it can go. Get manned up. You too, Andrews. I know you're not military, and we'll do what we can to keep you out of it, but I'll walk you through operating an assault rifle. Just in case."

"Good," Rachel said.

"So that's it? Decision's made?" Kelly asked.

"It looks that way, ma'am," Mulligan said.

She turned away and pushed past Rachel without saying anything further. She reached into a locker and she pulled out another set of body armor.

Mulligan nodded to Rachel. "Thanks for the assist."

"Just do your job," Rachel said. "For once." She turned her back to him and began pulling on a pair of kneepads.

14

ANDREWS SAT ON the floor of a darkened room, trying not to think about the aches and pains that still sung across his body, courtesy of the beating he'd taken at the warehouse. He was angry at himself for allowing the attackers to take him down so easily. Even though he'd been alone, he had been armed with an assault rifle and had gone through a fairly intensive basic training regimen that Mulligan himself had presided over. Andrews had thought he was ready for all eventualities, including having to kill another person, only to find that he had hesitated in the final moment. The only way to have avoided capture would have been to flick the firing selector to auto and open up on anyone not from Harmony Base. But he hadn't, and now it was time to figure out just what the hell he was going to do.

"Coach ...? How you doing?"

Andrews looked up. Sitting across from him was Spencer, his face battered and bloodied. He cradled his right arm against his chest. His wrist and hand were severely swollen, and the distended flesh there was already turning a vibrant shade of purple. Like Andrews, he had been stripped of all his gear, save for his uniform. Spencer tried to smile, but the expression turned into a grimace when his split lip started to bleed again.

"Compared to you, I'm sitting pretty. How're you holding up, Spence?"

Spencer looked down at his arm. "You think this is broken?"

"Oh, yeah. Don't move it, just keep it right where it is."

Spencer nodded. "I gotta tell you, the pain's about to get me, sir."

Andrews reached out and patted one of Spencer's feet gently. "Hang in there, man."

Spencer nodded, but his eyes seemed unfocused. After a long moment, he said, "What do you think they did to Leona?"

Andrews clenched his teeth and looked away. He squeezed Spencer's foot. Both of them had heard Leona screaming, a bloodcurdling series of shrieks that rocked them to their very cores. Andrews had immediately gone to the room's locked door and pounded on it—attacked it, really, kicking it with all his strength—but it was a metal fire door and wouldn't budge. They could tell from the screams that Leona wasn't that far from them, but with the thick cinderblock walls and the locked metal door, she might as well have been a million miles away. Her screams had stopped after a brief time, and they'd heard nothing for over an hour since. The light coming in from the room's single window high on the wall above Andrews's head had already faded to a dull amber. The sun had set, and night was coming.

"I don't know, man. I don't know," he said finally.

Spencer nodded again. "She's a strong chick. For her to scream like that ... they must've been doing something horrible to her."

"Don't talk, Spence. Save your strength." He wanted to add a platitude like *We'll get out of this*, or *Don't worry, the others are on their way*, but even to his own ears they would sound false. He settled for patting Spencer's foot again, though he knew the gesture would do little to dispel the swarthy crew chief's fear. He knew what Spencer was thinking. Even though they were both concerned for Leona's well-being, they were also deeply frightened of what lay in store for them. Death? Torture? Andrews didn't know, but he knew he would find out eventually. He had already decided to plead with their captors to let Spencer go and keep only him.

Or kill him first, so he wouldn't have to listen to Spencer's screams in the growing darkness.

But where's Mulligan? If they'd caught him, too, wouldn't he be here with us? Is he being held somewhere else? Or did he escape?

The last thought was a source of strength. If Mulligan had in fact escaped, there was at least a chance they could be rescued. Andrews had no doubt that Mulligan was the cold, highly skilled special operator he was said to be. If he had managed to elude capture and if he could get to SCEV Five and contact Laird and the others, then the chances of getting out of this mess alive went up a notch.

Unless he convinced the others to go for the supports and get the hell back to Harmony.

That last thought didn't leave Andrews feeling warm and fuzzy. He and Spence had made a silent decision not to discuss

Mulligan or his whereabouts—if he *had* escaped, there was no sense in giving their captors any intel on him. The possibility that he might have put mission success ahead of a rescue was something they didn't want to consider.

The sound of a metal bolt being drawn cracked through the darkness. Andrews rose immediately, facing the door as it slowly swung open. Spencer slowly clambered to his feet, cradling his injured arm; Andrews didn't move to help him. He wanted to be free and unencumbered in case he needed to fight.

Torchlight brightened the room. Two natty-looking men in threadbare clothing stepped inside. One held a torch in one hand and a spiked cudgel in the other. The second man held a machete, which looked like it had seen years of use. Both men were filthy, and their rank body odor filled the room quickly. Spencer muttered a curse and stepped away from them, grimacing. The two men were as thin as scarecrows, clearly malnourished, but Andrews didn't dare underestimate them. Though scrawny, they also appeared to be as tough as shoe leather—anyone who had survived in this dead city had to be.

A third man stepped into the room. His face was pockmarked and his clothing was old and worn, but he obviously tended to himself. His bearing told Andrews he was a man of some authority, such as it were. The bright gleam in his dark eyes conveyed to Andrews that he was as ruthless as any warlord who had ever lived. The man looked from Andrews to Spencer, then back again. He smiled broadly.

"Captain Michael Andrews? Commander of the Self-Contained Exploration Vehicle you've so graciously donated to us? The vehicle entry code is eight-nine-zero-two-four. It's powered by two Honeywell AGT2500 gas turbine engines and has an Arbalest millimeter wave radar system manufactured by Lockheed Martin—oddly enough, I'm familiar with those. You come from Harmony Base, a subterranean complex located in what's left of Kansas, some fifty miles from the Colorado border. You're here to secure supports for your geothermal heat conversion units. If you fail, then about three hundred seventy-five people will die." The man's smiled widened into a Cheshire Cat grin. "Feel free to correct me if I might have gotten something wrong."

"Where's the rest of my team?" Andrews asked.

"Lieutenant Eklund is being well taken care of, Captain. Don't worry—I know you must've have heard her screams, but she hasn't been permanently damaged. And your man Mulligan will be found any time now ... assuming he's still alive." The man's countenance darkened slightly. "He managed to kill several members of my family. He'll pay for that. All of you will."

Andrews heart leapt at the news. *Mulligan's still alive!*

The man smiled once again. "I wouldn't feel suddenly optimistic, Captain. He *will* be found. But listen, forgive the delay in our little meeting—I've been exploring the capabilities of your vehicle. Rather impressive collection of technology, isn't it? Sophisticated, but simple at the same time. Lieutenant Eklund has been *most* helpful in assisting me in understanding its more advanced operations. Allow me to introduce myself." The man actually *bowed*, as if Andrews was some sort of visiting dignitary being received by a civilized man in a civilized land. "I am the Law." He straightened and met Andrews's gaze with humorless eyes. "In both name and fact."

"Why did your people attack us?" Andrews asked.

"You invaded our territory. Perhaps you aren't aware, Andrews, but the world is a *very* hostile place these days." Law spoke almost conversationally. He looked down at his dark, long-sleeved shirt and brushed some dust from one of the lapels, as if Andrews was boring him.

"Granted, the world is absolutely a hostile place," Andrews said, and he heard the anger and frustration in his voice. "But now you *know* why we're here. Our mission has nothing to do with you. There's no reason for you to hold us—"

Law looked up and his eyes narrowed. The air seemed to crackle around Andrews, then a tremendous bolt of pain slashed through him, from head to groin. He cried out and doubled over, almost falling to his knees. He felt his bladder quiver and, for a moment, he thought he was going to piss himself. He'd never felt anything as intense as this in his entire life; it was like all his innards had suddenly burst into flame. His ragged cry dissolved into a series of hacking coughs as he gagged, his stomach turning. Then he did fall to his knees, and a moment later, his forehead met the floor as the pain increased.

"Don't lecture me, Andrews! This is *my* domain!" Law

shouted. "I ask, and you answer! That's how it works!"

With that, the pain suddenly disappeared. Andrews caught himself before he collapsed, feeling a hot sweat break out across his body. His gut churned, but he managed to hold back his gorge as he gasped for air.

My God, what just happened?

He felt a hand on his shoulder. "Captain ... Mike, you okay?" Spencer asked. "What happened, man?"

Andrews slowly pushed himself to his haunches. He nodded at Spencer, then rose to his feet. Law looked at him, smiling haughtily.

"Just a little trick I picked up years ago, before the war," Law said. "Yeah. 'Before the war.' There's something we don't talk about much around here, but I'll take a moment to fill you in. Interested, or—?"

"Go ahead," Andrews said, not wanting to contemplate what the "or" might entail.

"I was no one. I was a Marine for three years, but I hated it—I hated the service, hated the lack of individuality, hated being a tiny cog in a huge machine. I was one of the Corps' problem children—they couldn't make me into what they wanted me to be, and I wasn't inclined to let them. It wasn't exactly a match made in heaven, but I intended to serve out my enlistment. No matter what, I simply wouldn't quit—much to the Corps' displeasure, of course." Law smiled again. "But, as things happen, I was scouted by another agency. The CIA. Heard of them?"

"Yes," Andrews said.

Law nodded. "Anyway, I became a guinea pig for a new program. With artificial hormones and nanotechnology and some rather unpleasant rounds of microsurgery, my new employers gave me talents and abilities no other man has ever had. I was designed to be multifaceted. To be whatever the situation demanded—spy, soldier, interrogator, you name it—but then the war came. And this little guinea piggy was left to fend for himself."

Law indicated the two stinking men standing behind him, who watched Andrews and Spencer with hard eyes.

"Now, I'm the king. *Their* king, for whom they would do anything."

"Law ..." Andrews paused, swallowed, and licked his lips. He found he barely had the courage to speak. Would he be subjected to another round of horrible, terrifying agony? He would do almost anything to avoid that. "Law, please. Listen to me. You know why we're here, right? You understand what our mission is—"

"Your mission?" Law shouted, and Andrews took an involuntary step backward. "You think I give a rat's ass about your *mission*, Captain? You and your people live below ground in a sterile, climate-controlled environment, watching old movies, listening to music, eating decent food, living the good life while the rest of the planet fucking *died!* All your people did was kick back for ten years, not even *bothering* to help out the rest of us. You're hypocrites!"

"That's not so." Andrews kept his voice calm and rational. "That's not what Harmony's about. Our core mission statement is—"

"'When the world ends, our mission begins.' Yeah, I heard that already. I noticed your vehicle is armed with missiles and machine guns, by the way. Coming to offer help from the barrel of a weapon? I mean, you've already killed four members of my family, so why stop there?"

"Our weapons are defensive only, and *your* people attacked *us!* No warning, no attempted contact, nothing—just an outright attack while we were looking for what we needed. If you're so frightened of us, all you had to do was keep your heads down. We would've been gone in less than two hours!" Andrews spread his hands. "That's the truth, Law. Leona must have told you that, and I'm telling it to you again. We're not on a mission of conquest, we're here looking for what my people need in order to survive."

Law snorted, but he seemed suddenly calm. He regarded the two men before him for a long moment. "Yes, yes, you both sing the same song. But it doesn't matter, Andrews. It simply doesn't matter. I'm not willing to take the chance. I know that if you don't leave here, your people will die from a poisoned atmosphere. Kind of ironic that your impressive base actually becomes a mass grave, am I right?"

"Why? Why let that happen?" Andrews asked. "Harmony has everything you need. Food. Medicine. Building supplies.

Technology. We can relocate you to another place and support you in recovery. Listen to me, Law—if we die, then you doom your own people. We're your best chance at regaining what you lost in the war!"

"So you'd have us trade in what little we have left for the promise of a better future? Are you actually telling me that the *government* is back, and now it wants to help?" Law chuckled throatily, and Andrews could see he was actually enjoying the exchange. "I'm sorry, Captain. Those of us who managed to survive could never trust you. And why should we?" He turned away and walked out the door. As he passed the two men standing guard, he said, "Take them to the Pit."

When he stepped out of the room, more filthy survivors rolled in after him, overwhelming Andrews and Spencer like a putrid tide.

15

THE CAVERNOUS ROOM must have once been an arena of some sort, Andrews thought—perhaps a hockey rink, back when the world was still safe and sound. From the light of dozens of flickering torches that surrounded the rink, he could see that where there should have been a sheet of ice, there was instead desiccated earth dotted with sharp metal stakes. The bleachers surrounding the pit were filled with scores of wildly screaming survivors, ranging from filthy, scrappy men and women to twisted monstrosities—those who had been born with severe physical deformities, likely courtesy of the radioactive aftermath of the Sixty Minute War. He didn't understand how they had survived for so long. There were over a hundred people present, and they cheered and howled like crazed animals as Andrews and Spencer were dragged and thrown into the pit. Spencer cursed as he landed on his injured arm while rolling out of the fall, and he wound up lying on his side, cradling his wounded limb. Andrews hurried over to him and pulled him to his feet as the crowd began to pelt them with all manner of debris.

"Come on, Spence! On your feet!"

Once Spencer managed to stand, Andrews dragged him to the center of the pit. He tried to shield Spencer from the pieces of wood and stone that were hurled at them; most missed by a wide margin, but occasionally one connected.

"Man, this rates a solid ten point five on the 'Holy Shit' meter," Spencer said. "What the hell are these fuckers going to do to us now?"

"Nothing good," Andrews said. As he looked around the pit, he knew what was likely to happen. This was in fact an arena, just not for the sport it had been built for. Andrews and Spencer were going to be the entertainment.

At the far end of the rink, he saw Law mount a gangway that led to a decaying broadcast booth. Behind him, Leona was dragged along by two burly men. Her hands were bound before her. She looked down at them, and her eyes met Andrews's. Her expression was one of utter terror, and Andrews knew she had good reason to be frightened. Back at Harmony, Leona was considered beautiful. Here, in this shattered city where people still lived but humanity was dead, she would be a prized asset, perfect breeding stock. She would be passed from man to man until she could no longer provide what they needed. After that? Andrews wasn't sure, but he had no doubt she might spend years wishing for death.

Law held up his hands, and the jeering assemblage fell into a sudden, respectful silence, watching him with a mixture of religious reverence and bloodthirsty anticipation.

"It's been almost two years since this facility was last used, when survivalists from the north threatened our sanctuary with their tainted ways. And now, these two will meet their end in exactly the same manner!"

The crowd exploded into a barrage of cheers. Andrews could barely hear Spencer over the raucous din.

"Did he just say something about survivors from the north?" Spencer shouted.

"Yeah—I guess we were right, the Northwest might not have been hit so hard," Andrews shouted back.

"A shame, man. I would've liked to have gone up there, maybe see some real pine trees and Mount Ranier, or something." Spencer ducked as a dusty brick flew past his head.

Law held up his hands, grinning like a madman. When the crowd quieted itself, he looked down at the two men.

"The rules are simple, gentlemen. You fight until you are killed. Then, your carcasses will be divided up amongst my Family. After all ... a nutritious meal *is* hard to come by these days." To the crowd, he said, "And now ... *it begins!*"

As the crowd erupted yet again, Law continued walking to the old broadcast booth. Leona was dragged along after him, and the small group stepped inside. Law took a seat before the booth's open window, sitting up there like a demented Roman emperor settling in to watch gladiator games.

"You know, now would be a great time for Mulligan and the others to roll in and save the day," Spencer said, fear evident in his voice.

"The only thing Mulligan's saved in his entire life is a bad attitude." Andrews turned in place as he scanned the cavernous room, hoping to get an idea of what was going to happen next.

Surprisingly, he *did* see what was going to happen next. A

towering man leapt into the pit opposite them. He was even bigger than Mulligan, standing almost seven feet tall. He was extremely well-fed; his muscles rippled beneath scabbed, knobby skin, and just one of his thighs was almost as big as both of Andrews's. But all was not perfect; the man's right arm was a misshapen club of calloused flesh, and his left eye was missing, perhaps ripped out long ago in some past contest, leaving behind a scarred, empty socket. Completely bald, the huge warrior turned toward Andrews and Spencer and smiled hungrily, revealing rotting, black teeth.

"Missing an eye and a bum arm," Spencer said. "Maybe things are looking up. The guy's worse off than I am."

"Don't get too cocky, Sergeant," Andrews cautioned. "He's still going to be one tough customer. Keep to his left when you can, hang out in his blind spot."

"Hooah. What about you?"

"I don't have a busted arm. I'll try and tire him out, then we'll figure out how we're going to take him down."

If Spencer replied, Andrews didn't hear him. The crowd's cheering swelled, and the giant bellowed and charged before the two men had an opportunity to ready themselves for his attack. Andrews shoved Spencer aside and darted to his left, hoping to attract the giant's full attention before he zeroed in on Spencer, who would be the easier target. He needn't have worried; the giant was apparently looking for a fight, so he charged directly at Andrews, his club-arm held high, his mouth open wide as he released a guttural war cry. Andrews stopped short and waited for the disfigured warrior to close on him, his fists held out before him as he adopted a fighting stance. That encouraged the brute, and he pounded toward him with reckless abandon, his big feet stomping into the dry, packed earth of the arena, bearing down on Andrews like an out-of-control freight train. At the last moment, when the warrior was nearly on top of him, Andrews fell to his hands and knees. Unable to stop, the warrior tripped over Andrews and slammed face-first into the dirt, sending up an explosion of dust. The impact was strong enough to knock the wind of out Andrews and he floundered about on his back, frantically trying to take a breath while attempting to gather his feet beneath him and press his advantage. He rolled over onto his belly and pushed himself to his knees, his movements slow—

too slow. The giant was already recovering from his spill, and he awkwardly levered himself to his knees with his good arm. Andrews saw Spencer moving in, racing to tackle the brute before he could get to his feet.

"Spence, no!" Andrews croaked, but his warning was lost in the cacophony of the cheering crowd.

Spencer ran right into the warrior, slamming into him with his shoulder like a linebacker. He practically bounced off the larger man. The warrior howled and swung at him with his good arm. Spencer tried to duck under it, but the warrior was surprisingly fast. He took the swing right across the head, and the blow sent him sprawling across the arena's dirt floor. The crowd exploded with thunderous applause. The warrior grinned and hauled himself to his feet, stepping toward Spencer.

Andrews leapt toward him and delivered a powerful snap-kick to the giant's side, throwing as much of his body weight into the attack as he could. The warrior lurched sideways with a sharp grunt as Andrews's boot made solid contact with his ribs. Nevertheless, the warrior spun with uncanny speed and struck Andrews in the chest with his clubbed arm. The force of the blow was incredible; Andrews was literally lifted from his feet and went flying through the air. He landed on the hard-packed arena floor and rolled right toward one of the sharp metal stakes. The sharpened metal sliced open his temple as his head bumped into it. Andrews cried out and pressed his hand to the wound. When he pulled it away to struggle back to his feet, his palm was slick with blood. The crowd went wild at the sight of his injury, and dozens of natty survivors jumped up and down in the bleachers, shrieking in delight.

The warrior turned back to Spencer as he charged back toward him. He grabbed the front of Spencer's uniform in one big hand and swung him around like a rag doll. Spencer tried to twist away, but to no avail—the giant's grip was too strong. With a roar, the warrior lifted him into the air and hurled him away, as if the crew chief was no more substantial than a newborn infant. Spencer tumbled as he arced toward the arena floor, coming down squarely on one of the twisted metal stakes. The stake's sharp tip erupted through his chest. Spencer shuddered, then tried to get up. Dark blood spread across his uniform blouse. Heart blood, Andrews knew.

Oh my God.

Satisfied that Spencer was no longer a threat, the warrior pivoted and charged toward Andrews. Andrews grabbed a handful of dirt as he rose to his feet and hurled it into the giant's face. The warrior recoiled, rubbing at his eye with his hand while blindly lashing out with his clubbed arm. Andrews ducked under the first few swipes, then kicked the man-thing right in the groin. The warrior screamed and doubled over, sinking to his knees. Andrews stepped in and caught him with a fast uppercut that landed with such authority that the giant's jaws slammed shut. Andrews pressed his advantage, punching the giant in the face again and again, ignoring the pain that blossomed in his hands. The crowd booed, furious that their champion was taking a beating so soon after downing one opponent. The warrior's head rocked back and forth from the fury of Andrews's blows, until it finally toppled over onto its back, bleeding profusely from a shattered nose. With a gurgle, it spat out bloody saliva and pieces of broken teeth. Andrews reared back and brought up his right foot, intending to stomp on the giant's face, but a hurled brick struck him in the back of his right shoulder. He went down with a cry, stumbling across the giant's body. Feeling the shift in the tide, the giant lashed out with his legs. One of his huge feet caught Andrews under the right arm, and he was sent rolling across the arena floor. He came to a rest next to Spencer's spasming body. Andrews pushed himself to his elbows and, for a brief instant, his eyes met Spencer's. Despite the bloodied stake piercing his chest, the crew chief was trying to sit up, to get back into the fight. The light was fading from Spencer's face.

"I'm okay," Spencer said, smiling. Blood bubbled from his mouth and nostrils, and then he died.

Andrews heard the giant warrior grunt as he pushed himself to his feet. He looked at Spencer's body as it slowly relaxed, settling back onto the stake that had claimed his life. The crowd roared its approval, and Andrews knew the warrior must have been making his way back to him. Andrews felt a fire begin to burn in his chest, and he shoved himself upright, leaping to his feet. Hot rage fueled him, and he whirled to face the oncoming giant, ignoring the throb in his shoulder where the brick had struck him. He was surprised to find the warrior's approach was slow and measured—no more charging, no more howling.

Andrews had put a hurting on him, and he knew the warrior, despite his greater size and strength, was going to take his time. He had learned that Andrews was no pushover.

That suited Andrews fine. He was going to make the warrior suffer every moment until one of them was dead.

The tremendous din of the roaring crowd led Mulligan and the others to the arena like sharks following a trail of blood. The array of torches that illuminated the great ring caused their night vision goggles to wash out, so Mulligan whispered into his headset and ordered everyone to remove them. They had more than enough light to operate by, and with the vast majority of the opposing force focused on Andrews, the group could move with unexpected freedom.

He and Choi planted their charges on two stout I-beams that the big sergeant major judged were primary load-bearing components for the civic center. While eight pounds of C4 might not be enough to bring the house down under normal circumstances, it was his hope that the accumulated stress of surviving a nuclear attack, earthquakes, and changing weather might have weakened the structure enough so the blast would cause at least a partial collapse. As they made their way back to where Laird and Kelly waited with Rachel, Choi motioned to the arena, where Andrews and the impressively huge warrior continued their battle. Spencer lay motionless near the arena's center, surrounded by a pool of dark blood.

"Hey, shouldn't we do something about that?" Choi asked, not even bothering to keep his voice low due to the volume of the crowd.

Before Mulligan could respond, a filthy young man hurried out of a dark corridor, carrying a torch. His hair was long and matted, forming a natural set of grubby dreadlocks that hung down over his sallow face. The man stopped when he saw Mulligan and Choi crouching down only a few feet away. His mouth dropped open, and for a moment he gawked at them. Then he spun around and made to run back the way he had come. He didn't make it. Mulligan reacted instantly, grabbing a handful of his dirty, oversized shirt and yanking him off his feet.

The man dropped his torch and struggled; his shout was cut short by Mulligan's knife sliding into the back of his neck. The man kicked once, then went limp. The odor of urine made Mulligan's nostrils twitch, and he dragged the body to an abandoned refreshment stand. He hurled the corpse behind the concession counter.

"Damn, man! I thought we were going to give these people a chance!" Choi said, his eyes wide with shock.

Mulligan pointed to the arena, where Andrews and the big warrior were circling each other while the riotous crowd hurled all manner of debris at Andrews. "Yeah, like they did with Spencer? That plan's off the table. Use your head, boy!"

Choi considered that, then nodded. "Roger that, Sergeant Major."

Mulligan spoke into his tactical headset as he hurried down the corridor that ringed the arena. "Laird, this is Mulligan. Over."

"Go ahead, Mulligan. Over."

"Charges planted, and we just had to service one target. We're heading back to you now. Get ready to move out when we arrive. Party in thirty. Over."

"Good copy."

Mulligan abandoned stealth for speed and set an aggressive pace. They were living on borrowed time—even though there were no signs of firearms among any of the survivors, he knew that at least four assault rifles were somewhere in their possession, along with a multitude of bladed weapons that could be just as deadly if wielded by experienced hands. Though he would have liked nothing better, Mulligan's goal was not to get into a protracted fight—they had a greater mission to accomplish, and that meant the team from Harmony Base had to avoid becoming decisively engaged.

When he and Choi linked up with Laird and the others, he found they were still crouching in the darkened hallway that fed into the main corridor surrounding the arena. Laird was oriented toward the bleachers, M416A3 assault rifle at the ready; it was outfitted with an M320A1 forty-millimeter grenade launcher under the barrel, a double-action device equipped with its own pistol grip that allowed for more precise fire. Kelly Jordello's assault rifle was in a similar configuration, and she covered the rear of the hallway. Rachel Andrews had a vanilla assault rifle with no additional modifications, as Mulligan hadn't had the time to school her in the grenade launcher's use. She was in the center of the formation, and when Mulligan saw her staring at her husband fighting for his life down below, he wondered if he hadn't made a tactical error by not leaving her in the SCEV.

Mulligan motioned for Choi to stand guard while he squatted down beside Laird. "All right, it looks like Spencer's down, and Eklund's in that booth about fifty meters downrange. I want to go for her first, because I'm pretty sure things will get loud when we do, and that should pull some of the heat off Andrews. What do you think, sir?"

"Agreed," Laird said immediately. Either he had already formed the tactical picture by himself, or he was willing to do anything Mulligan suggested, as he was the expert. Mulligan didn't care which; he was just glad they weren't going to get into another debate.

"We have to help Mike!" Rachel hissed.

Mulligan fixed her with a seething glare. "We will. You stay here and hold this hallway, because we'll need it for our retreat. Are you ready to pull the trigger and ice some of these stinking fuckers, Andrews?"

She nodded immediately, with no hesitation. Mulligan liked that, but he had to be sure she was ready.

"They will likely come this way, or come up from behind you. You'll be on your own, and you might have to kill women and children. I'm going to guess that when you open up, they'll fade and try to get away from you. But you'll probably have to kill some of them. Are you *sure* you're ready for that?"

"Yes. I'll kill anyone I have to, Sergeant Major," Rachel said, her voice strong.

Mulligan pointed at her rifle. "Safety off, keep the weapon indexed until you have to shoot like I showed you. When it becomes necessary, put your booger hook on the bang lever and squeeze it. Shoot for the center mass, and do *not* hesitate—taking a second to think will only get you killed, and that just makes things harder for everyone."

"Yeah, getting killed would be a matter of importance to me too, Mulligan. Anything else?"

Have to admire the can-do attitude on this one. "Negative. Good luck, and if things turn south, contact us over the radio." He turned to the others. "Follow me. Remember your tactical spacing, and let's move fast."

He rose and started down the main corridor at a good clip, his rifle shouldered and held at the ready. Choi followed, then Laird, with Kelly bringing up the rear. They adopted a staggered formation, two hugging the right side of the corridor, two staying to the left. They moved at a jog and Mulligan dreaded every step, wondering if he was going crazy trying to pull off a rescue like this when the stakes were so high. He knew he had no choice, though. Even if the others could be convinced to cut their losses and resume the mission, Rachel Andrews would flat out reject the notion of not attempting to rescue her husband. And she had leverage—she was the one who had to decide which core supports were good enough to take back to Harmony. Returning with items that were damaged or the wrong size wouldn't help anyone back at the base.

They made it to the broadcasting booth's door without incident. Surprisingly, it was unguarded, even though Mulligan thought they must have known he had escaped. Had they thought he would just flee into the wasteland? That was a tragic miscalculation on the part of the city survivors, but he doubted they had to deal with incursions into their territory very often. Fine by him—their ignorance made his life easier.

Mulligan motioned Choi forward. "You get the door. Laird, you're in with me. Orient right when we go in, I'll go left. Jordello, rear guard. Everyone set?"

"Hooah," Choi said.

"Good to go here," Laird responded.

"Roger," Kelly said.

"Do it, Choi."

Choi reached for the door and turned the knob. Nothing happened. He tried again, turning it the other way. It wouldn't budge. He turned back to Mulligan.

"It's locked, Sarmajor. How do you want to play it now?"

"Get the fuck out of the way," Mulligan snapped. Choi obediently stepped aside, and Mulligan walked up to the door and kicked it with all his might. And this time, damn if the door didn't truly snap right off its hinges.

Leona was seated right next to Law, staring down at the pit below. Andrews and the hulking warrior clashed, kicking, punching, and charging. It was obvious the giant had strength on his side, but Andrews had skill and maneuverability. He was able to wind his way through the field of stakes sticking up from the arena floor with greater agility than the warrior, and he would close, strike, and retreat before the warrior could respond. And the giant warrior was tiring. His huge torso was slick with a sheen of sweat that gleamed in the torchlight, and even from her distant vantage point, she could see the warrior's chest heaving as he pulled in great breaths. Beside her, Law fidgeted and muttered, clearly agitated as he remained fixated on the fight. He had been initially elated when Spencer had gone down, an action that had brought Leona to her feet with a shocked cry. Law had laughed at her, reveling in her distress as one of her foul-smelling guards forced her back into her chair. He groped one of her breasts at the same time, gripping her painfully. She tried to shrug him off, and that made Law laugh even more.

But now, the gigantic warrior's assured win was no longer quite as certain. Leona could see that the deformed giant didn't have the same endurance as Andrews. He had probably never fought a well-nourished combatant before, much less one that had been formally trained in both down and dirty hand-to-hand combat as well as some of the more refined martial arts. Not that Andrews was in the best of shape, himself. He had clearly been beaten during his abduction, and he'd already suffered at the hands of his opponent; the cut on his temple was still bleeding, and a trail of blood had dripped across the front of his uniform. The giant was slowly herding him out of the center of the arena, which meant he would be at some peril from the crowd, who continued to try to pelt him with all manner of debris. But the tide of the battle had changed, and Law had become sullen and impetuous. Leona enjoyed his discomfort immeasurably.

Then the door behind her exploded inward.

Law was out of his seat in an instant. He charged through a side door as small arms fire filled the broadcast booth. The filthy degenerate who had groped her went down like a sack of potatoes from a single bullet to the head. Leona threw herself out of her chair, coming to rest on the cold concrete floor next to the man's still body. Two more shots rang out, and the second man guarding her crumpled. From her vantage point on the floor, Leona could see his right foot twitch erratically for a moment before a deep stillness settled over him. She realized she had just watched two men die—and she couldn't have felt happier.

A moment later, she was roughly hauled to her feet. "Eklund, you all right?" Sergeant Major Scott Mulligan asked as he produced a knife and sawed through the rough twine that bound her wrists together.

"The one that got away … he's psionic!"

"Yeah, okay, whatever," Mulligan said, and to Leona it appeared he had just decided she'd lost a ton of marbles.

She struggled to discover some frame of reference that Mulligan could understand. "Listen to me! He has mental abilities—he can cause you to feel pain just by *looking* at you! And he's absolutely insane, he thinks we're some kind of war party!"

"Good to know," Mulligan said. "Thanks for the hot tip." With that, he grabbed her by the wrist and hauled her toward the exit. Jim Laird fell in behind her, and from outside the booth, Leona heard a raging furor begin to build.

The gunfire sent a wave of shock through the entire crowd, and for a long moment, they seemed to forget all about their champion and his struggle with Andrews. The warrior himself turned in the direction of the shots, which came from somewhere behind him. Andrews looked past the giant's shoulder, and he saw commotion in the broadcast booth. Law bolted out of the cubicle through a side door and ran down a corridor without looking back, his arms and legs pumping. Through the booth's window, he saw someone haul Leona to her feet. It was Mulligan, and beside him, Laird stepped toward the opening and lifted his rifle to his shoulder, ready to fire on anyone or anything that might turn into a threat.

Dude … get this over with!

Andrews grabbed a nearby metal stake and pulled with all of his strength. Only its point had been sharpened, so he was in little danger of slicing open his palms and fingers, but the picket was stuck deep into the earth. He was elated to feel it give, bit by bit, until he had pulled almost three feet of rusted metal out of the dry earth. Holding the implement like a pike, he charged toward the warrior just as he started to turn back to him. He rammed the stake through the giant's neck, feeling the rusted metal grate against cervical vertebrae as it passed through soft tissue and tougher tendon. The giant shuddered with a gurgling cry as blood fanned into the air from a severed artery. He tried to fling Andrews off, squirming and thrashing like a wounded beast. Andrews hung on, pushing the stake even further into its neck. A gout of blood spurted across his hands and arms. The gigantic warrior shuddered once again and fell to his knees with a choking shriek. Andrews wrenched the stake from side to side, causing as much damage as he could. The warrior silently fell face-first to the arena floor, his limbs twitching as life fled his body. Andrews stood over the fallen brute and stomped on his head, again and again, throwing as much strength into each strike as he could. When the giant finally stopped moving and a pool of blood began to spread beneath his shattered skull, Andrews got control over the seething rage that filled him.

Spencer...

Several survivors leaped into the pit as Andrews moved to Spencer's side. He grabbed Spencer's wrist, seeking a pulse; finding none, he pressed his fingers against Spencer's jugular. He couldn't feel any trace of movement, and he looked down at Spencer's face. In death, the crew chief's expression was slack, as if dismayed by his demise.

Automatic gunfire ripped through the advancing survivors, dropping two of them. The rest shrieked and fled, forgetting all about Andrews as more bullets slapped at their heels. Several more stumbled and fell to the ground, writhing in agony from leg wounds. Andrews looked to his left and saw Rachel standing in the bleachers, a smoking assault rifle against her shoulder. The survivors nearest her shoved and jostled each other as they struggled to flee from the madwoman with the rifle. Rachel ignored them and leapt into the pit. Picking her way around the stakes, she raced over to Andrews and threw her arms around him.

"Thank God," she whispered into his ear. "Thank God,

thank God ..."

Andrews hugged her back. "Good to see you again, babe."

Mulligan loped up a moment later. He spared Spencer's body a quick glance, then pulled Andrews and Rachel apart. "Listen, this is touching and all that, but you'd better move your butts before you wind up giving the rest of us the celestial eyeball!"

He pushed them toward the side of the arena, where Laird waited, clutching his assault rifle nervously. He helped them climb into the bleachers while Mulligan stood guard behind them. As Andrews clambered up the side of the rink, he noticed a small group of people sticking to the shadows across the pit from them. They did not flee.

"Mulligan, see those guys across the arena?"

"Got them, Captain. So long as they stay there, I'll let them live." When the Andrewses were clear, Mulligan turned and pulled himself onto the bleachers. Once he had joined them, he grabbed Rachel's arm. "You were supposed to hold the hallway for us!"

"I decided to save my husband, instead. Have a problem with that, asshole?" Rachel shot back.

"Save this for later," Andrews snapped. He took the assault rifle from Rachel and looked at Mulligan and Laird. "We need to get the hell out of here."

"We sure do," Mulligan said. "We wired this place with demolitions—the sooner we can clear it, the sooner I can set off the charges and add some more confusion to the mix. We don't want to be around here when that happens."

"My thoughts exactly," Laird said. "Let's go!" He led the group back to the hallway, which was secured by Kelly and Leona. Down the corridor, several figures loomed in the flickering shadows cast by the torchlight. Andrews slowed when he noticed them, but Mulligan pushed him roughly from behind.

"Go on, I've got them!" the NCO snapped. "Laird, get them moving. Go for Four, it's closer. I'll hold these fuckers back for a bit, then I'll catch up with you. If I don't show in ten minutes, resume the mission!"

Laird looked back at Mulligan with narrowed eyes. "You're saying we should *leave* you, Sarmajor?"

"I'm saying you should finish what we started."

"We'll hold station for you as long as we can, Mulligan," Andrews said. "Don't screw around, just buy us enough time to get to the rigs."

"You can count on that, Captain." Mulligan raised his rifle to his shoulder. "Now shake a leg!"

Andrews nodded, and he pushed Rachel ahead of him as he and the rest followed Laird into the inky darkness of the hallway.

"Mike, here," Kelly said as she fell in behind him. She handed him a pair of night vision goggles, which he immediately powered up and slipped on over his head. He adjusted the monocle slightly, then shot her a quick thumbs-up. He could see perfectly, thanks to the light-intensifying technology of the NVGs. From behind them, Mulligan's assault rifle cracked out three rapid shots. Andrews didn't look back. The hulking senior NCO had their back, and he could take care of himself.

Mulligan watched as the group of survivors at the end of the corridor slowly picked their way toward him. He wasn't concerned about them just yet, since they were still a good distance away, but he had to question their intelligence. Who tried to sneak up on a guy holding an assault rifle, especially when their concealment was virtually nonexistent? He decided to illustrate their folly by firing three shots at the individual in the lead—two more than absolutely necessary, but he wanted to send a strong message that couldn't be misinterpreted. He was rewarded by two of the survivors going down. One of them lay still; the second one, who had been behind the first, writhed and screamed in agony on the floor.

"That'll learn ya," he said to himself as he reached into a cargo pocket on his uniform trousers. He pulled out the remote detonator that would trigger the charges at the other side of the arena and armed the device with a flick of his thumb. All he had to do now was press the trigger, and—

He lurched as something struck his M416, sending pieces of metal flying through the air. A second object slapped him in the chest an instant later, and yet another exploded against the concrete wall beside his head, pelting him with small pieces of shrapnel that cut open his face. He heard three reports from a firearm, then a fourth. Something went *snap!* as it blasted right past his head. Mulligan stumbled away and fell to his knees, thankful for the kneepads he wore. At his age, busting a kneecap would be bad news, though not as bad as being shot. He rolled away from the wall—and the hallway—and brought his rifle around. Sure enough, another group of survivors was closing in on him from the opposite side of the corridor, and one of them held a captured M416A3. Mulligan made to shoot the rifleman, but his own rifle was inoperative; he was disgusted to find that a chunk of the upper receiver had been damaged, right where the bolt carrier group was located. The result was that his assault rifle had been converted into a rather expensive club.

Motherfuck!

The makeshift rifleman opened fire again as he quickly advanced, grinning as he squeezed off round after round. The man had Mulligan dead to rights, and the only thing that saved Mulligan from being killed was the man's decision to fire while moving. As such, his aim was atrocious, and bullets pocked the concrete floor all around Mulligan as he frantically backpedaled. At the same time, he was being driven away from his escape route.

With no other choice available to him, he pressed the trigger on the detonator he still had in his right hand. He was rewarded with a tremendous thunderclap that seemed to blossom into existence right behind him; a heartbeat later, whirling shrapnel flew through the air as several torches were extinguished by the ensuing shockwave. He watched as several pieces of lethal debris slashed through the group of survivors. The gunman trying to kill Mulligan was almost beheaded by a spinning piece of metal that ricocheted off the corridor's concrete wall and buried itself in his neck. Plunged into inky darkness, Mulligan heard the creaks and groans of overstressed superstructure fill the air, loud enough for his ringing ears to register. The charges he and Choi had placed had done their job. The roof of the civic center was giving way, slowly collapsing. Great pieces of metal and thick, twisted girders fell behind him, striking the floor and the bleachers with thunderous impacts that kicked up a huge cloud of dust. Mulligan snapped his NVGs over his eyes and struggled to his feet, bolting for the hallway, weaving his way past falling debris. He had almost made it when something large and heavy struck him in the head, driving him to the floor and knocking the NVGs off his face.

Blackness engulfed him.

16

MUTED SOUNDS OF thunder caught up to the SCEV crew as they sprinted down the dark hallway, preceding the surprisingly strong shockwave that tore at them an instant later, carrying with it a great cloud of dust. Andrews grabbed Rachel's arm, supporting her as she stumbled and gasped in shock at the sudden rumble of the explosions. But the cacophony didn't abate; it intensified, and Andrews felt the floor tremble beneath his feet.

"Keep moving!" he shouted, his voice barely audible above the raging din. "Don't stop, the place is imploding!" But the light was failing, leaving the hallway in absolute darkness; their night vision goggles had nothing left to intensify. He was rewarded with vision a moment later as Laird switched on a flashlight, its harsh LED glow so powerful through the goggles that had it not been for the thick dust flooding into the passage, it might have overwhelmed the NVGs entirely.

"Follow me!" Laird shouted, as fragments of concrete began to fall from the ceiling. "Hurry, hurry!"

The team followed Laird as he set off down the hallway, wading through dust that only grew thicker with each passing second. The darkened passageway trembled and shook as the structure behind them collapsed upon itself. Andrews wondered about Mulligan's fate. He heard Laird trying to raise the sergeant major over the radio, but there was no response.

Finally, they left the choking clouds of dust behind, though the occasional sound of falling rubble followed them, echoing down the hallway. Andrews sneezed, his nostrils clogged with filth—he could taste it in the back of his mouth. Laird turned right and descended a wide flight of steps.

"This way," he said, voice pitched low.

"Where are we headed?" Andrews asked.

"There's a train station down below. It's open to the street, thanks to an earthquake or something. We can get out through there and go back to Five."

"What about Four?" Andrews asked.

"It's here, in a parking garage. It's a closer reach, but the thing is, the parking garage is locked by a big steel gate."

Andrews considered that. "Can we blast through it?"

"What, you mean with a missile?" Each SCEV was armed with AGM-114R Hellfire missiles that were packed with two hundred pounds of high-explosive. Originally intended as anti-tank weapons, chances were high that they would make quick work of the garage door. Laird nodded. "Oh, hell yeah."

"Let's go there, then," Andrews said. "We can't be leaving one of the rigs here, not if there's a chance we can get it out."

Laird hesitated, then nodded. "All right. We'll need to pull around the block to get my rig, though."

"Not a problem," Andrews said. "We're not going to leave any equipment behind if we can avoid it."

They descended down the next flight of stairs, moving as quickly as they could.

The garage was two floors below the arena level, and it looked mostly undamaged. With high ceilings and several different entrances—all of them closed by sliding moat doors, Andrews noticed—it was obvious this level of the parking structure had been intended for freight to be moved in and out. The carcasses of scavenged cars and big tractor trailer rigs lay about, stripped of anything useful. It was pitch-black inside, so Laird left his flashlight on, providing more than enough light for the team to see by with their night vision goggles. As they picked their way through the garage, Andrews saw SCEV Four sitting in a clear area on the far side of the parking structure. The rig was hooked up to a stout-looking tow motor by thick, rusted chains. He wondered how long it would take to free it.

"Looks pretty quiet here," Choi said, holding his assault rifle ready just in case. Even though he kept his voice pitched low, it still resounded with sibilant echoes inside the parking garage. Andrews motioned for him to be silent, then pointed at the rig, ensuring everyone saw the motion. He took the lead, jogging through the gloom toward the waiting SCEV.

Just as the group closed on the rig, Andrews heard a flurry of movement off to his right. Choi shouted a warning as a metal spear sailed through the air. It flew benignly past Andrews and struck Leona in the right thigh. She went down with a startled yelp, and the spear made a metallic clink as it struck the cement floor beside her. Choi fired at a car, cracking off five rounds in rapid succession. Through the NVGs, Andrews saw sparks fly as the bullets tore through sheet metal. Figures crouching behind the vehicle shrank back, fading into the gloom as they scurried between the rotting husks of long-abandoned semi-trucks.

"I've got her!" Laird said, stopping Andrews as he reached down for Leona. "You go get the rig open!" Behind them, Kelly fired a burst on full automatic at another motley group of survivors as they charged toward the SCEV crew. They fled beneath the gunfire, though none of them fell. Andrews was about to snap at her to stop wasting ammunition, then thought better of it. A few bursts of full automatic gunfire was a good deterrent to keep the goblins at bay.

Then more shapes loomed around the SCEV. A *lot* more.

"Oh, *fuck*," he said.

"What is it?" Rachel asked.

Andrews didn't answer. He grabbed her by the arm and pulled her down behind a nearby car that had been so severely stripped that it provided a questionable amount of cover. More gunfire sounded behind them. Laird appeared, half-carrying Leona. The spear was gone, but she had a hand clamped over the wound in her thigh, and her face was set in a rictus of agony beneath her night vision goggles.

"Problem?" Laird asked.

"Dude, we've got a substantial blocking force between us and the rig—yeah, that's a problem," Andrews said.

"You're kidding!" Laird looked over the car and saw the group arrayed in front of the SCEV. They maintained a degree of tactical spacing, which meant they had had some training. Andrews peered around the car's dilapidated bumper, and he saw several members of the group break off. They were going to try to flank them.

"Okay, let's fall back and try to get to Five," he said. "I don't want to get into a stand-up fight with these numbers."

"Damn straight," Laird snapped, frustration and stress evident in his voice. He had good reason to be short. Leona was wounded, and she would slow them down. "We'll have to get upstairs to the train station and crawl up through the debris field. We'll need to find someplace where we can get Eklund squared away first, though."

Andrews started to answer, but something whacked off the side of the car in a blurring flash. He had the distinct impression it was an arrow. A moment later, something flared out in the garage, and a small boy ran toward them with a bottle in one hand. A flaming rag stuck out of the bottle's neck. Andrews raised his rifle, but it was too late—the boy hurled the bottle at them and sped toward a car, vaulting across its empty engine compartment and disappearing behind its bulk before Andrews could establish a lane of fire. The bottle tumbled toward them, and he pushed Rachel aside as it shattered against the ground at their feet, erupting in a ball of flame that washed out the NVGs, causing them to whiteout from the overload.

Two dozen people emerged from the darkness, screaming war cries as they charged forward, holding spears, machetes, bows and arrows—and captured assault rifles.

Pushing his way upward, Mulligan eased his way out of the rubble that threatened to crush him. It took some doing, and clawing through the debris in pitch-black darkness didn't make things any easier. He knew he was severely scraped up; how many diseases was he exposing himself to? How much bacteria had gotten into his blood stream? As he dug his way out of the wreckage, he found he was laughing at himself. Of all the things to worry about now ...

His right hand found a void. He carefully pushed his way toward it, slipping beneath the twisted remnants of an I-beam, practically swimming in a sea of shattered concrete. His left shoulder met a piece of piping, and his progress was stalled until he could squeeze past it. He had to move slowly. The last thing he wanted was to cause the wreckage surrounding him to settle further and leave him forever entombed in San Jose.

Finally, he pushed into the void and found it was actually a way out of the rubble. Cool night air whispered across his sweaty, battered body as he clambered out of the twisted mess of metal, plastic, concrete, insulation, and wiring. Once he had fully extricated himself, he collapsed on top of the debris field, gasping for air. He hurt everywhere, so he just lay there, getting used to the pain. His eyes had adjusted to the darkness, and he saw more than half of the roof had caved in, leaving some stray supports remaining; they held up nothing but empty air. Night sky loomed high overhead, full of faintly twinkling stars. From somewhere beneath the wreckage on the other side of the arena, he heard other people moving through the debris with painful grunts and whines. They weren't his people, so he wasn't going to investigate. Slowly, he sat up on the hard rubble and checked himself for any serious injuries. He was phenomenally lucky— only scrapes and some small cuts. They were painful, but not life-threatening. The thick body armor and elbow and knee pads he wore had likely saved him from greater injury, for which he was deeply thankful. More troubling was the fact he had lost most of his gear. His rifle was gone, his night vision goggles were smashed, and his radio headset was missing, probably somewhere in the rubble. He was happy to discover he still had his knife and flashlight.

More than enough ...

In the distance, he heard gunfire—lots of it. He sat motionless for a long moment, listening to the sounds of combat. It definitely wasn't coming from outside, which meant the team from Harmony Base was trapped somewhere inside the building.

Mulligan slowly clambered to his feet. He pulled a long length of steel piping from the wreckage and, using it as a walking stick, slowly began picking his way across the field of rubble.

17

THE BATTLE IN the parking garage was hardly a one-sided affair.

Andrews was surprised by the ferocity shown by the survivors of the San Jose attack. Even though they were outgunned—mostly—they continued to attack the team from Harmony Base from all sides. They weren't terribly dumb about it, either. They would show themselves, feint a charge, then retreat as Andrews and the others opened fire. Then another attack would roll up on them from a different direction, forcing the SCEV team to divide their fire. The attackers moved like wraiths, fading in and out of the darkness so quickly that it was hard to get a bead on them, flitting from decrepit vehicle to support pillar and back again. The Molotov cocktails they occasionally hurled weren't particularly effective—Andrews and Laird kept the others moving so they wouldn't get fixed in place where they could be easily firebombed—but the weapons had an unexpected side effect. They caused the NVGs to overload occasionally, which deprived the team of their primary tactical superiority—night vision.

Then there were the two survivors with the captured rifles.

"Jesus, just how many of these guys are there?" Choi shouted as he reloaded. They were going through their ammunition much faster than planned. Even though Mulligan had instructed them to take as many magazines as they could carry, they had only a finite amount of munitions.

"A lot more than we'd thought," Andrews replied. He saw furtive movement in the darkness and raised his rifle, but he did not fire. Instead, he looked from side to side, keeping his weapon oriented on the original target, and he saw a group of four individuals running toward his position. They held axes and spears. Andrews turned to engage them and, as he did, one of the survivors with an assault rifle let loose a burst on his position. The gunman's aim was poor, and the bullets hit the car Andrews and Choi were crouching behind, but they slashed through the thin sheet metal. Choi recoiled, cringing.

Andrews kept his cool and squeezed off four shots at the group, which continued to advance. One went down, then another. The remaining pair split up and ran into the darkness, but Andrews followed one and fired two shots at the figure just as it slowed to hide behind one of the reinforced concrete support pillars. The body jerked as the 5.56-millimeter rounds passed through it before it slowly wilted to the floor.

"Choi, get on your weapon," Andrews ordered. "I want you to engage that shooter and take him out."

"Where is he?" Choi finished reloading his weapon, hit the bolt release, and brought it to his shoulder.

"Behind that truck over there, about seventy meters to your right. See it?"

"Roger, but can't see him!"

"Target the truck. Laird!"

"Go ahead!"

"Put a forty into that truck—the one Choi is targeting!"

"Got it!" Laird turned from his position with Kelly and raised his rifle. He put his hand on the M320's pistol grip and prepared to fire the forty-millimeter grenade downrange as Kelly sniped at another group of attackers. An arrow slashed right past Andrews's head.

Laird fired, the grenade launcher under his rifle ejecting its high explosive payload with a hollow puffing sound. A moment later, the truck was torn apart by a bright, sparking explosion that sent shrapnel whirling. The people hiding behind the truck fled in two separate directions.

"You want the guy with the rifle," Andrews reminded Choi.

Choi started firing immediately at the group peeling away to the right. *Crack-crack-crack-crack!* Andrews sighted on the group to the left and fired single shots, aiming carefully. Two combatants fell to the floor while the rest scattered, taking cover behind another truck.

"Got him!" Choi crowed. "*I got you, you stupid fuck!*" he shouted into the darkness. At the same time, something flashed to the right, immediately followed by another report. Choi grunted as he shifted sideways. Andrews spun and ripped off a burst on full automatic. Another shooter was out there, and he tried to fix him or her in place with full-auto fire. It didn't work; the assailant scuttled behind a distant row of dusty, cannibalized cars.

"Tony?" Andrews kept his sights on the cars, waiting for

the shooter to reappear.

"I'm good—the armor took it," Choi said. A moment later: "Oh, *shit!*"

"What is it?"

"The shooter I dropped—I was distracted, and someone else just picked up the weapon!"

We have to get out of here, Andrews thought. *And we need to do it now.*

"Kelly! Come forward with Choi!" Andrews put his hand on Rachel's shoulder as she crouched between him and Choi, keeping her head down. She was the only one who was unarmed. When Kelly joined them, Andrews waved her into his position, then scurried to where Laird had set up behind a thick support column. Leona was lying behind a nearby car, working on her leg with a medical kit. Like Rachel, she had no weapon, but she did her best to keep an eye out for any incoming bandits.

"Jim, we have to get to Five," Andrews said. "These fuckers are going to fix us in place, and then just wait until we use up our ammo. We can't get into Four, and we can't stay here. We need to get to Five."

"I'm behind you on that, but it's going to be one tough fight," Laird said.

"How many forties did you guys bring with you?"

"All of them, the full twenty-four in the ordnance locker." Laird paused to fire at shapes moving in the gloom. "But we lost Mulligan's, so that leaves us with seventeen now. You're right, we should start going through them and tear these bastards up."

"Negative, that's not what I was getting at. Law's people have been coming down on us hard, but so far, they haven't been able to circle around behind us—and that's where the garage entrance is. Any chance we can use the M320s to blast through the door?"

Laird's face lit up. "Jesus H. Christ, maybe so! Damn, why didn't *I* think of that?"

"I'll need you to take Kelly, Rachel, and Leona with you. You and Kelly can use your grenade launchers to try and blast a hole big enough for us to slip outside. Choi and I will hold them back. I'll need your spare magazines. We're going to have to pour it on big time to make them keep their heads down."

Laird frowned. "I don't think it'll take that many shots to

open up the door. One of us should be able to do it, and I can move faster on my own—"

"Lee's wounded and Rachel's essential personnel," Andrews said. "We can't care for them this close to the enemy, and they'll slow our fallback. Much better if you and Kelly take them with you—you'll be able to protect them as well as open up our line of retreat. And if worse comes to worst and things get too hot, you can take them to the SCEV."

Laird didn't seem to like that, but he didn't say anything as he and Andrews continued to scan the darkness through their NVGs. Andrews saw two scraggly fighters round a severely shot-up pick-up truck. One went to light a Molotov cocktail, and Andrews opened up on them with a quick burst. The bottle exploded in the man's hand as a bullet passed through flesh, bone, and glass, spraying both of them with whatever flammable liquid was inside. The bullet hit with enough authority to vaporize some of the fuel, and the flaming wick set it alight— along with the two fighters. They screamed and rolled around on the floor, and Andrews serviced both of them with two shots each.

"You keep shooting like that, we don't have anything to worry about," Laird said, suitably impressed.

"You have to get them out of here, Jim," Andrews said. "We need to open the back door, but if all of us can't make it, you need to get Rachel and Lee out of here. We've already lost Spencer and probably Mulligan, so you guys are the last game in town."

"I get that. All right, let's pass the word." As Andrews started to rise, Laird grabbed his arm. "I'm not going to cut and run at the first sign of trouble, man. But if I have to, we'll hole up in the rig and cool our heels for a few. Choi knows the way, so if we get separated, you can still find us. Hooah?"

"Hooah," Andrews replied. "Get Leona squared away." He got to his feet and returned to his original position. As he slid down beside Kelly, he squeezed Rachel's shoulder.

"How you doing, hon?"

"I'm hanging in there, sweetie," Choi said, between rifle shots.

"I'm good," Rachel said.

"Awesome. You're falling back with the others. Choi-boy

and I will hold the goblins back while you guys make a back door and get out of here."

"You and *who?*" Choi asked. Andrews ignored him.

"Where are we going?" Rachel wanted to know. "Aren't you coming with us?"

"Laird will give you the details, and yes, we'll be right behind you," Andrews said. He turned to Kelly. "Take Rachel to Jim. He'll brief you on what needs to happen."

"Roger that," Kelly said. "You ready to switch?"

"Affirmative," Andrews said. "On my count ... One, two, three!"

Kelly leapt from her firing position and Andrews replaced her. He shouldered his weapon and sighted on a target hiding behind the derelict hulk of an abandoned car. He fired two rounds through the sheet metal and was rewarded with a cry of pain. At the same time, another Molotov cocktail came cartwheeling toward him from the darkness to his right. Choi fired over his head, and the bottle exploded into a thousand glass fragments. The flaming wick still ignited the fuel the vessel carried, and liquid fire landed on the concrete. The glow ruined the efficiency of Andrews's night vision goggles, and he pushed them up on his forehead.

"Choi, I'm down to Mark One eyeballs," he said.

"Roger that, I've got good sightlines to our left, but the right is messed up for me too."

"Mike," Rachel started.

"All right, stand by to shift position," Andrews said. "I'm thinking that old truck over there—we might be able to climb into the cab and gain some elevation, so we're looking down on these fuckers instead of over at them."

"Movement over there," Choi said. He raised his rifle and fired into the darkness. Andrews could only see vague silhouettes.

"Mike!" Rachel said again. She grabbed his arm.

Andrews shook her off violently. "Are you fucking deaf? Go with Kelly. Go right now, Rachel!"

"Let's go," Kelly said, grabbing Rachel's arm. "We're leaving." Kelly yanked her to her feet, which was no small achievement, given that she was considerably smaller than Rachel. Rachel struggled against her for a moment, but Kelly dug in and yanked her toward her.

"I will fucking punch you in the face and carry you, Rachel," she threatened.

Faced with the threat of violence and the fact that Andrews and Choi were busy fighting, Rachel gave her husband one last glance. Andrews couldn't even spare her a quick nod, for at that moment a nearly emaciated woman came sprinting through the flickering flame to his right, carrying a sharpened metal spear. She shrieked as she bore down on him, holding the weapon like a pike, intending to run him through. Andrews twisted at the waist and fired two shots through her chest. Even though she couldn't have weighed more than ninety pounds, the 5.56 millimeter rounds didn't pack enough punch to stop the woman's flight, so she careened right into Andrews at almost full speed. But the bullets had done their job—her heart had beat its last before she crashed into him, and the metal spear made a clanging sound as it fell to the floor. As it rolled under the car he crouched behind, Andrews kicked the corpse off him—just in time. Several more shapes erupted through the flames, screaming like banshees and carrying all manner of weapons.

With a flick of his finger, Andrews set the M416 to AUTO and chopped them down. Kelly turned and fired into the mob as well, driving the survivors stumbling back into the darkness. Two fallen enemies lay nearby, clad in stinking rags, their limbs twitching as they writhed and moaned in agony. Waning firelight made their spilt blood glisten and gleam.

"Kelly—"

"We're gone, Mike." Kelly grabbed Rachel again and yanked her after her as she sprinted toward the waiting Laird. Once Rachel's back was to him, Andrews flipped his rifle back to SEMI and quickly killed the two wounded attackers nearby, shooting them in the head. He was surprised he felt nothing; only a day ago, committing such an act would have been far beyond him, something akin to an atrocity. Now, he simply considered it killing the enemy before they could kill him.

If someone presses your buttons hard enough, you'll find killing them is pretty easy. The words Mulligan had spoken to him back at Harmony came to him suddenly, and in hindsight, Andrews felt a sudden squirt of embarrassment at how he had reacted to the big Special Forces soldier's statement.

The voice over his radio snapped him back to the present. "Andrews, Laird. We're linked up, and we're going for the door. We look to be in the clear. Over."

"Roger, Jim. We've got the front door."

"See you outside. Out."

"Let's roll, Choi," Andrews said. "Let's give these goons something nice and mobile to shoot at. You ready?"

"No, I'm not *ready!*" Choi said, the scorn plain in his voice. "Does that count for anything?"

"Nope."

"Well, balls. Okay, I've got the lead." The younger man fired a quick burst into the darkness in one direction, then pivoted and fired off a grenade from his M320 in the other. The grenade struck a support pillar several dozen yards away and exploded with a sudden *boom* and a flash that cast shadows through the garage. Before the echoes had even begun to fade, Choi was on his feet, running toward the truck he and Andrews had discussed. Andrews swore and pulled his NVGs down over his eyes—the flames to his right were sputtering, so NVG effectiveness was pretty much restored—and he ran after Choi as quickly as he could. Just in time. The car the two men had been using as a fighting position was suddenly bombarded with fully-automatic rifle fire. Muzzle flashes lit up the garage far to Andrews's right. The shooter leaned into the weapon and turned it toward him, walking the rounds toward him as he ran. Andrews juked to his right as hard as he could and shouldered up against a nearby support pillar. Bullets slammed into the stout cement post an instant later, scattering concrete chips across the floor as a small cloud of dust billowed in the air. The gunfire ended abruptly, and Andrews knew this was probably his only chance. Placing his left heel against the pillar, he turned at the waist and brought up his M416. Through the night vision goggles and the low-light scope on his rifle, he could see the man with the captured assault rifle struggling to reload it. Andrews fired two rounds and hit him directly in the center mass. The man dropped the rifle and slowly crumpled to the floor.

"In place, Captain," Choi said over the radio. A moment later, his rifle barked, and in the dark distance someone yelped. "I've got your advance covered!"

Andrews pushed away from the pillar and sprinted toward

the truck, scanning left to right. He saw flashes of movement in the green-white world revealed by his NVGs. Several scraggly survivors were closing on them, leapfrogging from decaying car to decaying car, then flitting behind the thick concrete pillars. Muzzle flashes bloomed from the darkened cab of the semi-truck as Choi opened fire on the survivors. He continued to fire on semi-automatic, rationing his ammunition as well as he could. Andrews ran to the truck and slammed into its dusty fender. The rig's tires were gone, either having rotted away or been stripped off for another use. The big vehicle sat on its belly, which meant there was no way anyone would be able to crawl under it and use it for cover. Andrews pressed his back against the truck's sheet metal and fiberglass body and shouldered his rifle, scanning for targets.

"Choi, can you see movement to your left?" he asked, creeping toward the front of the truck.

"I see 'em," Choi replied. "They're trying to sneak up on us. How bad of a hurting are we going to put on these guys, sir?" His voice was neutral, as if he were discussing a menu item.

Andrews looked around the truck's grille, weapon at ready. "As much of one as we need to, Choi. If they don't back off, they die."

"Hooah. I'm engaging with a forty." Choi fired another grenade out of the truck's windowless cab. It arced through the air and landed in the shell of a car several survivors were hiding behind. The explosion was tremendous, made even more so by the relatively tight confines of the parking garage. Andrews's NVGs were once again overwhelmed by the sudden flash as the high explosive round went off, fairly decimating the car and turning it into one giant shrapnel generator. The goggles cleared instantly once the flare dissipated, and he saw several shapes writhing about on the concrete floor, shrieking in agony, their bodies flayed open by the fusillade of whirling metal. Men, women, and to Andrews's shock, children lay in the blast radius, their screams of pain echoing through the garage.

"Oh man, are those fucking *kids*?" Choi said from the cab. "They brought their *kids* to the fight?"

"Hold it together, Tony," Andrews told him. "They did it to themselves; you didn't do shit." He shouted into the parking garage, raising his voice so it could be heard over the cries of the wounded. "Back off and no one else gets hurt! We're not here to harm you, we just want to get out of here! You can send two people to recover your wounded—we will not fire on you!"

In response, another Molotov cocktail came spinning through the darkness from their rear. It burst open against the rear of the truck's cab, spewing flaming liquid across it. Choi swore as some of the flaming accelerant landed inside the cab.

They're behind us! As Andrews spun to face the new threat, something struck him in the chest with enough force to throw him back against the truck. He kept his grip on his rifle and looked down. A metal arrow stuck out from the body armor covering his chest, right between two pockets that contained magazines of 5.56 millimeter ammunition. That he felt no pain was little comfort—he had no idea if the projectile had penetrated the ballistic trauma plating that lay beneath the composite layers of bullet-resistant armor that covered the surface of his vest. Until he felt it, he wasn't going to stop fighting. Realizing he was silhouetted against the ribbons of fire that raged across the back of the semi-truck's cab, he ducked to his left. Just in time, for another arrow slashed past, and this one ripped right through the truck's sheet metal cab without even slowing down.

"Choi, we're taking fire from the rear! Laird, this is Andrews—we have OPFOR to our rear, they are between you and us! Over!"

"Roger that, Mike. We're at the door now, start making your way toward us!" As Laird finished transmitting, a loud explosion tore through the garage as a forty-millimeter grenade did its work against the steel mesh garage door. Then two more explosions.

Choi leapt out of the doorless truck's cab and landed beside Andrews. He fingered the firing selector on his rifle and ripped off a quick burst at a man standing fifty meters away, a huge longbow held in one hand. Both men fired at the same time, and Choi missed being killed by the man's steel arrow by millimeters. The attacker spun and dove away, and Andrews didn't know if he'd been hit or not. Choi glanced over at Andrews and saw the arrow sticking out from the center of his body armor.

"Man, that's some shit, Captain," he said, before returning

to the task at hand.

There were two more resounding explosions from the far end of the garage, and stroboscopic flashes of light peeled back the darkness for an instant. Andrews saw flurries of movement to their rear, and he stood up and peered through the open cab of the truck. More figures raced toward it, using its bulk to camouflage their advance. Andrews cracked off two rounds, then his weapon clicked empty. He ejected the magazine, pulled another from his vest and slapped it in, hit the bolt release switch, and was back in business. The attackers had disappeared. He knew they were crouched down on the other side of the truck, which meant he and Choi were practically within knife-fighting distance. But they weren't outfitted for close-quarters combat; their rifles weren't short-barreled, and they had no sidearms—those were not part of the SCEV weapons loadout. The only thing the two men could do was put some distance between them and their attackers. He slapped Choi on the arm and pointed in the direction of Laird, Kelly, and Rachel.

"Let's roll! When we get forty meters out, turn and drop a grenade on this thing!"

"Roger that," Choi said, already sliding another forty-millimeter grenade into the M320. Both men set off at a sprint from the vehicle, and just in time. With a war cry, the attackers on the other side of the rig swarmed over it, hoping to catch the two men from behind. Andrews half turned and fired a burst at the dusty wreckage, aiming as best as he could while on the run. He needn't have worried. When the bullets rained down among them, the attackers reversed course and dove back behind the hulk of metal.

"Laird, we're heading your way!" Andrews said as another explosion tore through the garage.

"Great timing—we're through over here! Speed it up! I'll drop back and give you some cover!"

"Negative—get Rachel to Five! We'll be right behind you!" Andrews ordered. Beside him, Choi slowed and turned, raising his rifle to his shoulder. At the same time, Andrews saw a burst of movement to his left and he spun, bringing his rifle sights on a small figure as it darted toward him. The boy was ragged and thin, his long, filthy hair tied back in a ponytail that seemed to go on forever. Through the NVGs, Andrews could see his every feature: wild eyes, foam building at the corners of his mouth, pockmarks on his face, the natty tunic he wore. He carried a single blade of steel that was patinated by time and use, and his feet were wrapped in scraps of cloth. His thin arms were exposed, and a sheen of sweat stood out on them. He looked to be only six or seven years old, but given the apparent malnutrition that stole through the group of survivors that had made the shattered hulk of San Jose their home, he could have been twice that age.

"Stop there, or I'll shoot you!" Andrews shouted. Behind him, Choi's grenade launcher thumped, and an instant later another explosion shook the garage. Dust rained down from the ceiling and the boy slowed, frightened by the sudden fire and fury as Choi's grenade destroyed the semi-truck the rest of the attackers were hiding behind. More cries and screams of shock and agony reached Andrews's ears. The boy looked at the conflagration behind Andrews, his pace slowing; then his face hardened and he accelerated toward Andrews again, blade held high. He released a keening wail as he bore down on Andrews, his eyes full of hate and fear.

Andrews shot him once through the chest. The boy stumbled and fell, skidding and rolling across the dusty floor, his blade clattering as it slid across the concrete. The small figure came to a rest on his back, chest heaving, a bloody froth spilling from his mouth.

Jesus ...

Andrews snapped out of it and turned to Choi. "Come on, Tony—let's get the hell out of here!"

The two men sprinted toward the far end of the garage, where they could see the ragged hole that had been blown through the entrance door. Choi reached it first, and he knelt beside the opening, rifle at ready. An expended forty-millimeter grenade casing rolled across the concrete ramp when he brushed against it with one of his boots, tinkling as it bumped over metallic debris. There was no sign of Laird, Kelly, Leona, or Rachel, and Andrews hoped they were well on their way to SCEV Five.

"Go on," Choi said. "I've got your back."

Andrews tucked his rifle close to his body and lifted up one leg. The hole was only four feet tall and just shy of that wide, so he had to step through it carefully, lest he cut himself on the ragged metal edges. The night on the other side of the hole was cool and dry, and a light breeze cooled his sweat the instant he was out of the garage. He reached back inside and tapped Choi's shoulder and, a moment later, he stepped out as well.

"Got one banger left. I'm going to use it to hold those bastards back," Choi said. "Just in case they decide to come after us."

"Roger that, but let's make tracks," Andrews said. The street was deserted, filled with the detritus of passing years—shattered glass from the buildings, collapsed facades, fallen light poles, and stripped vehicles. Several hundred meters up the street, he saw Laird leading Kelly, Rachel, and Leona away. Rachel was supporting Leona, helping her navigate her way across the debris-strewn street.

"Jim, we're out of the garage and coming up behind you," he whispered into his headset. "Keep going, we'll keep a watch on the back door. Over."

"Roger," came Laird's quiet response.

Andrews and Choi pressed on, gravel and glass crunching beneath their boots. Choi kept turning and looking back at the garage, but he did not fire off his last grenade. Apparently, their attackers weren't interested in pursuing them any further. Andrews was grateful.

Then he saw Laird stop. He turned and motioned Rachel and Leona to crouch as he and Kelly did the same thing. He brought his rifle to his shoulder and began firing bursts into the darkness.

Shit.

Behind him, Choi's grenade launcher went *thoomp* as it ejected its round, and a moment later, the harsh crack of an exploding grenade tore through the night. Andrews turned and saw several survivors writhing amidst the rubble, screaming in pain. Several more boiled through the hole in the garage door, and Choi clipped them with precision fire.

"Let's get to the other street so we can get a better angle on them!" Andrews said, hustling across the street's cracked pavement. Choi followed, walking backwards and firing a shot every second or so in an attempt to keep the rest of the enemy bottled up inside the garage. Andrews heard a scuffling noise from above, and he looked up in time to see several Molotov cocktails flying toward them, hurled by figures looking over the remaining portion of the civic center's roof.

"Choi, look out!" He raised his rifle and squeezed off a few rounds at the new set of attackers. They darted back behind the roofline as his bullets struck the retaining wall there, sending puffs of dust exploding into the night air. Then he and Choi were practically dancing in the streets as the bottles landed and shattered, spreading their flaming contents everywhere. From up the street, more gunfire sounded from Laird and Kelly.

"Mike, we've got a problem up here!" Laird said over the radio.

"Roger that, we've got goblins to the rear as well," Andrews told him as he flattened against the pockmarked wall of the building across the wide street. "Choi, keep the pressure on them, don't let them out of the garage!" He raised his rifle to his shoulder and targeted the roof of the civic center. He saw movement as several fighters slowly looked over the lip of the roofline, and he blew one of them away with a single shot. The heads dipped down again, and Andrews wished he had a grenade launcher of his own. He could lob a forty up there and ruin the rest of the night for several of the enemy. Beside him, Choi fired again and again, then stopped.

"Reloading!" he said, ejecting the spent magazine from his rifle. Andrews took up his firing position and drilled a survivor right through the chest as he started to shove himself through the ragged hole in the garage door. The figure cried out and fell back through the dark maw.

"Laird, how many combatants do you have up there?" Andrews asked. Beside him, Choi loaded a fresh mag into his rifle and resumed his position. Andrews returned to his examination of the roofline and saw someone quickly stand up to hurl another Molotov cocktail. Andrews shot him through the neck, and the figure fell away. An instant later, light blossomed as the cocktail exploded on the roof.

"Can't tell," Laird said, "but it's a lot of the bastards—we're taking some pretty accurate arrow fire up here, and they've got more of those Molotov cocktails as well. Our NVGs are pretty much garbage now. Over."

"Roger that. We're trying to keep the outbreak contained

back here, and we're taking Molotovs as well. Over."

Laird's response was lost amidst an ululating chorus of war cries as over a dozen people stood up on the civic center's roof, hurling Molotovs and firing arrows. Choi let out a frightened yelp as a metal arrow ricocheted off the wall beside him. Andrews flipped his rifle's fire selector to full auto and raked the crowd overhead, sending several reeling back into the flame-lit darkness. An arrow slammed into the sidewalk between his feet, and he felt a nick of pain as something tugged at his right sleeve, above his elbow. He ignored it and kept firing, squeezing off measured bursts and trying to break up the enemy offensive.

"Keep on the garage door!" he shouted to Choi. At the same time, he heard more automatic gunfire from Laird's position. A quick glance up the street sent a lance of horror through his chest. More survivors were advancing on Laird's position.

And they had an armored truck.

"Jim, hit that thing with grenades!" he shouted over the radio. His rifle stopped firing, the bolt locked back—it was empty. "Reloading!" He ripped the expended mag from his weapon and pulled a fresh one from his vest.

"Fuck, me too!" Choi said as his own weapon fell silent. From Laird's position, a grenade exploded, then another. Above the din, he heard a secondary noise, like a gunshot—but it didn't sound like five-five-six NATO.

"Taking fire up here!" Laird said. "They're using the truck as a combat platform!"

"Shoot it with a grenade!" Andrews repeated. He hit the bolt release on his rifle and cracked off two shots at the people emerging from the garage, missing them entirely.

He stepped to his right, realizing he'd been stationary for too long. The enemy had to know his position by now. He was right. An arrow wedged itself into the concrete facade right where he'd been standing, a shot that would have hit him directly in the forehead had he not moved. Choi was operational then, and he engaged the enemy combatants emerging from the garage. He missed just as often as he hit, and sparking explosions dappled the steel door as bullets flattened against it. Another detonation sounded from up the street, but Andrews couldn't check on the circumstances there as he fired on the enemy combatants who clung to the civic center's roof. He fired at one, and the bullet-riddled corpse tumbled off the edge and fell headlong to street.

"These guys are gonna get us, they've got the high ground!" Choi said, an edge of panic in his voice.

"Laird, SITREP!" Andrews said.

"We've hit that armored car with two grenades and we've managed to stop it, but the fuckers are using it for cover—we can't shoot through it, and Kelly and I can't take it by ourselves! We need you up here!"

Andrews heard the crackle of gravel down the street, as if something was making its way toward them. He started to look that way, but three archers stood up on the civic center's roof and raised their bows. He engaged them immediately.

"Roger th—"

"*Get down!*" Choi slammed into him suddenly, driving Andrews to the rubble-littered ground. An arrow slashed into the pavement only inches from his face, pelting him with concrete chips. He struggled against Choi, trying to pull his rifle out from beneath him and return fire.

"Choi, what the—"

The night erupted into fury as great gouts of flame seemed to arc up the street, turning night into day. A furious ripping sound cut through the air. Andrews turned, looking toward Laird's position, and saw the armored truck facing them was being slowly *demolished* in great, sparking explosions that sent bits and pieces of it flying through the air. Laird and the others cowered before the tremendous fusillade, and the enemies facing them jerked and spun as arms and legs were blown off their bodies. The corpses essentially disintegrated where they stood, and Andrews wondered what kind of hell had been unleashed upon the world. The ground beneath him vibrated, the shuddering growing with each passing second as the raucous din grew louder. He heard Choi whoop suddenly, an abrupt exultation of joy that seemed misplaced. Then Andrews became aware of another noise, a mounting whine that deepened into a bellow.

A gas turbine engine coming to life.

SCEV Five rolled to a halt right beside them, the turreted miniguns in its slanted nose spitting bursts of 7.62 millimeter death up the street. The opponents that faced Laird and the others broke and ran, but the firing didn't stop—the fleeing combatants were chopped down as they fled. The SCEV's outer airlock door cycled open, and the LED lights inside snapped on. The rig's armored bulk shielded them from the fighters on the rooftop, rendering their arrows ineffective. As if to underscore just how the tide had changed, the missile pod on the SCEV's back quickly extended into firing position, rotated toward the civic center, and promptly sent a projectile lancing into the structure's side. Riding a column of fire, the missile tore through the civic center's outer wall and exploded deep inside, causing the remains of the roof to suddenly bow upwards before it collapsed inward in a rising cloud of dust.

"Andrews, you guys had better get in. The meter's running, and I'm low on quarters," a voice said over his radio. Even in the heat of battle, Command Sergeant Scott Mulligan managed to sound completely bored.

"About time we rated door-to-door service!" Choi said as he pushed himself off of Andrews and climbed to his feet.

"Mulligan! You're not *dead?*" Andrews said as he bolted into the cockpit. Mulligan was strapped into the pilot's seat, so he slipped into the copilot's seat and buckled himself in. Mulligan looked like hell—he clearly represented the three Bs: battered, bloodied, and bruised.

"That's a matter of personal opinion," Mulligan said. A chime sounded as the airlock indicators went from red to green, and the big man pushed the control column forward. The SCEV responded like a tiger that had just slipped out of its cage, its engines shrieking as its huge tires spun, seeking purchase on the debris-littered ground. Every now and then, a tinny *tink* and *clunk* reached Andrews's ears. Despite the rig's firepower, the denizens of San Jose were still trying to put up a fight, launching whatever they had at the SCEV as it barreled down the street.

"I've got the guns," Andrews said, slipping on his headset and taking over the fire control systems. A window opened up on the infrared overlay that was projected on the viewport—a digital targeting system, which allowed him to control the turreted miniguns on the rig's nose. But there was nothing to fire on; all of Law's people were laying low.

"Roger, you have the guns," Mulligan said.

"Laird, Andrews—check your six, we're rolling up on your position. Get everyone ready to board. Over."

"Roger that," Laird responded immediately.

Ahead, Andrews saw Laird and Kelly marshal Leona and Rachel to the other side of the street so they would be in a better position to board the rig when it came to halt.

"Choi, override the inner airlock door! We're going to want to board them as quickly as we can," Andrews shouted.

"Roger that!" Choi responded. "I'm on it!"

"Get them aboard ASAP. We'll be vulnerable when we come to a stop, and it's not like we have three hundred sixty degrees of coverage," Mulligan said as he slowed the SCEV. When it rumbled just past Laird's position, he braked it to a shuddering halt. The huge vehicle skidded several feet across the loose debris. Andrews reached for the FLIR yoke and twisted it from right to left; the FLIR turret panned in response, and he watched the projected overlay, looking for any signs of life. Motionless bodies lay near the immolated armored truck, the figures glowing dully, still warm against the chilly night. Ghostly pools formed around them—blood, slowly cooling in the nighttime breeze. In the distance, he caught a glimpse of figures moving through the ground floor of a devastated building. He rolled the targeting bracket on them, his thumb hovering above the FIRE button.

Do it! They want us dead, so do it to them first!

He crushed the button beneath his thumb. The two miniguns blared, firing long streams of high-powered ammunition at the building. The infrared overlay revealed the destruction caused by the sudden salvo of 7.62 millimeter bullets as they slashed across the building's floor. Two shapes went down, blasted into pieces by the deadly hail of steel rain. More escaped being blown into oblivion, and Andrews felt a small— but not unexpected—twinge of relief in his gut. He knew he'd reached his limit, had had his fill of killing for the moment.

"Having an attack of the mercies, are you?" Mulligan said.

"What?"

"You didn't slew the guns to the left—you could have taken the rest of them down." His voice was neutral, revealing neither compliment nor reproach.

"All aboard!" Choi shouted from the second compartment. "Airlock sealed!"

Laird shoved his way into the cockpit. A big grin split his handsome, grime-covered face when he saw Mulligan.

"Well, I'll be damned. You must have an angel in your corner, Sarmajor!" He slapped the bigger man on the shoulder.

Mulligan winced at the contact. "The devil in my detail's averaging everything out."

"Jim, get everyone squared away," Andrews said. "We've still got some work to do, so we'll decon once we secure the supports and clear the city. Sarmajor, you good to take us back to the warehouse?"

"Absolutely, sir. I'm a hundred percent operational." He set the SCEV back into motion, accelerating past the wrecked armored truck. "And the sooner we get there, the better ... These guys'll figure out where we're headed soon enough, and we'd better get gone before they can corner us again."

"I'll give you one great big hooah on that, Sarmajor," Andrews said, as Laird retreated from the cockpit.

18

THE SUN WAS already kissing the eastern horizon by the time the SCEV made it back to the manufacturing complex, turning the sky from midnight black to cobalt blue, then to ever-brightening shades of red, orange, and yellow. As Mulligan drove the big rig across the parking lot, Andrews watched the side of the warehouse loom large in the viewports. Mulligan cranked the yoke hard to the left, and the big vehicle turned obediently, leaning hard to the right as it did so. Even Andrews was surprised by the sudden movement, and he was strapped into the copilot's seat. He heard Laird swearing up a storm in the back as he and anyone else who wasn't already strapped down had to scramble to find handholds before they were hurled off their feet.

"Take it easy, Mulligan!" Andrews barked.

"I'll take it easy when I'm dead," Mulligan replied. He brought the rig to a halt just shy of the door the team had entered through day before, then crawled forward until the entrance was directly across from the airlock. Laird stormed into the cockpit and glared down at Mulligan.

"Sergeant Major, what the hell do you think you're doing to my rig?" he snapped.

"Just breaking it in, Captain," Mulligan said, unperturbed. An ugly bruise was spreading across the right side of his face, and Andrews noticed his right eye was red with broken blood vessels.

"Mulligan, you don't look so hot," Andrews said, suddenly concerned.

"I'm good to go, sir. The second I start losing the edge, I'll let you know."

Laird bent down and looked at Mulligan closely. "Holy shit, you really *do* look like hell, Sarmajor." All traces of anger had left his voice.

Mulligan swiveled his eyes toward Laird. "Ladies, I'm touched by your never-ending concern for my well-being, but maybe you should stop commenting on my less-than-stellar looks and get the goddamned core supports?" His voice was a harsh rasp.

"We're on it, Sergeant Major. You stay put and keep an eye on things," Andrews said as he unbuckled his harness.

"You might find this useful, sir." Mulligan reached into one of the cargo pockets and pulled out a neatly folded piece of paper. Andrews took it and unfolded it. It was the manifest from the warehouse detailing the location of the core supports.

"Great work, Sarmajor. We'll have Eklund come forward and keep an eye on things with you."

"Gee, thanks," Mulligan said, turning away and looking out the viewport to his left.

"Is there a problem with that, Mulligan?" Andrews pushed the seat back and rose to his feet, crouching slightly to avoid hitting the overhead panel.

"Negative, Captain." Mulligan hesitated. "But please hurry. I think Eklund has the hots for me."

Andrews exchanged a look with Laird, and both men snorted. Andrews gently patted Mulligan's beefy shoulder.

"Well, I'm sure there are worse things in life, Mulligan."

"I can't think of any, sir."

It wasn't tough to find the supports, since Mulligan had saved the manifest he'd found during their earlier foray into the structure. Andrews, Laird, Rachel, Choi, and Kelly suited up and armed themselves for the extra-vehicular activity, and Andrews led the group to where the supports were supposed to be. He saw the signs of struggle from when Law's people had taken Spencer, and he wondered how long they had until they arrived. He knew one of the survivors' network of tunnels extended to the warehouse; it was the only way they had managed to get the drop on the SCEV Four team.

"Yes," Rachel said over the radio as she bent over the open shipping crate. "Yes, these are the supports. They're in great shape, too." She straightened and looked back at Andrews. "We should take four, at least. We only need two, but we need some safeties."

"How can we tell if they're structurally sound?" Laird asked.

"We can't, but they're extremely dense. It would take a

significant amount of energy to deform them, and this area of the city," she waved one arm at the warehouse, "didn't seem to get hit by a direct nuclear strike, so it's very unlikely their composition has been altered by ionization."

Laird turned to Andrews and shrugged. "Well, okay."

"Let's get going," Andrews said. "Rachel, go back to the rig. Choi, Jordello, you guys stand guard. Keep aware of what's going on around you at all times—we'll need you to provide security while Laird and I move some of these things to the vehicle. Questions?" No one had any, so Andrews turned to Laird and nodded toward the shipping crate. "Okay, let's do this."

Kelly and Choi escorted Rachel back to the waiting SCEV, then returned to stand guard over the two captains as they went to work on the supports. They had a special dolly with them that was motorized, so they wouldn't have to carry the supports all the way back to the SCEV themselves; since each support weighed almost four hundred pounds, that was a huge plus. Yet getting them out of the container was a struggle, and it took almost ten minutes to load one on the dolly. Then their return to the rig was limited by the dolly's slow rate of speed. Andrews was sweating profusely beneath his environmental suit and respirator assembly, and through the visor of his facemask, he could see Laird was as well.

"Man, this is going to suck," Laird gasped over the radio.

"You think it's bad now? Wait until we have to get them in the rig and store them in the locker," Andrews said. "We'll both have herniated discs by the time we're through."

"Thanks, man. Thanks so much."

Andrews was right. While extracting the core support from the container had been arduous, getting it off the dolly and into the airlock required some Herculean effort on their part. Stowing it in the SCEV's tight confines was a hellish nightmare; it seemed like there just wasn't enough room for them to move while struggling with the support's incredible weight. Rachel wanted to help, but both men warned her away; if someone lost their grip, the result would be a shattered floor plate, or worse, a crushed foot. They finally managed to wrangle the support into the floor-level locker without causing any injuries.

"Okay," Andrews gasped when they had secured the

support. "On to the next one."

"Man, this is kickin' my ass," Laird said.

"Better that than leaving everyone in Harmony to die, Captain," Mulligan said over the radio. He and Leona were listening in to their commo from the cockpit.

"You're a hell of a motivational speaker, Sarmajor," Laird said.

"I am a man of many talents, sir."

Andrews waved Laird to the open airlock door. A beeping alarm sounded every ten seconds, telling the crew the obvious: both doors were open, and the potential for internal contamination was increasing. Andrews led Laird outside, then he cycled the airlock closed.

They repeated the sequence twice more before they had to stop to rest. With three supports aboard, Andrews was motivated to bust some ass and secure the last one, but both he and Laird were almost dead on their feet. They drank from the hydration packs they carried on their backs and leaned against the SCEV for a few minutes, catching their breath and trying to regain their strength. Andrews's legs and arms felt rubbery, and his back and shoulders ached. His forearms burned, and he knew the pain would just increase over the coming days as abused muscles, tendons, and connective tissue grew inflamed.

But it's still nothing compared to what Law could do ...

"Mulligan, this is Andrews," he said.

"Go ahead, Captain. Over."

"Do you know anything about some special weapons programs that could turn a man into ..." Andrews paused, trying to figure out how to explain it. "Into some kind of super-warrior? A man who could inflict incredible pain just by *thinking* about it?"

"Lieutenant Eklund has been briefing me on the individual called Law, Captain. No, I'm unaware of such a program, but it wouldn't surprise me. I did know of a program called OMEGA, where soldiers were subjected to nanite treatments that increased their ability to heal and gave them superior strength and endurance, but as far as I know, it was never fielded. As a matter of fact, Congress passed legislation to outlaw activities like that, but I guess the CIA or whoever created this Law bozo never got the memo. Over."

"I wonder how he could have survived all this time," Andrews said, more to himself than Mulligan.

"Nanites are interesting little machines, sir. They can self-replicate and continue doing their job for as long as there's enough raw material to keep the process going. Have no idea if this is the case with that Law guy, but I'll tell you what—let's not hang around to find out. Are you guys about done with your smoke break, Captain? Over."

Laird pushed himself away from the SCEV tiredly. "Yeah, yeah, yeah," he groused.

"You guys want to trade places?" Kelly asked. "You can stand overwatch while Choi and I get the last one."

"Negative, there's no reason for all of us to risk getting injured," Andrews said. "We've got it. Just keep doing what you're doing."

"Take it easy, Mike," Kelly cautioned. "It's a long way back to Harmony, and I'd hate it if you guys were laid up for the entire run."

"We'll take care of it," Laird said, his tone terse and clipped. Andrews could tell his fellow officer was getting awfully close to his limits.

"Easy, man," he said.

Laird shot him a thumbs-up. "I'm all right, Mike. Don't worry."

"SCEV Five to all troops—once you've stopped sharing this tender moment, I'm going to have to ask you guys to cut some butt. We're being scouted. I have visual contact on several OPFOR glassing us from another building down the block. I can engage, but they're right on the edge of azimuth violation for the minis. Over."

"How many, Mulligan?" Andrews asked. As he and Laird struck out for the last support, Kelly and Choi flanked them. If they were going to be attacked, it would be while they were away from the SCEV. Both of them held their rifles at low ready. Laird towed the dolly along after him, kicking up dust as he ran.

"I see three, but that doesn't mean jack. There could be fifty more on the other side of the building. You guys need to decide if that last support is worth it. Over."

"It is," Andrews replied. "Mulligan, if we get into a furball, you need to leave right away. You got that?"

"Sorry, Captain. Your transmission's breaking up. Over."

Andrews almost laughed. He had expected a terse acknowledgement of the order and nothing else. After all, Mulligan was the one who was supposed to babysit the others and make sure the mission was completed. And here they were with goblins approaching, and he wasn't going to leave the others behind without a fight. Andrews had to admit he was impressed by the old soldier's attitude.

"They like to get up high and attack from there," Andrews said as he crawled into the crate and grabbed another support. "You guys keep your eyes open, and if you see movement, open up. There's no one friendly out here."

"Roger that," Kelly said, taking up a guard position on one side of the warehouse aisle. Choi hung back, positioning himself so he could see the doorway to his left and maintain watch on the other side of the warehouse.

Andrews and Laird grunted and strained, struggling to get the last support out of the crate. They finally managed to do it, but at the last moment, Laird lost his grip. With a yelp, he jumped back, and Andrews felt his end of the support slide out of his hands. The support slammed to the concrete floor with a tremendous crash, blasting a deep crater into the cement, sending chips flying.

"Goddamn it, Laird!" he shouted.

"Sorry," Laird said. "Come on, let's get this thing loaded up—"

"Captain Andrews? You there, my friend?"

The sudden voice over the radio made everyone freeze in place. Laird looked up at Andrews, the question visible in his eyes, as Kelly and Choi shifted uncomfortably. Andrews felt a stab of fear run through his heart.

It was Law. And if he was broadcasting on their frequency...

"Mulligan, position of SCEV Four!" Andrews shouted, panic plain in his own voice.

"Negative contact," Mulligan reported back, and there was an almost embarrassed quality to his voice. "Sorry, sir. We weren't paying attention to Four's transponder data. It's been shut off. Recommend you get back immediately. Over."

Laird bent over, struggling to get a grip on the support.

"Come on, let's get this thing—"

"Everybody back to the rig!" Andrews grabbed Laird's arm and yanked him away from the support. "*Now!*"

"Too late, my friend," Law whispered over the radio.

The warehouse became a living hell. From outside came the long, drawn-out ripping sound of miniguns firing, their six-barreled, electrically driven guns pumping out four thousand 7.62 millimeter projectiles per minute. The barrage ripped through the warehouse's shell as if it were made from wet paper towels, opening up great holes through which harsh sunlight poured. The bullets continued across the warehouse, decimating ancient shipping crates and sending splintered wood and fragmented metal whirling through the air like a vicious, barbed cyclone. Steel shelving units rocked back and forth, and as Andrews ran down the aisle, he heard all manner of shrapnel strike the crates and shelves around him. Outside, he heard SCEV Five's turbine engine begin to wail to life, and then another minigun blast exploded into being as Five opened fire on another target.

"Mulligan, SITREP!" Andrews yelled.

"Taking out their observers, Captain. No visual on Four, and I'm prepping to evac. Over."

"We're on our way!" Andrews followed Kelly and Laird as they turned the corner. Choi remained where he was, rifle at the ready, finger on the trigger. Another salvo of minigun fire tore through the structure from the opposite side of the warehouse, and Andrews flinched as something cracked past his head. He signaled Choi to head out, and the young Asian man did as instructed, running in a crouch for the door. Andrews turned the corner and saw the bright rectangle of light ahead of him. The SCEV's airlock was already open, and he watched as first Kelly, then Laird, vaulted up the short stairway and into the rig's interior. Then Choi emerged into the bright sunlight, and he skidded to a stop beside the stairway and squatted there, keeping an eye toward the SCEV's rear. He raised his rifle and started shooting immediately.

"They're coming up behind us!" he screamed over the radio, releasing a burst on full automatic.

"Get aboard!" Andrews shouted. Tinny *clanks* and *clinks* filled the air, and he felt projectiles hitting him with enough force to pierce his suit. A spiderweb of cracks filled one corner of his visor, and he realized Law's rounds were passing through the warehouse and slapping into the SCEV, disintegrating when they hit the rig's dense, armored hide. He scrambled up the stairs and launched himself through the small airlock, spinning around on the other side and reaching back for Choi. Choi bolted up the stairs and slammed into him, sending both of them reeling.

"Mulligan—*go!*" Andrews yelled. The SCEV lurched into motion and it sped away from the warehouse—in *reverse.*

"What are you doing?" Leona shouted from the right seat.

"They've already scouted us, so they know our orientation," Mulligan said tightly. "They probably have a kill box set up ahead, where your pal the Law is sitting pretty in SCEV Four, waiting to put a missile up our ass as we come around the corner. Sit tight, Lieutenant—unless these fuckers have an Abrams squirreled away somewhere, the other rig is our biggest obstacle."

"But he knows how to use it!" Leona said. She sat rigid in her seat, fear etched into her face, her eyes wild.

"He might know how to *drive* an SCEV, but he doesn't know how to *fight* in an SCEV," Mulligan said. "I'll bet you dollars to doughnuts he's sitting in a fixed position, hosing the warehouse, trying to flush us out. And we'll do what he wants, just not the way he wants us to do it." As he kept the rig hurtling backward, Mulligan's thick fingers danced over the center console. He raised the missile pod into firing position and brought up a targeting window on the viewport. He saw through the external cam feed broadcast to one of the displays on the instrument panel that Choi was right—there were about ten or so combatants behind them, obviously placed to add urgency to the situation and force the SCEV to expedite its departure. But they hadn't expected the rig to come right at them, and they dove behind the corner of the warehouse as the SCEV bolted backwards.

"Lieutenant, you want to hose those guys with some minigun fire while I tend to everything else?" Mulligan asked. "I'll pull past the warehouse and bring the nose to the right once we're clear, so all you'll have to do is fire. You don't even have to kill any of them, just get them out of our way. Hooah?"

"Hooah," Leona said, and she seemed to throw her fear into a corner as she pushed back her dark hair. She took hold of the fire control yoke on her side of the cockpit. "Guns up!"

"Stand by," Mulligan said. He held the control column back until it almost reached the control stop, and the rig's turbine engines bellowed with power. Then the vehicle flew past the corner of the warehouse, and he brought the column to the left while applying the brakes. The rig slewed crazily, its nose abruptly tracking to the right as a cloud of burnt rubber began to form outside. Leona pressed the firing button on the yoke, and the twin miniguns mounted on the SCEV's nose erupted as they vomited forth a salvo of destruction. The ten or so enemy combatants there didn't stand a chance—eight of them went down in spreading explosions of gore while the remaining two dived for the dirt and curled up in fetal positions, likely waiting for Death to tap them on the shoulder and inform them they were required elsewhere. Leona could have set up that meeting by depressing the guns just a few degrees, but she didn't, and Mulligan wondered why. Not that it mattered to him one whit. They had bigger fish to fry, then they would leave San Jose to rot in the powerful sunlight.

"Mulligan, what's the op?" Andrews appeared in the cockpit doorway, and he wedged himself between the seats.

"I'm going to see what I can do about SCEV Four," Mulligan told him. "We can't have that bat-shit crazy dude you guys say leads these morons taking us out from behind when we try to get the hell out of Dodge."

"I agree, but what are you going to do?"

"Don't know. Let's find out, shall we?"

"Uh—" Whatever sage advice Andrews was about to impart was cut off when Mulligan set the SCEV in motion once again, its big tires screeching on the parking lot's cracked surface as it accelerated forward, pulling parallel to the rear of the warehouse. The surviving combatants there tried to make themselves even smaller and, for a moment, Mulligan considered running them over, but he dismissed the notion. They were combat ineffective, and the team from Harmony Base had likely taken more than its pound of flesh during the night. The SCEV barreled to the other side of the warehouse and accelerated into the parking lot on the other side. A flurry of projectiles struck the rig's left side, and Mulligan grunted. Apparently, his opponent wasn't quite as predictable as he'd hoped.

Looking to the left, he saw SCEV Four slam its way through the rotting hulk of two cars, sending the metal carcasses tumbling across the parking lot. The miniguns on the rig's sloped bow were blazing away, raking SCEV Five with dozens of tungsten-cored rounds. If the SCEV had been more insubstantial—like the armored truck Law's people had tried to use as a gunnery platform earlier—then the crew from Harmony would have been in deep shit. But the rig's armor was thick and ballistically tolerant. It would take more than 7.62 millimeter to do anything but dimple its hide and mar its paint. Unfortunately, SCEV Four was also equipped with Hellfire missiles, and Mulligan wasn't keen on sticking around to see if Law knew how to use them.

"Time to boogie," he said, more to himself than Andrews and Leona. He kept the rig accelerating straight on, and it crashed through the fence on the other side of the parking lot and hurtled down a mostly vacant street. The rig's Hellfires were radar-guided, so if he could get Law to follow him down the comparatively narrow city streets, then the chances of him scoring a hit would be reduced. Even millimeter-wave radar was subject to ground clutter, and despite their versatility and high-tech systems, the SCEVs hadn't been designed for street fighting.

"Lieutenant, set the chaff dispensers to pop off automatically if we get a launch detection, and take the safeties off the root beers," Mulligan told her. Each rig carried six pan-shaped anti-missile warheads that could be launched from the rig's sides to intercept an incoming projectile. Essentially flying claymore mines, the AMWs—called 'root beers' by old timers such as Mulligan because AMW sounded a lot like A&W— would detonate in the path of an incoming missile or rocket and explode, sending a crescent of ball bearings flying into the projectile's path. The idea was that the missile would strike the steel wall and be damaged so severely that it would be unable to hit its target.

In theory, anyway.

"Done," Leona said.

From the rear of the SCEV, they heard something like hail hitting metal.

"Hey, we're taking fire back here!" Laird shouted.

"It's Four," Andrews told him. "Everyone strap in." He turned to Mulligan. "You planning on outrunning him?"

"Not much chance in that, sir. He's running a lot lighter than we are, so he's going to have the edge on us when it comes to speed and maneuverability. But I'm thinking I might have a surprise or two up my sleeve." He nodded toward a multistory building ahead, its exterior battered and worn by war and earthquakes and the passing years. It was a fairly tall and narrow structure, one of what had once been known as pocket skyscrapers—structures that were built on small parcels of land yet provided a remarkable amount of floor space due to their height. In heavily urban environments, they'd become wildly popular in the third decade of the twenty-first century. Many of them had been the cause of numerous lawsuits, because several had proven to be death traps. Mulligan hoped he'd picked a lucky one.

"You're going to lose him in that building?" Leona asked.

"Nope, but he's going to lose us. Captain, can you visually confirm everyone is strapped in?"

From the corner of his eye, he saw Andrews turn and look into the next compartment. "Roger that."

"You might want to hang on, sir. If this thing has a basement, we might wind up severely fucked."

"Yeah, well, maybe you might want to think about this again," Andrews said.

Mulligan shook his head. "Nah."

An alarm sounded, and something went *poof* from somewhere on top of the rig. Mulligan felt the pucker factor increase then, and half an instant later, a Hellfire missile ripped right over the speeding SCEV. It had passed through the radar-blinding chaff the rig had fired, and the seeker head in the missile's nose hadn't had the time to reacquire the vehicle when it emerged from the blinding cloud. With the target lost, the missile went into a steep climb so that it might be able to reacquire SCEV Five from a greater altitude. It never had a chance; it disappeared into a ball of flame and fury when it slammed into the pocket skyscraper. The building shook, shedding whatever layers of glass it still had, like a man brushing snow from his overcoat on a brisk winter day. A blizzard of rubbish cascaded to the street below like a filthy waterfall.

"How far behind us is that fucker?" Mulligan asked.

"A little less than two hundred meters," Leona reported. "Do you want the radar display added to your tactical overlay?"

"I'm good, Lieutenant. Too many pretty lights in front of me gets me all distracted." As the rig bore down on the building, Mulligan found he couldn't hold the tension back any longer. The palm of his left hand was slick with sweat, and if not for the light stippling on the control column's grip, it might have slipped out of his hand. He found himself pressing his back into his seat, and the harness's shoulder straps loosened a bit before the retractors took up the slack. As the vehicle sped on, he could see the building's lobby, empty of everything save some fallen ceiling tiles, shattered glass, an ancient reception desk, and several large empty pots that might have once held decorative saplings.

The SCEV crashed through the empty window frames, parting them like a ship's bow cleaving through a heavy sea. The rig bounced up and down as it hurtled across the marble floor and crushed the reception desk into thousands of splinters, then it burst through the framework on the other side of the building and into the street beyond.

"Lieutenant, your vehicle!" Mulligan snapped, and he released the control column. The SCEV began to slow immediately, and Leona hurriedly grabbed the column on her side of the cockpit. The SCEV accelerated forward again as Mulligan reached for the fire control yoke. A tactical overlay sprang to life on the viewport before him, and he activated the missile pod. He rotated it one hundred eighty degrees, deselected the missile safeties, and dead-fired two Hellfires right at the building. The two projectiles leapt out of the pod, accelerating to their peak velocity of Mach 1.3 within two hundred yards of launch. Not that the speed was really required; the building wasn't about to take evasive action, after all. Both weapons slammed into the structure within milliseconds of each other, right as SCEV Four drew near. Each missile was equipped with a blast fragmentation sleeve warhead capable of defeating reinforced concrete bunkers—in fact, the warhead had been developed specifically for that purpose. The dual explosions were nothing short of remarkable, and the concussive force of the blasts essentially gutted two of the building's lower floors, wiping out everything from sheetrock to thick I-beams that provided core support. The building began to pancake, instantly imploding in a gigantic cloud of dust that mushroomed into the air.

"Holy *shit!*" Andrews remarked, watching the video from the rear surveillance camera. "I don't believe it!"

"Me either," Mulligan said dryly, taking a moment to crack his knuckles. "Hopefully that son of a bitch drove right into it, so it'll be lights out for him." He looked at Andrews, still crouching between the seats and staring at the display. There was no sign of SCEV Four. "Don't worry, Captain. I'm sure Benchley will send us back to dig it out. The guy might be a general, but he's also a hell of a bean counter."

Andrews snorted, then looked at Mulligan directly. "I think the general might be a little more understanding of what the real world is about, Sarmajor. After all, he's the one who assigned you to the mission, and look what we ran into."

"Hey, I'm just glad it wasn't wall-to-wall boredom." Mulligan felt suddenly uncomfortable beneath Andrews's gaze, and he cleared his throat self-consciously.

When was the last time someone paid you a compliment? When was the last time you did something for someone else?

He shook his head and glanced at Leona. She glanced at him as well, and there was something in her eyes bordering on hero worship. Mulligan had to force himself not to groan in disgust.

"My vehicle, Lieutenant," he said, taking the control column in his left hand. "Captain, with your permission, I think it's time we head home."

"Damn straight, Sergeant Major. Damn straight."

19

TWO HOURS LATER, SCEV Five was slowly climbing up the rim of the Santa Clara Valley, leaving the shattered metropolis of San Jose behind. Mulligan refused to vacate the pilot's seat, so Andrews helped Leona out of the cockpit and asked Kelly to check her wounded leg. She had already cleaned and dressed the wound during the time they made their way back to the warehouse, but Andrews wanted it looked at again. The last thing they needed was for Leona's wound to become septic while they were out in the field. He then claimed the copilot's seat and strapped in while Kelly tended to Leona; Laird and Choi continued with decon procedures. He paid particular attention to the ground-search radar, looking for any sign of SCEV Four. There was no indication they were being pursued, which was a relief.

"How're you hanging in, Sergeant Major?" Andrews asked as the rig bumped its way toward the remnants of Highway 130, a twisting road that cut through the foothills surrounding the valley. Blocked in places by old mudslides, the road was just barely navigable. It was also fairly flat, which made it preferable to striking out overland.

"Still operational, Captain." Mulligan kept his eyes on the road, weaving around the occasional rotting husk of a long-abandoned motor vehicle. While he continued to handle the SCEV with impressive dexterity, Andrews was becoming worried. The sergeant major's face was puffy from swelling, and there was dried blood in his dark hair from a small scalp laceration.

"Maybe you should kick back for a while," he suggested. "Let Laird or Choi come forward and—"

"I'm good to go, Captain," Mulligan said.

Then his head dipped forward, and his hand slipped off the control column. The SCEV began to slow immediately, drifting to the left and bouncing over the remains of a rock-studded earth slide. Mulligan's head bobbed from side to side, and for a moment, Andrews thought the older man was joking, but it became apparent that he had passed out, held in place by his safety harness. Andrews seized the copilot's column and brought the rig to a halt.

"Mulligan?" Andrews reached over the center console and shook the sergeant major gently. There was no response; he was out cold.

"Guys, I need a hand up here!"

Laird appeared almost instantly. His hair was wet, and he wore only a mustard-yellow T-shirt and his duty uniform trousers. He had apparently just stepped out of the small shower in the rear of the SCEV.

"What the hell happened?" he asked, bending over Mulligan. He put his fingers against the bigger man's neck, feeling for a pulse.

"He just passed out," Andrews said, unbuckling his safety harness after setting the rig's parking brake. He pushed the seat back and got to his feet, crouching over the center console. "He still has a pulse, right?"

"Yeah. I guess that means he's really *not* a robot," Laird said. He unfastened Mulligan's harness and supported him when he slouched forward. "Hey, Sergeant Major! Can you hear me?"

Mulligan made a small groan, but didn't respond in a meaningful way. Laird looked over at Andrews.

"Looks like a concussion," he said. "Or maybe worse."

Andrews didn't like that. Everyone onboard knew first aid, and both Leona and Kelly Jordello were qualified medics, but a brain injury was something they were ill-equipped to handle.

"All right, let's get him out of here," Andrews said.

It took almost an hour for Law to extract SCEV Four from the collapsed building that had encased almost half the rig. Law had thought for certain he was going to perish in the collapse; even though he had slowed his pursuit of SCEV Five to avoid being crushed to death beneath the mass of the small office tower as it pancaked, several upper floors had suddenly tilted over, falling directly onto the street. Law had thrown the rig in reverse immediately, but the vehicle had been caught inside the debris field's leading edge.

Remarkably, he survived.

More importantly, so had SCEV Four.

It took time to back the rig out of its near-tomb. Reversing, advancing, reversing again, the big vehicle shuddered as its tires sought purchase in its bid to retreat from the wreckage's embrace. Finally, it did just that, and bright sunlight lanced through the dust covering the vehicle's viewports as debris rolled off its snout in a small avalanche. Law continued to back the SCEV away from the mound of rubble until it sat in the middle of the next intersection. Only then did he relax and roll the engine condition levers to IDLE. The twin turbine engines slowly spun down to a low whine, and Law knew it was absolutely miraculous that they hadn't ingested debris and destroyed themselves.

Shapes surrounded the idling vehicle, approaching cautiously, fearfully. Law watched them draw near, and he chopped the fuel to the engines, shutting them down. Cool air whispered over him courtesy of the vehicle's environmental system, and he sat where he was for a time, taking a moment to simply luxuriate in something he never thought he'd inhale again—clean, purified air.

He unstrapped himself and pushed the pilot's seat against the bulkhead, then left the cockpit. He cycled open the inner airlock and stepped inside the small room. The inner door closed and, after a moment, the outer clamshell doors opened, rising on well-oiled hydraulic rams. Law squinted at the harsh, unfiltered sunlight that greeted him, inhaling air tainted with dust. It was a warm day, almost eighty degrees now, and he pulled a filthy balaclava over his head. Direct exposure to sunlight was no longer a good thing; since the nuclear detonations had virtually eradicated the planet's ozone layer, it was taking Mother Earth quite some time to replenish it. Prolonged exposure to sunlight could result in all manner of vicious skin cancers, so Law and his family avoided it as much as they could. Indeed, those who walked to the base of the airlock stairs looked like extremely scruffy mummies, wrapped up from head to toe in thick cloth. Not even fingers or noses were exposed. Law pulled on the pair of dark goggles that hung around his neck and checked to ensure his gloves were tucked under the wrists of his jacket. Satisfied there was no exposed flesh for the sun to attack, he stepped down the small stairway as a tall, reedy figure wearing a patchwork of old military uniforms stepped forward to meet him.

"Xavier," Law said.

Xavier nodded and looked past him at the towering SCEV. His eyes were unreadable behind his goggles, and after a moment, he pointed them back at Law.

"Will you go after them?"

"Yes," Law said simply.

Xavier looked at Law for a long moment. When he spoke, he kept his voice low. "I don't mean to challenge you ..."

"Then don't," Law snapped. Xavier flinched slightly and stepped back. Law reconsidered his attitude an instant later and sighed wearily. "Speak your mind, Xavier."

Xavier swallowed, the action clearly visible behind the scarf he wore over his face and the hood covering his head. "Why?"

"Why what?"

"Why chase them?"

Law snorted. "You *know* why, Xavier. No one outside the family is to be trusted. We've met outsiders before, and they've always tried to take what we have—murderers, all of them, half out of their minds, looking only to kill and steal and destroy anything that's decent."

"They didn't," Xavier said softly.

"What?"

Xavier hesitated for a long moment. He was old now, but he was still a good soldier, and had served capably as Law's second-in-command for quite some time. Even though he still had to be punished on occasion—everyone in the family had to be disciplined from time to time, and Law was hardly stingy when it came to inflicting pain—Xavier had studiously avoided doing anything that might upset Law. But as he grew older, Law had sensed a change in Xavier. While he had no desire to experience the fields of pain Law could inflict, Law could tell Xavier had reached a decision some time ago to stop living in fear. Law smiled beneath his balaclava. An admirable choice, but the man was still eager to avoid the pain.

"They didn't come to murder us, Law. They came here only for what they needed, things we had no use for." Xavier's voice was level, reasonable. Just the same, the others standing nearby slowly began to back away.

"And what do think will happen if Andrews makes it back to this Harmony Base, Xavier?" Law asked. "He'll report to his superiors, as any good soldier will do, and what if they don't like what they hear? They'll send a force back to destroy us. You know the code we live by, my friend—*trust no one.*" He waved at the SCEV looming over them. "And if they return in more of *these*, or machines capable of even greater destruction, then the family will fall."

"We have no proof they would do such a thing."

"No proof? How many brothers and sisters have we lost, Xavier? Forty? Fifty? That was just from a small detachment of these soldiers. Imagine what will happen when *more* of them arrive!" Law felt the rage boiling up inside of him, that festering fury that was always close at hand, the poisonous anger that his handlers had unknowingly unleashed during their operations. The drugs and selective surgery and the introduction of thousands of tiny, microscopic machines that reorganized his brain had made him at once more than and less of a man. "To them, we're no longer men and women. We're *animals*! That's the mentality of Man, to destroy, to kill. It won't happen this time. I won't let it."

"But, Law—"

"*They destroyed the entire planet!*" Law shouted with such ferocity that he feared he might damage his vocal chords. "Look around you, look at what's *left*. We scrabble to survive here while *they* live in comfort, staying hidden for years until they were certain all of *us* had died. How many did they kill, Xavier? Billions! *Billions* of human beings died from that damned war, and now we're next!"

Xavier said nothing. After a time, he nodded slowly and looked down at the ground, his expression hidden beneath layers of protective clothing. Law stared at him, waiting for him to say something. He needed Xavier now more than ever, and he needed to get himself under control before he did something rash, something that couldn't be undone.

Xavier finally looked up. "What are your orders?"

"Take two men inside. Remove all the food and medicine, the bedding, the water, anything the family could use. But be quick about it. I'll need to leave within the hour."

"But how will you find them?" Xavier asked.

"They need to return to their base as quickly as they can, so they'll follow the same route they took to get here," Law said. "Simple, really—I'll catch up to them in the field and deal with them somewhere in the wasteland."

"And what will happen to us?"

Law looked at Xavier for a long moment. "I don't know," he said, finally. "That will be up to you, Xavier. I'm leaving the family under your care. I intend to return, but I don't know if I will. So you should do whatever you need to do to keep the family going. Do you understand?"

"Yes, Law. I understand." There was a mournful quality to his voice that touched Law. He stepped forward and put his hand on Xavier's thin arm. Xavier flinched at the contact, but Law held firm. He put his free hand on Xavier's other arm and pulled him into an embrace. Xavier stiffened, but he didn't resist as Law hugged him powerfully.

"They're yours to tend to, Xavier. I don't think we'll be seeing each other again, so lead them as best as you can. Be what I could never be. Be strong always, but also be what I never was. Compassionate."

"Are you certain this is the only choice we have?"

Law released him and stepped back, motioning to the SCEV. "Get started," he said, then turned and walked up the ramp and into the waiting rig.

20

AS THE SUN descended and slipped past the horizon, SCEV Five made its way across the former state of California, picking its way across the Sierra Nevada mountain range, sticking to roads wherever it could. Day died and night was born, but the rig continued its trek, bumping along through the darkness, unimpeded by the utter blackness thanks to its array of infrared devices. By the next morning, the burly machine had descended from the mountains and accelerated across the mostly flat deserts of Nevada. It then turned on a southerly course, aiming for New Mexico, where it would cut a path across the lowest part of the Rocky Mountains. Once clear of the rugged spires of rock, the SCEV would change course again, this time northeasterly, where she would return directly to Harmony Base.

It would take six days. If all went according to plan, the rig would deliver its precious cargo of replacement supports thirteen days after the Core had gone offline.

Andrews oversaw the SCEV as it sped into the glowing gloom of another night, and he wondered how many more friends might have perished waiting for them to return. As the lights grew dimmer inside the base, as the CO_2 scrubbers slowly failed, how many of the people he had known for the last decade had slipped away? None? A dozen? Fifty?

Bathed in the cold glow of the instrument panel, he found he didn't want to contemplate such things. Instead, he urged the SCEV onward, putting his trust in its computer systems to get them back to where they needed to go, to propel the hulking machine on the course they had mapped on their outbound leg.

The cockpit door slid open behind him, and he glanced back as Rachel slipped inside. She handed him a cup, and it was warm to the touch. He regarded it in the glow of the instruments as she settled into the copilot's seat and strapped herself in. She held a cup of her own.

"It's coffee," she told him.

He nodded and reached across the center console so he could squeeze her hand. "You're the bestest, hon." He was happy to have the caffeine. Shifts were longer now that Mulligan was out of commission. Everyone was already dog-tired from the voyage, not to mention the stress of dealing with Law and his people. Now that he had some time and distance separating him from the events in San Jose, Andrews marveled that several hundred people there had managed to survive. From the deformities he had witnessed, he knew Law hadn't been idly boasting when he said the survivors were fertile. Even though Law was obviously a psychotic madman, he had done an incredible job of keeping his people alive over the years, scavenging whatever they needed from the corpse of the shattered metropolis. It was truly a commendable feat.

Of course, that also included eating other survivors, he reminded himself. Viewed in that light, Law's accomplishment seemed a little less warm and fuzzy.

"How's Mulligan?" he asked, sipping from his cup. The coffee was hot and bitter, so strong it was almost overpowering—just how he liked it.

"Still out, but it looks like he's in a normal sleep, now. Kelly's keeping an eye on him." She paused and shook her head. "Well, whenever Leona isn't, anyway."

"Come again?"

Rachel looked at him and rolled her eyes. "Babe, you really need to pay more attention. Lee's got the hots for Mulligan."

"Eklund?" Andrews chuckled at the thought. "No way!"

Rachel shrugged and sipped from her own cup. "I can't imagine why, but it sure looks like it."

Andrews didn't know what to make of that—the two most disconnected people in Harmony Base had somehow managed to find one another after practically living on top of each other for years. Well, at least Leona saw something in Mulligan. It remained to be seen if it was a two-way street, especially since Mulligan was twice Eklund's age.

That ought to be something to see.

"Anyway, what are you going to tell Benchley about San Jose?" Rachel asked.

"Everything we know. Those ... people back there might not be what we were hoping for, but it's a start. And Law mentioned something about survivalists from the north, so that's something else we'll need to look into—"

A tone sounded suddenly, and the rig began to slow down. Andrews looked at the engineering display as he disconnected the autopilot and took control of the vehicle. He didn't like what he saw—a gear chip warning in the number two differential. The computers had automatically disconnected the faulted system, essentially placing the system in neutral to preserve the complicated array of meshing gears.

"That doesn't look good," Rachel said, looking at the same display.

"No, it's not," Andrews said. "We'll need to shut down and check it out. Without it, we've lost the center set of wheels. They'll still roll, but they won't provide any power, and that's going to screw us up big time."

"We could get stuck," Rachel said.

Andrews nodded, slowing the rig until it came to a halt. "Yeah. And getting stuck out here would be a permanent duty station."

While they didn't have Spencer's skills to draw from, both Laird and Andrews had enough technical smarts to figure out what had to be done, assisted by the SCEV's electronic system manuals. Rachel was able to pitch in as well; while her forte was not vehicular transmissions, she knew enough about them to be able to assist the two men as they pulled up the floor in the SCEV's center compartment to gain access to the differential. When they opened the case, they found that one gear had been partially stripped. Fishing around through the fluid in the case, they were able to find a few fragments, but were unable to recover all of them.

"It's definitely FUBAR, Mike," Rachel said finally. "I think we can still keep going, but we've got to be careful. Like you said, we get stuck now, it'll be permanent."

Laird regarded the failed gear. "I guess there's no chance of fixing this, huh?"

"Not out here," Rachel said. "We don't have any spares aboard, and I'm not familiar enough with these systems to jury-rig something. If I blow it, we might wind up worse off than we are now."

"You know, I don't think that would take a lot of doing," Laird said. He handed the gear to Andrews, who turned it over in his hand. It was still slick with lubricant, but the metal around the stripped teeth was sharp enough to cut skin. He sighed and wrapped a paper towel around the warm circle of alloy and placed it in a drawer by the engineering station.

"All right, let's button it up and get moving," he said.

"How much will this slow us up?" Kelly asked.

Andrews sighed. "Well, we're not going to be able to cruise as fast as we might, and we have to be damned careful about where we put the wheels. Getting stuck out here, especially in the mountains, would be a total bag of day old dicks. We'll have to be on our toes for the entire trip, and that means we'll have to take it slow."

"Mike, Harmony doesn't have a lot of time left." Leona looked at him with a grim expression that had nothing to do with the painful injury to her leg. Even under the numbing effects of the oxycodone Kelly had given her, she was still alert enough to understand the risks of arriving late.

"I know that, Lee," he said.

"You guys are all tired," she said, looking around the compartment. "Mulligan's still out, but I can pitch in and help out."

"Not while you're half in the bag from the pain meds," Laird said as he bent over the opening in the compartment deck. He matched up the seals they had disturbed opening the differential's casing and prepared to seal it up again. His hands were filthy with glistening, gray lubricant.

"I'll stop taking them," Leona said.

"Probably not an awesome idea," Andrews said, looking over Laird at Kelly.

Kelly shrugged. "It's not like she's going to be doing calisthenics, Captain. She'll be in some measure of discomfort, but as long as she takes it easy and doesn't tear open the sutures I put in her, she'll be fine."

"I can deal with it, Mike," Leona said.

"How long ago did you take your last dose?" Andrews asked.

Leona looked down. "Just before we came to a stop," she said, which meant a little over an hour ago.

He looked at Kelly. "How long until it gets processed by her system?"

"Six hours, to be safe. It does tend to make her a bit loopy, but that's an expected side effect for some patients. We can substitute it with acetaminophen, which won't be as effective at managing the pain, but there shouldn't be any side effects that could impair her performance."

"A little bit of the lightfighter candy all right by you, Lee?"

Leona nodded.

"All right. Go hit one of the racks, and we'll see about bringing you up front in about six hours," Andrews said.

"Hooah," Leona responded, and she slowly limped to the rig's third compartment. Andrews caught a glimpse of Mulligan lying in one of the lowermost bunks, wrapped up in a blanket. Half of his face was covered by an angry mass of black and purple bruises.

He picked up a torque wrench and bent over the differential casing as Laird fitted it back together.

21

THE WOMAN'S FACE *is still mostly smooth. The only signs of her true age are an array of laugh lines that crinkle whenever she smiles, which she does quite a bit, finding something humorous in almost every situation. Her hair is a tawny blond, its rich color diminished somewhat by the encroaching grays, the ones she's just not vain enough to try to hide behind the quick fixes of bottled hair products. The woman—and more importantly, the man who adores her—knows that youth and vitality are more about what's on the inside than what's on the outside. The interior is what's important, and only a precious few intimates get to see that. The exterior? Hell, everyone else on the planet can see that, free of charge.*

The girls look like both of them, a mix of her fair skin and honey-colored hair, but with his eyes and nose. He thinks the nose looks much better on them than on him. It confers an impression of quiet, regal strength that makes him wonder how they'll fare in the coming years when boys begin to circle around them. Would they take the males on head-to-head as he would, or would they instead use the mother's good nature and occasional guile? He finds he almost can't wait to find out, but he knows these things will happen sooner than he'll want. It's not going to be easy watching them winnow away the list of suitors until they find the right ones. And when that happens, they won't be his little girls any longer.

He pulls open the screen door on the small house they leased on the plains of Kansas, where the land is flat and seems to go on forever, broken only occasionally by trees or telephone poles that stand a silent vigil in the heat of the midday sun. From somewhere in the humid, sticky distance, a crow caws, and he feels a momentary portent of dread flutter across his heart. But why? The day is perfect, the weather calm, and his family waits for him only a few steps away in the small kitchen. He enters the room, and the girls shriek with delight as they leap toward him with no hesitation, even though he's been gone for so many years of their lives that he sometimes feels he barely knows them. His wife's smile is broad and welcoming, and her dark eyes twinkle as she turns from the kitchen counter, forgetting about the lunch she had been about to serve.

"Well, it's about time, stranger!" she says, laughing, her voice

bright and clear.

Behind him, the crow caws again.

The day explodes into bright white light that washes out all the color, turning everything into a hodgepodge of blacks, grays, whites. His daughters shriek, cowering before the brilliant, overpowering flare that scorches their retinas, decimating their vision in an instant. His wife staggers backward, the smile finally wiped from her face as her own eyes are immolated. She crashes against the counter, reaching out with both hands to steady herself.

From behind, a rumble draws near. He likens it to the roar of a subway train closing in on a station, pushing a gust of hot air through the tunnel as it advances. He senses death closing on him, something he's felt before, but this time it approaches with such surety that he knows there is no warding it off. No tricks to play to sidestep it, no weapon to defeat it, no training to help him prepare. He knows what's coming, and he knows his might is as insignificant against it as a drop of water holding back the desert.

The shockwave rolls over him, through him, and slams into the house with such force that the structure buckles immediately. The wave of superheated compressed air brings something else with it—burning, potent radiation that causes the house and those inside it to explode in flame. The girls' screams rise to a tortured keening that is impossibly loud in his ears, then his wife shrieks as well as her clothes disintegrate and her skin reddens and chars before the blistering onslaught. The shockwave does its work, tearing the house away from him before he can take another step, ripping his family away from him as the prairie catches alight—

Mulligan snapped to full consciousness, the ragged scream caught in his throat. The transition from the white-hot world of his nightmare to the semi-darkness of the SCEV's sleeping compartment jarred him, kept him mentally off-balance as he rocked from side to side in the slightly scooped bunk. He turned his head and found his neck was stiff, the tendons and muscles protesting the sudden action. His entire body was sore, essentially one giant ache. He saw a figure sleeping in the bunk across from him, and he recognized it as Jim Laird, his snores barely audible over the whining drone of the SCEV's turbine engines and the creaks and rattles of the rig as it bumped across the landscape. Mulligan slowly swung his legs over the side of the bunk and sat up, his movements sluggish. He sensed more than saw other figures in the compartment's tepid light—Choi, sleeping in the bunk above Laird, and Kelly Jordello, snoozing away in the bunk above his. Kelly murmured something in her sleep and rolled over, but other than that, none of them gave any indication that they had heard the strangled cry that he had tamped down on an instant before it became a full-throated scream.

Mulligan buried his face in hands and softly wept.

Leona looked up from her work at the Command Intelligence Station when the aft shield door opened and a disheveled Mulligan stepped into the second compartment. He looked like hell—bruised and battered, eyes bloodshot. He blinked against the compartment's bright light as he closed the door and moved toward the kitchenette, holding onto the padded rails mounted to the compartment's overhead. Leona smiled at him wryly, but if he saw it, Mulligan ignored her.

Fat chance of that, big guy.

"Welcome back to the world of the living, Sarmajor," she said. "How do you feel?"

"Like a rubber-billed woodpecker who's spent two weeks trying to peck his way through a petrified forest. How long was I out?" Mulligan reached into a cabinet and removed a mug, then slid it into the coffee machine bolted to one wall. He closed the metal fiddle rails around the mug so it wouldn't go flying as the SCEV trundled across broken ground. He stabbed the brew button on the coffee maker, and a second later, the scent of fresh coffee wafted through the air.

"Two and half days. We just came out of the Rockies a few hours ago," Leona told him.

He looked shocked. "Two and a half *days?*"

Leona smiled and shrugged. "Hey, you're not a young buck anymore, Mulligan."

Mulligan scowled and took his mug over to the dinette a few feet away. He slowly lowered himself into its confines, wincing in discomfort. Leona rose from her chair and hobbled over to him, grabbing onto one of his beefy arms with one hand while holding onto the overhead rail with the other. Mulligan's scowl deepened, and he pulled his arm away from her.

"I'm good, Lieutenant," he said brusquely. "Thanks for the assist."

Leona smiled and turned to the kitchenette at her back. She pulled out a bottle of water from the refrigerator and slid into the dinette across from him. "No problem. Mind if I join you?"

Mulligan released a world-weary sigh that said he did indeed mind, but he looked too damn beat to fight her. He carefully sipped his coffee instead, and regarded her over the brim of his mug.

"Any signs of pursuit?"

Leona shook her head. "Negative. Looks like you dusted that guy back in San Jose, Sarmajor. Good shooting. None of us would have thought to use a Hellfire in that way."

Mulligan merely grunted at the compliment and sipped more coffee. "Who's up front?"

"Andrews and Andrews."

Mulligan grunted again. "Thought they were going to keep to separate shifts."

"You and I were out of rotation, but I'm due to go take the right seat so Captain Andrews can knock off. Oh—I have these for you." Leona reached into one of her uniform pockets and pulled out Mulligan's dog tags and the eagle medallion. She fingered the medallion. "Your tags ... and this other thing. Where'd you get it? It's lovely."

Mulligan's bloodshot eyes bugged out when he saw the necklace. He held out one hand, palm up. "What in the hell are you doing with that?" he asked, his voice suddenly tight and constricted.

Leona frowned as she handed the necklace over to him. "I didn't want you strangling on them while you *slept*, Sergeant Major." Her voice was a frosty counterpoint to his.

Mulligan regarded the necklace for an instant, and she saw all of his attention was on the medallion. He looked up at her and nodded curtly. "Thanks for the thought."

Leona said nothing, just stared at the older man openly as he slipped on the necklace and hid it beneath his uniform blouse. *What the hell is it that I see in this guy? Father figure? Protector? Relic? What?*

"What the hell are you looking at, Eklund?" Mulligan asked

with a sudden ferocity that surprised her. She found herself recoiling at the barbs in his voice, and that pissed her off, though more at herself than at him.

"Nothing much, evidently," she managed to say.

Mulligan scowled and gulped some coffee, shifting on the dinette's faux leather wraparound couch. Something crinkled beneath him, and he reached down and pulled out an old comic book. A copy of *The Amazing Spider-Man*, one of Tony Choi's most treasured possessions—the kid had brought them into the base when he'd moved in with his family, and he carried them everywhere. Mulligan snorted derisively when he saw it.

"One of Choi's Asian encyclopedias, I see," he said, dropping it to the table as he took another swig. He regarded the cover for a long moment, then started trying to smooth out its creases. Why would he care about an old comic book, especially one that didn't even belong to him?

Because it's from before, she told herself. *It's like him. A relic.*

"What were you like before the war, Mulligan?" she asked suddenly.

Mulligan leafed through the comic book, keeping his eyes rooted on the somewhat faded but still colorful pages between its covers. She knew her question hit him wrong and pushed him into a space he didn't want to be in, and it was a funny sight watching the hard-bitten Special Forces trooper hide behind a slim edition of *The Amazing Spider-Man*.

"Lieutenant, I'm seriously in no mood for a game of Twenty Questions right now," he said, his voice surprisingly even.

"I watched you while you were out, Mulligan. You were having dreams. Nightmares. Things that seemed to terrify you." She paused to sip from her water. "That guy back in San Jose. Law. He did the same to me, the same thing your nightmares do to you. Break down the wall we've been hiding behind. Made me see things I never even wanted to think about ..."

"Great, we've both been mind-fucked." Mulligan didn't look up from the comic. "You think that means we're finally soul mates or something? Forget it, kid."

"You were crying. Why?"

Mulligan tossed the comic book onto the table and hauled himself off the dinette couch. If he felt any pain from the movement, it didn't register on his face as he got to his feet and drained the remains of his coffee mug, then turned and put the empty vessel in the steel sink. Leona rose as well. She knew that pursuing Mulligan like this was akin to cornering a wounded grizzly bear, but she didn't care. She was aware that of all people, she was incredibly ill-equipped to deal with a man like Mulligan, but she instinctively knew that to understand the man's pain was to know him, to glimpse his soul as it flitted between light and shadow.

"You lost your family in the war, didn't you?"

Mulligan froze for an instant, and Leona could almost see something flip inside of him like a circuit breaker. Mulligan whirled upon her like some thundering war god and seized her arms in his big hands. He swung her around as if she were a doll and pinned her against the padded side of the airlock, causing her to gasp in a queer mixture of fear and something bordering on delight. She'd found what made Mulligan tick, or at least found the path to it, but as she saw the uncontained fury break across his face, she suddenly wondered if she might take the discovery to her rapidly approaching grave.

"*Yes*, they died in the war, along with six billion other people!" Mulligan snarled, and his voice was as tight as a well-tuned snare drum. "And guess what, Eklund? After the missiles dropped, they were still alive for almost four hours! They were in Scott City, some little hick town that was only thirty minutes from Harmony, and I couldn't get to them because of my own *recklessness!*"

Leona writhed in his powerful grip, feeling his thick fingers dig into the flesh and muscle of her upper arms, but there was no escaping the towering man's grip. She would have bruises—if she survived the encounter. Mulligan's eyes were wild, filled with a mixture of pain and rage and despair that had festered unchecked in him for a decade, and even she knew such a combination was as volatile as unstable nitroglycerin.

Suddenly, Mulligan released her and stepped back, his fingers curled into fists, his feet spread wide apart against the swaying of the vehicle. He glared down at her, his chest rising and falling as he took in great deep, ragged breaths.

"Get what you wanted, Lieutenant?" he asked finally, his voice barely audible over the sounds of the rig's passage. "Any other action news updates I can provide, now that we're finally having that warm heart-to-heart you've been after?"

"Don't you ever touch me again," she said. She tried to put steel in her voice, but it sounded pathetic and weak after his fury.

"Then take the hint, girlie—stay the hell away from me."

He turned and marched past her, heading for the cockpit.

Andrews and Rachel were in the cockpit. The day beyond the viewports was hardly bright and accommodating—it looked like another storm was beginning to brew, coalescing on the horizon. He glanced down at the instruments, paying special attention to the radar display, which showed a deepening wall of clutter that rose almost twenty thousand feet into the air, and it was climbing.

"Mind if I sit in on the last leg, Captain?" Mulligan asked.

"Mulligan! How do you feel?" Andrews asked, looking up at him from the confines of the left seat.

Rachel stiffened when she heard his voice, but he ignored her. "Like shit, sir, but that's normal."

"Yeah, well, you should be resting. I hear you're recovering from one hell of a concussion," Andrews said, facing forward.

"Concussion, hangover—who can tell the difference, these days?" Mulligan said, trying to adopt a jovial tone and failing miserably.

"I already have Eklund ready to come forward," Andrews said. "You should rest, Sarmajor."

"I've been out for over two days, Captain. I've had more than enough rest, and I'm a hundred percent operational."

Andrews chuckled. "You said that right before you passed out."

"Yeah, well, that was then, this is now. How about it, sir?"

Andrews glanced up at Mulligan again, then down at the instruments. After a moment of consideration, he nodded slowly. "All right, Sarmajor. But if you start feeling messed up, you let me know and Eklund will take over. Understood?"

"Roger that, sir."

"Take the right seat. Just so you know, the number two differential's blown. It shit the bed about two days ago."

Andrews nodded again, this time to Rachel. Slowly, hesitantly, she unbuckled her safety harness and pushed back the copilot's seat.

"Can it be fixed?" Mulligan asked, twisting to one side to allow her enough room to leave the cockpit. It hurt like hell, and he could feel Leona Eklund staring daggers into his back. Mulligan came to the wry conclusion that he was caught between two women who probably wanted nothing more than to stab him repeatedly in the heart with dull pencils.

Andrews seemed mostly unaware of his predicament, though he did watch Rachel with a casual expression. "Negative, it's completely fragged—can't be repaired without a lift and a hardstand. It's put us another seventeen hours behind schedule." He nodded out the viewports. "And there's another treat: a storm building up to the east. Eklund says it's a big one."

Rachel pushed past Mulligan, her eyes downcast. He released a small sigh. At least she didn't make a dramatic exit, which meant she was either extremely exhausted or her husband had spoken some words of wisdom that she'd taken to heart. Either way, Mulligan was happy to ease himself into the copilot's seat and close the shield door.

"Well, I can tell you one thing, Captain. This mission wasn't a bore."

Andrews rubbed his bristly chin with one hand and nodded. "I'll give you that, Sergeant Major." He studied the instruments and made a small noise in his throat. "That storm's coalescing pretty quickly. The front goes right off the scope."

Mulligan checked the rig's position on the moving map display, and he was surprised to discover just how close they were to Harmony Base. "We're not that far from the signal repeaters. We should have voice contact with the base pretty soon, assuming they have enough power to transmit. No sign of pursuit from California, right?"

"Negative," Andrews said.

Mulligan put some confidence into his voice. "Then we're almost there. We'll make it home without a hitch, Captain. Maybe we should switch on the transponder, so the base'll know we're coming. Just in case we can't make voice contact."

"Good idea," Andrews said, and he pressed a button on the panel before him. "You a man of faith, Sarmajor?"

Mulligan bit back his immediate reply and took a moment to actually consider the question. "I don't know about faith, sir. But the odds look good."

Andrews nodded. After a moment, he looked over at Mulligan, studying him as the enlisted man looked out the viewports. Mulligan watched him from the corner of his eye, wondering why the hell everyone found him so interesting as of late.

"Thanks for coming back for us, Sarmajor," Andrews said finally. He turned forward and monitored the rig's progress as it traveled on under the guidance of the autopilot. "And I'm sorry we didn't at least try and return the favor."

Mulligan was surprised by the sudden sentiment, but he didn't let it show. Besides, his face was so battered that adopting a surprised look would probably hurt like hell. "Forget it, sir. If I had any sense at all, I would've died back there. You had five people to take care of, and a mission to complete. If I'd been in your boots, I would have made tracks, too." He paused for a moment. "Besides, life hasn't been a barrel of laughs, lately. Dying's nothing I'm afraid of, believe me."

"Maybe you ought to alter your outlook a bit? You're still alive, and some folks care—"

"Yeah, sir, thanks a lot, but let's not go there, okay? We're still on an ongoing mission, so let's keep our minds focused on that." He faced Andrews directly. "Okay, sir?"

Andrews met Mulligan's gaze evenly and held it. "Roger that. But I want to tell you something, Mulligan. I was wrong about you. Having you on the roster wasn't such a bad idea, after all."

Mulligan snorted. "Who're *you* trying to kid? Letting Benchley talk me onto this rig was the biggest mistake I've made in years. I'm way too old for the Iron Man act. I should've stayed in the dark with everyone else." Almost against his will, Mulligan was surprised to add, "But, uh ... thanks anyway, sir."

Andrews nodded and turned away, apparently satisfied with Mulligan's response. Mulligan busied himself by running some diagnostics on the rig's drivetrain components, hoping that if he looked busy enough, Andrews wouldn't be tempted to make any more maudlin chitchat.

LAW EXAMINED THE growing storm with some trepidation, watching as it billowed and grew on the horizon. While the SCEV had handled itself admirably—it even continued rolling along its course when Law had, very much against his will, fallen asleep in the pilot's seat—the storm front was simply gigantic, stretching from horizon to horizon ... and it was still over fifty miles away. Great flashes of lightning illuminated the pulsating formation's innards, and a wall of wind—a gust front, he remembered from his earlier days—had already swept over the SCEV, sending clouds of dust flying across the vehicle's viewports. To say the tempest was intimidating was a massive understatement.

Will this be the end? he wondered. *Will this storm destroy the vehicle, or just give Andrews enough cover to return to this base of his?*

Either way, I'm dead.

Law had not taken the time to stop at any of the caches on the way back to Harmony Base, so the SCEV was critically low on fuel. He had only a couple of hundred miles left, then the rig would be reduced to battery power. After that, he would have—according to the computer display in front of him—another thirty hours of power before the SCEV became inoperable. Given the rather toxic environment outside the vehicle, it was obvious he wouldn't survive for long after that happened.

There had been no sign of his quarry. Had Andrews and his remaining crew taken another route? Had they been delayed somewhere in their travels, and he had passed them by in the darkness? Had he been wrong in assuming that his lightened rig would be able to catch up to Andrews's heavier one? Had they deviated from their course to take on more fuel at one of the caches?

He just didn't know.

But I'm close. He regarded the moving map display. Harmony Base was only a hundred or so miles to the east, buried beneath the gently rolling landscape of dry earth and desiccated grass and the occasional twisted, rotting tree. *I'm close, so even if I get there ahead of them, I can simply wait for them.* He judged that he could extend his survival by several days if he shut down the rig and conserved fuel and power, laying in wait for his prey. The interferometers positioned along the rig's exterior shell—basically a series of antennae designed to receive electromagnetic pulses along certain spectra—would alert him to SCEV Five's approach, presuming Andrews was running with the ground-search radar enabled. And why wouldn't he? There was no reason for him to disable it. Even if he was operating it at minimal power, as Law was doing, the SCEV's receivers would detect the pulses of millimeter-wave radar energy long before Andrews and the others could get a solid return that showed his location. While in the Marine Corps a lifetime ago, when the planet was still green and fertile, Law had learned that radar energy was detectable far beyond the range of its own receiver, which was one reason that pilots and warships had practiced emissions control, limiting their use of technologies that could give away their location before they were ready to engage the enemy. Perhaps he could use that to his advantage—

A chime sounded over the cockpit speakers and, for a moment, Law was overcome by terror. Had Andrews found him? Was his vehicle being targeted by another rig, hidden somewhere out on the landscape?

He scanned the displays and saw he had been given a remarkable gift. SCEV Five's transponder had been activated, and it emitted a string of data.

Including the rig's position, just seventeen short miles ahead of him.

Law almost laughed out loud. The other vehicle was moving at less than forty miles per hour, which meant he would catch up to it in less than sixty minutes. He reached for the map display and zoomed out, examining the surrounding terrain. There was a small line of ridges that stood above the plain twenty-five miles ahead. If he could get to them in time, they would provide Law a clear view of the area, and he would be able to look down on SCEV Five as it rolled past.

Law dropped a waypoint onto the ridged area by dragging a finger across the map display's touch screen, and the SCEV obediently altered its course.

Soon, Andrews. Soon.

As they closed to within fifty miles of Harmony Base, Andrews slipped on his radio headset, switched one of the radios over to the approach frequency, and pressed down on the TRANSMIT button on the control column. "Harmony Base, this is SCEV Five. Over." He released the button and heard nothing but static-tinged emptiness crackling across his earphones. He tried again. "Harmony Base, this is SCEV Five. We're inbound to you now. Can you give us a SITREP? Over."

A faint voice came through the static interference, vague but distinct. "SCEV Five, Harmony Base. Stand by for Harmony Six. Over."

"Roger that, Harmony. Over." Andrews looked over at Mulligan. "Well, we get to talk to the Old Man himself."

"The wonders of modern communications technology never cease to amaze me, sir," Mulligan said. He donned his own headset and adjusted the boom microphone. "I hope he picks up soon. We're going to lose commo once that storm hits."

A low whine came across the radio as Benchley spoke, his voice barely audible above the background noise.

"SCEV Five, this is Harmony Six. SITREP. Over."

"Harmony Six, this is SCEV Five. We have three supports. One soul and one rig lost. Number two differential is gone, but all other systems are green. ETA in just over one hour, but we're on a storm run. Is there any way you can you boost your signal output? We can barely read you. Over."

Lightning flared in the storm, and the radios were awash with static. Benchley responded, but Andrews couldn't make out the words.

"Harmony Six, negative contact. Over."

Again, Benchley's voice came across the radio, horribly distorted and drowned out by the rising tide of white noise. Andrews repeated his situation report and again reported negative contact, hoping that those in Harmony Base might be able to hear it.

Mulligan stirred in the copilot's seat. "We should still be able to establish voice contact at this range," he said. "They must've burned through the auxiliary power faster than they thought."

"Damn," Andrews said. He had an ominous vision of a darkened Harmony Base, the air stale and filled with the stench of sweat and untreated waste, the personnel inside the subterranean fortress fighting to draw enough oxygen from the carbon dioxide-saturated air. Had more people died? Would even more die over the next hour?

Could they even send the vehicle lift to the surface to retrieve them?

"Transmit our status over the data link," he told Mulligan. "Ask them to raise the lift, so we can at least make it that far."

Mulligan's fingers flew over the instrument panel as he executed the captain's command. "Done."

Andrews pressed the button that opened the pressure door separating the cockpit from the second compartment. "Leona, you still back there?"

She appeared at the doorway a moment later. "You want me to come forward?" she asked, glancing over at Mulligan.

"Negative—we're close enough to Harmony that we'll keep the staffing as it is right now. Get everyone else up and ready. We've got about a hundred klicks to go, and that storm is going to be on the doorstep by the time we get there. Let me know when everyone's awake and strapped in. We've got to move a little faster."

"Roger that." She looked at Mulligan again. The big NCO ignored her, but there was some tension there. Andrews found himself wondering what was up between them.

Later, he told himself as Leona withdrew. Andrews sealed the pressure door again and peered through the viewports. Dust was blowing across the dead fields, driven by the storm's gust front. It wasn't heavy enough to vastly reduce visibility, but that was coming. By the time they made it to Harmony, they'd be half-blind despite the radar, infrared, and the rig's rather impressive array of floodlights.

"We're good to go back here," Leona said over the intercom a few minutes later. "Everyone's strapped down. Open her up."

"Cool. Thanks," Andrews replied. He switched off the autopilot and pushed the control column forward. The SCEV accelerated, picking up speed until it was dashing across the landscape at almost fifty miles per hour. He had to slow when it rolled up to a series of ridges, but he stuck to the narrow defiles between them, using them as avenues to shield the rig from the mounting wind. It took only a few minutes, then they were back on the plain. Andrews pushed the control column forward again, coaxing the big rig into an all-out sprint across the more-or-less flat terrain. Even with the rig's sturdy suspension, the ride was hardly a comfortable one.

A series of loud *bangs* cut through the air. Andrews swept his gaze across the instrument panel and reduced power, thinking the machine's drivetrain was experiencing another failure. But the combined moving map and radar display froze up, and a single message flashed across the screen: SYSTEM INOP: HARDWARE FAILURE.

He was trying to process what had happened when he felt the control column move forward with such intensity that it was almost ripped from his grasp. Mulligan had slammed the copilot's control column full forward, until it literally banged against the control stop.

"We're taking fire!" he snapped.

It couldn't be more perfect.

Law positioned the SCEV atop one of the ridges that overlooked the plain and eased it slightly downslope, where he hoped the miniguns would have a full field of fire. Just to be sure, he slewed them from side to side once he had set the SCEV's brakes, then checked elevation and depression. Both weapons would be able to engage SCEV Five, which approached Law's position from the southwest. Thanks to godsend of transponder technology, he was able to monitor his enemy's progress across the wasteland without needing to resort to the millimeter-wave radar system to paint the target. That would only serve to alert Andrews and his crew, and Law was in no mood to sacrifice surprise just yet. While the SCEV carried several thousand rounds of tungsten-cored 7.62 millimeter bullets, he knew they would be mostly ineffective against the SCEV's armored hide. In fact, they couldn't even reliably defeat the rig's tires, which were constructed out of a self-sealing honeycombed polymer. But the radome on top of the vehicle wasn't armored at all, beyond a fiberglass shell that was transparent to radar. Beneath the shell lay the radar scanner itself. Law knew if he damaged that, he would also take out the vehicle's anti-missile defenses, which the helpful electronic manuals he had read during his voyage informed him required a radar contact to act against. With both the radar and AMW system down, Law could target Andrews's SCEV with a Hellfire missile. Since the weapon was designed to destroy even densely armored main battle tanks, SCEV Five would be easy prey.

All too easy.

There was no indication that Andrews and the rest of the crew aboard SCEV Five had seen him as he dashed past them, his vehicle a vague phantom in the storm-blown dust that swirled over the plain. He had come within five hundred meters from SCEV Five, and he had caught momentary glimpses of it through the roiling dust. It was moving much slower than his own vehicle. Was that because Andrews was being conservative in their approach, or was the vehicle damaged? Was there something about the local topology that necessitated a more deliberate speed? Law found nothing unusual in the vehicle's electronic navigation system, and it had updated itself during the outbound voyage from Harmony Base. By the time he had reached the top of the highest ridge, he knew he had nothing to fear. The speed of SCEV Five was nothing of importance; he would simply have to wait in his ambush for several extra minutes until the target drew past.

There it was.

SCEV Five emerged onto the flat plain below, no more than eighty yards to the right of the ridge Law's vehicle sat on. He had only seconds to act before the other rig's radar detected his vehicle amidst the clutter of the ridgeline—the hard, metal shape of SCEV Four would be difficult to conceal in such an elevated position. But he had prepared himself for quick action, and the miniguns on the rig's nose were capable of being aimed and fired optically, so he merely slewed the turreted weapons to the right, laid the electronically-generated crosshairs across SCEV Five's form, allowed the computer to correct for windage, and fired. Two muted columns of flame erupted from the rig's nose as the electrically driven miniguns unleashed their salvo of rounds, and SCEV Five was suddenly besieged by a hail of muted sparks as the bullets struck it at a quartering angle. Law fired the rounds across the top of the vehicle's MEP, where the radome was located, and he was rewarded by the sight of fiberglass exploding into shards that whirled through the air, before the wind caught them and sent them fluttering off to the west. For an instant, he caught a glimpse of the radome's interior parts, including the millimeter-wave scanner array. Then it too disintegrated as several rounds smashed through it, shattering sensitive electronics, before the SCEV began executing a series of clumsy evasive gyrations. More bullets pelted the vehicle, raking across its side and rear. Law ceased fire and tracked the target, then ripped off several more bursts as it accelerated away. The rounds struck the rear of the rig, but other than shearing off an antenna, denting some metal, and tearing away a coating of slick paint, they did nothing more than further mar the already dirty vehicle's appearance. Law secured the miniguns and went for the missiles. He raised the pod and switched SCEV Four's own radar array into targeting mode, his fingers dancing over the fire control system, then across the display he had dedicated for the purpose of engaging SCEV Five with the Hellfire missile system. The radar locked onto SCEV Five's fleeing figure instantly, but he was surprised to discover he couldn't fire on the vehicle—the firing button on the display was grayed out. He tried the physical button on the control yoke, but the results were the same: no missile would launch. He understood the problem quickly. The fire control computer had image recognition capability, and it had automatically refused to fire on an SCEV until Law cleared the warning message flashing on the touch screen display. He did so, and the firing button became active again. Law pressed the button and was rewarded with a chime indicating positive launch. A brief *hiss* sounded as the missile left the launch rails and arced toward SCEV Five.

All too easy, Law thought again.

Andrews silenced the blaring alarms, content to allow Mulligan to do whatever he needed to keep the vehicle from being hit again. He thumbed through the engineering display and found the radar was, in fact, quite dead; there were warnings that said the dome was unlatched, but he knew that wasn't the case. It had been destroyed by a hail of steel rain. More importantly, the sensitive components inside it had met a similar fate. More bullets raked across the SCEV's back, making scattered pinging noises as they ricocheted off the rig's armored hide. Andrews put the AMW system under manual control; without the radar, they wouldn't deploy automatically. They could still be fired from the cockpit, just without the extreme precision of a radar launch.

"Stand ready on those things," Mulligan said. "If your friend lobs a missile at us, it's the only system we've got that's going to matter. Can't be sure that chaff will work very well in this wind."

Andrews grunted, then spoke into his headset microphone. "Harmony Base, SCEV Five—we're taking fire, rig status coming your way now! Over!" As he spoke, he transmitted the SCEV's engineering condition to the base. There was no response, of course, as the storm's static discharges were interfering with the communications, filling the frequencies with ululating bursts of white noise. He hoped the data burst would make it through, but there was no guarantee of that, either. He set the system to rebroadcast the rig's status every two seconds, in the hope that one of the data bursts would make it through.

Another alarm sounded, one that Andrews had only heard in training: one of the IR receivers mounted on the rig's hull had detected a sudden heat bloom, which meant a missile had been launched. The tactical display indicated the shot had originated approximately three hundred meters behind and to the left; he immediately deployed two bursts of chaff, waited a half-second, then popped off one of the anti-missile warheads. The unit leapt out of its niche and, a moment later, a dull explosion could be heard somewhere to the rear of the rig. Andrews held his breath for a couple of seconds, then released it in a rush. They were still alive. A Hellfire would have caught them by now if it hadn't been destroyed by the AMW or lost its radar lock from the chaff.

Can it reacquire us in this?

He hoped the obscuration generated by the storm would work to their advantage. He knew the radar-seeker in each

Hellfire's nose would energize upon breaking target lock, and that the weapon would climb to reacquire the rig with its own internal millimeter-wave system.

Apparently not. Another alarm sounded, indicating a second launch. Andrews repeated the procedure, feeling a cold, clammy sweat break out across his forehead and scalp as his heart pounded in his chest. Mulligan muttered a curse, working the control column and sending the rig into a series of violent gyrations. There was another distant *thud* as the AMW exploded, but Andrews kept pumping out the chaff anyway as the radar warning receiver continued to trill its song. Mulligan cranked the rig hard to the left, almost seeming to turn it in the middle of the plain—

The world seemed to explode right outside the viewport beside Mulligan, and the rig lurched in an odd way, rising up on its left tires as something slammed into it. The horizon rolled, and the thunderous cacophony of screeching metal and shattering plastics filled the air. The displays flickered, and the master caution warning alert blared as Andrews reached for the control column on his side and pulled it hard to the right, only to find it was already contacting the control stop.

"Fuck!"

The SCEV rolled over onto its side and, victim of its own momentum, continued rolling until it skidded across the plain on its back, the view through the viewports dimming as earth and a cloud of dust washed across them, turning almost black.

23

THE WORLD HAD turned upside down, and Andrews couldn't quite make sense of it.

The cockpit was mostly dark, illuminated only by glowing warning annunciators and the anemic flickering of LED displays. Something kept going *beep-beep-beep* with a metronomic regularity, but Andrews couldn't figure out what it was. He felt confused and disoriented, and there was a growing pressure in his head. The straps over his shoulders felt incredibly tight, as if the gravity reels had attempted to retract the entire harness, pulling him against the seatback. He blinked in the semi-darkness; all he could hear above the beeping alarm was the *tick* and *pop* of cooling metal and electronics. Outside, the wind howled, loud enough to be heard through the rig's thick hide.

The wind blew away a coating of dust on one corner of the viewport, and Andrews knew that the world was actually right side up. It was the SCEV that was upside down.

Oh, fuck ... we're on our back!

"Come on, Andrews!"

Andrews saw movement beside him, and he looked over to see Mulligan brace himself against the cockpit overhead before he hit his harness's quick release. He tumbled out of his seat and sprawled across the overhead, the weight of his body snapping off several plastic switches on the panel. He squirmed around on the panel until he was able to sit upright, and he looked at Andrews hanging down beside him like some ridiculous giant bat.

"Captain, are you hurt?" he asked.

Andrews considered the question, and decided he felt mostly fine. He shook his head. "I'm good."

"Then let's get the fuck out of here, sir. We've got battery power available, but that's it."

"What happened?" Andrews put a hand on the overhead—now below him—as Mulligan had done, and released his harness. He half-fell out of his seat, braced by his arm and his legs slamming into the bottom of the instrument panel. That hurt.

"Must've been a near-hit by that last missile," Mulligan

said. "I guess it broke lock, reacquired it, but couldn't maneuver fast enough to put steel right on target. Must've hit the deck right next to us as I was turning, and the blast flipped us over." Mulligan regarded the instrument panel, then flipped a switch to shut off the beeping alarm. "We're not going any further in this crate, unless you happen to have a Triple A membership."

Andrews extricated himself from beneath the instrument panel. "What are you talking about?"

"Never mind," Mulligan said dryly, pulling open the pressure door. It squealed in its track, then stopped suddenly when it was only halfway open. Mulligan tugged on it with both hands and wrenched it open a few inches at a time, until there was enough space for the two men to slide into the next compartment.

The lounge compartment was a mess. Lockers had burst open, spilling their contents. The rest of the SCEV crew lay on what once was previously the overhead. Laird and Leona lay in a bleeding, twisted heap just outside the cockpit door. Andrews reached for them and gently began to pull them apart.

"Jim? Lee? You guys all right?"

"I think so," Leona said, blinking in the dim emergency lighting. She seemed dazed and unfocused.

Laird was anything but, and he shoved her in the shoulder. "Then get the hell off of me!"

Andrews found there was enough room to stand, so he got to his feet and picked his way past the pair as they unwound themselves with Mulligan's help. Across from the dining settee, Rachel and Choi tended to Kelly, who lay quite still. The precious core supports sat next to her, having exploded out of their locker and shattering the dining table in the process as they hurtled from one side of the SCEV to the other. Andrews picked his way to Rachel's side and put a hand on her shoulder.

"Babe? You okay?"

She nodded and glanced over her shoulder, looking up at him for a moment before turning back to Kelly. "I'm good, but one of the core supports tagged Kelly in the leg. I think it's a bad break."

"Christ. Can she be moved?"

Rachel watched as Choi gingerly felt along one of Kelly's legs. Andrews noticed it was bent at an unnatural angle near the base of her thigh, the flesh there hard and mostly unyielding beneath Choi's probing fingers. Choi looked up at Andrews, his usually affable features marred by concern.

"I don't know about that, sir. This looks *severely* messed up," he said.

"Make a hole, make it wide," Mulligan snapped. Andrews stepped aside as far as he could, and Mulligan squeezed in beside Rachel. He knelt next to Kelly and examined her injured leg, and none too gently. "Choi, you have knife?"

"Yeah." Choi reached around and pulled a folding knife from his pocket, opened it, and handed it to Mulligan. The sergeant major cut open her uniform over the injury site and ripped it open, baring her entire leg. Choi started to remove her boot, but Mulligan stopped him with a wave. He turned the knife back to Choi and continued exploring the wound. Sure enough, there was an angry red impact site on her leg, just above the knee, and it was swelling considerably. Mulligan shook his head with a sigh.

"It's a closed break, so that's better than her bleeding out. We'll need to get a splint on her right now, and have something ready for the pain if she comes to. If we take it easy, she'll be okay." Mulligan turned and looked back at Leona as she pulled herself upright, wincing at the pain in her own leg. "Lieutenant Eklund, you're a medical officer ... What do you think, codeine?"

Leona nodded. "Choi, there should be some injectable codeine phosphate in the medical locker behind you." The locker's door was bent inward, probably from one of the core supports crashing into it. "If you can get it open, I'll give her a dose right now. The vacuum splints are there, as well, in red bags. Pull out a medium unit and the pump."

"I'll treat her, Lieutenant," Mulligan said. "I've done this sort of thing before, and the codeine's an intramuscular injection, so that's easy. Just tell me what dosage to administer."

"Sixty milligrams should be enough for the next few hours, Sergeant Major," Leona said. Her voice was curiously brittle, but if Mulligan picked up on it, he didn't show it.

"So what else did they teach you at Fort Bragg, Sarmajor?" Andrews asked.

"A little of this, a little of that. You want to see something really special, remind me to whip up some of my famous five-alarm chili. It killed a Texan once." He looked up as Choi yanked open the medical locker and pawed through the disorganized contents. He found the splint first, then the small bottle of pain medication. He handed them over to Mulligan, who looked at Choi expectantly.

"I need a hypodermic, dumbass," he said finally.

"Oh. Sorry." Choi turned back to the medical locker, rummaged through it a little more gently this time, and pulled out a plastic of individually wrapped hypodermics. Mulligan filled one with the prescribed medication.

"Mike, what the hell happened?" Laird asked. "Did we actually take fire out here?"

Andrews nodded. "Affirmative. Looks like Law and some of his pals are still in possession of my rig. The bastard must've been chasing us across half the country, then split off and set up an ambush when he caught up to us."

Laird's eyes widened. "But we've been averaging almost a hundred klicks an hour and had a day's lead time, at least!"

"He must've stripped down the rig to increase its speed. Once we lost the differential, it was only a matter of time until he caught up to us—he just had to follow the e-nav. He's still out there, too. We can't stay here."

Leona frowned. "Mike, there's a storm front moving in. Even in full gear, the sievert count'll be high enough to kill us!"

"We're not going to survive in here either," Andrews said. "We just happen to be the proverbial sitting duck." He turned to Mulligan. "You're the survival expert here, Sarmajor. Any tips?"

"Don't look at me—I've used up my quota of miracles on this trip." Mulligan administered the injection, then capped the used syringe and tossed it into the plastic box. "We'll need to suit her up before I can put on the splint. Choi, you're going to help me. We need to be careful, because we could pop an artery if we move her too much."

"And I could scream," Kelly said breathlessly. Even though her eyes were closed, she was coming out of it. She was sweating slightly, and her blond hair was stuck to her forehead. Deep circles were forming under her eyes.

"Hey, take it easy," Andrews told her. "We'll do our best to make sure you don't get hurt any further, all right?"

"That'd be awesome," Kelly said, her voice faint and weak.

"Don't worry, XO," Laird said. "I'll bust heads if anyone does anything stupid."

Kelly smiled vaguely, then seemed to drop out again.

"All right, let's get suited up. We're abandoning the rig," Andrews said. "We'll go with full environmental gear, including respirators. I don't like the fact that someone might be shooting at us while we've got air tanks on our backs, but we're not going to live very long without them."

"Aren't you forgetting something?" Laird asked. "The supports?"

"Too heavy. We'd never be able to hump those things out of here and our wounded at the same time."

"Mike—those are the things we need to get back to Harmony!"

"They'll be fine," Rachel said. "Even if the rig is destroyed, they'll survive. You already know how heavy they are, and the weight is because they're extremely dense. Fire won't harm them, and only shaped charges would be likely to make them unusable. It's safe to leave them here, Captain."

Laird shrugged. "Well, you're the SME," he said. "All right, crew. Let's suit up."

Andrews looked at Rachel and smiled at her as the others started prepping to leave the overturned rig. "I'll bet you're glad you came, huh?"

She took his hand. "I wouldn't have missed this for the world. Besides, for better or worse, right?"

"Yeah, well, I hadn't thought things could get much worse, but here we are," Andrews said, turning to the suit locker and pulling open its heavy door.

24

THE AIRLOCK WAS inoperable, and they discovered the SCEV's tailgate was also not available for use—the big loading door had been jammed shut in its frame when the rig rolled onto its back. That meant everyone would have to disembark via one of the side viewports in the cockpit, which could be used as an emergency exit. Loaded down with respiration gear and weapons—as well as one immobile crewmember and one walking wounded, exiting via the cockpit was no small chore. It took Andrews almost a minute to clear the vehicle and emerge into the wind-torn day. He conducted a brief security scan— there wasn't much to see, especially with all the loose dust blowing around—then turned back and assisted Leona in exiting the dead SCEV. Rachel and Choi came next, then Mulligan, and they all helped him pull Kelly Jordello's still form through the opening, handling her as gently as they could. Andrews saw her eyes were open but glassy behind her visor. Either she had slipped deep into shock, or the codeine was strong enough to dope her up. Laird was the last to emerge, and it took him quite some time to fumble his way out of the vehicle. Once he did, the crew looked toward the eastern horizon.

Through the blowing dust, Andrews saw the brewing storm squatting on the horizon, a dark mound illuminated by brief bursts of internal pyrotechnics. A malignant mass, pregnant with the promise of death.

"Look at the size of that front," Leona said, awe clear in her voice when she spoke over her mask's transceiver.

"I see it," Andrews said. He turned in a half-circle, trying to get an idea of the terrain. He recognized the general area, but it wasn't until the wind ebbed for a moment and the dust began to settle that he saw a low-lying ridge several hundred meters to their left. He pointed it out to Laird. "Jim, get everyone to that ridge over there. Hide in the rocks. Choi and I will hang back and give you some cover for as long as we can." He turned to Mulligan. "Sarmajor, you go on ahead. Try to make it to Harmony's perimeter. Someone's got to be watching for us."

Mulligan scowled behind his visor. "What? I can't leave

now."

"The odds are what they are, Sergeant Major." Andrews felt suddenly weary, and he wished he could rub his burning eyes, but the full facemask of his respirator prevented it. "They won't change very much if you stay. And you've got the skills—if anyone can survive in this shit, it's you."

Mulligan stood where he was, looking directly at Andrews. His scowl was gone now, replaced by an odd look Andrews hadn't seen before. Was it respect, or something else?

"Hit the road, Sergeant Major," he said finally, when Mulligan made no move to obey. "That's what we call an order, just in case that flew over your head the first time."

The two men looked at each other for another moment, then Mulligan shifted his rifle and reached into the knapsack that hung from his side. He pulled out three forty-millimeter grenades and handed them to Andrews.

"Here, take these. They're old, but they'll still work. Standard M441 rounds, nothing fancy and nothing that'll be likely to take out an SCEV. But if you can get a shot at the radome, take it. Otherwise, they'll be about as effective as a frying pan."

"Hey, better than nothing," Andrews said. He had two of the SCEV's original loadout of forty-millimeter grenades, and Choi had the last one. He handed two to Choi and kept one for himself.

"Good luck, sir. I'll be back," Mulligan said. Without further ado, he ran off, keeping to a crouch and heading due east.

"Jim, get the others to the ridge," Andrews said.

Rachel took one of his gloved hands in her own. "Mike, I'd really like to stay with you."

Andrews shook his head. "No way, hon. There's nothing more you can do down here. Get to the ridge and hunker down. Help will come, believe me." He smiled at her, even though she couldn't see the lower half of his face. "No heroics here, I promise."

She looked at him keenly for a long moment. "I hope not." She reached out and touched his mask. "I can't even kiss you good-bye."

"Then kiss me hello later," he said.

"Andrews, I'm going to need help with Lieutenant Jordello,"

Laird said to Rachel.

"Get going," Andrews told Rachel. He nodded to where Laird and Leona stood over Kelly's supine form. She wore a vacuum splint on her injured leg, which had in turn been bound to her uninjured limb by several cravats.

"On it, Captain," she said to Laird, slowly turning away from Andrews. She helped Laird haul Kelly into a fireman's carry, despite the fact the splinted leg made the action awkward. Laird didn't seem to notice, and he set off toward the rock-strewn ridge hovering in the distance. Leona followed, hobbling on her injured leg, an assault rifle in her hands. Rachel looked back at Andrews for a moment, then turned to join them. The wind began to blow again, and the billowing dust swallowed them from view.

"Choi, ready?" Andrews asked.

"You know it, sir," Choi responded immediately.

"All right. About three hundred meters to the south, there's that region of rocky outcrops. You know which one I'm talking about?"

"Yes, sir."

"That's where we're headed. Follow me, and keep low." Andrews headed off in the opposite direction from Laird and the others, keeping low and moving as quickly as he could through the flying dust. He glanced back occasionally to ensure Choi was still with him, but he kept moving. They were out in the open and, for the life of him, he couldn't understand why they weren't already dead.

Law had laughed aloud when he saw his second missile strike the ground near the SCEV and the resulting explosion that lifted its right tires high into the air. The rig seemed to hang there for a moment, like a stunt driver doing a trick in one of the mindless adventure films he had watched as a youth, and for an instant he thought it would slam back to the ground and continue on. But slowly, inexorably, the rig leaned further to the left until the chance of recovery died. The SCEV grounded on its left side, tearing a huge gash in the dry earth as it slid along for several meters before turning turtle, crashing onto its back in an explosion of dust. Bits and pieces of the vehicle flew through the air as panels and antennae and even the forward-looking infrared scanner and one tire were shorn off by the force of the impact. The vehicle ground to an abrupt halt, and columns of steam and smoke erupted from its undercarriage.

Law had to confess, it had been quite some time since he'd seen anything so beautiful.

He moved to fire a final missile, which would surely strike true and blast the vehicle into flaming wreckage. Right before his fingertip touched the button on the LED display, he stopped, pulling his hand back to his side.

I want to see them. I want to see them die with my own eyes, if I can.

In order to do that, he would have to reverse course and navigate around the ridges. The upthrust he was parked on had far too sheer a face to safely maneuver the vehicle across, and he had no intention of dying out here with Andrews and the others. So, he cautiously reversed the rig in the direction he had come.

Andrews and Choi set up in the rocky abutments several hundred meters from the overturned SCEV. The wind continued to mount, and dust swirled through the air. Andrews made sure the dust cover on his assault rifle was closed, then checked to ensure the grenade launcher was ready to go. He hadn't heard anything from Laird or the others, nor did he expect to; they were to observe radio silence unless something untoward occurred. Even though their channels were encrypted, Law had military experience, and it was conceivable he could use the signal-hopping radios in SCEV Four to find the channels reserved for their use. Not very likely, of course—while Leona had been very informative in describing to Law how to use the vehicle, he had only had access to her for a few hours, and something such as spoofing an encrypted communications channel likely hadn't been one of his priorities.

In the distance, through the billowing clouds of dust, Andrews caught a glimpse of movement.

SCEV Four appeared, bouncing out of the ridgeline. Once it made it down to the flat plain, it accelerated toward the overturned hulk of SCEV Five. Andrews looked to his left, where Choi was positioned about fifty meters downrange. Choi met his gaze and he nodded, pointing at his grenade launcher. Andrews motioned for him to hold his fire. There was no sense in alerting Law to their presence if he already thought they might be dead.

He turned his attention back to the SCEV as it advanced through the dimming light of the day. It stopped two hundred meters from the wrecked vehicle and sat there, its turbine engines whining, missile pod extended, miniguns oriented toward SCEV Five. The FLIR turret on the rig's nose slewed left and right, as Law used the optics to surveil the area. After thirty seconds or so, the rig began to trundle forward, slowly bumping its way across the plain, drawing closer to SCEV Five's shattered form. It circled the dead rig, slowing every now and then, the FLIR turret turned toward it, as if Law thought he could use the device to peer through the armored hulk and see what lay inside. The rig circled around the wreckage twice before it accelerated back toward the ridge. Two hundred meters away, it turned back until its snout was pointing more or less at the destroyed SCEV.

Come on, guy ... Get it over with.

Andrews didn't have to wait for long. Seconds later, another Hellfire missile leapt out of the extended pod on SCEV Four's back and roared across the darkening plain on a pillar of fire. Andrews had only an instant to crouch down behind the rocks he was using as cover before the projectile climbed up, gained altitude, and nosed down. It slammed into the overturned rig's belly and exploded. Even several hundred meters away, Andrews was shocked by the ferocity of the explosion. One moment, the wrecked SCEV was there, the next, most of it vanished in a gout of flame and smoke and thunder that sent a shockwave racing across the wasteland. The missile managed to decimate the rig's self-sealing fuel tanks and ignite the propellant that remained inside. The remains of the SCEV began to burn, bright and furious, the flames dancing in the gale that carried the black smoke to the west. A moment later, pieces of debris began raining down on him. Something clanged against one of the rocks beside him, and Andrews saw it was an access plate to one of the MEP electronics racks, twisted and burned.

Just like the remainder of SCEV Five.

Andrews peeked around the rock, exposing half of his face. He knew the suits the team wore would help mask their thermal image, but the FLIR on SCEV Four was extremely sensitive; if Law knew what to look for, he might see a small sliver of heat through the gloom. That would be bad news for all of them. He watched as the SCEV sat unmoving, while SCEV Five continued to burn. A sudden series of pops erupted from the flaming vehicle as the 7.62 millimeter rounds in its magazines cooked off in firecracker-like detonations, which were made tinny and insignificant by the howling wind. Andrews studied the idling rig for a full minute, watching the vehicle's FLIR slew from side to side.

What the hell is he waiting for?

Law sat in the cool, climate-controlled environment of SCEV Four's cockpit, his right hand on the FLIR control yoke. The immense heat given off by the burning rig distorted a good portion of the infrared picture, and the mounting wind began to drive flying dust even harder, which made visual inspection of the conflagration even more problematic. The vehicle's millimeter-wave radar returned nothing suspicious; there was no sudden movement in the wasteland other than that driven by the winds, and the only sizeable metallic signature was on its back before him, burning away.

Still, Law wasn't convinced. Andrews and the others had had ample time to evacuate the overturned SCEV, unless they had a procedure in place to sit tight and wait for rescue. But would they do such a thing when they were under attack? Would they follow the usual SOP when they knew an armed aggressor was closing on them? Had they all been killed, or so severely injured during the rollover that they had been unable to exit the vehicle?

Judging by the sturdy straps that kept him anchored to the pilot's seat of SCEV Four, and the numerous straps and handholds spread throughout the rig, he rather thought death and injury, while possible, was unlikely. At least for the entire crew.

He began tracking the FLIR to the left, away from the burning remains of SCEV Five. To the left, the landscape rose slowly into a series of small, low-lying ridges. Law panned the sensitive infrared device across them, zooming in occasionally when a feature caught his interest, but for the most part, the landmarks were rather unremarkable and, like the rest of the plain, exhibited a definite lack of life.

Something moved among the rocky ridgeline. Law zoomed in on it immediately, and he caught a quick glimpse of a head peering over the rock, a head that was hidden beneath a white hood and a gas mask of some sort. Definitely a person, and whatever he or she wore very closely resembled the same suits Andrews and the others had been wearing in San Jose. The heat signature was barely above the ambient temperature of the ridge itself. If he hadn't been paying close attention, he would have missed it. As he watched, the head dipped down behind the rock, disappearing from view.

Law slewed the miniguns in that direction and ripped off a burst, watching as the 7.62 millimeter rounds pulverized rock and earth, sending great gouts of dried soil exploding into the air. He walked the turrets from side to side, strafing the entire area until it disappeared beneath a cloud of dust and fragments of shattered rock. He ceased fire. He was down to just over seven hundred rounds of ammunition in the SCEV's magazines. He would have to be less indulgent in the future. Zooming in with the FLIR, he surveyed the target site, looking for any sign of life. As the dust cleared, he saw no movement, nothing that resembled a human being. That could mean they were either dead, or the attack had been ineffective—there was a good amount of rock sticking out of the ridge, and if the survivors from SCEV Five had managed to dig in or find a depression in which to lie, the minigun attack might have been useless.

A missile should take care of that.

When SCEV Four suddenly opened fire on the ridgeline he had directed the others to, Andrews knew the gig was up. Law had seen something up there that had attracted his attention, and the target area was too close to where he believed Laird had led the others. He gauged Four's position to be just inside the max range of a forty-millimeter grenade, but figured the wind might give an attack a little more reach. When he saw the Hellfire missile turret rotate to the left, Andrews figured he had no time to sweat it. He had to act.

He raised his rifle, flipped up the grenade launcher's windage sight, aimed for the missile pod, and fired.

And prayed.

Law jumped back in his seat as something exploded against the copilot's viewport, filling the cockpit with a thunderclap of sound and fury that left him with ringing ears and a headache. The viewport itself didn't buckle, but the explosion gouged several deep chips out of it and ripped the wiper blade from its mount and sent it hurtling through the dirty air. The LED displays on the copilot's side of the cockpit flickered for a moment, then resumed their normal operation. No alarms sounded, but several caution lights came on—one for the FLIR, which was now apparently stuck in a fixed position, glaring up at the ridgeline Law had just attacked.

Another explosion erupted right in front of the SCEV, causing it to rock on its suspension. A beeping alarm sounded, and the FLIR display went dark, fatally damaged. Law pulled back on the control column and sent the SCEV hurtling in reverse for a hundred meters until he braked to a shuddering halt. Without the FLIR, he was now dependent on the millimeter-wave radar and his own eyes. He had already noticed the effectiveness of both systems was being slowly compromised by the approaching storm; the tempest's electromagnetic discharges were sufficient to degrade the radar's performance, and the blowing dust was most certainly reducing his visibility.

But Law had another tool at his disposal.

"All right, Andrews," he said aloud. "All right. My turn, now ..."

He learned back in his seat and relaxed as much as he could. Reaching into himself, he clicked on the switch in his mind that allowed him to extend himself, to let his mind detach itself from his body and float into the distance, connected to his body by only a small thread of consciousness. He became hyper-aware of his surroundings: the susurration of air moving across him from the cockpit vents, the smell of sweat and metal and oil, the light but steady vibration of two turboshaft engines running at low idle power. Then more, from outside the vehicle: the surprising dry heat of the air, the pressure of the wind as it continued to build, the vague sensation of dust whispering across his phantom hand as it reached out across the wasteland with probing fingers, reaching for something—anything—that might indicate life outside of his own. It took a great physical toll upon him, extending his consciousness in such a way; his body began to break down fat reserves to provide fuel for the action, and his heartbeat and breathing elevated, as if he were in the middle of a hotly contested marathon. Law was only peripherally aware of these things; the vast majority of his attention was focused on that great hand of his, reaching out from the SCEV as it explored the environment outside. One of those phantom digits brushed against something that possessed a restrained bioelectric field, something he had been altered and then trained to detect, even if it lay outside his field of view. Law focused on the signature, bringing all his talents and decades-old training to bear. As he did so, he caught spectral glimpses of other bio-signatures in the area—four on the ridgeline he had attacked, and another closer to the first. All diminished by the suits they wore, he knew, but still detectable, despite everything.

Law fixed on the first signal and redoubled his efforts, sending a suggestion along the ethereal connection he had established, even as his body screamed for him to stop, to disconnect, to stop himself from pushing past his limits. He ignored the warnings for as long as he could, hoping he could maintain contact long enough to do what was needed.

Andrews felt a queer sensation in his gut, and he had the disconcerting notion he was being watched. A wave of panic crested in his breast as he realized he had felt that sensation before—when he had first met Law, only moments before that horrible, terrifying pain had taken hold of his body and threatened to decimate his mind. Andrews felt the bolt of wild-eyed fear begin to take hold, and he might have actually cried out, but mysteriously, Law's presence retreated, fading but not disappearing, growing dimmer with each passing second until it was barely a glimmer of memory. Andrews gasped for breath, surprised at the fear and loathing he had felt, but thankful that unendurable agony had not come.

How did he do that?

"Skipper ..." Choi's voice was soft and somewhat slurred over Andrews's radio earphones as he broke radio silence. "I feel really funny ..." There was a peculiar lilt to the younger man's voice, as if he were drugged, swept up in some sort of narcotic dream.

It's Law. He's got a fix on Tony!

"Choi, I'm headed for your position now!" Andrews pushed himself to his feet. Keeping to a crouch, he ran toward Choi's position, but found he couldn't see him any longer—the wind had picked up to at least sixty miles per hour, and the thick dust was flying hard and fast. Andrews stumbled as the gale tore at him, like a living thing trying to grab him and throw him to the ground. He pressed on against it, fighting his way through the maelstrom, his crouched position not helping, given the heavy environmental gear and body armor he wore. He concentrated on putting one foot in front of the other, moving as quickly as he could and stumbling over grapefruit-sized rocks and loose earth. Through the deepening murk, he saw Choi kneeling behind his cover. He was facing Andrews, but he gave no indication he saw him. He trembled and shook, as if deep in the grips of a seizure. As Andrews drew nearer, he saw Choi's eyes were wide and panicked behind the visor of his facemask. Inexplicably, he slowly pulled his rifle against him, the collapsible stock fully retracted. Andrews slowed, and a worrying thought wormed its way through his mind.

Is Choi going to shoot me?

"I can't stop myself," Choi mumbled. "Help me, I can't stop..."

He watched as Choi placed the barrel of the rifle under his masked chin. Andrew lunged forward, stumbling over a large stone as he reached out to knock the rifle away. His gloved fingertips barely grazed the weapon's upper receiver as he lost his balance, collapsing to the hard ground right in front of Choi.

He grabbed Choi's boot and pulled with all his might, trying to jar his aim. The rifle barked, and he knew he was too late. Horrified, he watched as the 5.56 millimeter round punched a hole through the top of Choi's skull, blasting his mask askew and ripping apart the protective hood. Choi shivered once, then slowly listed to the right until he collapsed to the parched earth. Dark blood pumped from the horrible wound in his skull for a moment before it stilled as his heart beat its last. Andrews cried out and scrambled toward Choi's corpse on his hands and knees, but it was far too late for him to do anything. Choi's eyes were still visible through the crooked visor, and they were wide and staring, one looking to the left while the other stared straight on behind a half-closed lid.

"Choi. Oh, Tony ..."

Another voice came over his earphones. "Mike, are you all right?" Rachel asked.

Andrews squeezed his eyes shut, both to shut out the grim visage before him and to bite back the scathing response that came to him automatically when she broke radio silence. But it didn't matter—if Law could somehow exert enough influence over someone to force them to commit suicide, then a little something like chatter on an encrypted radio channel wasn't going to weigh heavily against them.

"I'm all right," he responded. "Choi's dead ... I don't know how, but that fucker in my rig made him kill himself."

Rachel started to respond, but Laird stomped on her transmission. "Four's on the move again—you'd better break off and get up here," he said. "We can hide out until the storm's pulse effect craps out the rig's radar. He's not going to be able to find us when the shit really starts to fly."

Andrews pushed away from Choi's cooling body and peered around the rocky outcrop he had been hiding behind. True enough, SCEV Four was slowly rolling forward. As he watched, the vehicle disappeared behind a filthy halo of light as its floodlight array snapped on, cutting a brilliant swath through the dust-filled air. It turned toward the ridgeline and Andrews lost sight of it momentarily as it disappeared behind the smoldering ruins of SCEV Five. It emerged on the other side of the smoking conflagration and deviated again, resuming its slow progress toward Andrews's general position.

"Roger that," Andrews said. He turned back to Choi's body and pulled the rifle off the corpse, then fussed with the tactical carry rig strapped to Choi's body armor. He figured he would need every magazine and grenade he could get his hands on. He pulled the body into a sitting position, trying not to watch as Choi's ravaged head tilted toward him, exposing the hole the round had made as it passed through his crewmember's skull. He unfastened the rig's Velcro tabs and pulled it off the body and hooked it over his left arm. He slowly lowered Choi's body back to the bloodstained ground as gently as he could and bowed his head for a moment.

Looks like I'm going to have to leave you here, buddy. I hope you won't hold it against me, okay?

Laird spoke again, this time with greater urgency. "Come on, Andrews—move it! He's closing in on you!"

Andrews raised his head and looked toward SCEV Four. It was still coming, though very slowly. Andrews wondered if Law might have lost the FLIR. That would explain why he had switched on the lights. If he was relying on those to see with, then Andrews saw no reason to let him keep the advantage. While the SCEV and its various components had been built tough, the floodlights weren't especially immune to physical damage.

"Laird, you have an angle on the rig?" he asked.

"Roger. What do you need?"

"I think he's lost the FLIR. He's half-blind, and when the storm gets closer, he's going to lose a lot of MMR capability."

"Roger that, but is there something you need us to do?"

"Take out his fucking lights," Andrews said. "Let's leave that fucker blind, so I can make a run for the rig."

"Ah, roger on the lights, but what's this about running down the rig? You figure you're just going to walk up, pop the airlock, climb inside, and bitch slap the guy?"

"Pretty much." Andrews opened his M320 grenade launcher and pulled out the expended cartridge and loaded a fresh one. Then he pulled the M320 off the rail on the underside of Choi's rifle barrel. He removed the magazine from the M416 itself, ejected the round in the chamber, and leaned the rifle against the rock next to him. He didn't need it any longer, and he didn't want to lug around its weight.

But the grenade launcher ... that, he decided to keep. He ensured the weapon was loaded, then clicked on the safety and shoved it inside his knapsack. It might be handy to have it nearby.

Just in case.

25

"EKLUND, YOU CURRENT on the M416?" Laird asked as he made a quick system check of his own rifle. As he had no grenades, he had no grenade launcher attached, only a forward hand grip to give him better control. The weapon was loaded, charged, and ready. He flicked off the safety.

"I am," Leona said.

"Then you're with me. Andrews, stay here with Jordello. Keep down, don't move a fucking muscle until someone tells you otherwise. You get me?" Laird looked over at Rachel, taking note of her wide eyes. She nodded fractionally, not looking at him, but at the SCEV moving across the darkening plain below. The harbinger of death, slowly stalking her husband. Laird was sure she was torn up inside, so he grabbed her arm and forced her to look at him.

"Andrews, do you read me?" he asked, his voice brusque and full of iron, even though he didn't feel it in his heart.

"Yes," she said finally. "I heard you the first time."

"Then listen to this: if we don't make it back, you need to bury yourself and Jordello with as much earth as you can. You'll run out of canned air in an hour, so make sure this," he pointed at the filter can in the flexible composite hose that connected his air tank to his respirator face mask, "is exposed to the environment. Don't bury it. It'll filter out all the particles that you could inhale. It's got a threaded connection. Just unscrew it when your tank runs dry, then do the same for Jordello. Bury yourselves and leave the filters on the surface. Can you get to your entrenching tool?"

She reached around and pulled it from the magnetized hook it hung from on her back and held it up for him to see. "Yes."

"Know how to use it?"

"What is this, a job interview?" Her voice sounded shrill over the radio.

"Rachel, do what Jim tells you." Andrews's voice was calm and rational over the radio net. "Just answer his questions. We've got stuff to do, and arguing with Jim is only slowing us down."

"Yes, I know how to dig a fucking hole!" she snapped. "I know it needs to be big enough for both of us, we need to be covered by at least twenty-four inches of dirt, and it has to be packed as hard as it can be so the wind won't scour it away."

Laird grunted. "Okay, sounds good to me." He raised his head slowly and looked down at the plain. He had gotten sloppy before, exposing himself when Law was clearly surveying the ridge and causing the group to be on the receiving end of a withering fusillade of 7.62 millimeter minigun fire. Thankfully, the rock had been dense enough to prevent anyone from getting killed. A missile strike, though ... That would be a different matter altogether.

"Let's roll, Eklund." He pushed himself into a crouch. "I want to move at least a hundred meters downrange. Keep up as best as you can."

"Roger," Leona said. She got to her feet and hobbled after him as he set off down the ridge.

Law was bathed in sweat, despite the cool, conditioned air that whispered across him. His hands trembled, and he felt vaguely nauseous. Extending his senses over such a vast distance and at such amplitude to take over one of his enemies had taken a remarkable toll on him. He had no idea who it was he had found; such knowledge was available to him only at close ranges, and it had been a miracle he had been able to interact with the target's mind at all. It would have been easier to induce a fatal cardiac infarction, as he had been trained to do, but he had no idea of the team's medical capabilities. So he had merely compelled the mark to commit suicide, something he had done numerous times in the past while keeping the family in line—it prevented any blowback among the family, because it could never be proven that he had forced the individual to hang himself, or slash her wrists on a piece of rusted metal. But overpowering a man's sense of self-preservation over such a vast distance and forcing him to shoot himself had been enormously taxing, leaving Law shaken and weak, as well as ravenously hungry and thirsty. He would need to replenish his body's energy stores as soon as possible.

Was it Andrews? he wondered dimly as he lay gasping in the pilot's seat. *Was he the one I killed?* He tried to recall the more intimate aspects of the connection, but there was nothing much to pick over. It had been as empty and impersonal as a simplex radio connection where the caller could speak, but could hear nothing back.

Through blurry eyes, he looked out at the terrain beyond the viewports. The skies were growing ever darker as the massive storm loomed closer, radiating bursts of lightning that flickered and flashed across the landscape. Still struggling for breath, Law hunted around the instrument panel until he found the switches for the rig's floodlight arrays, located on the overhead panel. He flipped them on and was rewarded with a substantially brighter view of the bleak environment outside. He noticed that the radar display was reading more and more clutter, garbage through which it could not see. That worried Law. He would have to try to get a hold on himself and finish the task at hand. There were still others outside to hunt down, and he would be best served by starting with the grenadiers first. He knew he had killed one; now, he had to do the same to the others.

Rubbing his eyes until his vision cleared, Law sat up in the seat and pushed the control column forward. The SCEV slowly rumbled forward, swaying slightly in the wind. The hunt was once again afoot.

Slowly, the rig drew closer to a brief line of rocky outcroppings. Law peered through the viewports. The floodlights revealed more detail as the vehicle approached the formation in the landscape. He decided this would have made an excellent position to attack from; not only did upthrusts of stone provide more than conceal-only cover, he got the distinct impression the plain rolled away gently on the other side. The decline would provide additional protection, from both weapons and radar.

Something winked in the darkness to the left and above the SCEV. He heard several objects slam into the SCEV's nose. The floodlights suddenly went dark as glass exploded. Sparks played along the SCEV's nose as several pockmarks appeared in the viewport right before his eyes. Law made a strangled, enraged sound as the floodlight array was destroyed. He reached for the radar display and tapped the screen, highlighting the area on the ridge from where he believed the weapon fire had originated. He heard a distant whine as the missile pod automatically spun and locked in on the site, and one of the Hellfire missiles homed in on the spot. Law pressed the fire button on the display, and was rewarded with a brief hissing sound as the missile leapt from the rail and blasted across the darkening sky. A quick second later, a bright flash of fire and smoke signaled the weapon's impact as it powered into the ridgeline and exploded, sending great chunks of rock flying through the air. Debris rained down from the sky, peppering the SCEV as a column of smoke-filled dust rose into the air from the impact site. Law stared at the ridgeline for a long moment, looking for any movement, any sign that a follow-on attack was underway from that side. He saw nothing, but he held his position for a moment, watching and waiting, knowing the idling rig made an attractive target. He briefly considered expanding his consciousness again, allowing his mind to brush against the ridgeline, but that part of him was reluctant to function. He had severely overstressed himself, and to reach out with his phantom hand and explore the landscape would leave him incapacitated and unable to proceed any further with his plan. At least, until his attackers drew nearer.

Come on, Andrews. Show yourself, you coward ...

A chime sounded, followed by a male voice: *"Incoming. Incoming. Incoming."* Shocked, Law turned to the radar display and saw a pipper rapidly approaching the SCEV, arcing toward it from the sky above. There was a vague rumble as one of the anti-missile warheads erupted from its niche and curved upward to meet the incoming object, but the angle was wrong; the defensive system fired up and out from the SCEV, whereas the incoming round was coming almost straight down. It slammed into the top of the rig as the AMW projectile curved away, climbing uselessly into the sky where it detonated benignly fifty meters overhead. At the same time, another explosion rocked the SCEV, and the rig trembled on its suspension as the radar display went dark, replaced by a flashing legend that told him the array had been destroyed, no doubt by a grenade. With a shout, Law pulled the control column backward, backing away from the ragged line of rocky outcroppings, cursing himself over the loss of his last remaining targeting system. Now, the remaining Hellfire missiles were of no use, and he would have to fire the miniguns the old-fashioned point-and-shoot way.

Still enough to kill them all.

Another chime sounded, and Law swept his eyes across the displays, looking for the source of the notification. When he saw what it was, he slammed on the SCEV's brakes and reached for his harness release before the big rig had come to a full halt. The assault rifle propped up in the copilot's seat went clattering to the floor as he reached for it, and he groped for it while staring at the engineering display in the center of the instrument panel.

The outer airlock door had opened.

Someone was aboard the SCEV.

Andrews whooped when he saw SCEV Four's floodlights disappear into explosions of shattered glass that sprinkled across the rig's top and nose like a sudden snowfall, leaving the rig bathed in darkness save for where its LED position lights still gleamed. The rig ground to a halt less than twenty meters to his right, and Andrews could see the FLIR was knocked askew, its flat pane of mirrored glass turned away from him, pointing more or less at the ridgeline where Laird and Leona hammered the vehicle with aimed bursts of 5.56 millimeter rounds. He saw a vague outline behind the rig's viewports, a small, slender figure craning its head around, looking for his attackers. It was Law.

Time to pay the piper, pal.

Andrews pushed himself away from the clump of rock he was hiding behind and hurried toward the SCEV, keeping to a low crouch. "Good job, guys," he said over the radio. "I'm on the move now, closing on the vehicle—you should relocate."

"On it," Laird said.

Andrews was only five meters from the rig's nose when he saw the missile pod slewing to the left. "Look out, he's going to use a Hellfire!" He dropped down and knelt, raising his rifle. As he did, one of the missiles erupted from the launcher, riding a plume of flaming exhaust that was incredibly bright against the darkening sky. He heard a microphone key open, perhaps as Laird started to reply, but the transmission was cut off as the Hellfire slammed into the ridgeline and exploded. A small mushroom cloud of spark-filled black smoke erupted into the air, its shape a short-lived affair as the wind tore at it, breaking it apart and pushing the cloud downrange. Pieces of rock—some small as pebbles, others as large as a grapefruit—rained down around Andrews as he estimated the range to the SCEV. He would have to fire the grenade on a very short but high arc, one that was certain to be detected by the rig's millimeter wave radar. He had no idea if the anti-missile defense system would be able to intercept an object as small as a forty-millimeter grenade, but he had no choice. Rachel was up there, and if Law got off another shot, she would likely be killed. He pulled the trigger on the M320, and the grenade fired with a brief thumping noise. Almost immediately, one of the AMWs in the rig's side exploded away from the vehicle, curving up into the air. Andrews didn't wait to see what happened next. He pushed himself to his feet and made a mad dash toward the vehicle, more or less certain he was inside the radar's small blind spot. If not, he would find out the hard way.

Two explosions tore through the darkness, the first coming from directly atop the SCEV, the second from much higher as the AMW warhead detonated. The SCEV bounced on its suspension as Andrews ran toward it and flattened himself against its metal hide. Payload from the expended AMW pinged off the rig, and small eruptions of dust exploded all around Andrews as a portion of the weapon's load of ball bearings hit the ground. None of them struck him, and he knew just how lucky he was—the projectiles were moving almost as fast as bullets, and were quite capable of killing him. More material rained down from above, and he saw it was pieces of shattered fiberglass. He didn't know if he had destroyed the rig's radar, but he had definitely destroyed the radome that encased it. He popped open the keypad access panel next to the airlock door, but before he could type in the entry code, he heard the rig's turboshaft engines begin to spool up. Next to the airlock was a series of maintenance access steps, hidden behind hinged dust covers. Andrews pushed his right foot into the lowermost step and boosted himself up, reaching for the next handhold. He grabbed it just as the SCEV's tires began spinning, and the rig rocketed backward. Andrews hung on for dear life as the vehicle roared away in reverse. He reached for the open keypad, but the vehicle was bumping so much that he would never be able to type in the code. Instead, he reached for the yellow and black handle next to the keypad, marked with the word RESCUE in red letters. He yanked on it, but it refused to move. He pulled harder—and almost succeeded in losing his grip on the maintenance ladder. Swearing and fighting to maintain his tenuous grasp on the SCEV, he pulled again. This time, the handle pulled outward with a pop, and Andrews felt the airlock's drive motors engage. The airlock door popped open, and he flung himself inside. He bounced off the hard wall inside the cubicle, and he grunted as he opened another panel, revealing the secondary emergency access. He yanked on it, and it pulled out from the recess easily. The inner door slid open into its pocket just as the SCEV slammed to a shuddering halt, throwing Andrews across the small aisle, where he crashed headlong into the science station. His helmet smashed into one of the displays there, fracturing the durable, coated plastic screen. An alarm blared, indicating the rig's pressure seal had been compromised, and that it was exposed to the hostile environment. Both pressure doors at either side of the second compartment began to slide closed automatically. Andrews reached across the science station and pressed down on the command override there, and both doors withdrew into their pockets. He whirled toward the cockpit, and there was Law. Their eyes met for an instant as the smaller man pulled an assault rifle off the cockpit floor and pointed it at him.

Well, this could end pretty badly for me—

Andrews lunged toward him just as Law fired. Two rounds struck him right in the chest, making him falter, but his body armor stopped the small bullets cold, and the ballistic plates inside the tough Kevlar composite dissipated the shock across his entire torso. It felt as if someone had punched him hard in the chest, and his breath left him in a rush. Despite this, he charged right into Law, using his entire body as a battering ram. Law shouted as Andrews crashed into him, driving him back against the instrument panel. The rifle went off again, discharging into the copilot's seat. Andrews pinned Law against the panel and reached down with both hands, fumbling with the weapon as Law tried to pull it away from him. Realizing he'd never be able to take control of the weapon in such close confines, he hit the magazine release and tore it free. The magazine dropped to the cockpit floor with a clatter. Law howled and released the weapon and slammed a fist against his facemask. Andrews felt the air seal pop, and a red light came on just below his visor. Contaminants were now able to enter the suit's closed system. He responded by slamming into Law again, fists flying as he punched the smaller man in the face once, twice, three times, shouting incoherently as blood exploded from Law's nose. Law sagged and fell to the left, across the pilot's seat. Andrews reached for him, but Law grabbed the control column and pushed it fully forward. The SCEV's turboshaft engines shrieked as they dutifully spun up, delivering full power to the transmission. The rig's knobbed tires spun as they sought traction. They found it, and the rig lurched forward.

Heedless of the SCEV's uncontrolled roaming, Andrews grabbed Law and battered him relentlessly. He grabbed Law's neck in both hands and slammed his head into the instrument panel, tearing open his scalp. Law released the control column and lashed out with an elbow, slamming it into Andrews's face. Andrews's head snapped back from the impact, striking the cockpit bulkhead hard enough to stun him. He felt his legs go weak, and he reached out to grab the copilot's seat. He noticed the impact of Law's strike had, rather serendipitously, resealed his respirator facemask. Law kicked Andrews in the chest and drove him out of the cockpit. As the SCEV lurched across the landscape, Andrews felt his balance slipping away, and he fell half inside the open airlock. He thrashed about on the cold deck, which was already patterned with a sprinkling of dust. He grabbed a handhold and hauled himself to his feet and tried to unsling his rifle, but his movements were made clumsy by the heave and sway of the uncontrolled SCEV.

Law appeared in the airlock's doorway, blood streaming from his nose and his lacerated scalp. He glared at Andrews as the veins in his forehead pulsed with a sudden power. Andrews felt that peculiar electrical sensation building around him, and he released the handhold, grabbing his rifle in both hands and raising its barrel, intending to fire on Law from the hip. He never made it. Before he could do more than raise the weapon, his nerves erupted in a blinding, searing agony that brought him to his knees. He screamed, loud and long, caught up in the embrace of an exquisite agony he had prayed he would never feel again. Andrews started to black out, and he looked up at Law, seeing him as if through a rapidly lengthening tunnel. He tried to will himself to raise the rifle and fire, but his arms refused to comply; his body was shutting down in a final attempt to ward off the agony. Then it was gone, as quickly as it had come, leaving Andrews gasping for breath. A sudden bout of nausea grabbed him, and for a moment, he feared he might vomit into his facemask. He reached out for the handhold, and the assault rifle slipped out of his grasp as he lolled against the side of the airlock. It was right at his knees, only inches away. He reached toward it with a trembling hand, but the SCEV heeled upward and the rifle slid away from him, coming to a rest against the blood-splattered deck at Law's feet. The smaller man fell to his knees and grabbed the weapon, pointing it at Andrews. Law looked drained, diminished; dark circles had sprouted beneath his eyes, and the blood continued to flow from his nose and scalp, leaving him wearing a mask of bloody gore across his face.

"Did you really think you could beat me, Andrews?" His voice was barely a ragged whisper above the beeping alarm, the howling wind entering the open airlock, and the slowly winding-down engines. "Did you *really* think you would win?"

Without waiting for an answer, Law raised the assault rifle and aimed it at Andrews's head.

The SCEV heaved once again, this time with great violence as the deck tilted upward at a crazy angle. The rifle fired a burst on full automatic, right across the airlock's overhead, missing Andrews entirely as he fell backward. He bounced off the airlock's ledge, then tumbled out of the vehicle as it crashed to a brutal halt. Andrews heard rock crumbling and metal screeching as the SCEV bucked to an explosive standstill, then he slammed into the hard ground. Fire blossomed along his right wrist and he grunted, but the pain was nothing compared to the tapestry of agony Law had crafted with his inhuman powers. As a cloud of dust boiled across him, he pushed himself to a sitting position. He felt a strange buzzing sensation in his head, and he wondered if he had suffered a concussion somewhere along the way. He looked up at the SCEV towering over him at a drunken angle. The rig had impaled itself on a spire of rock, and one of its front tires was tilted at a crazy slant. He could tell just by looking at it that the rig's front axle had been shattered. The SCEV had gone as far as it could go.

"Mike! Mike!"

Rachel's voice sounded tinny and distant over the radio. Andrews made to answer, but he couldn't form any words. He cleared his throat, staring up at the SCEV. He felt like he was swimming in a world full of cotton, and most of it had managed to wind up in his mouth.

"Rachel," he croaked. "Stay where you are. I love you, baby." He tasted blood in his mouth, and he felt more pain in his chest when he breathed. *Cracked ribs, if I'm lucky.*

Law appeared then, slumping against the doorway of the opened airlock. He looked down at Andrews with bleary eyes, moving unsteadily. His face and the front of his dark, rancid garments were soaked in blood, but he still held onto the assault rifle. He slowly raised it, bringing it to bear on Andrews.

"Why?" Andrews shouted suddenly. "*Why?* All we wanted were the core supports. If your people hadn't attacked us, we would've been gone by sundown!"

Law smiled crookedly. He paused to spit out a bloodied, fragmented tooth, then looked down at Andrews as he sat in the dust. "After all we've been through ... after years of disease, famine, violence ... you expect me to believe your intentions were nothing but *honorable?* Tell me another one." He waved an arm, indicating the dark, storm-torn wasteland surrounding them. "Look at all you've done. Look at the legacy of mankind. Your kind's a *plague* on the planet!"

"Your people are going to die anyway!" Andrews shouted.

Law shook his head. "Think so? That we can't survive another day without your supposed help? We've sucked it up for a decade, Andrews! Though the sickness still claims many of us, with every generation, we become stronger. We adapt."

Andrews laughed. "Adapt? Adapt for *what?* Take a look around, pal—there's nothing left to inherit! You've got all these mental powers—you *know* we could've helped all of you to live as people again!"

"People destroyed the planet, Captain," Law said wearily. "My family will live. They'll be better than what we were before. Something admirable."

"Admirable, huh?" Andrews chuckled humorlessly. "Try amoral, you sick fuck. It's a much better fit."

"History's written by the winners." Law seemed to gather

his remaining strength. He pushed himself upright and stepped away from the airlock's sill. He shouldered his rifle and aimed it squarely at Andrews's head. "I'm sorry, Andrews. But it's just too late for me to take any more chances."

Light flared suddenly through the gloom, shining across the SCEV's battered frame. Law looked up, and his mouth opened in frank shock as the illumination grew in intensity. A growing wail could be heard above the wind, and gravel crunched behind Andrews. He turned and looked over his shoulder, wondering if what he saw was a mirage or merely wishful thinking.

Emerging from the clouds of dust behind him were two SCEVs. Their minigun turrets were fixed on SCEV Four as they braked to a halt fifty meters away, their engines spooling down, their floodlight arrays blazing.

"No ..." Law's voice was barely audible above the din of the storm and the idling rigs sitting nearby. "No, no, no, *no!*"

Andrews snapped out of his funk. He reached into his knapsack and pulled out the M320 grenade launcher. Grabbing its pistol grip in his right hand, he flicked off the safety and raised it, pointing it right at Law. Law became aware of this a moment too late, and both men fired at the same time. A hail of bullets slashed at the ground right in front of Andrews, peppering him with debris. At the same time, the grenade launcher bucked lightly in his hand, and the forty-millimeter round slammed into Law's waist and exploded, blasting the man right in two. Ribbons of gore splattered across Andrews before he could move, and he closed his eyes instinctively. When he opened them, Law's ragged torso lay right before him. As he watched, Law's remaining arm flailed about, grasping at air, fingers curled into claws. Their eyes met, and Law's lips moved soundlessly. Blood bubbled upward from deep inside him, and whatever Law was trying to say was lost as he choked on his own fluids. The light faded from his eyes, and Andrews watched as dust covered the mutilated corpse, turning the warm blood into a pasty crust.

He became aware of someone calling his name. He looked up as a figure loomed over him. It was Mulligan, and his white environmental suit was almost brown with filth.

"Mulligan," he said, stupidly. "You made it."

Mulligan nodded, looking down at the disfigured corpse. "So

did you."

Other suited figures appeared. They reached down for Andrews and, as they hauled him to his feet, another jolt of pain from his injured ribs made him pass out.

26

LAIRD, LEONA, KELLY, and Rachel had been taken down from the ridgeline. All were alive, though Laird and Leona had been injured in Law's missile attack. The Hellfire had detonated thirty meters from their position, and both had taken shrapnel and shock damage from the blast, but were expected to survive. They were conscious and mostly alert when they were brought aboard SCEV Seven, which had been designated as the medical evacuation vehicle. Andrews, Kelly, Laird, and Leona were stationed in the vehicle's rear compartment, where two medics and the base surgeon tended to them. Andrews had suffered a broken left wrist and, as he had thought, several cracked ribs, but his injuries were considered light. Laird and Leona both had concussions and lacerations that needed to be cleaned and sterilized due to their exposure to the elements, and Kelly was in severe pain from her fractured femur. The surgeon elected to wait until they returned to Harmony to set the break, but his portable X-ray and follow-on ultrasound diagnostics revealed she hadn't suffered any major blood vessel damage. She would have a difficult recovery, but she would live.

Once everyone was stabilized, they returned to the base in SCEV Seven. Mulligan remained behind to assist in the recovery of the core supports, and by the time the rig returned to the base, he had already reported that the supports were in good condition. Rachel had been right; while they couldn't stand up to an immeasurably more powerful earthquake, the objects were tough enough to survive an explosion caused by an anti-tank weapon. Upon their return to base, Andrews and the others were transported by litter down a personnel evacuation stairway, one that had lain dormant for almost ten years. There wasn't enough power available to operate the vehicular lift, so they had to be transported to the base by manpower. Andrews wanted to walk and save everyone the effort of carrying him, but the base surgeon overruled him. He would be transported like the rest of the wounded, his dignity be damned.

"Look at it this way, you get a hero's welcome no matter how you get home," Rachel had said to him on the way down the dark, winding staircase. She had been ordered to return to the base with the others, even though she had offered to assist in the recovery operation. It had been decided that she had been in the field more than long enough, and for that, Andrews was thankful. With the storm bearing down on them, he didn't want her exposed to the environment any longer than she already had been.

SCEV Three remained on the surface for another day, the core supports secured safely aboard as her crew weathered out the storm. There was no way they could enter the base while the storm raged above in full fury; there were far too many obscurants, and the radioactive fallout stirred up by the storm was lethal even through an environmental suit. Rachel had told them the core supports would be lightning magnets, and that settled the issue. No one was willing to venture out with the supports; not because they might be killed, but because Mother Nature might deliver some award-winning examples of bolt lightning that could compromise the supports, wasting the team's hard work and sacrifice.

The base was dark and gloomy. Air quality was poor even though some intrepid engineers had pulled the batteries from the remaining SCEVs and used them to power the air scrubbers. They had to be run in staggered shifts to preserve the batteries. Recharging them required starting up an SCEV, and no one wanted to add poisonous exhaust to the mix, so power rationing was the standing order. The air smelled of sweat and oil, just like an SCEV after a long foray into the field. The difference was that there was the added tint of untreated sewage, which Andrews found more than slightly unpleasant.

But hey, at least I'm alive.

Which was better than three other people who had passed away while he was out on the mission. The injuries they had sustained during the earthquake were too grave, even with the sophisticated medical expertise available. Sometimes, Andrews knew, it was just a person's time to go. He thought about Spencer and Choi and felt guilty about their loss, regardless. At least they had gone down fighting. Fate had just given them the short straw.

Once the core supports had been brought into the base, it took another two days to install them and test the power generation equipment in the Core. After the systems had been validated, power was slowly restored to the base, level by level, with a few exceptions. The medical section was given priority for power allocation, as were the environmental systems. Over the course of another two days, Harmony Base came alive again, with heat, hot water, sterilized air, and light. Repair work continued day and night, and Andrews thought that after a month or so, no one would even be able to tell that the base had been severely damaged.

On the eighth day after recovery was completed and all systems were stabilized, a memorial service was held in the Commons Area. While all the bodies of the dead had been incinerated as soon as possible—the base's designers had provided a mortuary as well, because even when the world ended, survivors would continue to die—the command group had decided that funeral proceedings were to take place. To provide a degree of closure. A large memorial had been erected on one wall just after the war. Previously, only a small handful of bronze plates had been affixed to it, but dozens more had been added over the past few weeks. Each plate bore the inscribed names of the deceased, their birthdates, and the day they died. All the new additions had passed away in the first two weeks of June. Andrews, his wrist in a cast and his ribs bound, joined the line of survivors who filed past the memorial. He knew every name there, some better than others, but each bronze nameplate equaled a hole that would never be filled. Even though he had intended to be strong, to be the rock, he found that when he finally made it to the end of the line, he couldn't hold back his tears any longer. Seeing Spencer and Choi's names, and knowing how young they had been, was just too much. Even though they were a few years younger than him, they had grown up together, and he would always feel their absence.

"We've all been through hell and back—twice," Benchley said in his address. From the front of the Commons Area, he regarded the assemblage with clear eyes, his voice strong. "We've all lost people near and dear to us—twice. First in the Sixty Minute War, then on the earthquake of June ninth, and two more in the mission to recover the supports we needed in order to survive. The very fabric of our society here has had a hole blown right through it. But we're a strong people. We have to be, because our work is just getting started. We know now that there is life out there. It may not welcome us, it may fear us, it may distrust us, but it's life nonetheless, and we need to do everything in our power to help those who survived the war. It's what we're here for. It's what we're all about.

"I want all of you to look to the people next to you. I want all of you to reach out to each other, and help those who are in need get through the coming weeks and months. We all grieve together, regardless of rank or position or occupation. We are Harmony Base, and even burdened by the weight of our sorrow, we have a mandate: *quando mundum finit, opus nos incipiet.* When the world ends, our mission begins. We need to remember our fallen, but we need to keep putting one foot in front of the other." The general paused, then looked at Mulligan, who stood at attention nearby. "Look around you. Find those who have lost their way and help them get back onto the path because we need to walk it ... together."

A lone bugler clad in a spic-and-span Army Class A uniform played Taps. Mulligan, whose own Class As were accentuated by his green Special Forces beret, held rule over a formation of honorary pall bearers. All wore black arm bands. Andrews watched the assemblage as they picked up the ceremonial interment flag and neatly folded it into a tight triangle. Mulligan took the flag and marched toward Benchley, presenting it to the base commanding officer. Benchley accepted the flag with a grave expression, then returned Mulligan's sharp salute. Mulligan turned and dismissed the detail tersely, and they filed out of the Commons Area, preceded by the base's colors. Benchley and the command staff exited as well, marching in step in keeping with the protocols of a military service. Others slowly followed, but many more remained, sniffling, grieving, weeping.

Jeremy approached them, his eyes red, his expression downbeat. He looked up at Andrews and Rachel and forced a specter of a smile to his face as he embraced both of them. "I'm proud of you two," he said. "So incredibly proud, you have no idea."

"Thanks, Dad," Andrews said.

Jeremy released them, then reached out and touched Rachel's cheek. "Especially *you,* young lady. You really proved your stuff out there, and in a big way. Think you'll go military now?"

Rachel blinked. "Why do you ask that?"

"You're young, and you have an adventurous spirit. Don't get me wrong, I don't want to see you leave the Core," he said, sparing Andrews a wink, "but who knows? Maybe you're cut out for field work, yourself."

Rachel favored both of them with a pale, distracted smile. "I hadn't really thought of that. Maybe that's something to consider. Excuse me for just a second." She turned and walked toward the line forming in front of the memorial wall.

"Well, maybe that was the wrong thing to say," Jeremy said.

Andrews shook his head. "Nah. She's not upset with you, Dad. She's just ..." He shrugged. "She's just not herself, these days."

"That'll change. She's young. She'll heal."

Jeremy embraced him again and planted a kiss on his forehead, a display that would have embarrassed both of them weeks before. But after the earthquake and the reminder that life was so incredibly fragile, things like that no longer seemed to matter.

"I've got to get back to the Core," Jeremy said, his voice full of apologies. "There's still a lot to be done. Tell Rachel she has a couple of days off if she needs them."

"I'll pass it on."

Jeremy clapped his son on the shoulder. "Are you really my son? I can't believe I got so lucky with a winner like you."

"Blame Mom," Andrews said, smiling weakly. He found he suddenly missed his mother, even though he hadn't thought of her in weeks. He felt a strong pang of guilt when he realized that.

"Nothing to blame her for," Jeremy said, looking down at his feet for a moment. "She did right by both of us, but you got the best part of her. And thank God for that." He cleared his throat and wiped his eyes. "All right. I've got to go."

Andrews nodded. "I'll see you later. Take care of yourself, Dad."

Jeremy clapped his shoulder again. "Don't worry about me, son. I'm fine. Look after Rachel." He stepped away, walking toward one of the exits.

Andrews turned to the memorial and saw his wife standing at the end of the huge wooden plaque. For Rachel, the loss of the past few weeks were tragic, but none were as painful for her as the fact that the names of her parents were at the front of the list. Not for the first time, Andrews wondered how she'd been able to handle it, growing up in the base and going through the transition from childhood to womanhood under the care of watchful friends and well-wishers, but devoid of a parent's guiding hand. Andrews's mother's name was on the wall, as well; she had succumbed to ovarian cancer three years after the base had been sealed. He'd had his father to see him through the tough spots; Rachel had no blood relatives. Despite the hardship, she had grown up to become a woman to be reckoned with, as she had shown during the mission to San Jose. He could tell by the arch of her back and the set of her shoulders that she was grieving all over again. In that moment, he doubted he had ever loved her more. He walked over and joined her, and she folded her hand inside his.

"Babe? You okay?"

Rachel reached out and touched the plates that bore the names of her parents—Peter and Catherine Jane, who went by CJ. Though he had seen dozens of photos of them, he could only vaguely recall meeting them a few times in real life, during their first base orientation sessions, back when the Andrewses and the Lopezes had been selected to be part of Operation Harmony.

"I'm fine," she said, and she turned to face him. Her eyes were bright, but she hadn't shed any tears. The pain lingered just below the surface, like it always did. Andrews leaned forward and kissed her forehead.

"Really?"

"Really. How are you doing?"

Andrews shrugged, suddenly uncomfortable with telling her the truth. He did it anyway. "A little guilty, I guess."

She looked at him through narrowed eyes. "Guilty? Why? About Choi and Spencer? What happened to them wasn't your fault, Mike."

"I beg to differ. I was their commanding officer. It was up to me to bring them home safe."

Rachel nodded. "Yeah, you were. And you did everything

you could. The odds were just stacked too high. Trust me—I was there."

Andrews made a noise in his throat. She was right, of course, but that didn't do anything to stave off his remorse. He wondered how long it would take for him to be quit of it, but as he turned to look over the slowly thinning crowd, he decided he already knew the answer—he would never stop feeling responsible. Choi and Spencer were his crew, and he had been powerless to save them. They died under his watch, and that was a responsibility he would take to his grave.

He put that burden aside and kissed Rachel on the cheek. "Let's get out of here."

She nodded. "Yeah. Let's."

They turned to go, but Mulligan appeared in their path. The big man still looked battered, slowly-healing bruises and cuts on his face, but his appearance had improved considerably over the past several days. He regarded Andrews and Rachel with his dark eyes, his expression inscrutable. Andrews glanced at Rachel and saw she was staring at Mulligan with a cold, unreadable expression that was nearly as enigmatic as Mulligan's. When Andrews turned back to the sergeant major, he was surprised to find his eyes were uncharacteristically downcast.

"Can we help you with something, Sarmajor?" he asked.

"Ma'am, I'd like to talk to you, if I could. I know you're probably not feeling too hot, so I'll keep it short." Mulligan looked up and met Rachel's emotionless gaze. "I need to tell you about something that happened a long time ago. You might think you know everything about it, but ... well, I figure it's time you hear it from the guy who was there."

Silence descended, heavy and uncomfortable. Rachel stared at Mulligan for a long moment, ignoring the curious gazes of those who walked past. The history of enmity between them was well known, even though it was considered to be mostly one-sided. Mulligan stood before them, stoically enduring her cold, impenetrable glare, even though Andrews supposed it must have been embarrassing for him. As the seconds ticked by, he did not prompt her for a response; he merely stood there and looked back at her, his face a mask of disciplined composure.

Rachel finally favored him with a curt nod.

Mulligan cut his eyes over the Andrews. "Sir?"

"I think I'd like to hear what you have to say as well, Sarmajor. If you don't mind." Andrews looked over at Rachel to see if she had a different opinion, but she kept her gaze rooted on Mulligan.

The tall senior NCO took it in stride. "Very well. Would you like to go—"

"Here is fine," Rachel said, her voice taut as a banjo string, belying her impassive expression.

Mulligan met her eyes once again and nodded. He removed his green beret and stepped closer to Rachel. Even though their expressions did little to illustrate their internal feelings, Andrews nevertheless felt the uncomfortable tension between the two of them as if it were a physical thing. He glanced down and saw Mulligan was slowly twisting his beret in his hands, and he wondered if whatever the sergeant major was going to say would be a good thing, after all.

When he spoke, his voice was pitched low, but he kept his gaze on Rachel. "After the bombs dropped, I tried to get to my family with SCEV One. By *stealing* it, actually. Your folks cared enough about me to come along, to try and help. I was, uh—pretty crazy, then. I was within three weeks of retirement. Two days from terminal leave. I was basically just marking time, waiting for my replacement to show up. All of us were marking time back then, you might remember." He paused, but Rachel gave no indication she was going to speak, so he continued. "Visibility was zero. Radar and communications were useless, because of the electromagnetic pulse effect. Anyway, I was driving balls to the wall—all I could think about was getting to my wife and daughters before the fallout rolled over them.

"We got extremely unlucky when a ground burst went off only about a mile away. I'm not sure what they were aiming at—the best I can come up with is that one of the weapons heading for Wichita malfunctioned and came down way short. Your mother happened to be looking in the general direction of the blast when it went off—she went blind from the flash. Your father was standing between the cockpit and the science station. The EMP fried a good amount of the rig's systems, despite the shielding, and we stopped dead. Before I could do anything to get the rig moving again, the shockwave hit us. The SCEV rolled three times, tossed around like some kid's Tonka toy.

Your father was killed instantly. One of the gravity belts on your mother's harness broke, and she was ejected from her seat. When it was over, she managed to hang on for another three hours. I had no voice contact with the outside world, and the rig was demolished. I figured there would be at least an attempt at a rescue, but it didn't come soon enough. CJ died in my arms." Mulligan looked down then, and the muscles in his jaw clenched as he gritted his teeth. Andrews saw the nightmare of pain and guilt in the big man's eyes, and he realized the Green Beret was something of a kindred spirit. They shared a deep responsibility for those they had lost.

Rachel stared hard at Mulligan, her face carved from porcelain. Mulligan hesitated for a moment, then looked up and tried to force a smile. It died stillborn when he met Rachel's unflinching glare.

"Do you remember how we were friends?" Mulligan asked, raw pain in his voice. "Your parents and me, we hit it off really well. You used to call me the Jolly Green Giant, because you thought I was so tall and always wore a duty uniform. Whenever I saw you in the corridor, I'd go 'Ho, ho, ho! Rachel Lopez!' and you'd laugh. Do you remember that?"

Rachel's expression didn't change, but she balled her hands into fists. As she continued to stare up at Mulligan, her knuckles were turning white. A small shudder went through her and tears rose in her eyes, but she didn't take her eyes off of Mulligan for an instant.

"Do you remember?" Mulligan asked again, bending toward her slightly, his voice hardly more than a whisper. There was a peculiar pleading quality to the question, and Andrews realized that Mulligan—the strongest, biggest badass in Harmony Base, and maybe in the entire Army—had been dying inside for years.

When she didn't answer, Mulligan straightened, transforming once again into the base's enigmatic command sergeant major. "So, anyway. Your family died trying to help me rescue mine, who died because I couldn't get to them. Somehow, the only son of a bitch who managed to walk away from it was me. God must've been laughing his ass off." Mulligan's voice was back to normal, the no-nonsense deadpan it had been for the past ten years. He displayed all the outward emotion of a robot, as if he were reading a readiness report aloud. It was as if he didn't care anymore; he had done his job, and that was all there was to it.

Rachel lunged at him, pounding on his big chest with her fists, making small, agonized sounds as she lashed out at him. Mulligan endured it, taking no steps to defend himself. Bystanders surged forward, shocked by the sudden display. Andrews pulled Rachel away from the towering soldier, wrapping his arms around her and ignoring the jolts of pain from his tortured ribcage.

"Why?" Rachel fairly shouted. "Why didn't you tell me this back then? Why did you let it drag on for so damn *long?*"

Mulligan looked down at her, ignoring the inquisitive looks from the other people standing nearby. His body language told them all they needed to know, and they stepped back, returning to whatever it was they had been doing before. But they kept looking toward the tall man and the crying woman, and Andrews saw expressions of sympathy among them. For Rachel. And for Mulligan.

Mulligan sighed heavily. "I should have told you. I should have tried to look after you. But I ... I couldn't. I always thought that was kind of funny, because before everything went to hell in a fast sports car, I was always a responsible guy. I always tried to do the right thing, even if it was hard. But this time, I decided to do the easy thing, and ignore what had happened to Peter and CJ. And I ignored you, and pretty much everyone else in this damned place." He looked at her and shook his head sadly. "Anyway, that's it. That's all there is. Your family left you because they wanted to help me, because they thought they'd be safe, that I'd do the right thing. I wound up killing them, and I let you down when you needed me the most. I just thought you should know." He paused for a moment, looking at Rachel. "I'm sorry. I'm so very, *very* sorry."

"So you think I should forgive you now?" Rachel asked, her voice quavering.

Mulligan shook his head. "I just want you to remember one thing: I miss them, too. Every day."

Mulligan turned on his heel and walked away, shoulders square, his heavy footsteps echoing in the large room. Almost everyone turned to watch him make his exit, then they turned back to Andrews and Rachel. Andrews ignored them and touched Rachel's face, wiping away her tears.

"Sweetie ...?"

She hugged him tight for a moment, then looked up at him. "I'm fine," she said, and her voice was stronger. She wiped her eyes with the heels of her palms and smiled vaguely. "Actually, I feel better than I've felt in a long time."

"Then let's get out of here. I'm starting to feel like we've been on exhibit for the last few minutes."

"Yeah. Let's go home."

Leona lay in the narrow bed she had been allocated in the medical section's recovery ward. The injury she had acquired in San Jose from the spear attack had become infected, and the base surgeon had wanted her to remain under his staff's direct care until her fever subsided and the wound started to show substantial improvement. That had been days ago, and the fever had finally broken the previous night. Her appetite had come back, and she was thrilled to discover that not only could she now eat and not immediately throw up, she had her choice of almost anything on the menu because full power had been restored. Even if it was the same chow as what they served in the Commons Area's commissary, she found it to be mighty tasty after enduring almost two weeks of SCEV chow, followed by a few days of not being able to eat at all.

In the bed beside her, Kelly Jordello was recovering from her own injuries. Her broken femur had been set, and her leg was in traction for the rest of the week. After that, the base surgeon would decide whether or not to insert pins to assist in her recovery. The two of them joked that since both of them had only one working leg each, the only way they could make a run for it was if they taped themselves together. They had watched the memorial service on the base's video network, and both were feeling more than a bit melancholy. Leona was staring up at the ceiling, lost in her own thoughts when Kelly suddenly said, "Well hello, Sergeant Major."

Leona looked up, and when she saw Mulligan standing between their beds, she felt as if her heart had jumped into her mouth. He was still in his Class As, and he held his green beret in one hand. Leona stared up at him, marveling at his attire. She couldn't remember seeing him in anything other than his Army combat uniform.

"Lieutenant Jordello, how are you coming along?" Mulligan asked, giving Leona a quick glance before looking down at Kelly.

Kelly indicated the traction rig that held her leg suspended in the air. "Well, I'd try and get out of here, but I don't think I'll get very far on foot."

Mulligan grunted. "Better stay where you are then, ma'am."

"Sharp threads, Sarmajor. What brings you here? Bedpan patrol?"

"No, ma'am. I flunked the candy striper test. Just as well, I hated the duty uniform. Excuse us, please." Mulligan yanked the privacy curtain between the two beds closed, hiding Kelly from view as he turned toward Leona. She looked up at him, confused.

"Sarmajor?"

Mulligan scowled at her. Combined with the mass of bruises on his face, the expression made him look positively ferocious. "Stop gaping, girl. You look like you've gone feeble." Before she could make a response, he stepped closer to the bed and held out the eagle medallion to her. Leona looked at it, watching as it swayed and twinkled in the room's antiseptic light.

"Uh, what—"

"My wife made that for me, out of a coin," Mulligan said, cutting her off. "An Eisenhower dollar, actually. It seemed to attract your attention out in the field, and I ..." He paused for a moment, then sighed. "Well, I thought you might want to have it, is all."

"Why would you want to give it to me?"

Mulligan considered that for a long moment, then shrugged. "My day to make amends, I guess. I treated you pretty badly out in the field, and you didn't really deserve it. Sorry."

"Oh." Leona looked from the medallion to Mulligan as he towered over the bed. "Well, look, Sergeant Major. I'm not going to report it or anything, because I pretty much stepped over the line ..."

"So you're not interested, then?" Mulligan asked, his voice flat.

Leona hesitated, uncertain of what to do. She couldn't think of what to say, so she slowly raised her hand and took the medallion from him. She looked at it, turning it over in her hand. The details of the eagle were finely crafted, and even though she'd never seen such a creature before, she knew it was a symbol of strength and honor. It fit Mulligan perfectly.

"This has got to mean a lot to you, Mulligan. I mean—I'm flattered that you'd think of giving it to me, but that won't bring absolution, you know? Your family will still be dead." She wondered if she was saying too much; after all, the privacy curtain wasn't exactly soundproof, and she had no trouble imagining Kelly hanging on every word.

"That's not exactly what this is about," Mulligan said, "but the offer stands, anyway."

Leona regarded the medallion again, then looked up at Mulligan. He seemed different to her, now. There was something akin to humor in his eyes, and while it seemed foreign to her, it also seemed *right,* as if she was glimpsing the real Scott Mulligan for the first time. Despite his cuts and bruises, he seemed more alert, as if he'd just awakened from a very long, refreshing sleep. Leona still didn't know what he was up to with this impromptu visit and unexpected peace offering— she couldn't quite get her mind around the possibility that he was giving her a *gift*—but she knew what she hoped for. If this was her shot at getting it, then she had to take it.

"Thank you," she said, hesitantly. "It's very lovely."

"Well, it's not a wedding proposal or anything, so don't mess up the sheets, okay?"

"*What?*" Leona suddenly laughed, in spite of herself. When Mulligan allowed a ghost of a smile to cross his lips, she knew he was teasing her. Humor from Scott Mulligan was something she'd have to get used to. "I wasn't about to, Sergeant Major. But ... just what *does* it mean?"

Mulligan crossed his arms and considered her question for a long moment, his gaze locked on hers. "Well, Lieutenant, I guess it means that maybe we'll sit down and have a talk sometime, once you get out of this overblown band-aid factory. If you can make the time, that is."

"Yeah, I think I can make the time," Leona said automatically, and the sudden eagerness of her reply left her feeling foolish and embarrassed. She felt her face grow warm. Either her fever had returned, or she was blushing.

"Cool," Mulligan said, and he touched her arm briefly. His hand was warm and dry, his touch surprisingly gentle. "Catch you then, and get well soon."

With that, he swept aside the curtain. Kelly lay in her bed with her eyes closed, mouth open, so obviously pretending to be asleep that it was almost laughable. Mulligan looked down at her, shook his head with a sigh, then headed for the door.

Leona called out to him before he could make a clean getaway. "But what'll we talk about? Force protection in post-holocaust America? Diplomacy versus firepower? Mercury in retrograde?"

Mulligan stopped at the doorway and turned back to her. He looked at her frankly, and he allowed himself a vague smile. "You're a funny girl, Eklund. I like that. But I'll leave the topic of conversation to you—I can't lead all the time. See you around campus."

Then he was gone. Leona stared at the doorway for a moment, her mind whirling. *Did Mulligan just—*

"Did Mulligan just ask you out on a date?" Kelly asked, very much awake.

"I ... I guess?"

Kelly smiled and clasped her hands behind her head, looking up at the ceiling. "Well, in that case, I guess you'd better get well soon, Lee. I don't know much about these things, but I'd say the big man still has a lot of *rawr* left in him, if you get what I mean."

Leona wanted to ask her what she meant by that, but then decided she didn't need to know. She would find out herself. All in good time. Her gaze returned to the medallion. She studied it for a long moment, and she realized a soft smile had spread across her face.

27

REPAIRS HAD BEEN underway for an entire month. Benchley paid attention to every detail, and ensured that Jeremy Andrews and his team of engineers had enough manpower available, not to just fix what had been broken in the earthquake, but to reinforce and strengthen the outpost's power array. No one wanted to go through another event like the one they had just barely survived, and Benchley made it a priority for the engineers to move quickly and expeditiously. For weeks, everyone labored to put the base back together, and everyone had a hand in its restoration. Even Benchley had pulled on coveralls and spliced wire, welded piping, and serviced heavy equipment. No one was allowed any slack. Bit by bit, the station was patched up and made fully operational again.

But while Harmony Base was healing, it would bear scars for the rest of its life.

At night, in his quarters, he avoided sleep. Not because he feared his dreams—he had long since grown inured against them—but because Mike Andrews had finally delivered his mission log. And the things Benchley found in the report were shocking. Frightening. At times, even outrageous.

And most surprising of all, the report contained hope.

Unconfirmed reports of other survivors from the Northwest. Benchley found himself circling around that again and again. That there were survivors eking out a bare existence beneath the desolate rot that had once been San Jose had been surprising enough. But the mention—the mere *rumor*—of other survivors in the Northwest, where all the models and simulations had suggested that nuclear fallout would be less than anywhere else in the nation, set his mind roaming. San Jose was their first target, of course. But after that, Benchley knew the Pacific Northwest was their next destination.

There could be a society there. So why wait?

The notion took him by surprise. He had been planning on concentrating all the base's energies on contacting the survivors in San Jose, making peace with them, and even outright providing for them, if they would allow it. Harmony had tons of bounty in its stores, all manner of items that the remaining residents of San Jose would need. But they were likely a small group, smaller than Harmony's population. They wouldn't need much, comparatively speaking. It wouldn't take long to get them squared away, living like human beings again, as opposed to cannibalistic savages.

We can do both.

Benchley thought about that for a long time. Life after the Sixty Minute War had served only to refine his normally conservative approach to issues like this. Determine the mission. Plan the mission. Launch the mission. Support the mission. Sustain the mission. Exit the mission. Repeat.

But Benchley knew time was running short. Even though Harmony would survive, the next catastrophe that befell the post might be substantially worse. Mother Nature had already done what Mankind had not: wound the base, hurt it, send it a signal. There may not always be another tomorrow. And if the worst were to occur, the people of Harmony would need to find a place where they might be able to have a second chance.

The Pacific Northwest.

He nodded as he sat hunched over the log book and his tablet computer, his Spartan quarters illuminated only by the lamp on his desk. The Pacific Northwest. It was a veritable beacon flashing in the murky darkness as the sun slowly set across the decimated United States of America. He decided to make it the first order of business at tomorrow's command staff meeting. While he had to let the command staff weigh in on it, he saw another mission departing from Harmony, one commanded by Mike Andrews. The kid was a star performer, and there was no one better suited to carry the torch.

The world had ended.

And Harmony's mission had finally begun.

AFTERWORD

Earthfall had an odd conception. Originally, I'd written a bare-bones novella in very late 1982, which I used as a kind of outline for a screenplay in the summer of 1983. It didn't take me long to write, as the adventure in the piece was so compelling that it kept me up at all hours, banging away on my shiny, new electric typewriter—personal computers were things of fancy back then—in between classes and dates and bottle after bottle of Pepsi. (It was sold in glass bottles back then, *real* glass bottles, not this tacky plastic we have today.) Back then, I was focused on writing a story that would combine the best of *The Road Warrior* with what little good there was to be found in the movie *Damnation Alley*...which basically amounted to some cool looking vehicles, and maybe a score by Jerry Goldsmith. I worked on that screenplay, off and on, for years.

Hollywood remained uninterested.

I put it away for at least twenty-plus years and forgot all about it, as one should when holding onto an unsalable property. Every now and then, I'd think back and reconsider it, but I always pushed it aside in favor of more contemporary projects, meatier projects that I could sink my teeth into. There are always new stories to be spun, and I try my best to look forward. After all, at my age, the road ahead is much shorter than the one in the rearview mirror, so I'd best keep my eyes up front. No telling what a guy might hit when blasting down the highway of life at 85 miles an hour.

Curiously, it was one of these "meatier projects" that led me back to *Earthfall*. I was working feverishly on a novel called *Tribes*, a Chricton-esque adventure novel with a sprinkling of science fiction dusted over it. At the halfway mark, I began to lose steam, and the project started to wander. The story wasn't as lifelike as I'd hoped, and the characters were approaching insipid. No, that's not right. They *were* insipid. When a writer can recognize that in his own work, and can't write his way of the box he's written himself into, then it's time to step back and reevaluate.

Serendipitously, *Earthfall* came to mind again.

I pulled out the script—the novella has long since

disappeared, and is nowhere to be found—and reread. Parts of it made me grimace in embarrassment. To think I'd actually shown this around! No *wonder* I was never the next hot thing in Hollywood. My skills sucked! The dialog was horrible, some of the sequences absolutely juvenile. I mean, twenty years after the bombs dropped, and people are turning into pumpkin-headed *mutants*? (Though in my own defense, I didn't have 50 foot scorpions leaping out the wasteland sand.)

But still...there was a story there. A very rough one, but a story, nevertheless.

So I put *Tribes* aside and resurrected *Earthfall*. And while it was trying at times, it was also fairly easy—I knew where I'd wanted it to go back in 1983, but I hadn't the chops to steer a story back then. I'm still unsure if I do three decades later, but I decided to make a go of it. It's not survivalist fare, and it still retains a patina of 1950s pulp science fiction about it, but I did try and toss in as much weight as the story could handle and still move like a cheetah with a Saturn V rocket shoved up its butt. If you've made it this far, I hope you agree. Or, at the very least, didn't find it too overwhelmingly odious!

Thanks are in order...

From 1983: Big shouts out to Rick Sylander, Kevin Slater, Marc Schliesman, Tim MacNary, Jill Ferrari, Caryl Dailey, Doug Aho, Leah Creatura, Todd Webster, Carolyn Payne, Gordon Dailey, Ann Juliano, Leonard Scott, Jackie Soma, Hank Netherton, and Bill Mellott. You all read the scripts, and for some reason, neglected to tell me every draft sucked. I've lost contact with many of you, but I love you all, and your friendship, love, and support will never be forgotten.

And now, in 2013: Joe LeBert, Fred Anderson, and the long-suffering Derek Paterson, for your reviews and views. Will Allen for your beta—your comments were significant. Bobby Cooper and Scott Campos, for the sanity checks. Craig DiLouie for the blurbs and kind words of encouragement. Jeroen ten Berge for some awesome cover stuff, and Nathan Carlisle for his depiction of the SCEVs. Editors Sean Fox and Lynn MacNamee at Red Adept for your editorial efforts, as well as Diana Cox at novelproofreading.com for the final burnishing. And a salute to former Navy officer Paul Salvette and his lovely wife for formatting the ebook release.

Author disclaimer: despite the efforts of those above, the final result is all my doing. Mistakes and assorted grief are all mine. Accolades, if any are coming, are shared with all.

And the biggest thanks to you, the reader. It's been a ball corresponding with you all, via email, via Facebook and Twitter, and on my modest blog. You make a guy feel all right about himself, even when he steps in it.

Which is often.

Stephen Knight lives in the New York City area.